THE DARKNESS FALLS

A Lythinall Novel
Book Three

THE DARKNESS FALLS

A Lythinall Novel
Book Three

MICHAEL D. NADEAU

THE DARKNESS FALLS

Copyright © 2022 Michael D. Nadeau

"Skullgate Media" and associated logos copyright © 2022 Skullgate Media LLC

www.skullgatemedia.com

ISBN 978-1-956042-20-7

Ebook ISBN 978-1-956042-21-4

Cover art licensed from DepositPhotos

Cover design and internal layout by Chris Vandyke

THE DARKNESS FALLS

A Lythinall Novel
Book Three

ACKNOWLEDGEMENTS

To my wife Sheila, for putting up with Karsis the bard, my friends for always having faith in me, and my children. Our many adventures play out in my head as I write these exciting stories.

To Gwen and Lexi for continuing to inspire me with my faeries—your energy and imagination is refreshing. I'm almost sad to have come to the end.

And to Michael R., Brett P., and Alan P. for the continued help with talking me through things and helping me out. You guys rock.

MAP OF LYTHINALL
And Surrounding Regions

CONTENTS

WHAT HAS COME BEFORE

Once sealed away, the Incarnation of Death, Dar'Krist, crawls his way out of his earthen prison, free again. As he marches towards civilization and descends upon the frontier villages without mercy, a young warrior named Rhoe and the legendary bard, Karsis, travel south to Everknight to warn King Arian of this great evil.

Meanwhile, in Everknight Princess Allissana hears of the newly arisen evil at a council meeting and takes it upon herself to go and confront it. High General Carana, who has trained Allissana to be one of the best fighters in the kingdom, goes with her as she sneaks out of the castle in the early morning hours. Allissana faces the Incarnation of Death, standing with the young warrior Rhoe at the bridge. All three fall into the spring-fed waters of the river when the bridge rots away and are washed downstream.

Roe and Allissana—now going by Liss—are found by faeries. They attend a faerie Revel, in which they accidentally get married. They warn the faeries that a great evil is coming and the former queen of the faeries, Irilyn, chooses to fight the Incarnation with the combined power of all the faeries burning inside her. She tricks him into a faerie ring that transports them far to the north. She dies at Dar'Krist hands but succeeds in leaving him wounded hundreds of miles away from Roe and Liss.

Back at the capitol, King Arian is attacked but the old priest Ralavin saves the day, giving his life to slay the traitor. Karsis leaps to the priest's side and gives him the Vial of Eternity, which not only restores the priest but gives him back his youth as well. The king finds some children living on the streets and brings them back to the castle to train them to be the King's Messengers—a better life for certain.

Rhoe and Liss leave the faeries and make their way south towards River Vale, but are attacked by a wolvren. Badly wounded, Rhoe is taken to River Vale to be healed by Caerlyn, with help from Karsis. They meet up with a homeless man named Graf and flee the city when the corrupt duke attacks them. When Rhoe is attacked by a southern sorcerer, Caerlyn is wounded by an evil blade that threatens to consume her very soul. Karsis goes into her mind to help and they vanquish the demon within her. With the unconscious heroes in their care, Rhoe, Liss, and Graf travel to Everknight, finding trouble along the way. Karsis and Caerlyn wake up as they near Everknight and finally everyone is reunited—including Rhoes' parents, whom he thought to be dead. But there is terrible news as well.

Messengers from Keragan Hold bring with them a name that forces the heroes to assemble and plan for the worst— Ill'-lyth G'harr, the great elven archmage. While everyone is distracted, the man in black finally strikes, revealing himself and going after Karsis. With war looming on their southern borders, and their only hope the elves who vanished hundreds of years ago, it is up to Rhoe and Liss to gather allies and save the land from tyranny...

PIECES ON THE BOARD

She stepped out of the magical portal and felt her heels sink into the earth, the cold dirt spilling over the rim of her footwear and onto her pale skin. She was ready for the crisp air at this altitude but was unprepared for this little annoyance. Shaking her head in disgust, she whispered to the earth and pulled her foot free as the soft dirt hardened beneath her. The ground solidified before her like a dark carpet and she smiled despite the filth on her foot.

Madam Ill'lyth G'harr straightened her back and walked confidently down this small path, heels now clicking softly on the enspelled ground. She hadn't been in the Shield Mountains for centuries and it still had the same effect on her: it bored her to death. The scenery was all the same: rocks, rocks, dirt, and—if you were lucky—some scrub. This high up nothing grew worth a damn. The only things that liked it up here were the ogrann. But the ogrann were why she was here.

Ill'lyth turned a corner and saw an ogrann guard standing there with his dumb grin and tree trunk of a club resting on his massive shoulder. Ogrann were about eight feet tall and smelled of rotting meat. They were grotesque and ruthless, not to mention packed with more muscles than an elephant. The beasts usually roamed the lower hills, making sport in hunting the humans in the outlying villages, but they lived up high in the mountains. This was the main reason hunting parties never found the ogrann villages. The various knights and soldiers that protected the lower hills would attack their hunting parties but never found their homes.

The ogrann finally noticed her and smiled, its cracked teeth showing bits of some sort of meat still stuck in them. "Hey, it's one of the littles. Have you come to get eaten?"

"Certainly not," Ill'lyth said as she pointed and called to the earth. "Ash'anti dir haeth dosit crean." The ancient elven arch-mage never broke stride, walking past the brute as the very ground beneath its feet rose up and fully encased the creature. As his last muffled cries as the dirt poured into his mouth and covered his head, she couldn't hide her smile.

Another whisper to the air blew the crude wooden gate wide open as she walked on, her confidence an almost palpable thing. Smaller ogrann—probably children—took off and ran for the larger thatched buildings as warriors came rushing to the front to see what was going on.

Ill'lyth continued, calling to the various elements as they came at her. One warrior went down gasping for air, clutching his large throat and gagging on nothing. Another suffered the same fate as the gate guard, dropping his spear to vainly fight the very dirt that was engulfing him. The other ogrann fled to the rear of the village, putting as much distance between themselves and this horrible threat.

"Stop!" Kragth came around the Speaking Hut and saw the devastation. He feared that the children had been attacked, but it seemed that this little was only defending itself as his warriors attacked. Thankfully, Kragth was a smart ogrann—in that he had the capacity for *some* forethought. The warriors backed away, except for the ones that died within seconds as the little walked by them. The little had long, bone-white hair tied up in a bun, held by a wrought-iron pin, and her long black dress looked ripped up the side revealing her delicious legs.

"What does this little want here?" he asked. Ill'lyth was having fun until the big one had to go and ruin it. Still, this was what she was trying to accomplish after all.

"I'm here to speak with you, actually. I assume you are the leader of this village?" He was a little larger than the others and had all of six teeth. His mangy hair was caked with mud and she was pretty sure that was a human femur tied to the end of his filthy locks. Interesting to say the least.

"Me the leader. Name is Kragth. Who is you, little?" Kragth was a bit confused. He had asked her a question, but then she asked him one... he wasn't sure if he should've answered, or just smashed her. Leading—like thinking—was hard sometimes.

Ill'lyth smiled and took stock of the size of the village. There were about fifty warriors here, not counting the children and females. The females were scarce, as the ogrann only kept them for breeding and cooking: if they couldn't breed, they cooked them. "I am called Ill'lyth, and I'm here to recruit you to my cause." She saw his look of confusion and laughed quietly. If only her own generals were this stupid. "Here, let me help you." She walked forward a bit, so that she was within arm's reach of him, and closed her eyes. "Ash'anti ethir, lok dosit a'ren," she whispered to the ether, taking control of his mind. She chuckled softly at the clouded nod that he gave her; he was hers now. She walked up to him and took his arm in her own, ignoring the filth and slime for a show of superiority to all his followers.

"Now, come dear—we have plans to discuss," Ill'lyth said. He followed without complaint and the rest of the village returned to normal. Within an hour, the children had planted a rock garden on the two large earthen mounds that marked where the dead had fallen.

Inside Kragth's hut, she gleaned where most of his warriors were currently located, then had him send runners out to call them back to the village. Her forces were laying siege to Keragan Hold as she spoke, so she had to move quickly. She gave him the orders she had readied, detailing the plan as simply as she could for his tiny mind. Once he had the numbers she was looking for—roughly one hundred ogrann—he would start a long, forced march upon the city of Everknight. With their long strides, it would take a little over a day's march to get there; if they started in two days, they would get there ahead of her main force. More importantly, they would hit the northern gate, where a meager force would be holding it against the attack.

Feeling satisfied that most of the ogrann in the entire Shield Mountains were now doing her bidding, Ill'lyth walked back to where she arrived. She closed her eyes, concentrating on her bedroom at the Golden Palace, and opened a portal home. She could've left the old one open, but hadn't wanted any surprises coming through while she was busy with the ogrann.

She dreamed of a hot bath and maybe some torture before looking for the Incarnation of Death, and—upon stepping through and seeing her servants' expression—knew she needed that bath. They didn't say anything though; they knew that their lives were more important.

"Bath!" Ill'lyth screamed, sending them all scurrying. Sitting down on her bed, she relaxed for the first time in a long time. The servants would take about ten minutes to ready the water, so she could take a good breather and think. Her plans were set into motion—nothing could stop her now.

THE HIDDEN VALE, EASTERN LYTHINALL

Liss tossed and turned in fitful sleep, unable to awaken no matter what she did. She was standing in the streets of Everknight and watching her city fend off an attack from a horde of ogrann. It seemed to be almost over when she saw *him*. Rhoe came leaping over one of the blockades with a grace that took her breath away. His robe was ripped and torn. Blood from a dozen minor wounds soaking through, and he was spinning and kicking with a fervor that sent chills down her spine. Behind him came the Incarnation of Death himself, looking almost as battered. It was clear that they had seen their share of fighting. The scene changed and Rhoe was on the ground, his skin turning black as it rotted away. His father, Gareth, crawled to him, wasting away as well, yet determined to make it to his son. Another figure was behind them that was unaffected by the wasting power of death, yet his face was obscured; there was no sign of Dar'Krist anywhere. Liss rushed towards them, fighting a powerful wind she couldn't see, but she was too late—Rhoe died before her eyes.

Liss screamed as she woke in a rush of panic and sweat, looking around for Rhoe. He was just sitting up as she turned to him, panic and concern written on his face. "Oh Rhoe," was all she could say as she hugged him tight to her. Then she remembered that they were both naked.

"What's wrong Liss, bad dream?" Rhoe asked as he took a breath, finding his center and calming down.

"Yes, but it's over now. You're here." Liss still hadn't let go, despite being naked. They were in a hollow tree again—like the last time they were here—and had finally given in to their desires last night after having fun at the Revel thrown to honor the return of Karsis. She felt closer than ever to this caring, wonderful, man next to her. She had made sure to stay away from the drink *and* food last night, eating only what she had brought herself. Rhoe had no defense when she came at him last night, stripping his robe off and pushing him down. It wasn't her first time, but she remembered that it was his, so she was gentle and soothing; he surprised her by not being shy at all.

Rhoe finally eased her back, holding her at arm's length. "We should really get dressed, Liss. Karsis will probably be searching for us and I would rather not be naked when he finds us." Rhoe couldn't believe he was here with this gorgeous woman, never mind that he was in a faerie land, sleeping inside of a tree. He watched Liss as she tried to find her clothes. She was slim and toned, and her long golden hair fell over her shoulders as her copper eyes danced in the darkened hollow of the tree. Rhoe pulled his robe over his head, just as they both heard the singing.

"Oh, Gods above!" Liss exclaimed, fighting desperately with her clothes. She saw Rhoe smile at her as he stood, pulling on his breaches. "Oh sure, you have two things to put on. Cheater." Liss saw him wink and laughed as she looked him over. Rhoe was a little over five feet with a solid but wiry frame. He had trained all of his life as a warrior, like his mother, and had kept his body in shape. But his most striking feature was his long, flowing hair. It reached down to his lower back and was as white as bone. It enthralled Liss to no end and she had no idea why.

"I'll try and stall him, but hurry," Rhoe said as he kissed her forehead and ducked out of the tree. He squinted as the tiny rays of sunlight stabbed through the thick canopy of trees above him. The Hidden Vale was beautiful beyond words and Rhoe didn't think he would ever get over the sight of it. Their tree was right next to the Council Tree area and it soared up into the high canopy as far as he could see. Rhoe saw Karsis coming towards them and marveled at how comfortable the bard seemed here in this place of myth and fairy tales.

Karsis the Bard stood a hair above five feet, with long, auburn curls draped over his slender shoulders. His clothes were finely made, especially his burgundy longcoat that he was very fond of. He wore a ruffled shirt with tiny pockets and his black pants were tucked into black polished high boots, which were decorated with tiny charms. That would be enough to make the man stand out in any crowd, but it was his mannerisms that most people found disturbing, the look on his face that said he had seen everything and still wasn't impressed. It helped that he wasn't bluffing.

Karsis was walking through a massive clearing filled with all manner of sylvan creatures. Pixies, sylphs, and dryads all lounged in a huge circle, in the center of which stood the Council Tree. The Council Tree was massive, its canopy covering the entire clearing, while buzzing faeries of all shapes and sizes flittered through its branches high above the ground. The carved throne beside the Council Tree stood empty this morning.

Karsis saw Rhoe come out of his hollow tree and smiled at the boy's timing. Karsis was in a great mood this morning, as he had danced and played the night away with good company he hadn't seen in many years. The bard had found a cute little water nymph to steal away within the wee hours of the morning and was just now coming back. He wasn't even hung over if one could believe that. Gods above know he couldn't.

He was singing a little shanty about a faerie fiddler and a young dancer but stopped when he got within arm's length of Rhoe. Something was different about the boy. He looked nervous and fidgety, his eyes darting to all the faeries. *He must be worried that someone would see Liss getting dressed,* Karsis thought with a smile.

"Good morning to you, Rhoe. Isn't this a splendid day?" Karsis bowed with a flourish and came up with his arms out wide. He winked at the boy and... wait. Karsis used his *sight* and looked at the boy with a bit more scrutiny. Though it was frowned upon in wizard society to do this, he needed to see if he was correct... and he was! "Rhoven Whiteheart, you truly astound me."

Rhoe, as usual when dealing with Karsis, was confused. "Are you hungover, Karsis?" Rhoe honestly had no idea what the bard was about this early.

Karsis walked around the young man, looking him up and down. "I'm not—though I'm as shocked as you on that front. No, what astounds me this morning is that you have once more done something very hard, and with ease." By now a small gathering of faeries had come to see what all the fuss was about, mainly because they had nothing better to do.

"Are you going to tell me what this amazing feat was or will I have to guess?" Rhoe thought he might know what Karsis was talking about now, but he didn't think it was that big a deal. After all, he was a boy and Liss was a girl.

"Yes, yes. Guess!!" The faeries chanted all around them. Oh, how they liked a good game, especially when it involved humans.

Karsis looked around and smiled, bowing in mock consent. "Let the young one guess then. But only three tries, then we shall have to tell him." The faeries cheered and flittered about in excitement. Karsis could never figure out what it was about a good show that got faeries riled up like this.

Rhoe smiled and took a breath, fairly certain that he knew what Karsis was talking about. He saw that the faeries wanted— no, *needed*—a show, so he decided to play along. "Was it that I was born a sparrow?" The faeries howled and laughed at the inanity of it and he waited until they calmed a bit before he put his hand upon his chin. Rhoe heard Liss come out and turned to see her questioning face. "Or is it that I fell in love with a royal

Princess?" The faeries all drew breath in mock shock, then they all laughed out loud at the look on Liss's face, but stopped when they realized she was crying.

"OhmyTrees'youhurther!" Liana flew in and hugged the Princess's neck, glaring at Rhoe. The other faeries all made noises like 'Ooohhhh', and 'Aaaaahh,' but made no move towards them. The faerie, Liana, was only about fourteen inches tall, with gossamer wings and curly hair, but her heart was much bigger than that, especially when it came to her friends.

"No, Liana, I'm all right. They're happy tears," Liss said, staring at Rhoe. He had said he loved her. More than that, he said he had *fallen in love* with her. She felt honored, even though she was the one with the royal bloodline.

Rhoe looked at Liss, and in that moment he knew that she loved him too and that made him smile even wider. He realized that the game was still on though and nodded to her before he spun around towards Karsis. The bard was looking at them both with an odd look. "Wait... I have it! Karsis was talking about the fact that I have become a wizard." The faeries all hushed in one miraculous second, holding their breath for Karsis's reaction. The final judgment was his.

Karsis bowed deep, bending at the waist and letting his auburn curls lightly brush the ground. "I concece that you have guessed, dear Rhoven. Know that what you have done has not been achieved in centuries as counted by the elves themselves."

"Wait...what?" Rhoe had spun to embrace Liss, but turned back to Karsis slowly, noticing that the faeries were held like snakes to song. "What do you mean?"

Karsis stood, brushing the wrinkles from his longcoat. "What I mean is that when a wizard takes that last step and banishes the darkness completely, it's usually done in a complicated ritual that spans a month of training; some actually die from it." He tried to keep his voice light, but the shock at seeing this young man standing before him, a prodigy like he was yet so much more, was too heavy for light words. The faeries looked at one another, bored already, but were too vested in the conversation to fly away.

"Oh." Rhoe felt like he was going to be sick. Then Liss actually *did* get sick and that broke the tension. Rhoe held her hair back. Her skin was warm to the touch.

"Ewww, look at what she ate last night!" Liana flew down and held her little nose, but the curiosity was overwhelming.

Karsis cleared his throat and turned to the faeries. "All right, party's over. Let's get back to whatever you faeries do and give them some room." He walked over to the kids and couldn't help but think he was missing something, but he had no time to try and figure it out. He knew it had something to do with these two, so that meant it could wait a little bit... he hoped.

Liss stood up and wiped her mouth. "I'm sorry. I don't know what came over me." She straightened her shoulders as the faeries were looking at her whispering. "Gods above, it feels like I'm back in court all over again."

Karsis patted her on the shoulder. "Pay them no mind, dear, they don't see much of this sort of thing around here." He motioned for them to follow him and walked towards the throne. "We're going to have to leave very soon, and not solely because Everknight is depending on us."

Liss wasn't going to ask, but she needed something to distract her from the faeries looking at her. They were still staring, and it was getting intense. "What's the other reason?"

"For one, the time difference."

"The what now?" Rhoe asked, turning to look at Karsis with wide eyes.

Karsis sighed heavily and floated up a little so he could pull his legs under him. Sitting cross-legged in mid-air made him feel more comfortable than actually sitting. "Faeries, by their very nature, disturb the natural order of the world. By themselves they are harmless. However, gathered in one place like this, they tend to warp certain things around them. Things like time." Karsis kept his voice down, not wanting to draw an audience for once. "As such, anyone who stays here ages faster than normal, as time passes quicker here than outside the Hidden Vale." He saw the alarm on their faces and had to laugh. "Don't worry— the effect is very slight, barely noticeable at all. It's more like every day spent here is like four months to you, but only you. Your body can stand to age a couple months faster, and no one would ever notice. But that's why I want to get going; you've already spent a couple of days here the last time."

"Are you scaring them, Karsis?" a voice asked from above. Lurien floated down from a high branch, her smile as radiant as her wings. The Queen of the Faeries was a little under five feet with gossamer wings and a crown of leaves upon her head. She wore a white gown that just grazed the ground, and her feet were bare. Her long, golden hair seemed to move as if there was a light wind, and her smile was like a soothing ray of sunshine.

Karsis turned his head as he floated around to face her. "Perish the thought, dear. We were just going to find Liana and Avaryn so we can get going." Karsis was actually going to enjoy this trip. The last unicorn, a hyper faerie, a princess that wanted to be a wizard, and a wizard that was a warrior. Good times.

"I'm here Karsis!" Liana flew in like a frantic sparrow, dive-bombing them with a giggle.

As am I. Avaryn projected the thought to all of them at once. *Let us depart on this excursion so that I can return and find a quiet place to sleep for a couple of years.*

Karsis dropped, stood on the ground, and spun, his longcoat fanning out behind him. "Very well. Off we go to the city of the elves!" Karsis patted his shoulder and Liana flew over and sat down. They were off—now all they had to do was survive the journey.

MEETING PLACE OF SYLL, SOMEWHERE IN THE HEAVENS

More of a constructed reality than an actual location, it was brought into being the moment *she* thought of it. This place was created by the will of the being called Syll, Goddess of Nature and Magic. This time she assumed a form with black hair, entwined with leaves. Her cloak was covered in stars that seemed to move over the cloth-like they were alive. She was a kind being, loving all creatures big and small, and was as old as the very stars themselves. Elves and faerie folk all worshiped her, as did most wizards and even sorcerers. It was her turn to host the Gathering, as there were still things she and the others needed to work out; she knew her peers would behave, as the ancient rules were still set in place.

They couldn't scheme here, nor could they use their powers against each other. The gods had been working on a project for years now—the first time they had worked together since they created the Incarnations—and it was almost done. Syll smiled to herself at the term *years*. To them, it was no different than a blink, but they had been keeping track as of late.

Her fellow gods would be here soon. They would sit and discuss things until one or more of them grew bored, then they would break again. As host, the meeting place was hers to form. This time it consisted of a large rock, twenty feet in diameter, that rested in a clearing of her favorite trees: beautiful pines and dark birches. Every time they met—and this would be the fourth since they had come up with this plan— the host would stylize the meeting place to their liking. Syll smiled at the notion that some of them would be bothered by being this close to nature but knew that the next location would bother her just as much.

Trees. Why am I not surprised? Norar projected as he stepped into the newly created realm. He was known as the God of Thieves and Shadows and he had chosen a form hooded and cloaked in darkness. Long, black, hair spilled out of the hood and his gloved hands flexed nervously. He sat at the table and though his face was concealed, anyone could tell he was scowling. Norar was a secretive being, loving whispers and hidden truths the way most people loved sunsets. He adored sarcasm, and nothing out of his mouth was ever direct.

Because nothing surprises you? Syll retorted calmly. Of the five, she expected this reaction from Norar the most. Syll turned as a pair of beings formed at the table, not even bothering to even step in from elsewhere.

Greetings sister,—we have come, Ollian thought as she sat in unison with her eternal mate, Davalar the Just. Ollian was the Goddess of Beauty and Love and her form was stunning, even to beings such as the gods. Ollian had flowing platinum blond hair laced with golden thread and a cape of silver covering a gown made of pure light. The light showed off every detail of her perfect form. She was a haughty being, not really caring about the needs of others. It was all about her, all the time... and twice at night.

Indeed. Let us discuss this and move on to our own business. Davalar seemed agitated, probably because he disliked the deal he had struck when this all began. Davalar was the God of Protection and Honor and, as such, hated these meetings, which he considered trivial. He had a form made for combat, all muscles and strength, and his long, white hair fell over his golden cloak. His hand never left Ollian's. He was generally a good being, guarding all life as sacred, and had a flair for following rules, never breaking his promise, and always coming through in the end.

Just waiting for our brother. Rest easy—our task is near the end. Syll couldn't wait for this to be done so that they could go back to ignoring one another once more. Still, truth be told, she looked forward to these meetings, if only to see the others in a neutral setting for once. *What drove us apart?* she thought, raising powerful wards to keep the thought from the others.

The room darkened, then brighten once more, as if a surge of power had flooded through it. Syll held up a hand and strengthened the reality of the place with but a thought and looked around for whatever had tested her strength. Even her god-enhanced senses detected nothing, but when dealing with beings of her caliber, she knew she wouldn't be able to sense anything if one of her fellows didn't want her to. By process of elimination, she knew it had to be the one they were waiting for. On the other hand, the surge of power could have been one of the others trying to stop him from coming. They all loathed him. She was the only one that knew he was necessary.

Waiting for me? The thought came from everywhere at once, and the others frowned at the show of power. Krist arrived with his usual bravado, his form an ebony-skinned elf wearing gleaming mail and carrying a scythe. The God of Death and Corruption had long, white hair, and his eyes blazed a vivid blue. He was beautiful in his own way but had always been jealous of Davalar and Ollian.

Krist sat down and folded his hands, smiling at each of his brothers and sisters in turn. *So, are we ready for the end of our plan?* He was the darkest of beings, reveling in the death of all things and coveting power only for himself.

Turns out there may be a problem, Syll thought to the group. She envisioned birds flying overhead and smiled as they appeared. *Your Incarnation is being stalked, Krist and the chances of him being taken are growing with every mortal breath. You told us that wouldn't happen.*

I said it wouldn't matter, Krist thought back, his smile darkening. *Davalar gave them the prophesy so that they could prepare for this possibility and I, for one, have faith in his creatures.* Krist tried not to sound magnanimous, but it had been a long couple of decades with these sniveling beings. Even if he had agreed to go through with this plan, he had his own ideas. After all, he *was* getting the better deal out of all this. He wouldn't have agreed to help if that hadn't been the case.

Davalar sat up straight. *The plan is unchanged. I know how it will unfold and there is nothing that can thwart our will now.* He looked askance at Norar, who sat cowled and hidden, and wondered if the God of Shadows would try to stop them after all.

Norar didn't bother to acknowledge his brother. *So not all of them, but some of them?* He asked quietly. Norar was on board, but he wanted to make sure they knew he wasn't pleased. Usually, he didn't bother with the world, but this time he was perturbed. He just hoped he wouldn't be disappointed in the end.

Syll smiled at her brothers and sisters, knowing that they had all made sacrifices. *That is correct brother, and fear not—the plan will be for the better. Too long have we been absent. A little guidance will refresh the world. Now, on to the events with Ollian. Are you sure you have guided them down the right path?*

Ollian looked bored as her hand lightly grazed Davalar's face, even though he was ignoring it. *Yes, sister. And now it is up to your creatures and the powers they hold to further the plan.*

The God of Shadows scoffed. *I still can't believe you forced them together,* Norar thought, shifting his feet from the floor to the top of the stone table. He saw Syll scowl and barked a laugh at her expense; he loved irritating her the most.

Davalar leaned forward, his eyes flaring. *We didn't* force *them—it happened naturally. We just sped up the process a little*, he thought. *I saw them together when we started this, but it would've taken them years. Instead, they are together when we need them to be.* He sat back as he finished this thought and almost smiled. Almost.

Syll rose, spreading her arms wide as a sign of peace among her peers. *Then we are done for now. We will meet one last time when the plan is finished.*

I do believe I have the pleasure of hosting next time. Krist smiled darkly, savoring the looks from around the stone table. *I look forward to meeting you all in my little piece of heaven.* And just like that, they were all gone, the beings that would-be gods, along with the forest around them. Only a single bird was left flying in the void of nothingness. It smiled to itself, as a bird cannot, and reflected upon his children and all they had wrought. It could've gone better, but as it stood, they were finally making up for their past mistakes. He grew larger and more distant, then vanished as if he were never there. With no one to witness it, who was to say he was?

2

ONWARD TO GLORY

He scanned the battlements of Keragan Hold once more and counted at least fifty archers left. His troops were just out of arrow range but were getting anxious to attack once more. Commander Elis frowned and waved his hand for a messenger.

"Yes sir?"

"Tell General Pondar that he is safe to send his forces in from the west this morning. I'm going to bait them here," Ellis said and dismissed the messenger with a wave of his hand. The commander had close-cropped hair that was quickly turning grey and his aging, broad shoulders held his southern cape very well. The reinforcements had been here for over a day and already that foolish general had lost more than five hundred men. Ellis shook his head as he thought of those foolish charges against the fortified walls and all of the arrows that came raining down. He had tried to tell Pondar, but the man would take no counsel. Ellis had done the same thing just three days before and had learned his lesson the hard way.

General Pondar had charged the wall as well, losing a good number of men, but that wasn't the worst part. The worst was the second charge. That damnable Lord Keragan had wrapped rocks up in burlap tarps and placed them on the battlements, and the southern forces couldn't tell what was in the sacks until it was too late. The defenders unrolled them once the soldiers came close to the wall, raining chunks of stone down on their heads. As the men ran back to their lines in a full route, the archers picked them off like sitting ducks on a still pond. After that, General Pondar took seven hundred men and went west with the sorcerer, Khaz, leaving Ellis with roughly eight hundred men.

"Think he's going to change his mind and not tell you?" Franc asked beside him. He hated Pondar on general principles, something that most people said Pondar didn't even have, but Franc still tried to respect the oaf. Franc was Commander Ellis's second-in-command and loved working with the gruff but respectable leader. Franc had curly hair, a bubbly attitude, and was never afraid to say what was on his mind.

Commander Ellis furrowed his brows, turning towards Franc. "If he changes his mind and attacks from another direction, then he will lose more of his men." Ellis sighed and turned towards his own soldiers. "Prepare the men!" He looked over at the construction crew and made a fist. "Gather shields!" Ellis watched the men pick up their hastily made work and come running over. It was a group of tower shields slipped over long beams and lashed together. The six shields, held over the men, would protect them from the arrows raining down from above. Hopefully.

"Won't they be looking for the sorcerer, Commander?" Franc asked, remembering what happened to the first sorcerer the minute he stepped forward and tried to take down the walls with his magic. The arrow was sticking right out of the man's throat before anyone knew what was going on. Franc swore they weren't in range, because no one could've made that shot otherwise.

Ellis sighed and turned towards the shorter man. "Probably, though it's not our concern. We have to draw their fire long enough for General Pondar to get Khaz near the west wall and bring it down." He saluted the construction crew as they brought the second shield roof over. Ellis had twenty men under each one, enough to start working on the main doors at least and give the hold something to focus on. The rest of his men would be three hundred yards away, a safe distance from arrows and close enough to storm the hold if the door ploy worked. He saw the lead men nod as they gathered under their new protection, then Ellis signaled to the caller. The young man let out a blow from the war horn and the men were away.

Up on the battlements of Keragan Hold, Storn frowned at the things coming towards his front doors. Storn had surprised the southern forces with rocks when they came at him, but now it seemed they had a trick or two of their own. The women and children were safely away, as were the old and infirm, so that left him with one hundred men, almost all of them competent archers. *I only pray that Thanier and Ellen are all right leading the women and children into the Shield Mountains.* That was when the runner came bolting up the stairs interrupting his thoughts.

"Lord Keragan!" the man yelled, trying to catch his breath.

"Slow down, it's all right." Storn would've laughed at the poor runner, huffing and puffing, if they weren't all going to die horribly any minute now.

"I'm sorry, sir. It's just that we only have twenty quivers left. The guard captain said you needed to know that."

"Damn! Yes, you're right. Thank you very much. As you were, man." Storn turned again and looked at the contraptions coming at the hold. He had two volleys left, and by the look of that thing, they wouldn't pierce it at all. Things looked bleak indeed until he saw the thin column of smoke to the rear of the encamped army. As he watched, it slowly turned into an 'S' and then changed back again. "Tanan, that has to be you. You sly demon!" Storn raced down the stone stairwell shouting for every man to take arms. He passed the caller and set the man to ring the bell and slid into the outer courtyard, snatching his favorite bow and yelling for his men. In five minutes they were all at the front gate awaiting his orders, and wondering how they were going to fire arrows over the wall from here.

Guard Captain Rozzen stepped forward and saluted. "Lord, what are your orders?"

"One moment, Captain. Just let me think a few seconds more." Storn paced back and forth, then pointed to the old siege catapult that had graced the courtyard for years. "That! Perfect." Storn spun and smiled and every man shifted his feet a little bit; Lord Storn Keragan smiling was a rare thing indeed. Storn stood there, wearing a simple dark green cloak over his white shirt and woolen breeches. He had very dark skin and his black hair and beard were trimmed but not lavishly. Storn Keragan wasn't a big man, but he stood over five feet and was well muscled. His main attributes were his keen eyes and quick thinking; at least Karsis had always said so. "You three. Get that rolling and get it set in front of us. I need thirty men to push it out the door and we will follow as fast as we can."

"But it doesn't work, sir." Rozzen was even more confused. The catapult hadn't worked since he had come to the hold—as far as he knew it wasn't even functional.

"It rolls. That's all you need for now." Storn had an idea, but he would need it to be going pretty fast. "All right, now for the fun part. I'm going to tell you the plan, and you're probably going to hate it. However, we have friends close and honestly, there is no other way." He turned to the gates and kept going as the men worked. "They split their forces late last night and Gods above know where they went. So have faith and follow me once last time, and know that I'll be there with you, come what may."

A cheer went up, and as he told them his plan they nodded their heads solemnly. This was it—their last shot. Ride into the jaws of your enemy and take as many as you can with you.

BACK ON THE FIELD, THE FORTY MEN WERE ALMOST AT THE front gate and not one arrow had been fired. They were nervous at first, but as time went on, they went from nervous to confident. So confident that when the gate was thrown open and the men ran out, they were completely dumbfounded. Arrows came racing straight at them, dropping them as fast as they could turn around, then another burst dropped the second team. In less than a minute, forty men were dead and Storn's desperate ride had begun. "Gather up these shields, men!" Storn said as they got rolling once more.

Commander Ellis stared open-mouthed for a couple of seconds, then snapped his mouth shut and turned on his heel. This crafty lord had outsmarted him at every turn. He had to admire him, but he didn't have to like it. "Franc, take half of the men and charge. They will be in arrow range soon, so meet them upon the field and slaughter them before they can riddle our army from afar." They couldn't use the cavalry efficiently across the pock-marked ground, so infantry it was.

"Yes sir!" Franc spun and started barking orders for the men to form up. Within seconds they were running as carefully as they could over the pocked ground. They charged with spears and swords out, determination in their eyes.

Commander Ellis called for his own archers to come forward and set up. Unfortunately, they only had short bows, so their range was limited compared to the longbowmen of the hold. It was only a backup move, however, as Franc would cut them down with his almost four hundred men to their paltry hundred.

Franc was halfway across the field when he saw what had happened to their shield constructions. It seemed that they were attached to some sort of rolling...something, and it was coming right for them. He signaled for the men to spread out and watched the contraption keep on course. With one set of the shields on the front, and another on the rear, it would be impossible to hit them with arrows at range. That was when he saw the men fan out behind the thing and drop to a knee.

"Arrows!" Franc called out, but it was too late. Franc fell with an arrow in his leg and chest, feeling the cold creep in on him slowly. Then his body was crushed under the wheels of Storn's desperate ride.

Storn was yelling at the top of his lungs; he couldn't believe he was doing this. A stunt like this... well it was usually something Tanan or Karsis would come up with. He was more of a thinker and planner and this was just too spontaneous for him. He had to admit that it was working thus far, though. He had thirty men pushing this thing as hard as they could, and with the improvised shields that the ten men riding it held, they would be safe from arrows as they approached the main force. They speared clean through their devastated, confused foes who were now leaderless; the remaining arrows would be used by the sixty other men running alongside when they got closer. He guessed that the men left behind—half running to catch them, and half staring dumbly after the others—only numbered two hundred and fifty. Not too bad at all. They were still dead if the second part of the plan failed, though, and that was the worst part; it was based on a guess.

Commander Ellis felt his blood rise. The lord of the hold had come up with some sort of contraption himself, then used Ellis's own shields to protect it! "Archers, target their infantry and take aim!" Ellis yelled as he walked down the line of soldiers. He guessed that those improvised shields would stop most of the arrows, so he was going to have them target the men on foot instead. He was about to order men with polearms to set their weapons against that contraption when he heard someone clear their throat behind him.

"Ahem." Tanan saw the old man spin and reach for his sword, only to miss as the harness slipped off his shoulders—Tanan had undone the clasp seconds before he alerted the old soldier. Tanan threw off his southern cloak and watched the man step back, weaponless. "Good sir, if you could just surrender, that would make my job a whole lot better." Tanan swung his short sword back and forth in short swipes to show the man he meant business and saw the man's eyes narrow. He had expected the commander to shout for the soldiers to attack, but he didn't—he wasn't complaining, mind you, it was just disturbing that his luck was holding for once.

Ellis couldn't understand how this man had walked past all of his soldiers. Worse, he had announced himself. That meant he *wanted* Ellis to call for an attack as a diversion. The commander backed up and reached slowly for one of the archer's swords. Every archer carried a short sword for close combat, and even though it wasn't Ellis's weapon of choice, he was more than proficient with one. He noticed the man was dressed in a black silk tunic with black breeches and sported a long, dark-blue cape. Broaches and pins adorned his clothes and his high black boots were silent when he moved his feet. The man's steps were light, almost graceful, and his thin wiry frame said he had seen action before.

"Sorry, surrender is not an option. Whom may I say I have the pleasure of killing today?" Ellis asked as he drew the archer's sword.

Tanan let him draw the sword and smiled, unfazed at the scenario. He wasn't here to kill anyone. "I am Lord Tanan, of the Companions of Everknight, also called the Lilac Lord in some very elaborate circles," Tanan said with a flourish that would've made Karsis proud. He looked around—the other soldiers had drawn their weapons, but they didn't attack. They simply watched. None of them looked worried that their commander was going to face him. Maybe this man was better than he appeared? "However, I have to warn you—I do not wish to fight you."

Commander Ellis knew that the Lord of Keragan hold was almost in arrow range, so he had to make this quick. "Well, prepare to be disappointed." He lunged forward twice, lightly landing on the balls of his feet, then retreated just as quickly. He had caught Tanan off guard, tearing his shirt with the tip of his blade, but the man's smile never faltered. All of a sudden, Ellis wished he was twenty years younger.

Tanan baited him perfectly, even letting the man get the first strike. Now all of the soldiers were watching—all eyes were on him. "Thank you for the entertainment, good sir; it was a pleasure meeting you." Tanan glanced at his ripped shirt and frowned. "I'll pay you back for the shirt at a later date, be sure of that." Tanan bowed again and put his fingers up to his mouth. He gave a shrill whistle and ducked into a backward roll as a volley of five-hundred arrows rained onto the commanders' ranks. He sprang to his feet and fought his way back south and east to his main force, then gave the command to pull back. He took a couple of minor hits but he was alive...for now.

Ellis knew the first thing they had to do was stop that charging lord. "Arrows away! To arms men!" he yelled over the screaming soldiers as his men dropped around him. The front ranks let loose and cut into the approaching archers from the hold, but also cut into the men chasing them. Meanwhile, Ellis's forces were in disarray as Tanan's force flanked them, hitting hard even as they ran a controlled disengagement; the G'harran's fell apart quickly.

Ellis felt a stabbing pain in his leg and looked down to see an arrow embedded in his thigh. He tried to rally his men, but the soldiers from Lythinall were already on the move, fighting an organized retreat to the east. His men were confused, wounded, and caught off guard. The archers yelled, and Ellis turned to see an unmanned contraption thundering towards them. The shields had fallen off; he could see it was a large catapult rolling helplessly towards them, a weapon of uncontrolled damage amongst his unorganized force.

"Damn them all to the Deep Hells." Ellis scowled as he tried to regain some semblance of control. He limped out of the way of the siege engine gone wrong and saw the Lord of Keragan Hold and his men striking out east on foot to meet up with Lord Tanan. Ellis still outnumbered them, but it would take a couple of minutes to get his men in any kind of shape to give chase. Now he had to think of what he was going to tell General Pondar when the General got back from the west wall.

WESTERN RIDGE, KERAGAN HOLD

Janna Suris and Dren sat on a small ridge behind Keragan Hold. They watched General Pondar's force as the men marched around wide to the west wall. Janna remembered seeing the force arrayed against the hold and wondered how they were going to help. The force from Lythinall had stopped half a mile behind the G'harrans; there was no way to alert them without giving away their own position. Tanan asked her to enchant some wood so when they burned it the smoke would turn into an "S." He'd had it was something they did years ago, but she thought he was just making it all up.

Janna played with her long, brown ponytails as her piercing green eyes stared out over the soldiers lining up to face the west wall. Her confidence betrayed her small, thin, frame, which was only a little over five feet and weighed only seven stones. Janna's harp was slung on her back, and her clothes were cut high to show more skin than fabric. *Now let's just hope I haven't misjudged the power of the general's sorcerer.*

"There he is," Dren said as he shifted his feet to get comfortable. He wasn't going to come with Janna, but when he heard there was a chance to kill a G'harran general, he couldn't say no.

Janna rolled her eyes. "Yeah, yeah. Just settle down and kill the sorcerer first. We jump out there without getting rid of him and he may just take us out first." Janna didn't really believe that, but she had to rein Dren in from time to time. She was worth four southern sorcerers, but she also wasn't stupid. "When he steps up to take down the wall, take him out. I can hit the general after that." She whispered to the air to make Dren's arrows fly faster, then sat back and waited for the sorcerer to give his position away. Although Dren looked like just another guard captain, she knew that he was special. He had black hair and dark eyes, but it was his passion that put him above others she had known. When his best friend had given his life so that they could escape, it had broken his heart. He had loved the man, though she doubted that anyone besides her ever knew,.

Dren tested his longbow. It was well made with a good pull; it was his skill, not the weapon, he was worried about. He wasn't half bad with a bow, but it wasn't his best weapon by any means.

"Gods above, make my aim true," he whispered to himself. Then he saw movement in the enemy ranks as a lone man, dressed in a black cloak, hesitantly walked out.

Khaz took two steps and held his hands up as if they could stop an arrow. After three breaths—when he realized he was still alive—he took three more steps. Still, no one appeared on the battlements. Khaz commanded the air around him to shield his front against attacks, then confidently strode towards the wall. This was going to be *his* day and he was going to make a grand show of it to impress General Pondar.

"Obren sonn, brak..." he started, then felt a sharp pain in his side. His breath caught before he could finish the spell. Screams came from behind him and the sound of swords clearing their scabbards rang in his ears as he looked down at his side. His vision dimmed as he saw it was an arrow, pierced neatly through his ribs and into his lung. *But I warded... the front...*he thought in his last waking moment. Then he hit the dirt and never rose again.

Dren swore under his breath as the arrow sunk deep into the sorcerer's side but he didn't go down. Janna had warned him the man had shielded himself with air in the front, so Dren had fired as soon as he had a clear shot to the man's unprotected side. He may or may not have shot with his eyes closed, mainly because he heard the man already chanting. As the soldiers drew weapons and looked for the assassin, the sorcerer looked down at his wound and finally fell.

"Yes!" Dren did a little dance and hurried back to where Janna was hiding. He ducked as a hail of arrows sailed over his head and thanked the Gods above that they all missed him. Janna was concentrating so he knew she was taking care of the general, but her face didn't look happy.

Janna saw the arrow find its mark and breathed a sigh of relief. She used her *sight* to focus on the general and whispered to the air to leave his body. As an Incarnation, she had more raw power than most wizards, but even so, she always gave her foes the benefit of the doubt. This was one of those times. She saw him gasp, but then his mouth moved and he started to breathe easier once more. He turned his head and looked, smiling right at her. *Crap,* she swore to herself, *how did he do that?*

General Pondar called out to the earth and commanded it to engulf the assassin. She was pretty enough, but she had tried to kill him and forced him to reveal his secret. If any of the men around him told the bitch queen about his magical talents, his life would be forfeit. As it was, they were all staring at him as he had shouted the words to stop the air before he lost his voice. No one knew that he was an accomplished sorcerer except his tutors, and he had them all killed once they had taught him what they knew. General Pondar saw her shake off the earth and frown. He had her, he could feel it.

Janna cursed as the earth fell away from her feet. The man was a sorcerer! "Damn him to the Deep Hells!" She called out to the heat in the air, fanning it and emboldening it, then unleashed it in a torrent of flame that consumed his legs and worked its way up his body. She saw him scream and closed her eyes. She hated fire. It always gave her the creeps, but she needed it now. The flames crawled up his legs like little gremlins of fire, leaping and dancing in their work. General Pondar didn't have the concentration to put it out while he was burning.

Hells, not many people do—except Karsis and maybe the Sorcerer King, Janna thought as she sat down and collected herself, shivering in disgust. She looked up as Dren came over and smiled, weakly. "Got him."

"I see. Nice work there, girl." Dren saw she was exhausted and helped her up, but he was distracted by the army of angry

G'harran's approaching their position. "Shall we get back to the others?"

Janna nodded. "Yeah, they should be on the move to the east now, so we will have to go around the long way to avoid the chasing army." She really was weak, which was odd, since she was the Incarnation of Beauty. Incarnations healed faster and were generally tougher than most humans. That General must've been stronger than she thought. Dren's face fell and she followed his gaze down to her stomach. There was the reason she was so weak. . She had taken an arrow and it had gone in deep. "Well, crap," she exclaimed, then promptly sat back down.

"What can I do?" Dren asked calmly. He knew she was a wizard of sorts. He had heard her use the elven word for please, something sorcerers never did. *Look at me, a couple days with heroes and I think I know stuff,* he thought sarcastically.

"You can hold my hand as I fix it because this is going to hurt worse than sex with an ogrann." She grabbed his hand and whispered to the heat in the air, focusing it down tight, like a needle, trying to ignore her terror of fire. She hit the shaft with the focused flame and incinerated it, cauterizing the wound as she did. Janna screamed, then clenched her teeth as she started to shake. Unfortunately, she also burned some of the tissue on the inside as well. Thank the gods she healed faster than normal, otherwise that little stunt might have killed her. But she knew the enemy soldiers had heard her scream and would be here soon.

Dren held her steady and tried not t look behind them. "I think we're going to hide for a while and let the others carry on without us," he said as she went pale and sat down.

"No... can't." She tried to sit up, then thought better of that idea, as her equilibrium decided then and there to go on a short vacation. "They're going... to be coming... here for us," she finally got out through ragged breaths. Then she was in the air as Dren picked her up. *Is he seriously carrying me? What book have I found myself in?* she thought as she slipped into a breathing routine that would help the pain.

Dren shook his head. "Forget it. I lost Stard, I'm not losing anyone else." He took off at a slow pace back where they had come from. It was a tough walk along the mountain ridge behind the hold, and he could hear soldiers behind them already. Then he saw their chance.

"Hold on, Janna. I'm going to do something a little crazy." He turned up the mountain path and climbed a good fifty feet, then backtracked along a higher ridge. He didn't want to leave her alone, but he needed to stay low and couldn't do that while carrying her.

Janna couldn't believe he was going back towards the enemy—but then again, she couldn't really see what was going on, just the direction. "What are you doing Dren?" She bit her lip as he set her down and crept along without her. He was moving towards a large boulder and she suddenly knew what he was up to. She heard the soldiers below and saw Dren trying to move the rock with everything he had. Janna used what strength she had left and whispered to the air to help shove the rock. It gave way and toppled down the ridge, raining stone debris upon the soldiers below. It hit them like Davalar's fist and scattered them.

Dren felt a strong wind behind him and smiled as the rock went down. Leave it to Janna to help even when she was hurting. He watched as the southern soldiers scattered uselessly. Out of almost fifty men, only ten were unscathed, and most of them turned back to the main force. "Teach your grandmother to eat dirt!" Dren called after them.

"Hey, settle down and come pick me up." Janna teased. Dren had probably saved them both but damned if she was going to let him know that. "What kind of insult was that anyway?"

"It was something I just came up with. We can't all be bards you know." He smiled and picked her up once more. Now they just had to figure out how to meet up with Lord Tanan again. *If it was easy, it wouldn't be worth doing now, would it?* he thought as they climbed out of the mountain ridge.

HUNTING PATH, LOWER SHIELD MOUNTAINS

Thanier stumbled for the hundredth time and shook his head. He was not cut out for exploration of any kind, but here he was. He was short, only about five feet tall, with a shaved head and grey robes. Not athletic whatsoever, he was more brains than brawn. He had led the women and children, along with the old and infirm, out of Keragan Hold and up into the Shield Mountains. The plan was to find a safe haven and wait out the siege, hoping for the best but expecting the worst. The one glitch in the plan was that the lower Shield Mountains were home to wandering ogrann. They hadn't actually seen one yet—the Gods know he would've passed out from fear—but he was constantly scanning the horizon for any signs.

"How are you holding up, Than?" asked the slight woman approaching from behind him. Ellen Falkwind was dressed in traveling clothes of earthly colors; her favorite bow was slung around her shoulder. Ellen's short, brown hair was more boyish than stylish, and she took nothing from no one—ever. She was the Scout Captain of Keragan Hold and her skills in the wilderness were unmatched in this region. Ellen gently rested her hand on his shoulder, a true sign of respect. She had teased him the first few days but he had proven his worth, leading with an intellect that had surprised her. Sure, she was a tracker with survival skills that most would marvel at, but he had already saved them. Twice. Right when they set out, they came across a gap that they wouldn't have crossed if not for his quick thinking. They would've had to go back and gods above know what would've happened. The second time he didn't just save them all... he had saved her.

Thanier nodded. "I'm fine, Ellen. Just keep your eye out for those bent trees I was talking about." He knew the signs of ogrann, though he had never before seen one in person. Books were his weapons, and he was very good with them. When ogrann traveled, they usually leaned on the surrounding trees. This high up the trees were weakened by erosion and would lean permanently when pushed. They had been traveling for days and so far no signs. Unfortunately, they hadn't found any caves they could stay in either, but the distant ridge-line had promise. Their people were tired and scared, but determined.

Ellen patted him on the back. "I will, Than, I will." She jogged ahead, scanning the tree line out of habit. Her head still hurt from the falling rock, but thanks to Thanier she was alive. It had caused swelling in her brain, apparently, and he had some of the older women make a poultice out of herbs that helped her to live through the night. He'd actually cut into her with his knife. Ellen shuddered at the thought, but smiled at the memory; they told her Thanier had passed out after seeing her bloody scalp.

Ellen came out of her thoughts and stopped dead, still fifty feet ahead of the line of refugees. Ogrann tracks, and dozens of them, all heading in one direction and coming from all over. They had gathered here and set out somewhere *en mass*. Ellen signaled for the group to stop and waved Thanier forward.

Thanier's shoulders sank. He didn't think he could handle any more bad news. He felt as if he'd had three nervous break-downs already and was sure that if he had any more stress his heart may give out. He trudged up with a half-smile anyway "What did you find, Ellen?" He was so tired of walking that Ellen looked blurry in the fading sunlight.

Ellen pointed to the tracks with a concerned look. She didn't want to give him anything else; he seemed to do better without presumptions. "What do you think?"

Thanier walked around the tracks. He wasn't a tracker, but he saw something in their grouping. "They come in all bunched up, but leave in an odd three-by-three pattern. Marching?" It was all he could think of, but for ogrann to band together and march was almost unheard of. Almost.

Ellen nodded in agreement. "I would've said that, but ogrann never band together like this." She saw his smirk and knew he was waiting for her to say this. Times like these are why she always used to want to punch him, but not anymore.

Thanier placed his hands behind his back like he always did when he lectured. "I wouldn't say 'never.' In the old wars against the elves there was one Archmage who gathered a group of ogrann and used fear to drive them at the elven camps. They were, of course, slain out of hand, but it gave the attackers a chance to wear down the defending elves." He looked to the distant east and knew that they were being herded towards Everknight. "Care to guess that Archmage's name?"

Ellen was there when her Lord told them, but honestly, she was terrible at remembering things that didn't directly involve her. "Is it the woman that Lord Storn says is leading G'harr?"

Thanier smiled wide. "Give the girl a ribbon." He turned back to the group with a frown. "Problem is... what do we do now?"

Ellen narrowed her eyes. "Wait—how is it that you read that in a book? I thought all the stories from that time had disappeared?"

Thanier was proud, but he was too tired to boast. "I have a

stash of rare books taken from raids that Lord Storn used to make on G'harr. The things I've read would make your hair turn white." He was starting to sweat profusely and the exertion was making his heart pound in his chest. He was glad for this slight pause.

"Is that how you lost your hair?"

"As a matter of fact, no." He stuck his tongue out at her as he caught his breath. "By the way, thanks for giving me some lead out here. I was sure you would just shout at me until I fell off a cliff."

"No problem, Thanier. You have really pulled your weight —and mine." Ellen paused before she continued talking. Once she started it was hard to stop, and being mushy was the last thing she wanted to do out here. "Now, this is what we're going to do. You are going to find a safe place for this group to shelter until it's safe again, and I'm going to follow this hoard of ogrann and see what mischief I can cause." Her blood was up now. The whole way up here she'd been ready for a fight; she needed to shoot something.

"Ellen," Thanier stopped himself short. He had known her for years and there was absolutely nothing he could say to make her see reason. "Be safe. Once we are settled, I will follow the tracks as best I can to help." He even kind of meant that.

A few days ago she would have laughed, but after seeing how brave he had been despite the physical exertion, she was proud that he cared enough to help. "Very well, Than. You find me, all right?" She embraced him, feeling his awkward squirming, then gathered a pack from a horse and set out.

Thanier felt a lump in his stomach. It was hard seeing her leave; he was on his own now. *They are depending on you—pull it together,* he thought to himself as he trudged back to the line of people. He led them down one of the opposite trails that the ogrann left on and it only took another two hours to find a cave large enough to shelter them all. It was dark by then and it took even longer to get a fire started and everyone settled in for the evening. They set guards and handed out provisions, then Thanier stood by the cave mouth, staring at the blossoming stars in the night sky. He would leave in the morning and try to find Ellen. He just prayed that she hadn't done anything foolish. Sadly, he knew the possibility of finding her body was just as good as not. "I'll find you, Ellen, I promise."

SERPENT RIVER BRIDGE, SOUTHWEST OF EVERKNIGHT

Tanan's forces could see the Serpent River Bridge but the enemy was too close. To cross the bridge with this many people his forces would have to stop and go over in smaller groups; by the time they were finished, the commander's forces would be right at their backs. Not for the first time, Tanan missed his old blade, Morlan. It had been destroyed by the Incarnation of Death, even though Tanan was sure that nothing could've touched that blade. It was one of a kind, pulled from the back of a dragon. *Now that was a fun day,* he thought to himself.

"Last stand?" Storn was only half kidding. He saw the dilemma as well and knew these soldiers had only one chance of getting across this bridge.

Tanan laughed despite himself. "Always with the self-sacrifice—though, sadly, this time you may be right. If Janna were here we would have a chance, but I haven't seen her or Dren." Tanan didn't want to think that something had gone wrong. After all, the other general was not behind them, but they should've been back by now.

Storn looked back at the approaching dust cloud. "They'll be all right, Tanan, Dren seems like a solid man in a tight spot, and that girl is a force of nature all by herself." He remembered when they had saved his life not too many days ago, and knew that anyone who went against them would be very, very sorry.

Tanan laughed. Janna was an Incarnation herself and very hard to kill. "If you only knew!" Tanan called for a halt with a raised fist and then gave orders to form up in the rear while the others began crossing as quickly as they could. The bridge was solid oak and wide enough for a merchant cart, but there were almost three hundred and fifty soldiers and they were exhausted. He spied one of the captains approaching and knew what the young man was going to say. Tanan smiled at the man who had never dealt with the stubbornness of Storn Keragan.

"My Lords, you should be crossing with the first wave." Hennet was a first-year, a rising star in the Everknight Guard. He wasn't a knight yet, but he was close to becoming one.

Storn laughed right in the man's face. Literally. The old archer strode up and clapped the man on the shoulder and barked at him, inches from his stunned expression. "You *must* be new. I am Lord Storn, of the Companions of Everknight. I do not leave the battlefield like a haughty noble, leading from his ivory tower."

"But... sir?"

"New *and* deaf." Tanan knew he shouldn't instigate, but he was having way too much fun.

Storn leaned into the man, making poor Captain Hennet back up meekly. He knew guys like this and hated the type of officer they made. Young and rich, he probably bought his way to the position and had never even seen combat. Storn knew just what this young officer needed. "As a matter of fact, captain—it is captain, isn't it?" Storn waited for the man to nod. "As a matter of fact, I think I should show you exactly what it means to be in charge." He put his arm around the man and led him to where the rear guard was forming up. He felt the man start to shake in his boots.

Hennet was doomed. He had only fought mock battles, rising in rank through his family's connections more than his deeds. Now here he was, walking to the battle line like a grunt at the side of a legend. Hennet couldn't say no, for fear that the king would get wind of his family's interference, so he tried not to cry and looked for something to hide behind.

COMING IN HARD ON THE HEELS OF THE FORCES FROM Everknight, Commander Ellis had all of his men, as well as the late General Pondar's men, behind him. He had assumed command and chased the lords all the way to the Serpent River Bridge. He had found Franc's crushed body and had vowed to cut down the dark-skinned Lord of Keragan Hold personally if it was the last thing he ever did—especially if it was the last thing he did. Ellis was so consumed with vengeance that he almost didn't stop in time when Lady G'harr appeared in front of him out of thin air. *No, not thin air,* he thought as he saw a shimmering door behind her.

Ill'lyth had felt Pondar's death and had located Ellis with her *sight* after resting for a bit. She opened a portal, which took effort since she was still drained. Ill'lyth could've just sent him a message, but she had to come in person. She needed to get her point across and she didn't think the man would give up this close to his prey unless she made her point face to face. "Commander Ellis—or should I say, *General* Ellis?"

Ellis knew he should bow or something, but it just wasn't him; never had been. He saluted and inclined his head in respect but then his hard eyes came up to match hers. "What can I do for you, my Queen? We're in a bit of a hurry to catch the enemy before they get behind those walls." If he died, so be it; he was angry and didn't care.

Ill'lyth tilted her head. "Actually that is why I came. You see, I have a surprise for them and want them to get back in one piece. Besides, waiting for the other generals and their armies would be a strategic move and help your own men out as well." She pointed behind him to show him how weary they all looked. "To be more precise, I command it. Relax and rest up for the moment, but do not let anyone from Lythinall back this way; they are to stay there."

Ellis sighed. He had to admit that she was right. He had let his emotions take hold of him and drive him without thinking of his men. Typically, he always put the men first, but just now he hadn't and he felt stupid.

Now you look like a real General, the voice in his head said in Franc's voice.

Shut up Franc, Ellis thought back. He knew it was probably his guilt, but sadly, he welcomed it right now. "As you command, My Queen. How long do we wait until we start the advance?"

"I should be back in two days. That should give my... surprise time enough to get where I want them to be." Ill'lyth saw that he wanted to ask, but held his tongue. She turned and headed back to the shimmering door. "Oh, and General Ellis? Tell Haldir and Kasson that you are in charge until I arrive. I have another errand to attend to and will be bringing it with me when I come back."

"Yes My Queen," Ellis said, but she was already gone. He let out a breath he hadn't realized he was holding and turned to the weary runner next to him. The poor lad was white. "You heard your queen—inform the men that we are resting. Set camp and call for watch while I get ready." The boy was gone in a heartbeat and Ellis was left to contemplate his field promotion with just his ghosts for company.

I'm not a ghost.

General Ellis closed his eyes, trying to ignore the voice in his head. Then it started whistling. *Shut up, Franc.*

As you wish, General.

TANAN WAITED WITH THE REAR GUARD AS THEY WATCHED the dust come towards them. Spring was giving way to early summer and the heat was already drying up the roads. As such, heavy traffic would kick up clouds of dust, and a force that size made quite a cloud. As they watched with nervous anticipation, the dust settled and dispersed. A rumble passed through the ranks as the rest of the defenders made their way across the bridge with alacrity. Tanan heard the speculation of why the G'harran had stopped and knew he had to quell these rumors before they got out of hand.

"Are you thinking what I'm thinking?" Storn asked gravely as he approached. The Lord of Keragan hold was still dragging Captain Hennet around with him, but at least the little man looked a bit more confident.

Tanan smiled and winked at the captain before answering his old friend. "Yeah, they have something up their sleeve and it's making my stomach very unhappy." Tanan turned and signaled the last half of the rear guard to start falling back towards the bridge. "I'll save the speech till we get to Everknight though, just in case." He heard the right side of the rear guard call out a warning and turned to see two men on foot approaching their flank. Scratch that. A man and a very beautiful woman.

Janna saw the men arrayed before the bridge and smiled. They were still here! "See Dren, you always think the worst." They had seen the G'harran forces about a half-mile away suddenly stop and took the chance to run around their blindside and get to Tanan. Janna had healed up fairly well and wouldn't even have a scar. It helped that she had the power of the Goddess Ollian running through her; more like galloping, actually.

Dren sighed in defeat. "Yeah, well, I still think we got lucky. That commander had them dead to rights at this bridge." He was utterly shocked that Tanan's forces were still alive; he was sure they would've been wiped out.

"Maybe they are waiting for more reinforcements?" Janna didn't fully understand war tactics, but she knew that they couldn't take the city with what they had here.

"Well, let us hope that's what it is." Dren waved to Tanan and Storn as they came over and knew that this was only the beginning of what was going to be a very hard fight. "At least we can get to the city; I really could use a drink."

"Or five." Janna winked and started to skip towards Tanan as he smiled at her. *Maybe I'll even have some fun with the so-called Lilac Lord tonight.*

LORD'S MANSION, RIVER VALE

Aeric looked over the complaint for the second time, and for the life of him, he couldn't see what the problem was. It was basically a register from one shop owner demanding that another shop be kept from opening at a certain time. He would pass it along to Veddick, one of his men. That man had a flair for this type of thing. He stamped it and set it into a wooden bin, then sat back and sighed. Aeric Savar, acting Lord of River Vale, had been having a harder time with politics than he could've imagined.

Aeric was a dedicated man with black hair and hazel eyes, and a stare that made people either stand up or walk away. He had taken over governing the city after he had killed the former

Lord, Brenscomb. Aeric had slain the man in defense of Princess Allissana—and for retribution. The corrupt Lord had sent men to ambush his patrol and killed several of his men. Of the whole patrol, only he and five others still lived. Even his horse was gone, taken by Karsis and the princess to chase down the sorcerer behind the whole thing. It had been a tenday since they left and he had received ominous news from Everknight in the meanwhile.

It seemed that G'harr had acted openly against Lythinall, and Everknight was sending armed reinforcements to Keragan Hold. "Damn the devils to the Hells, I should be there!" Aeric stood and strode to the window, looking out at his city. *His*—it seemed his position wasn't just temporary anymore. Along with that dire news was a message that King Arian had given him the city permanently. He was officially the Lord of River Vale; he should be celebrating instead of worrying. Being the King's Marshal was his dream, mainly because he never even thought he could become a Lord. Now that the entire city was his to protect, however... well, it was a little daunting. Thank the gods above that he had at least five trustworthy men under his command, as they had been invaluable to him so far. Aeric had placed them in all of the positions that had come up, and so things were running smoothly, but he just wished that he could help his king.

Unfortunately, when the corrupt Lord Brenscomb turned against the king, he took a good many soldiers here with him. Then Karsis, Caerlyn, and the princess killed over half of those that remained. Aeric remembered the bloodshed from when he had charged the south gate. Even though he was still running on adrenaline, he would never forget the princess's smile as she wiped her sword on a used cloak. Allissana had come a long way from the little girl he knew years ago.

That fiasco had left him with a very diminished barracks,

meaning he barely had enough guards to keep his city safe. His numbers didn't count the dozens of new recruits that had come forward after the corrupt Lord was slain, but they were barely trained and over eager. They would help in the long run, but he would need weeks to train them before they could fight, and his guards needed a break now.

"Busy sir?" Veddick leaned in with a half-smile. Veddick was whip-lean and short, barely cresting five feet. He had run his horse almost to death to get the lady Caerlyn when they brought that boy in after the wolvren fight and was considered to be the best rider in the whole patrol. He had short brown hair and brown eyes. If you passed him on the street you probably wouldn't think him special, and he liked his anonymity.

"Never too busy for you, old friend." Aeric sat down and put his feet up on his crowded desk, trying not to scatter papers everywhere. He still needed to go through half of these today. "What can I help you with?"

"Well, I was thinking of your problem."

"Which one? Gods above know I've got enough."

Veddick laughed and shook his head, "The one I know you've been wrestling with—how to help Everknight." He saw Aeric's eyes open and knew he had his Lord's interest.

"Go on." Aeric sat up and placed his feet down solidly. This just might cheer him up.

"As I see it, you would need to take a force across the river and head east for a little over sixty miles, with no roads, and across scrub. Taking the uneven terrain into account, it would take you a little over a day and a half to reach the city with time to cross the river."

"You're not telling me anything I don't know, Veddick." He had gone over the numbers to see if he could spare enough guards to go with him. Sadly he couldn't.

"Well, what if you took your time and made the trip last two and a half days? Hear me out," Veddick said, holding up his hand to forestall any objections. "Instead of taking any guards, you take the dozen or so trainees and work with them on the trip. It will take an extra day to whip them into some sort of shape, but it would do them good to get out into the field. Plus, the North gate of Everknight shouldn't be a target if G'harr is coming from the southwest, so the new recruits won't be on the main front. Instead, they could hit what little forces are probably used as a distraction from the flank and get some much-needed blooding."

"Veddick, they're so young." Aeric didn't think he could lead kids like that into battle. Then he saw the look his friend gave him and he remembered that they were kids once too. "All right. I have to say that sounds like a plan that could work. They do know their way around a sword. They just need discipline."

"And they would get that under your direct command."

"True." He smiled at the compliment. "Send a page to the barracks and ready the gear. You'll be in charge whilst I'm away. Let's just hope that Everknight isn't under attack as we speak, or I'll be the one in for a surprise."

"Right away, Milord," Veddick said mockingly, bowing as Aeric threw a paperweight at him. He left the room and couldn't help but be proud of his idea. He hadn't seen Aeric smile in days, and now the man couldn't stop. He probably didn't even know he was doing it.

3

HELPING HANDS

Karsis played his lute slowly, as he weaved around the trees, singing a lively tune.

> *The man did come*
> *Walking with death in his eyes*
> *And lo did the wizard laugh, calling upon fire*
> *Why do you mock? asked the man of death*
> *And the wizard answered him with a smile and*
> *   a quip*
> *I do not mock, only slay*
> *And he did, then was on his way.*

Liana clapped her tiny hands and flew in circles above Karsis's head. "Againagainagin!" She was so excited to be traveling with her friends that any control she had been working on was thrown over the cliff and dashed upon the rocks below.

Rhoe smiled at the carefree attitude that surrounded them all. It eased the weight off their shoulders a bit, and gods above knew they needed a break from worrying. They had to convince the elves to help Everknight or the city may well fall to the forces of G'harr. The problem was that the elves had hidden away from the troubles of the wide world for centuries and hadn't poked their head out to help *anyone* since.

"Is that one about you, Karsis?" Rhoe asked, trying to distract the little faerie. If she wasn't distracted once in a while, she might explode.

"Indeed it is Rhoe. Very astute of you." Karsis put away his lute, sliding it inside his long coat, the long-handled instrument disappearing into his tiny pocket. "Now, as we approach the end of the Watching Woods, there are some things I need to discuss with you all." His voice lost its carefree tone and turned serious as he slowed his pace a bit.

"This can't be good," Liss said as she walked beside Rhoe.

Karsis ignored the quip and continued. "Society in Tir-Lanan is different from what you are used to. As visitors, you will probably be surprised at some of the... *stranger* rules of conduct, but you won't be held to them as long as you have an escort. Namely, me."

Liana couldn't take it anymore. "Elves!" she screamed in her tiny voice and flew in wide circles.

Avaryn sighed mentally and shook his head. All the way here he had tried to get her to show some calm and discretion in her thoughts and actions, but it was like trying to hang mud by a string. He would rather teach a purple squirrel tricks. *Calm little one, we don't want to scare the elves away, now do we?* Avaryn thought in her mind alone. He could project to everyone at once but decided to keep his tutoring private. Besides, he didn't like being inside Karsis's mind; it was like a hallway filled with locked doors. He had never experienced a mind like that before, and he was old, so he had seen a lot of minds.

Liana stopped and closed her eyes, concentrating so hard that she started to shake. Not talking out loud turned out to be the hardest thing she had ever done. *All right, Avaryn. I'll try and do better.* She tried to imagine a pout as she thought this to Avaryn; his snort told her that it worked.

"If I may continue?" Karsis looked from Rhoe to Liss and wondered why they weren't asking more questions. *Oh yeah, they know I'm an elf and don't want to give anything away. Good for them.* "Most elves have trained since very young in the use of swords, so they carry one around the city as common practice. Most are ornamental, but still function if necessary. Even the young carry knives. Remember that elves live for a very long time, so anyone with a weapon is probably much better than they appear, as they've had decades of practice."

"Don't they have blademasters?" Liss asked shyly. She was trying to avoid the topic of elves, focusing instead on the speech she had to memorize from the time she was sixteen winters old. However, the thought of that many skilled citizens intrigued her warrior instincts. It also helped that she was trying to forget the fact that she had been sick again a mile back. She tried not to think about what it implied, especially with the revelation about the time difference. She must have eaten something bad while with the faeries. No one else had noticed, so she kept it to herself. It was probably nothing.

Karsis nodded as they walked on. "Indeed they do, and you would never want to cross blades with one, although you may be one of the only humans I would put money on to go more than a minute with one. Besides myself, that is."

"Thanks... I think." Liss smiled but suddenly wanted to test herself against one of these blademasters, or just a skilled elven warrior. Just to see.

"Don't mention it. Being trained by the Incarnation of Protection is a mighty big deal in my book, and I saw you fight in River Vale. You're very good, Princess." Karsis looked at Rhoe again and wondered what was going on in the young wizard's head. "But I digress. Now here is one custom you *will* find alien. Hair length is a sign of station among the elves. The longer the hair, the higher the station. Most commoners have short hair, while nobles have very long hair. Wizards usually have *very* long hair, while the high king has the longest; all the way to his knees, actually."

Rhoe was taken aback at this. In all the books he had read he had never heard of anything like this. It seemed trivial, but at the same time, he couldn't discount its simplicity. You could never mistake someone for anything other than what they were in society. "Should I cut my hair Karsis?"

The wind went out of the bard before he could answer. For the boy to even suggest this implied that he grasped inter-racial politics far deeper than some professed scholars. Rhoe had obviously never cut his hair, but here he was, ready to get rid of his birthright for the sake of diplomacy. *Oh, Rhoe, when will you stop impressing me?* Karsis thought to himself.

"No dear boy, I would never ask that of you, nor would any elf. You are a visitor and as such will be treated like a dignitary. Besides, you are a wizard and have the appropriate length for one."

"Anyone goes near his head with so much as a sharp fingernail and I will personally send them to their graves," Liss blurted out. She adored his hair and would kill anyone that made him get rid of it. It was a part of him.

"Well, aren't we just a bit protective," Karsis said with a chuckle. "Nonetheless, I stand with you, my dear. His hair is a symbol of who he is." Karsis wouldn't go into detail, even though Rhoe looked like he was curious about the odd statement. "Lastly, the laws in elven society are basic, yet very strict. The taking of life is the most heinous crime an elf can commit, other than taking that life with magic. The penalty for either is death — and on sight. The elven wardens—who you would call knights—carry out this swift justice and are capable of casting a truth spell that determines if someone is guilty. Trials are held for most other crimes, which include theft, assault, and treason, with penalties varying according to severity. Treason is always dealt with swiftly and usually with life imprisonment, which for an elf is extremely horrific." Karsis looked around and saw that they were finally coming out of the ancient forest. The Silver-sword Pass was just ahead. Then things would get interesting.

"Karsis?" Liana said, the breath going out of her. She pointed off in the distance, her eyes wide. She thought she had just seen a weird mountain, but then it had moved.

"Yes, my little one?" Karsis hadn't turned towards her yet, as he was still scouting out the land before the pass for any patrols.

Rhoe looked to where the little faerie was pointing and gasped as well. He fell back a step, then another as his mind wrapped around what his eyes were perceiving. He grabbed Liss's arm and tugged as the breath was stolen from him as well. In fact, he felt fear wash over him like a physical force, a wave. Everyone seemed affected except Karsis and Avaryn.

Karsis, I do believe we have found a dragon. Avaryn sent to everyone, just to see if he could break through the fear inside their heads

Karsis turned slowly. He knew this could be bad. Sure enough, lying embedded in the side of a hill was a huge dragon. Its glistening, deep-red scales covered his bruised and ravaged frame, and with each ragged breath more scales fell off to litter the dirt. Dragon scales changed color with age, and this dragon was indeed ancient.

Karsis tried to keep his voice calm. "Well, that is something you don't see every day."

SILVERSWORD PASS, NORTHERN LYTHINALL

Illiandral shaded his eyes against the rising sun once more and tried to see what had made the ground shake two tendays ago. They all thought he was crazy, but he had seen a huge shape come down out of the clouds and disappear into the low mountains around the pass somewhere. The wardens said it was the earth shifting or some nonsense, but he knew it was something else.

Illiandral was on duty in the Silversword Pass, and that usually meant staying on the elven side and making sure no one wandered through accidentally, even though no one had come through the pass in ten years. He had gone out every day since then, looking for a sign of what had fallen from the sky, but had found nothing.

"Brooding again, Illiandral?" Warden Ives'rhan asked. He knew the young elf meant well, but this theory of his was getting him nowhere.

"No, sir. Just scanning the range before I head out again, sir." Illiandral knew the elves behind him were snickering; he could hear them. He saluted Warden Ives'rhan and smiled at the older elf. The warden wore his white hair shoulder length and his leathers were dyed off-white, the better to hide in the northern snows. Everyone respected the warden, and his skill with shorter swords was legendary.

"Well, I can't stop you from your free time, but you only have a day's leave. If you don't want to spend that in the city with your family, then so be it. For the record though, I think you're crazy." The warden patted the young soldier on the shoulder and turned to regard the others. They all stopped laughing immediately. "Weapons aren't going to clean themselves, now are they?"

Illiandral walked away with his head held high. He was

young for an elf—almost forty years old. He had bright green eyes and wore his hereditary white hair cut shoulder length. His leathers were simple brown, and his pouches hung from small hooks all around his waist. He was a simple scout, but he had dreams of becoming a warden someday. His training in wizardry was coming along well, and in another twenty years, he could attempt to banish the darkness within himself; then they wouldn't laugh at him anymore. Illiandral turned towards the pass and traveled down past his last checkpoint. He had tried every path into the mountains to see if there were any craters of debris but hadn't found anything. *Time to go farther down the pass this time,* he thought, as he steeled himself against the unknown.

He had never been this far into the pass—if the Sran'en Kith were right, then there could be humans just waiting to ambush him at any minute. Illiandral smiled as he thought of the isolationist faction and their warnings of the many dangers that could befall the wayward elf. *All nonsense if you ask me,* he thought. He turned the bend and continued towards the end of the pass that exited into Lythinall.

His world turned upside-down as he saw a group of humans pointing at the side of the mountain before the entrance of the pass; then a wave of fear hit him like a wet blanket of terror. Illiandral turned and his eyes went even wider as he stared into the immense eye of a dragon!

"Dra... dra... dragon!" Illiandral called out as the breath left him.

Karsis not only heard the elf but saw the dragon turn his eye to the elf and raise his eyebrow. "Rather loud aren't they?" Karsis asked the dragon. He hoped it wasn't starving at least He really didn't want to tangle with a dragon this old right now. Scratch that—ever. *Last time I did, I lost my hand,* he thought with a smirk.

Kanthalianar was alive, but barely; he wasn't even sure how long he had been here—fading in and out of consciousness would do that. Then he felt the presence of scmeone behind him and worried that the Incarnation had come to finish him off. Not that he could do anything about it, but Kanth hadn't worried about anything in so very long that the sensation was new to him. Then he saw the unicorn and faerie with a bunch of humans and knew that his day had gone from vrorse to.... well he didn't have a word for it yet, but it was bad.

Kanth was about to speak to the auburn-haired foppish one when he felt another presence from up the pass. Hearing the scream of *Dragon!*, he turned his eye and saw an elf. *Maybe this little elf is a wizard and can help me?* He thought, but the elf lost his breath and fell to his knees. *Fantastic... Just my luck—a scaredy elf.* He heard the foppish one ask if they were loud. The man spoke clearly and precisely, without fear whetsoever.

"Why as a matter of fact, yes," Kanth answered. He tried to turn his head to face the man better but it was no use; he had no strength left. "Mind shutting him up while I try to turn my head again?" Kanth asked, trying to buy some time.

Rhoe couldn't move. It seemed worse that the thing was speaking. That was when he recognized the dragon. Rhoe focused his strength inside and down to his center, sent an angry letter to his feet, and a complaint in triplicate to his brain. He concentrated on the cloud of fear around his heart... Snap! He was free! Rhoe spun towards Liss and grabbed her shoulders. "Liss, look at me. In my eyes." Rhoe was going on instinct now, letting the magic within him guide his thoughts. When her trembling face met his, he closed his eyes, holding the image of her eyes, and sent his center out into her, cuttir.g through the threads of fear like fire through spider webs.

Liss was rooted to the spot with an overwhelming fear. She could think of nothing except what stood in front of her; that it shouldn't be that big. Then suddenly *he* was there—her Rhoven. She heard his words and moved her eyes to gaze upon his and was shocked sane by the sight. Tiny fires danced within Rhoe's eyes and then they came towards her and into her own. She flinched, but couldn't even blink. Then it was over. Allissana Everknight stumbled back and felt renewed. She felt Rhoe's power running through her veins and clearing the fear from her like a blast of cold water. "Rhoe, is there anything you can't do?" Liss asked, humbled.

"Well, I can't walk along a river without falling in." Rhoe turned and looked at Karsis. "This was the dragon I saw in the mountains Karsis. The one fighting the Incarnation." He noticed that Avaryn was touching his horn to Liana and it seemed to free her as well. Rhoe winced at the thought of her being unafraid of the dragon and what she might do now. Apparently, Karsis had the same thought.

"Stop!" Karsis said in a fairly loud tone. He was staring right at the tiny faerie as he strode towards her with one hand out, his other suddenly holding an old charred staff that had appeared out of nowhere. He had a pleading look on his usually stern face. "Liana, please contain yourself and stay away from the dragon." It wasn't phrased as a question.

Liana was no longer afraid of the massive creature; she also wasn't stupid. She turned her face towards the bard and put on her best *Who, me?* look. "Karsis, don't worry," she started, talking very slowly, like she was afraid she would spook the rather large beast. "I'm curious, not suicidal."

"There's a difference?" Rhoe couldn't help it. These kinds of remarks were what Gareth always scolded him for.

Liana stuck her tongue out at him and fluttered her wings.

"Are all of you mad?" Illiandral couldn't believe what he was seeing. They were actually arguing amongst themselves in front of one of the most feared creatures in existence. Illiandral was shakings o hard he still couldn't feel his feet. He wasn't even sure he had feet at this point.

"No, just me," Karsis answered the elf without looking at him, his gaze now fixed upon the dragon. The bard walked around so that the eye wasn't straining to see him. "So it would seem that you know our mutual enemy," Karsis said casually, holding the charred staff in both hands now and leaning on it. It was one of his safeguards against fire, and it was very powerful, but only in certain situations. Legend said it used to be one of the three sacred treasures of a lost city to the west, but he couldn't find anything about what happened to it.

Kanth could hardly believe his withering ears. A human had seen him fighting in the mountains? He knew there was no one else around them, so that left only magic—and powerful magic at that. Kanth had heard of wizards *seeing* from afar, but those that did were masters at their craft, not this young. The dragon sniffed the warm air and drew in the boy's scent. It was mingled with the girl's. That's when he noticed the hair. The boy somehow had elven blood! He turned his focus back to the bard, who seemed a lot more powerful than any bard he had ever known. "Yes, I left him piled under a cliff, but the damage had been done. I fear I don't have long on this world."

Karsis saw that the dragon was infected with the same rotting disease that the Incarnation used, and by the looks of it, the disease had been gnawing at the dragon for a long time. "How did you survive until now?"

"I used my breath to heal what I could, but the fire has finally given out inside of me. Now that I have exhausted the flames within me, I shall succumb fairly soon." Kanth wasn't ready for the twilight that dragons went to when they died, but he was out of options.

"Can't Avaryn heal him with his horn?" Rhoe felt that this creature deserved more than a death like this.

"Do we really want to heal a dragon that might devour us?" Liss had only heard stories, but they all seemed so very plausible looking at the size of this great beast.

Kanth was impressed with the young boy. "Good thought, but a unicorn's horn, though powerful, can't heal a wound this strong." Kanth swung his eye towards the girl and saw that she stood like a warrior. "But don't worry, young one. You humans taste horrible. Gamey really, especially the young ones."

Karsis laughed, knowing that dragons rarely ate people. They killed them, yes, but usually after the human had done something foolish or stupid. The Companions of Everknight had stopped a few dragons in their time, but never once had to fight them to the death. It was *very* hard to kill them. He wished he could think of something to help the dragon, but even *he* was out of ideas; his magic wouldn't even touch this level of decay. Karsis knew that Rhoe was able to stop the decay from affecting people, but that was *before* they were touched. Then Rhoe opened his mouth and shocked them all.

"Well, if I'm supposed to be the one that can stop the Incarnation's power, what if Avaryn channels his horn through me?" Rhoe didn't actually know if it would work, but he was almost positive the dragon would die if he didn't try.

Karsis, this boy just floored two of the most magical beings in the land. I fear that he could be right. Avaryn sent to everyone,. He mentally shrugged, then stared again at the young wizard, trying to figure out if his power would overwhelm the boy before he could use it. It wouldn't hurt him, but he might pass out.

"Well, the unicorn is right—I'm floored." Kanth knew suddenly, and without doubt, that he was in the company of someone destined to become one of the most powerful wizards ever known. He had powerful mages before, in ages past, but they never had the compassion that stirred within one so young.

And the control he had! This half-grown human broke through his fear like it was nothing. "All right young one. If you are willing to try it, then I'm ready."

"Rhoe are you sure?" Liss was still in awe of the dragon, but now that Rhoe was involved she was a bit more focused. It's not that she wanted it to die, but she was worried about Rhoe.

"Well, no, but it's worth a shot if Avaryn will try." Rhoe looked at Karsis and saw the bard staring open-mouthed at him. He thought it was weird that Karsis had been so quiet. "What's the matter Karsis? Is it going to kill me or something?" Rhoe had never seen his mentor with that look on his face before.

Karsis was trying not to cry. He had been surprised by this boy before, but this went beyond that; the bard was truly moved. This young wizard was ready to try something possibly dangerous just to save another. It didn't matter that it was a dragon or a pig, the thought was the same because Rhoe didn't know that he would be fine. The boy would be safe, as a unicorn's power could never hurt someone so pure, but Rhoe didn't know that. "I'm just truly proud of you Rhoven. No, it won't kill you. You'll be fine. But hurry, he doesn't have long." Karsis saw the dragon shudder.

Rhoe stepped up and laid his hand upon the rotting scales of the dragon's head. "What is your name?"

"Kanthalianar, but you may call me Kanth." The dragon tried to keep his eyes open, but he just couldn't. Kanth could feel his scales rotting faster and faster. Beneath them, his flesh was writhing in agony.

"Then hold on, Kanth. I don't know what this is going to feel like... for either of us." Rhoe turned to see Avaryn walking reverently towards him and Liana staring quietly in awe— quiet for the first time in her whole life. "Hit me, Avaryn, before I change my mind." Rhoe laughed at the quip; he knew he wasn't going to change his mind.

Liana flew over to Liss and buried her little face in the girl's neck. "Ican'twatch."

"Hush, Liana. He will be fine. I think he just did something like this to me. This will just be on a grander scale, that's all." At least she hoped so.

Avaryn touched his horn to Rhoe and flooded him with its healing power. The unicorn sent the power flowing through him and into Rhoe, linking to the boy's mind, and sending calming thoughts. Avaryn was shocked yet again to find a sort of calm center already there. *It's all right Rhoe, I'm here now, let it go.*

Rhoe felt Avaryn touch his horn to his shoulder and flood him with power. Rhoe envisioned the power flowing through his center and into his arms, then hands, willing it to spread outward. He felt Avaryn's shock and almost laughed. *I know, Avaryn. I have it now. Let me know if it gets to be too much.* Rhoe opened his eyes and let the energy flow into Kanth, the power rushing out in a torrent, washing over all of the decay and rot that infected the great beast. Still, he could sense it wasn't enough. Rhoe had to think of something. Then he remembered what the dragon said about fire; Kanth had fire *within* him.

Rhoe concentrated and whispered to the darkened, fiery core inside of the dragon, asking it to help him. He could feel it there, a part of the elements that he had been working with, just dormant. Rhoe had never thought of asking the other elements for anything like this before, as Karsis had always told him Ether was for healing, but in a second the fire leaped up to meet Rhoe's power combining with it into a holy, white flame. It spilled out of his hands and washed over the dragon's scales in a cascade of healing fire. Rhoe could feel it burning the darkness away, but he could tell it this wouldn't be enough. He *still* needed more power.

"I need more Avaryn. May I?!"

The unicorn felt the power combine with the fire and flow through the boy. He was amazed. Then he heard Rhoe ask for more. Suddenly, he knew what the young wizard meant by 'may I'. Avaryn mentally sighed. This would be as close to anyone he had ever been, yet to save a life he was ready.

Yes, Rhoe. I give you consent.

I've got you. Rhoe reached down and pulled more power from the horn with the will of his mind, pulling it from the depths of the majestic beast's heart. Rhoe channeled the unicorn's force through his own power again and felt the dragon shudder in relief. It was over in less than a minute; as Rhoe pulled back, he sensed it would snap both Avaryn and himself if he let go too fast. Clamping down on his will, Rhoe let the power go slowly and gently until it was all gone.

Then it was over. Sinking to his knees, Rhoe saw the faces of his friends and wondered if he was in one piece. They looked horrified. *I hope I'm not naked,* he thought as he closed his eyes and breathed deep to reset his center.

No one could move, not even Karsis. When Rhoe channeled the power, his hair was lifted up as if by a strong wind. Karsis heard him whisper to the fire and the breath went out of his lungs—Rhoe was going to use fire to heal the dragon! No one had ever tried anything like that, but in theory it would be the perfect way to heal a dragon. He hadn't even known that dragons healed themselves with fire until today, so there was no way Rhoe could've known.

Is he still going on instinct...? His thoughts were interrupted when Rhoe burst into flames as well, a brightly burning beacon of holy flame.

"*No!*" Liss lurched forward, but her hair caught on something. It was only Liana. She reached for the faerie but the little one evaded her grip and pulled her hair again.

"No, Liss! Heisonfireyouwillbeburned!" Liana couldn't

calm down, not faced with the imminent death of another friend. Then Karsis was there, his charred staff disappearing in a pop of displaced air. Liana let go of Liss's hair and slowly flew down to the ground to cry.

Karsis wrapped his arms around the princess, holding her tight. "It's all right, Allissana. He is channeling it. The fire won't hurt him unless he lets go, and he is smarter than that. Hells below, he is smarter than most people I can think of at this point."

"Smarter than you?" Liana asked sincerely through tear-streaked eyes as she sat on the ground.

"Let's not get hysterical." Karsis laughed and held onto the princess, just in case she tried something stupid. It ran in her blood.

"I need more, Avaryn. May I?!" Rhoe shouted. More fire arched into the mighty dragon. Seconds passed as they all stared in horror as Rhoe's clothes burned away but his flesh remained untouched. Flames licked his hair, which flailed like there was a thunderstorm. Suddenly the roar of the fire dwindled, his hair fell, and slowly, ever so slowly, the fire went out. Avaryn stumbled back and lay down on his stomach, resting his horn on the ground. Rhoe looked up with a quizzical look on his face.

Illiandral stumbled and fell to his knees, tears streaming down his face. He had never heard any story of humans that bespoke of such courage, such compassion. He had seen this young boy, who was obviously somehow a wizard, risk his life for a dragon. What's more, he had seen the boy use fire to heal—even though his magic was just beginning, he knew that was impossible. "Who are you people?"

Karsis spun around, letting his coat fan out as usual. "I am known as Karsis the Bard." He paused for dramatic effect; he always did. "You may have heard of me?"

Illiandral decided right then that it would be a perfect time to pass out, and his brain complied generously.

Liss ran over to Rhoe after Karsis let go of her and wrapped her cloak around him, helping him up. "You all right there, Rhoe?"

"Well, I'm apparently naked, but I feel like I just showered in very hot rain. Am I making sense? It doesn't sound like I'm making any sense." Rhoe couldn't even tell if the two dragons were moving. *Two dragons? That's it—I need a nap,* he thought, and promptly sat down once more, this time with feeling.

Liana was torn. She had three people that she wanted to fly to and console, but she was only one small faerie. *This is what it must feel like to rule,* she thought, in a moment of perfect clarity. She choose Avaryn, feeling responsible for him since she was the ambassador to the faeries and all. "Avaryn, are you all right? Did your horn burn out?" She was trying to speak slowly and clearly, just like he always told her to. She didn't know why she felt like she should.

Avaryn felt like he had just fallen off a castle, hit the ground, then rolled for five miles... over small rocks. Everything hurt, yet at the same time, he had never felt *cleaner.* The unicorn felt like everything had been burned away, except obviously the aches and pains. *Yes, little one. I fear I will live,* he thought only to her. He was pleasantly surprised that she was so attentive, though he worried about what that meant for the universe.

Kanthalianar stretched out and slowly pulled away from the hillside. Dirt and rocks rolled down, but he was careful not to shower the people around him too badly. Especially this young wizard. He had never, nor would he again for that matter, feel that kind of power course through him. This boy was more than just a wizard—he had known his share of archmages as well— and none of them could've done that. "Are you in one piece, young wizard?"

Rhoe looked up and finally saw only one dragon. *That statement says a lot about my tenday, doesn't it?* he thought to himself with a chuckle.

"Rhoe."

"What now?" Kanth wondered if the boy had burned out his brain.

"My name is Rhoe." He tried to stand and felt a hand on his shoulder. He looked and saw that it was Karsis holding him down.

"Stay down, Rhoe, you can talk from there." Karsis turned to face the now healthy dragon and put on his best smile. "So how does it feel?" Karsis couldn't imagine what was going through this creature's mind right now. Well, that wasn't entirely true, but he liked to think it wasn't thinking what he was thinking at least.

"I've never felt better. Now, Rhoe." Kanth turned his eye directly towards Rhoe and lowered his head even more. "I haven't seen courage like that since I wore green scales. I owe you a debt of life, and to a dragon that is a mighty thing indeed. Know that you and your family are always safe from me, and I will always try and help when I can. You have but to ask the ether and call me by name, and I will hear it."

There was a long, uncomfortable pause. "Rhoe, say thank you to the nice dragon," Karsis said. He couldn't believe what he was hearing. A life debt? He had met others with those kinds of debts before, but never with a dragon. Karsis tried not to feel jealous and failed miserably.

The young warrior-turned wizard was too stunned to speak. Finally, Rhoe bowed his head and tried to stand, brushing off Karsis's hand and leaning on Liss. "I am honored, Kanthalianar, and I do not take this pledge lightly."

"Farewell then, and may your wings always keep you aloft." Kanth gave a warning look, and they all backed up. He flexed his powerful legs and shot up into the sky, waiting until he was well above them to flap his wings. The powerful motion still whipped dust and dirt around, but it wasn't as bad as it could've been. He shot up into the sky and decided he would find his cave and take a good long nap. Or five.

Karsis was the first to break the silence after the dragon's departure."Well, now that we have that out of the way..." He turned towards the unconscious elf. "I was going to take the back way into Tir-Lanan, but now that he's seen us, I fear a quiet visit is over with." The last time he was here over ten years ago, he had fought with his father about hiding his identity within the city's walls. It had ended badly and he hadn't been back since. He hoped that all was forgotten between them, but it probably wouldn't be that easy. It never is after all.

Illiandral came around slowly, sitting up and rubbing his head. He must've been dreaming because he *swore* that the man had called himself Karsis the Bard. Then someone else called him by name. It *was* him! He couldn't believe Karsis was back. What had it been—ten years or so since he caused that huge uproar among the factions? Illiandral adored the bard back then; Karsis was the main reason he started on the path to becoming a warden. He was ashamed that he hadn't recognized him by his coat and hair.

"I can bring you right into the city by the pass gate, Karsis," Illiandral said. "I'm sure your father would be there to meet us." Then he saw a tiny flying thing coming at him.

"I can make sure he doesn't talk Karsis, let me at him." Liana flew angrily at the elf. She was ready to fight for her friends if need be. If he was going to stop them from getting in, he might have to disappear.

Liss couldn't help it. She burst out laughing at the prospect of Liana attacking the poor elf. "Liana, it's all right. I'm sure Karsis knows what he's doing."

"Is that a faerie?!" The elven scout was going to pass out again. Faeries had left so long ago that most elves had never seen one. When this group walked in the gates to Tir-Lanan, there were going to be a great many surprises indeed.

Karsis looked at both Liana and Illiandral. "No, yes, and we can talk about the rest on the way. Can you travel noble steed?" he asked Avaryn. He was worried that the unicorn hadn't stood up yet. *Please—let's not lose the last unicorn on my watch.,* he thought sarcastically to himself.

Liana backed off and landed on Karsis's shoulder, folding her arms and frowning at the young elf.

Yes, great bard. I can walk, just give an old steed a second or two, he thought to the bard, ignoring the shot at the fact that no one could usually ride a unicorn. He slowly stood and shook his mane out. He snorted at the looks the others gave him. *Enough staring. Let's start before anything else decides to pop up and test us.*

TEMPLE OF DAVALAR, CASTLE EVERKNIGHT

He walked around the statue once more and shook his head; he still didn't *feel* anything. Griff closed his eyes and opened himself to the God Davalar once more, desperate to know more about his own powers before the attack—before people would be relying on him or his friends could die. A tear leaked from his eye, mainly from built-up stress, and he wiped it away with his white sleeve. Griff was maybe fourteen winters old with freckles, wavy red hair, and green eyes. He never quite remembered his birthday, but he thought he could be fourteen at least; his early life was fuzzy. *Davalar, I call to thee. Please bathe me in your heavenly light and give me a sign. Show me that everything will be all right,* he prayed. Griff dropped to his knees without even knowing that he had done so. His chest was warm through his white robes. He looked up and there was a figure standing in front of him, bathed in a bright light. The figure reached out a hand and touched Griff's face lightly. Griff was in awe, barely finding the compulsion to breathe. Then the figure spoke.

"He sent me to save you," Rythal said as his hand lightly touched the young healer's face.

"You!" Griff lurched to his feet in shock as his godly image turned into the broken boy from the North. Rythal was around the same age as Griff, with sparkling blond hair and golden eyes. His darker complexion stood out with his tanned skin, but the eyes that used to sparkle with delight at the world had faded with the death of his twin brother.

Rythal saw everything—he always did. He screamed endlessly for his brother, but Innal was dead. His brother was just a pile of ash and dust, and he wouldn't hear anything anymore. It didn't keep him from screaming in his own mind though. Rythal had seen the young boy praying and it had the same effect—the same clarity— that he had experienced with that pretty blond lady. He took another step and touched the young healer, *No, not just a healer. An Oracle. That is what he is...but how do I know that?* Rythal tried to think through the cloud of ash and death that was his fractured mind, yet all he could see was his rotting brother. Rythal gripped the young boy's arm tight and tried desperately to connect with him, to find his way through to that clarity.

Not yet, Rythal...

The voice boomed inside of his skull and he went stiff with pain and shock, almost going blind from the power behind it. Rythal dropped to his knees, yet still held the boy's arm. "He sent me to save you!"

Griff was horrified. The boy had grabbed his arm like he wanted—no, needed—help. Before Griff could say anything, Rythal went ridged and collapsed, still holding fiercely on to

Griff's arm. Griff wasn't sure that he had the strength to pry him loose, and wasn't entirely sure he wanted to. *I should help him,* he thought, yet he knew what happened when others had tried to look into Rythal's mind; he was there for both attempts. He still felt like he should try something. *Well, at least there isn't anyone else here to get hurt.*

"Oh great Davalar, bring ease to this soul, who is ever in your care." Griff found his warm center and focused the power through his hand, touching the young man's shoulder, taking great care not to touch his head as the others had. Griff felt the power flow into the boy and saw a dark halo of ash surround him, then turn a bright yellow hue. This lasted only a second, and Griff was sure that no one else would've been able to see it, but then he heard a grating voice, almost like it was coming from the boy's head, inside his own skull and he screamed with the intensity of it. It wasn't Rythal's voice.

Brave one, there isn't anything to fix. He is as he needs to be. Still, We commend you on the attempt. Go in peace—but never try this again. Rythal's grip loosened and he went limp, letting go of Griff and letting his hands drop to his sides. Griff followed a second later, dropping to all fours and breathing heavily.

Ralavin came running when he heard the scream. He was way down the outer hall that led to the temple, and he sprinted all the way there. What he saw stunned him to his core. Rythal usually moved around the castle at his own whim, but he had never seen the boy in any pose other than just standing there. Now, though, Rythal was on his knees in front of Griff like the young healer could be his salvation. His arms were limp at his sides and tears fell slowly down his ridged face. Griff was on his hands and knees, breathing as he had just run all the way from Daelyn.

"Griff!" Ralavin ran over, not even out of breath, thanks to his new young body. "Are you all right?" Ralavin looked at the boy and saw nothing amiss, yet he still had that feeling that he had been hurt.

Griff was in a state of shock. Who was that voice and what did it mean when it had said 'We'? He saw Ralavin and came to his senses before the priest shook him right out of his clothes. "I'm all right, Ralavin, just spooked is all." The sound of drawing steel echoed in the temple and they both spun to see Lan standing at the door with his sword out. A larger man came huffing behind him and drew his own sword a second later.

Lan heard the distant scream and turned from the practice field and bolted towards the sound. He heard Trav sigh behind him and start running as well. He turned a corridor and saw Ralavin running ahead of him and put on a boost of speed. When he slid into the temple he drew his sword, looking for danger. He only found two people staring at him, and a figure on its knees. "I heard a scream," Lan said in the way of an apology for his entrance.

"I ran all that way for nothing?" Trav was trying to get his breathing under control and failing miserably. He was a big man, and it had been a long time since he was in the best shape. He took being a knight as a kind of free pass, and as a result, had let himself go.

"Thank you for responding Lan—it seems like everything is under control. For now." Ralavin walked over and checked Rythal for signs of life. He was breathing regularly, and his heartbeat seemed strong.

"Someone spoke through him, Ralavin." Griff crouched down and smoothed the hair out of Rythal's eyes. The boy looked tormented, even unconscious like this.

"Someone familiar?" Ralavin asked, concern edging into his tone. This he did not like one bit.

"No, but they referred to themselves as 'We'." Griff saw that Lan was walking closer, so he stood to shake his hand in thanks.

"Coming to my rescue again, huh?" Griff smiled warmly remembering their time on the streets. Griff could always count on Lan to get him out of trouble. He missed those days if you could believe it. It was a time that he wasn't responsible for saving lives or being this supposed Oracle.

"Don't mention it. I just wanted to make sure everyone was all right." He turned as the regular guard came in to inspect the noise, and saw Trav wave them away in his knightly manor. Lan shook his head at the prospect of being bound to this ingrate. It was his choice though—it was that or watch Carana beat him senseless and he couldn't, in good conscience, do that. It was his hope that he could show the man that the ways of the knight were not just words to get a job or a free pass. They were a way to live life every day

Ralavin had Rythal standing again and brushed him off lightly. He was worried about this supposed voice, but he had other concerns at the moment. "Well we should get going, Griff if we are going to talk to the other healers that came up from the city." They had fifteen healers ready to learn whatever they could from the priests. It was Ralavin's hope that some of them could at least cast the smaller healing spells; they needed anything they could get with war looming. Ralavin wanted Griff there as a sign that the God works in mysterious ways. It was the truth after all. They all walked out of the temple, each lost in their own thoughts; not one of them noticed the smirk that came upon Rythal's face as he looked up at the statue of Davalar.

As Lan and Trav walked down the halls of the castle, they saw a page coming straight for them. Lan heard his partner click his tongue in irritation. "I'll handle this, Trav. Why don't you go get some food and drink? I'll catch up to you later." Lan watched Trav walk away with a disgusted look and frowned. Would that oaf ever learn that he wasn't better than others?

The page handed Lan the scroll and bowed his head before

turning to leave, obviously in a hurry to get somewhere else. *Must be bad news*, Lan thought as he undid the wax seal. The note was clear and precise: Carana wanted to meet with him this evening to see how Trav was coming along and check if there were any problems. Lan rolled the note back up and let out a heavy breath; he would have to tell her the truth but hoped it wouldn't reflect poorly on him. He still had a couple hours before he had to find Carana, so he trudged back to the city below and found Trav.

Down the other hallway, Kari was standing off to one side, watching them all go. She was lonely and couldn't shake the feeling that she didn't fit in anywhere. Kari had started training with Mistress Jerina, the Queen's most competent bard, and had surprised even herself with her voice, but she just couldn't *feel* the music when she sang. Without that, she was just a good singer. Kari did have a good ear for memorization, but no spark of bardic talent.

Jerina had told her such talent was rare in children this young and to have hope that when she got older it could come out... but Kari doubted it. She moved on to try every type of weapon around the castle, but she was just mediocre with them, not good. Even training with Carana let her down. She did well enough, but she was the worst student of all the children. Kari did the best with her sticks, which pleased Carana because she hadn't seen anyone fight with those in a long time. Still, Kari just couldn't get the right moves to fight well with them.

I'm just not good at anything, Kari thought to herself, as she turned around and wandered away down the hallway. She thought about going to see the head priest about healing, but got cold feet and stopped before she went in. She sighed as she turned a corner and went to sit in the upper balcony to practice her singing. Like it would help.

❦   4   ❦

TIME FOR REFLECTION

The King of Lythinall paced the room with his hands behind his back. Arian Everknight wore his full plate armor and seemed ready for war to strike at any minute, but in truth he knew they had a couple of days at least. Arian was tall, well over six and-a-half feet, and it was all muscle. His golden locks fell just above his shoulders, brushing his armor but lightly, and his piercing blue eyes seemed to hold one's attention involuntarily. Even though he was now past fifty winters, he could still keep up with all the day-to-day activities that came with being the king—though he had to admit the present troubles were pushing him to his limits. His runners had returned saying that Tanan had made it back with the survivors of Keragan hold, but the enemy wasn't advancing. Lord Norhil had scouted out the G'harran camp and estimated that it would take almost two days to assail the capitol from where they were, once they finally started marching again. Still, all that wasn't why he was pacing.

"If you don't stop pacing you will chaff in that armor," Tierra said from her comfy seat in the back of the council chamber. Her slim build and long flowing hair gave her an almost

70

dainty look to her short frame. She was sitting and holding her twin braids, playing with the two steel balls tied into them. The 'clack clack' of the steel balls echoed in the relatively empty chamber. "It's just a speech. Haven't you given like hundreds of those already?"

Arian winced and turned to the woman, trying to put on his best smile. Under her scowl, his facade died quickly. She was a warrior of the Fra'hir so her whole body was a weapon, but her gaze seemed like the most deadly thing about her. No one else thought so, but to him it was something he always feared... along with his wife's frown.

"Those were mostly ceremonial—fluff, if you will. I've never had to tell my people that they could *die*." There, he said it. Arian was worried about the coming war, not for himself or his city, but for the normal folk that depended upon him to keep them safe. The women and children had been moved to the castle's lower floors and hallways, and the men that could lift weapons were stationed at the castles main gate and inner chamber. If he and his soldiers failed to keep the G'harrans out, the men here would be the only defense left.

Tierra stopped playing with her hair and stood up with a fluid grace that would've amazed most fighters. She walked quickly over and thumped him on the breast plate with a sturdy finger. "Now look here! You are going to march in there and address your people like a King, and if you don't I will person-ally kick you in the shins until you do."

"You really would, wouldn't you?"

"Just ask Gareth."

"Where is the big man, anyway?" Arian hadn't seen him for at least a day. That wasn't unusual, but with war looming he liked to keep tabs on his best fighters.

Tierra laughed and sat back down. "He is still in the armory trying to find a suitable replacement for his axe the Incarnation ruined." She rolled her eyes, pouted her lips, and made a cradle motion with her arms that implied her husband was being an infant.

Arian laughed and leaned on the council table for support. He could imagine the big man sorting through all of the swords and spears looking for a good axe and throwing them aside with no care for their upkeep. Worse, he could see the Quartermaster having a fit over it. "Oh Gods, that's good. He should've just asked; I have a nice axe in my room on the wall."

"*Now* you tell me," Gareth said from the doorway. He had finally found an axe that was functional, albeit a little small, and had came up here to find the king and apologize. Gareth was huge, well over six feet tall, and his corded muscle stood out prominently through his woolen shirt, stretched tight over his barrel chest. He had shoulder length brown hair that always looked like it could use a combing but no one dared to get close enough to try. In essence, the man hit things for a living—preferably with weapons, but he didn't need them.

"Sorry about the room... I mean armory. Oh, and by the way, Reginald should be fine. I think he just passed out." Gareth laughed as he pulled up a chair to the council table and sat. "That poor Quartermaster was running after me, picking up all of the discarded weapons that I was throwing this way and that, yelling about how 'everything has a place' or something like that. Then, when I yanked this off the wall, he just fainted." He held up an axe and worried when Arian's face did something weird. The axe was double-bladed and had white leather wrapped around the lower end of the haft. A small ruby was placed into the handle above the leather, with runes in elvish that went all the way up to the blade. It was well balanced and very sharp.

"Off the wall?! Oh good Gods, that's why!" Arian grabbed a chair and sat himself as he started laughing and coughing at the same time. It took a while before he could speak, and he could tell Tierra and Gareth were just dying to know what he was talking about. The king took a deep breath and steadied himself. "That axe was my great grandfather's and was put there as a memorial when he passed on. Reginald's main duty is to keep *that* heirloom safe from all harm."

"Oh, Gods, Arian—I'm so sorry!" Gareth didn't know what to say. He felt horrible and jumped up to go right back down there to put the axe back on the wall. He didn't get that far.

"No, Gareth. It's all right. Look, sit down." Arian stood again and chuckled at the irony of the situation; Karsis would've called it fate. "That axe was placed on the wall of the armory because my grandfather said it was never to be used until this city needed it. Now, with the imminent war coming, there was never a better time for you to wield it." He had a really good idea as to what his speech was going to entail now. "In fact, I'm going to need you by my side in a couple of minutes."

"Where are we going?" Gareth still felt bad, but if it was going to help the city, then he was all right with it.

"Just to talk with a couple of people." Arian winked at Tierra as they left the room, already talking to Gareth about duty and honor.

Tierra watched them go, smiling to herself, mainly because she knew her husband hated speaking to large crowds, but also because they were getting along again. They had spent a lot of years not speaking and had lost so many good memories together, but now they were catching up. Tierra sighed and made a decision herself. She had wanted to find Carana and spar with her to see how good the woman who trained her new daughter-in-law was, but had been busy helping the people in from the city. Now, though, she was free for the rest of the day. *All right Carana—let's see what you can do.* She thought, as she found her way down to the training area.

TRAINING ROOM, CASTLE EVERKNIGHT

She ducked again and rolled, just like she had been shown, and came up on wobbly legs. Sprout smiled at her trainer and bounced on the balls of her feet. It felt weird but she had to admit it did give her better balance. The stick came again and she slid to the right, then ducked and rolled towards her opponent. Sprout came up and grabbed the stick with both hands near her opponent's grip, took a quick second to breathe, then fell backwards, pulling it with all her might. The staff gave a little resistance, then popped out of Carana's hands and went with Sprout.

"Good, little one—very good! Now remember, if that is a sword, you're going to have the sharp end pointing at you. Roll to the side and throw it out of his reach before you hit the ground. Then you will have a good chance at living when your opponent comes at you again." Carana was easily six feet tall with short, dirty blond hair. It matched well with her sun-darkened skin and brown eyes, but even these features paled in comparison to her physique. The woman was built slender, but had packed that slight frame with every ounce of muscle possible.

She stepped up and kicked out at the tiny girl, not hard but a solid blow that Sprout would remember. Her boot connected with the little one's side and she saw the girl's eyes go wide with pain and shock. Carana had started training Sprout a little bit each day after Karsis had left, knowing full well that she would be easy prey if they couldn't hold the gates. So far the young one had grasped the easy things rather well, and that was all she needed to survive; that and the Gods own luck.

Sprout rolled over and over to get away, throwing the practice staff away from her. She had rolled over on it twice before she could throw it, but she would practice that later. Right now she had to get rid of those feet coming at her. She decided to try an old street trick and changed her direction and rolled even harder; straight at Carana. At only eight winters old, Sprout was four feet tall and weighed about ninety stones. Her short blond hair still looked dirty despite being washed daily, and her skin was a dark tan from being on the street all that time.

Carana was just swinging her foot again when she saw what the girl was doing. She kept from laughing, as the little one thudded into her other foot, but not hard enough to trip her up. "Good try, Sprout. But with your size that just won't work." She looked down and saw that she wasn't moving. "Playing dead huh? Not a bad move, but soldiers won't fall for that one." She reached down and pulled her up, then took a step back to throw her harmlessly away... and fell right over onto her knees. Sprout was up like a wild animal then, climbing up her chest to get at her throat and screaming playfully. Carana managed to mostly hold her at bay and started laughing along with her. The little girl had tied her boots together in record time. After a second or two they both heard clapping from the entrance and turned, still laughing.

Tierra saw what the little one had done the minute the high general fell and she was impressed. She clapped at their escapades and walked in as they got up, Carana more slowly as her boots were still tied.

"You know that won't work on armor, right little one?" Tierra had come to see the great warrior in action, but so far she only saw a caring woman helping a little girl barley old enough to wield a stick.

Carana got up and saw that Tierra was standing at the ready. She hadn't been that way in the council chamber, though she was skilled enough to be ready at a moment's notice anyway. No. She had come here looking for a fight. Not many other people would've picked up on it, but Carana wasn't just anybody. She stood and kicked off her boot, bending down to untie the other one as she spoke.

"So what brings you here, Tierra?" Carana kicked off her other boot and stood bare foot on her own practice floor; the cold stone as comfortable as a lovers caress.

Tierra knew instantly this woman was deadly. It was her tone, her stance. Carana knew what she had come for. "Well, I just thought I would see who trained the person my son married," the warrior said off-handedly. Somehow this caring woman had gone from laughing to downright dangerous in a few seconds; Tierra saw that even Sprout could tell there was something different in the room as the little girl backed away quickly. Tierra circled around the wall, keeping Carana in front of her, and found her center. She was grounded and ready. At least she thought she was.

Sprout felt like she was outside when a storm was about to hit. Like when your tummy gets all woozy and you can smell the rain coming. If there were any animals in here they would be gone by now. "I'm going to go sit over there while the big people talk." She couldn't believe that she just said that. *Maybe I am growing up,* Sprout thought, as she backed up to the far side of the room and sat down, curling her feet under her and getting comfy. She still wasn't sure if she should be watching, but it felt too intense to miss.

Carana flexed her arms and stretched. "No weapons I assume?" She saw Tierra nod and smiled. If the warrior thought she would catch her off guard she had another think coming. She had trained in various styles over the decades and was quite good in all of them. Carana gauged her opponent's reach with a few easy swipes and kicks, moving in and out quickly without any intension of striking. Carana hadn't fought without weapons in a very long time, but it came back to her instantly. Within seconds they were at it and she found that she actually had to try. They traded blows, Carana getting in a bit more than Tierra, but then Carana was pushed back to defensive moves as the woman came at her savagely. The slight woman was quick, and her moves were eerily familiar. She could tell that the hair with the steel balls was dangerous and watched as the woman used them all in deadly concert.

"I see how you could've have stood against the Incarnation. You're excellent and can adapt to your enemy quickly. Let's see how you handle full contact though." Carana changed her stance, jumped up, and swung her right foot around and straight down at the small, but remarkable warrior. Using her hair braids and quick strikes, Tierra had backed Carana up and was ready to hit her with a flurry when the woman spoke.

"Ready when you are," Tierra answered, trying to bait the warrior in front of her. It wouldn't work, but she had to try; she knew that she was facing a master. Still, she wasn't without tricks of her own. Instantly Carana's stance changed, and when the high general jumped Tierra knew where the woman had learned to fight. In the split second she had to react, she used the only maneuver able to counter the lightning fast strike that her own master had always used.

Tierra abandoned offense and rolled backwards into a ball and tried to get away. Standing up she felt the floor shake as Carana's foot hit where she would've been, then the dangerous general did something completely unexpected. Carana used her momentum and spun once more, transferring the energy from the first kick into her other leg and brought it around at her. Tierra had never seen anyone have enough strength to even try this. Tierra dropped down on her back with a thud to avoid getting slammed with that kick, then flipped up a second later. She was breathing hard and still hadn't even really landed any decisive blows on her opponent. Time to step it up.

Carana wasn't shocked that Tierra knew how to escape that

kick. She thought that the woman's fighting style was familiar. Carana knew things that Tierra didn't know, however, and she was sure that she would surprise her with the follow up kick. Seeing that Tierra had escaped that as well she nodded to the smaller warrior and came at her once more, but Tierra charged her, swinging her braids. There was no sidestepping, no counter measures. Tierra just came at her like a wild animal. *Is she falling apart already?* Carana thought, as she deflected blow after easy blow. She had fought people like this before and when they know they are done for, they use a desperate gamble that never pays off. She ducked as those deadly steel balls arced over her head in a vicious swing. Standing back up, Carana realized her mistake immediately; it was a trap.

Tierra had feigned chaos and desperation to get Carana to lower her guard. The first swing of those braids was a ruse; the second one, however, came in like a falling dragon. *Gods above this is going to hurt.* Carana braced her legs and raised her arm. The hair wrapped around her arm impossibly fast, ending in the steel balls slamming against her arm with finality. With a loud *Snap*, her arm broke and she screamed in rage and pain, yanking on the hair with everything she had.

Tierra knew she had her, then watched in horror as Carana took it on her arm instead of ducking a second time. The second time would've been enough for Tierra to rush and kick her hard enough to make even an ogrann dizzy. No one told Carana this though. When the woman screamed and yanked, it took Tierra off her feet and slid her right to her opponent's feet. A second later, a bare foot was pushed into her face, covering her nose and mouth with force.

"Yield, brave warrior. These feet have been in boots for a tenday at least," Carana said wincing in pain.

"MmMmmmmmmm."

"What was that? I couldn't hear you over the sound of my

arm bleeding." Carana wasn't really worried about the arm. She hadn't had a sparring match like that in years. Not since Arian's graduation. She lifted her foot a little so Tierra could speak.

"Ok I give up." The foot was taken away and a good arm was given to the warrior to help her up. Those feet *were* bad. Tierra rubbed her head where the braids were, thanking Syll that Carana didn't rip them out all together. She had a head ache that would probably be with her for three years, maybe four. That was when they both remembered Sprout.

The little street child had seen a lot of violent crime and fighting on the streets of Everknight, yet this was something far worse. What she was watching was more like a fire raging out of control and spreading to the buildings next to it. Sprout was crying, not out of sadness or fright, but for an unnamed emotion racing through her memory of a woman with long white hair and knives.

Could that have been my mommy? she thought, as the tears rolled down her face unasked for. The two woman rushed over and asked her over and over if she was all right. After a couple of moments Sprout had calmed down. "No, it's all right, I was just thinking of my parents. They drowned when I was very little." Sprout tried to stop crying and be brave, but it was hard.

Carana frowned. She had heard from Arian that Sprout's parents were taken by some 'very bad men' and had actually started looking into that a few of days ago, before this whole war thing had started that is. Carana would have to speak to Lan about this and find out what was going on. She was meeting him later on to discuss Trav and it would be the perfect time to question him on this as well.

"Speaking of the past," Tierra began, turning to Carana once Sprout was feeling a little better, "I see that you studied under my old master, Master Bizu." He had taught Tierra the Changing Wind style years before she had joined the Companions of Everknight. The sect of Fra'hir warriors used to be located in the Shield Mountains, until the Oran destroyed them and killed her old master. She was the only one to survive.

Carana laughed out loud. She didn't mean to—it was just that with these heroes knowing that she was an Incarnation made things like this a little easier. "*Master* Bizu? Well, good for him. He always did want to get out from under the shadow of defeat." She saw Tierra's face drop—well more like crumble—and composed herself. "Sorry, let me explain. Bizu and I both studied under Master Yui Fan, a warrior from the far southern continent. We competed to be the best and he never could beat me. He developed that strike kick—called the Spiraling Wind—just to best me. He lost when I came up with the second attack, aptly named Death from Above." Carana walked away towards the weapon rack, a tear of memory falling on her own face. Those were the good days, the beginning days, when she didn't appear to be Immortal. "Bizu came with me, back here, and went into the mountains to start his own sect, while I watched the kingdom here grow. I heard about his death years ago, but I never visited so never got to say goodbye. I assumed that he grew to despise me."

Tierra was smiling. She knew who Carana was now. "Well, then it would be glad tidings indeed to tell you that he taught all of his students this mantra when they left to wander the world." Tierra stood straight and put her finger in the air like some sort of teacher. "*When you wander, please if you will, watch for my Canary. It will not appear as a bird, but instead will be a creature of deadly skill. Tell her that I miss her.*" She lowered her hand. "We never knew that it truly wasn't a bird." Tierra saw that Carana had turned and was crying openly, sobbing like a little girl.

"He called me that every day... his Canary. Oh Tierra, you have made me so happy." Carana hugged the small woman, crushing her and not caring at all. Her old friend had remembered her after all.

"Can I call you Canary?" Sprout was crying again, not knowing why. She thought the name sounded pretty though.

"Why yes, dear, you certainly can. Now let's go and find us a king and see what he needs us to do." Carana's arm had already started healing but would be sore for a couple of days. It was so worth the win though. She took the little girl by the hand and Tierra by the shoulder, wincing in pain, and walked up to the throne room.

A LITTLE WHILE LATER, LAN WALKED INTO THE HIGH General's quarters and stood at attention. He only held that position for about three seconds before Carana sighed and threw a pillow at him. She was seated on a small couch, opposite a high backed chair, with a pot of what could only be spiced wine by the smell of it. Carana leaned forward as he moved to the chair and sat down, the look on her face telling him that she was in need of something and wasn't in the mood for pomp and circumstance. "High General, what can I do for you?"

Carana sat back and kicked her feet up on the small table in front of her. "I've been hearing stories about you berating Trav openly about being a knight and wanted to make sure everything was still going well with you two," she said taking a sip from her glass.

"Trav is doing better. He just has to stop and realize that the word knight is supposed to mean something," Lan said. "And I wasn't berating him, so much as correcting him at times."

"It's fine Lan. I just wanted to make sure he was behaving." Carana was glad that Lan was taking responsibility for Trav, but she would step in if it got bad again. If it weren't for Lan stepping in and stopping her, Trav would've been dead.

"No need to worry about that. Every time I mention that I'm meeting with you he goes white as a ghost," Lan said with a wide grin. They both laughed at that, but then Lan could see there was something else on her mind. *Weird, I've never been able to read her before,* he thought. *She must be worried about something.* "Anything else I can help you with, High General?"

"I was actually hoping to ask you something about Sprout. Any chance we could talk about her past?" Carana asked.

"Sure," Lan said with some trepidation. He had to wonder what Carana could want to know about street kids. "What would you like to know, High General?"

"Just call me Carana when we're talking like this, Lan." She put her feet down and leaned in, setting her spiced wine down gently. "It's not anything too important, but I was wondering about Sprout's parents." Carana didn't know why it felt important, but somehow it did.

"Oh. Let me guess—she told you they burned in a fire?"

"No. Did they?" That was horrific for a small child to go through and Carana could only imagine what it had done to the small girl. Her own experience with fire was very traumatic and she had only gotten through it with the passing of many years.

Lan chuckled to himself, then realized that it might look bad to someone that did not know about the little girl's stories. He saw Carana's look and cleared his throat. "Sorry. No, to our knowledge her parents didn't burn in a fire. You see, none of us know what happened to them, not even Sprout. As best as we can figure, she tells these wild stories about how her parents died, or were taken, because she doesn't remember what happened."

Carana didn't understanding this at all. "You might want to

elaborate on that... and go slow, it's been one of those days already."

"Well, one night she told Griff that they were killed by a guard. Kari overheard her and called her out because she was told that they had been kidnapped. Once that came out we all traded stories and found out that she had told each of us a different tale." Lan paused in reflection, remembering how funny that night was; the look on the little girls face was priceless. "That was when we found out that she doesn't know what happened to them, so she makes up a wild story to make herself feel better."

"Why would that make her feel better?"

"Because it's not just that she doesn't remember. She says she feels like she lost them and doesn't want people to think she lost her own parents, as silly as that sounds." Lan knew that probably wasn't true, but he didn't know for sure.

"All right. That makes a little more sense now." Carana couldn't believe that the little girl thought she lost her own parents; more likely they abandoned her. "Thanks again. And don't tell her that I know. I will keep her secret, don't worry," Carana told him as she stood up.

"I'm not worried about you knowing, Carana. If that was all?" Lan asked, standing as well.

"Yes, and thank you again, Lan." Carana watched him walk out of her quarters and had to smile. These children were getting more and more fascinating by the day.

CRYSTAL GATE, TIR-LANAN

Karsis was irritated and had been for the last day and a half as they made their way to Tir-Lanan. He didn't plan to walk in through the main gate of the city, let alone to the fanfare that arriving with the Princess of Everknight, a unicorn, and a lost faerie brought. The famous bard saw the lines of waiting elves and frowned again. He was home, for the first time in over ten years, and he wouldn't be here unless he absolutely had to. Last time he had stayed in his Karsis persona and had inflamed the already petulant factions into an all out war—something his father was not pleased at whatsoever. He would be staying as Karsis again this time too, and hoped that it would be a little better; they had to pull this off.

Everknight would be hard pressed to stand against G'harr's might, even if it wasn't being led by an ancient elven wizard with a gods complex. So here they were, at the elven city of Tir-Lanan, to see if they could get the elves to fight against their old enemy alongside the humans; they would have better luck kissing a dragon. *Well, come to think about it, Rhoe probably could've after that display of power,* Karsis thought, as they passed the great crystal gates of the city's main street. The city was huge compared to Everknight, and the cobblestone street welcomed them without prejudice; that was what the elves were for.

Once again, Karsis lamented the fact that they weren't able to sneak in the back way like he wanted, arriving at his father's tower in secret and planning everything before the elven council even knew they were here. Now the entire city would be trying to get at them, trying to gain their allegiance for the varying factions on this or that vote. Oh, how they loved their voting days! They never really accomplished anything, but it made the people feel like they were at least trying. He saw his father's serving maiden, N'vea, weaving through the crowd and waving. She was short even for an elf, standing at only four and a half feet. Her white hair was a little shorter than shoulder length, and her long silver dress flowed out behind her. Karsis grabbed Liss's shoulder and guided her towards the little elven woman, waving to the other elves and grinning to hide his disgust; he still had a part to play. Karsis reached out and grabbed Liana as she floated, mouth open, in stunned silence. He wasn't worried about Rhoe—that love struck boy would follow Liss even if his eyes were gouged out. Avaryn... well if the unicorn strayed away from the group Karsis would feel sorry for the elves that cornered him. *I'm just glad that there are so many things to divert the elves' attention and give them other things to gossip about other than me coming home once more,* Karsis thought with a smile.

N'vea waved as she saw them coming over, shocked that Karsis was wearing his human guise once again. The last time he was here it caused so many problems between him and his father that she was sure that he would never have it on when he visited again; she was wrong as usual. N'vea spotted the tiny faerie and unicorn and had to look twice. She was told they would be with them, but she still couldn't believe her own eyes. Then she saw the young man with the long white hair and her breath caught. He was walking along like anyone else, but he had an aura about him that he probably didn't even know he had; it was almost majestic.

N'vea shook her head to snap herself back to reality and greeted Karsis in elven, then stopped as he gave her that look that said not to do that again. She had seen that look enough coming from his father so she switched to the common tongue among humans. "Glad to meet you all. I am N'vea and I will take you to see Adrilian. This way, please, and stay close." She turned and walked briskly through the crowd, which was now trying to stop them all and ask questions. A loud bell tolled over the street then, silencing the entire crowd at once.

Rhoe looked around at the sound of the bell and marveled at the reaction from the crowd. It was like they were trained to obey that tone. Then he heard the whispers of Adrilian and his tower and he thought he understood. Whoever Adrilian was he was powerful, and these elves knew it. It probably sounded to let everyone know his guests were to be left alone. A lot of the whispers weren't kind as the elves sauntered off in various directions.

"Well, that didn't gain Adrilian any favors," Rhoe muttered to himself. A hand caught his arm and spun him around without warning and Rhoe reacted with instinct, twisting his body, ducking under the arm, and coming in tight. Rhoe placed both palms upon the elf's chest and pushed hard, sending him backwards.

Maldren was outraged. How dare this *human* say something so rude about their society that he knew nothing about. He stepped behind the boy and grabbed his arm, to spin him around and berate him before everyone. That would show them these humans were nothing but unlearned barbarians once and for all. Before he even knew what had happened, however, the boy spun, twisted and shoved him! Maldren fell back and heard a collective gasp. He caught his balance asked the air to hold this impudent whelp while he drew his slender sword.

Rhoe heard the man cast and knew what was coming. While the elf spoke he whispered his own little surprise. "Ash'anti fra, tur ea hayen," Rhoe asked the air around him. Unlike other battles, Rhoe wasn't countering the air sent at him—he was just giving it another purpose. Shock passed over the elf's face as the air failed to hold Rhoe and instead spun him around impossibly fast. As he spun, Rhoe extended his foot, planting it in the center of his aggressor's chest. The elf went spiraling back into the crowd as Rhoe called to the air and set himself down. He remembered what Karsis had said about hair, and his was longer than whoever had grabbed him. Rhoe was hoping that would work in his favor. People scattered as whistles shrilled and three elves dressed in white leathers ran up to the group. Karsis just smiled and held Liss back. Rhoe nodded to him and faced the newcomers passively.

Malden got to his feet with a shaky stance, gasping for air through a bruised rib or three. His purple robes were ruined and his long white hair was in his face. He had never been so humiliated in his life, and he was very old. He didn't even know where his sword was.

"Seize that human!"

The wardens slowed their pace when they saw who it was that had been assaulted; they were not fans of Maldren Ulryntar. The man was a councilman, yes, but he was also a gigantic loudmouth and pretentious ass.

"On what grounds, sir councilman?"

"On the grounds that he assaulted me!"

They turned to the human and noticed his hair for the first time. He didn't seem to be elven, but he had the hair. "Did you assault Councilman Maldren sir?"

Rhoe smiled and held his hands out like the faeries did when they greeted someone. "I was only defending myself." He knew this councilman was going to keep screaming, but he wanted to stay calm.

"He used his sorcerous powers to command the air and kick me!" Maldren looked around and saw the bystanders weren't nodding along with him. It looked like he was losing his standing on the street with this escapade.

"Actually, he grabbed *me*, then I pushed him. I only used magic when he asked the air to hold me. I asked it to spin me, then kicked him away."

"Wait, you *asked* it?" The guards were confused. Humans couldn't use magic, and when they did it was to command, not ask. "This looks like a council problem—if you would come with us..."

"The boy will do no such thing." The sentence was spoken

plainly, without inflection, yet it carried so much weight that most of the people backed up. Adrilian stood among the companions and pointed at Maldren. "The boy is under my charge and so I can—and will—act in his stead. I believe the infraction of attacking a councilman is grounds for a duel? I would be happy to indulge you, Maldren. Right here and now." Adrilian brushed a strand of long white hair out of his face and stared, slowly smoothing his bright red robes that hung loosely on his lithe frame. Adrilian almost laughed when his *sight* told him this powerful child had attacked an elf, more so when they revealed it was Maldren! He couldn't have been happier with the way the boy held himself in a strange land; Rhoven had come a long way in a very short time. That was the way with prophesy—it tended to mold those that it needed, and quickly.

"No, no—of course not, Adrilian. I wasn't aware he was in your charge. All charges are dropped." Maldren turned to the wardens, as if to give them orders, but they were already walking away. He turned back to congratulate the young man through bitter teeth, but he also was walking away. Maldren stood among the whispers and giggles of elven society and vowed to get payback from that insolent whelp of a human. The councilman stormed away, walking back to the council chambers to fill them in and see how many he could get on his side before Adrilian got there.

Liss was completely lost. The great gates made of crystal were one thing, but when she saw the elves waiting for them just inside those gates she did a double take. Not only were they all dressed in silks and very fine clothes, they all had weapons of some sort. Karsis had told her that would be the case, but to actually see it was another thing altogether. Then she was led away with Karsis and turned her back for ten seconds, only to have Rhoe get into trouble. She had no idea what happened—one second everything was fine, then Rhoe was kicking this guy across the street. As fast as it happened, it was over. Now another elf was leading them away, Adrilian she thought his name was. She found Rhoe and wrapped her arms around him tight, needing a sense of familiarity in this strange city.

"Good job, anyone else you want to start a fight with?" she teased.

"Hey, I tried to just push him away. He was the one throwing magic at me after I've had a rough couple of months." Rhoe smiled weakly at Karsis, who shook his head. "Oh, don't tell me you wouldn't have floored him for grabbing you, Karsis."

"Oh, most assuredly. Although if I did it, he wouldn't get back up." Karsis winked and tried not to make eye contact with his father. He really wanted more time to prepare for this. Then he remembered how quiet Liana was and started to worry. "Hey, how are you doing little one?"

Liana heard him but was still looking around It was all too much. Her mind was going so fast that she was having a hard time even speaking... which had never happened. Ever. The dragon had shocked her, that she expected. He was a big scary thing with more teeth than she had the nerve to count, but this city was over her threshold. The crystal gates that were almost thirty feet high? A touch overwhelming. The crowd of elves dressed like it was a revel? Heart stopping—or tongue stopping if you think about it. Then, when she was just starting to get a grip on herself, Rhoe got into a fight with an elf and then the red robed guy showed up. "OhmygodIcan'tevenbelieveI'mhere!" There it was. "OhKarsisI'msorryI'mtalkingsofast."

Karsis laughed and shook his auburn hair in the light summer breeze. "It's fine little one, I expected it. I was just worried that your mouth might be broken."

If only, Avaryn sent to everyone. Everyone except Adrilian, whose wards were absolutely magnificent. He could've pierced them, but with elven archmages there tended to be nasty surprises waiting for anyone who tried.

"Hey!" Liana countered, then buzzed off to hide on Adrilian's shoulder. "Can you believe how rude that was?" She had slowed her speech now that she had snapped out of her funk somewhat. Now she just perched there, like it was something she had done every day for years. It was a gift she had.

Adrilian stopped dead in his tracks, turning his head to look Liana straight in the eyes his long white hair falling in his face as he stared. He tried not to smile, even when she sheepishly brushed his hair out of his eyes, like she was apologizing.

"Faeries. Gods above how I've missed you." Adrilian turned to them all, now that they had covered a good distance towards his tower. "Let us make haste to get off these streets and into the privacy of my dwelling. The amount of eyes and ears that will be upon you after that display is astounding."

"I'm sorry sir, I should've just left things alone." Rhoe felt bad, being human in an elven city was bad enough; starting a fight was not helping things. He was worried now that he had spoiled their chances at getting them to help at all.

"Sir!" Adrilian glared at Karsis with mock hateful eyes that danced with delight. "Just what have you told this young wizard about me?" He waved N'vea ahead to open the door to his tower, smacking her on her arm to get her attention away from the unicorn; he couldn't blame her. What he wouldn't give to talk with that one for years on end.

Karsis closed his eyes and wondered what kind of trouble he would get into on this visit. His father hated the fact that he wore a glamour inside the city, and one tied to his soul at that; it just wasn't done. Honestly he would've dropped it this time if it weren't for Liana and Avaryn. Hells below, just Liana. Avaryn could keep a secret. "Nothing. Trust me, you never came up at all." They all walked into the tower of Adrilian Everence and Karsis's thoughts were dark indeed.

Liss was very good at reading people. Usually Karsis kept his emotions carefully hidden, but something was making him unstable, and it showed. She pulled his coat a little, not enough to alarm him, but just enough to get his attention. "You all right?" she whispered

"He's fine, dear," Adrilian answered for the bard. "He just hates visiting because he knows he is going to get a lecture, among other things."

"Gods above, Karsis. He is just like you!" Rhoe knew he shouldn't have said it, but he couldn't stop himself. It was just weird to see Karsis being treated like he treated everyone else.

Karsis stared at Rhoe with mischievous glee. "You will pay for that one, dear boy."

Adrilian put his arm around Rhoe and pulled him away from Liss. "Oh, don't let him scare you. I taught him everything he knows. Now let's sit and chat whilst N'vea brings us some wine and juice." Adrilian walked into his antechamber and the torches lit by themselves. He did like to show off sometimes.

"So, Adrilian—what can we tell you that you haven't already seen in your scrying pool?" Karsis knew that his father had been keeping tabs on them. It was what he would've done if he had the time and resources. Karsis sat back and watched Liana circle around and find a comfy spot on the floor. This was going to take a little bit of time and he knew that events were unfolding in Everknight as they talked. It couldn't be helped though—the elves had their ways and they weren't quick to do anything. The bard took his lute out of his inside pocket, throwing a wink at Liss as he did, and began to play a soothing song as the others filled in the blanks for Adrilian. Yes, it was good to be home.

THE GOLDEN PALACE, G'HARR

He crawled out from behind his old throne and looked around cautiously. He hadn't seen his captor in a while and was wondering if it was safe to come out of hiding for a little bit. Not that he could go far, mind you—the shackles he was bound in kept him within a tight radius to the throne. A throne he used to sit in.

Ran'cian Ashren was the former Sorcerer King of G'harr, and his once handsome features were lost behind a film of dirt and grime. His long black hair was disheveled and his torn clothes barely kept him covered these days. For the hundredth time since he brought Ill'lyth G'harr back from the dead, he wished he could go back and fix it. Ran'cian had known that he had found an ancient elven Archmage buried under the G'harran palace. He'd even guessed it was the very Archmage that started the elven wars all those years ago, but he honestly thought he could control whoever it turned out to be. Then everything had gone to the deep Hells once she was free. Ill'lyth broke every magical confinement he tried, even three at once, and in the end, despite his shield, she just blew him down with the very air in the room despite his shields. She created the manacles he was now wearing out of a metal rod she had on her person and he was shackled then and there. He'd had been her slave ever since.

Ran'cian looked to the large windows and lamented his choices. Before he had raised Ill'lyth, he had been trying to find his long lost child somewhere in Everknight. A servant had run away years ago, pregnant with his offspring, and he had never found the child. The servant had died, but somehow the child had lived and escaped his grasp. Ran'cian tried everything, yet all his attempts were thwarted; he never had the chance to look again. They had done the summoning the very next day and his life had been these shackles ever since. The former Sorcerer King looked down at the restraints and frowned. The metal was unique in that it canceled all the power he had, which was quite a lot. To say that the situation he found himself in was life changing was an understatement.

Ran'cian had never allowed the darkness to consume him, like other sorcerers usually did. Quite the contrary. He always kept the darkness right at the edge, baiting it, promising it, then filling his heart with purpose to keep it at bay. It was the secret to what made him so powerful. However, once he had started to really think about that child, his thoughts drifted away from absolute power and ran more along the lines of raising her in this world. Now that he had seen his kingdom enslaved, he vowed that if he had the chance to reclaim it, he would do better; at least he thought he would.

Ran'cian sat back on his feet and raised his head up, staring at the golden ceiling and the large chandelier hanging there. It was a massive structure, held aloft by magic and crafted out of silver and polished wood. A dozen candles flickered within the solid frame, magically burning forever by the enchantments placed upon them ages ago. *How old was she now? How long have I even been in these shackles? Years?* His thoughts were morose, but he wasn't angry for once. The former Sorcerer King chuckled as he remembered exactly why he needed to release an elven Archmage. He had found a very old text about a powerful beast that could ravage the land and where it was imprisoned. His plan was to control it and force Lythinall to concede to his whims, merging their land and his and granting him even more power. Then, with both nations under his dominion, he would wage war against Miran to the southeast and finally Sirr to the northwest; back then it all seemed so easy to imagine.

Once he was shackled though, the plans kept going without

him. Ill'lyth, along with his conspirators, released the beast, which she knew was the Incarnation of Death, but had no immediate concerns for leashing him. Instead, she let those lack-wits in Everknight, led by Othren, try and assassinate the King of Lythinall. She was using the Incarnation, and her hidden assassins, as a distraction to keep the rulers of Lythinall too busy to realize she was back; never mind that most of them wouldn't even know her name. So Ill'lyth let this thing of nightmares go on its killing spree, and Ran'cian had to listen to the reports of the death and destruction that lay in its wake. He had to hope that this new young warrior—and if reports could be believed, Karsis himself—would actually stop the dark thing they had released. *And when I get out of these shackles everything will be different...* Now he just had to convince his mind of that as well.

GOL'ROUN, TIR-LANAN

He walked around the Gol' Roun and couldn't help but smile. Sinaron had dreamt about the humans coming to Tir-Lanan, but the faerie and unicorn that arrived with them were complete surprises. He rarely was surprised these years, so it left him in high spirits. Sinaron Hana'ryr was a priest of Davalar, God of Protection and Honor. He was also an Oracle, a rare individual handpicked by the gods to be a beacon of their faith. It was said that they were a form of lesser Incarnation, but that was just conjecture. He had it on good authority that Oracles were here to preserve certain individuals who had a destiny to carry on into the future. For centuries he had been the only one, ever since the Half-elven Oracle of Ollian died saving the Incarnation of Beauty from a horde of ogrann in what was now called Sirr.

Now, however, there was another one. Sinaron's dreams told him that a human child in Everknight had been called by

Davalar and he wished he could go to him. Sinaron knew first-hand how hard it was to come into these powers and he longed to comfort this boy. It hadn't looked good, until Karsis walked in with the human princess. He knew what they were going to ask for, and Sinaron would be the first out of the gate at a dead run.

The Oracle moved out of the way of a busy merchant, begging pardon for the inconvenience, and stopped at a cart selling exquisite hand mirrors. Sinaron picked one up—a silver handled beauty with engraved symbols of the Goddess Ollian—and gave the merchant five gold coins. Sinaron spun back to the center of the Gol'Roun and looked at himself in the polished glass. His long white hair was bound in a single braid, woven with white leaves, and his deep green eyes shone like emeralds; not bad for over three-hundred winters. He polished the glass on his white robe and placed it in the sling bag that he carried everywhere he went; you just never knew when you would need it. He saw a familiar face in the crowd and skipped his way over to say hello even though he knew how the elf was going to react.

"Why, Ciril'ven, you are looking positively enlightened this morning," Sinaron said with a bow, extending his arms out wide.

Ciril'ven Draken'ar was quite possibly the most notable elf in all of Tir-Lanan, only beating Karsis's reputation because he always left to spend time among the humans. She was almost two-hundred and thirty winters, and by sheer personality alone she dictated the style of the entire city. If she was wearing it, *everyone* had to be wearing it. She heard her name and knew immediately who was speaking to her. Sighing loudly, she turned and regarded Sinaron pleasantly.

"Why thank you, Davalar's Mouth. And what else does your god wish to tell me this morn?" Ciril'ven's venomous tone showed exactly what she thought of the self-proclaimed Oracle. It's not like she didn't believe in the gods—quite the opposite—

but for one man to be chosen among all of the people? Preposterous.

Ciril'ven was a slight woman, about five-feet tall and weighing only about seven stones, but she made up for that with her personality. She was a force of nature, and her clothing reflected her nature every single day. Today she was wearing a short, white-silk wrap around her tiny waist and a white silk coat.. and that was all. Her skin was painted with white paint under her bare breasts with white stripes down both legs; her coat was left unhooked on purpose.

People moved away from both of them, almost like they knew there would be a standoff, but Sinaron would not be bated this day. "Oh, dearest Ciril'ven, you know He doesn't speak right through me—that would rattle my teeth something fierce. No, I was just wondering if you heard what had befallen our fellow councilman, Maldren?" Sinaron took an apple out from his sling bag and bit right it while waiting for her to respond; it was a horrible faux pas. Gossip travelled quickly in the city, especially when it pertained to new comers.

Ciril'ven wasn't rising to his games this day; she was more controlled than that. "No, I haven't heard yet. Pray tell, Oracle, what has that stuffy dog gone and done now?" She hated not being up on the hot gossip, and if she had to get it from this over-inflated windbag... well, then she would have to grin and take it.

"Seems Maldren went and had an altercation with one of the humans under Adrilian's care—worse, he used magic on the poor boy." Sinaron was leading her on, inviting her in, but not for the reasons she would assume. He was trying to get an audience to spread the news faster than it already had spread.

"Oh, that poor boy! Did Adrilian save him?" Ciril'ven asked with mock pity. Not that she didn't like humans. She was a member of the Ari'en Brekith, a faction that believed the rights to come and go should be given back to individuals. If an elf wanted to leave the city and venture out, they should be able to choose that without having to petition the council. They didn't think building new elven cities throughout the land was the way to go, but hiding away in stagnation was just as bad.

"Davalar's mercy, no! Can you believe the boy bested Maldren by altering the magic himself?" The words halted at least a dozen passing elves and more were walking over to listen. "The young human just took the wind and spun right around, kicking Maldren at least fifty feet across the street." Sinaron was embellishing, but he knew how to work a good story. Karsis had taught him to weave a good tale for an audience decades ago.

"The boy is a sorcerer?!" Ciril'ven was no longer smiling. This was a serious offense—and inside Tir-Lanan at that!

Sinaron placed his hand on his chest and staggered back. "You would think so, but no. The boy *asked* the wind to help him. Asked! The boy must be a wizard, but I'm not sure how that can be." It was working. The people around him were already running off to tell everyone they could find. It was the price of keeping a people bottled up in the same area for centuries; even a patient race like the elves. Boredom was a constant enemy, so they loved to gossip. "Alas, I see that the sun has moved to another time, and I have prayers. It was good seeing you Ciril'ven," Sinaron called as he danced through the crowd. This was another bad move publicly, as no one left the woman who dictated style standing alone in the middle of a conversation, but he didn't care for that kind of style. His god knew his worth, and that was all he needed.

Ciril'ven was in shock, but she pulled herself together at the last second and wrapped her style around her like it was a palpable thing, cloaking herself in power that almost radiated outward. Ciril'ven ignored his escape and walked towards the center of the Gol' Roun. She thought about what the name of this place meant in the common tongue of the humans and laughed a little. It literally meant *Trade Circle*, and the fact that the news was flying around this circle was not lost on her. The elves dealt in gossip like most cultures dealt in goods, and thus had perfected it. Ciril'ven walked back to her villa to change her outfit and ponder what could be done to get this human wizard on her good side.

THE ELIEN SHIR, TIR-LANAN

He sat in the back of the tavern, at a round table facing the entrance. He wasn't paranoid, or even paying that much attention—it just seemed the most dramatic place to sit at the moment. To be fair, he was waiting for someone, but it really wasn't as clandestine as all that. Noro'sin Olendir was the head of the Yaw Worl'aren, a faction that wanted the elves to open their gates and blend with the world once more in complete harmony. It wasn't the most popular faction, but it had been around since the day the elves left the humans behind and came here. Of late his faction was losing ground, but the current gossip was that humans were here once more, and that always helped his cause.... if he could get them on his side that is. It had been over three decades since the last visit from the human prince of Lythinall.

Noro'sin had curly white hair that hung down to his shoulders, and his deep violet eyes were a contrast to his chalk-white skin. He always dressed in dark blues and purples, mostly silk, and could always be found with a drink in his hands. Other elves always complained that he seemed disconnected to reality. They said it was the hallucinogenic wine he was always drinking, but he wasn't convinced. Then he saw the two elves he was waiting for and he signaled the serving maiden to bring him another bottle. She made a face but went to get another from behind the bar.

"I see you're already half into your cups, Noro'sin," the tall elf said, pulling a seat out and making himself comfortable. Boril'ran Silverleaf was well past his four-hundredth winter and was the head of the wardens in Tir-Lanan. He was a very powerful wizard and his long white hair was held back in a single braid that ended in a small ruby. He rested his staff against the table and motioned for his companion to sit. "You asked for us and so we are here, Noro'sin. Now what do you want of us?" Boril'ran tried not to sound bored, as the man sitting here technically held more prestige than he did, but it couldn't be helped. No one summoned the head warden these days except the high king, and even then it was rare. No, this had to be about the humans.

The other elf beside Boril'ran sat down and tried not to hyperventilate. Illiandral was ready to go back to Silversword Pass when the Boril'ran stopped him and told him to follow. Illiandral tried not to pass out, figuring that it had something to do with the humans he led into the city, but he daren't ask; it was far beyond his pay grade to do so. Illiandral kept his eyes down and shifted his feet. He had never dreamt of being in the company of elves this powerful, and it scared him more than a little. Then he heard someone say his name and looked up to see both elves staring at him.

"Well?" Noro'sin asked as he swirled his wine around in his glass slowly.

"I'm sorry, Lord. I was trying not to pass out." It was the only thing he could think of to say.

"I asked you if you witnessed this *magic* for yourself." Noro'sin had heard from his contacts that the young boy had used magic to tussle with Maldren and he wanted proof before he tried to convince the child to join his cause.

Illiandral looked to the head warden with eyes that asked, *What do I say now?* He had been told not to say anything about the dragon or magic, and it had been his superior's orders. He honestly didn't know what to do.

Boril'ran sighed, knowing the young elf probably had been told to keep quiet. "It's all right boy—just tell him. He will find out eventually. Someone in his position always does." Nobles bothered him, especially ones that thought they were entitled to a better life simply because they were born into it. Rubbish, all of it. You should be judged by your accomplishments and hard work, not birth. What did *he* know was that Noro'sin was only one of the most powerful wizards in the city.

"Well sir, " Illiandral began slowly, "I wasn't there at the gates when he fought Lord Maldren, but I did witness the young human use magic." He stopped short when he saw Lord Boril'ran look at him with raised eyebrows. Boril'ran didn't know. It came to Illiandral that his superior hadn't told *anyone* about his report, either because he didn't believe it or because he wanted to suppress it. But it was too late now. Illiandral swallowed hard and continued. "You see, they found a dragon buried into the side of the pass, apparently dying of something caused by an Incarnation..."

"A *what?!*" Noro'sin was fully awake for the first time in at least fifty years, and stone cold sober out of nowhere. He wasn't sure which word had done it specifically... *dragon* or *Incarnation*. Both were equally as bad.

As much as Boril'ran echoed the statement in his own head, he had more restraint than this drunken tart. "Ignore him. Go on." He would get the full story from this young guard later.

"Well, they were trying to heal the dragon and the boy thought he could channel the unicorn's horn through him. Then he used the fire within the dragon and ignited himself, healing the great beast." Illiandral was crying again without knowing it. He felt the tears sliding down his face and smiled at the thought of the selfless bravery he witnessed. "The human didn't even know he would be all right—he just wanted to help. I have never seen such bravery." That was when he saw that the Head Wizard was staring at him open mouthed. "Sir?"

Boril'ran was floored. *With fire.* Those two words were counter to everything he had ever known about the magic he'd used every day for the past four-hundred years. The boy healed with *fire.* Granted, it was dragon fire and used on a dragon, but how on Syll's green world would a young human boy know how to do that? It only made sense after hearing it; he never would've thought of it himself.

"Illiandral, did you catch any of their names?" He had to know what was going on, even if he had to knock on Adrilian's door himself.

"I think the boy was called Rhoe, and of course there was Karsis. But that was when I fainted." Illiandral smiled when he thought of meeting his hero, but his thoughts were interrupted by a loud crash.

Boril'ran stood up and his chair went flying back, crashing into the table behind him. The room went eerily silent. "Come. With. Me." The wizard ignored Noro'sin and thundered off, dragging the poor young guard behind him. He was angry at himself for not knowing that Karsis had returned, and vowed to check his contacts at the pass. The commander was also going to answer for the matter of not telling him about a dragon. It was going to be a busy tenday to say the least.

Noro'sin sat there, trying to digest what he had heard. It was too much. He noticed there was a bottle sitting next to him, ready to be opened. He hadn't even seen the maiden bring it over. "Well, time to work through everything I just heard," Noro'sin muttered to himself, as the noise of the tavern started up again. He would have to push his contacts about this Incarnation. If he remembered this in a couple of hours that is.

A STRANGE LAND INDEED

She had fallen asleep after eating some weird bread and drinking some very good wine. Karsis, Rhoe, and Adrilian were talking about the council—what the ruling body would be inclined to hear and what they would believe. Liss wanted to stay up and listen in, but she found her eyes closing despite her resolve. Suddenly, she was up and running for the privy, then throwing up everything in her stomach. Liss wasn't even fully awake yet, but somehow she was focused enough to not hit the floor. Rhoe was there in seconds, holding her hair back and whispering to her softly. "Sor—sorry Lord..." Liss tried to apologize to their host as Adrilian walked over, but he was laughing before she finished.

"Dear Princess, are you actually *apologizing* to me for being sick? Well, I guess I have missed some of the traits of you humans." Adrilian really liked this princess, even more than he liked her father, Arian. That man was unforgettable and he remembered the speech he gave to the council like it was yesterday. "Do you think it was the wine?" the powerful wizard asked, suddenly worried that maybe someone had infiltrated his stores in an effort to kill his guests. She had been asleep for a while, so if it was poison it couldn't have been a fast-acting one.

"No, I think it may have been the bread," Liss lied. She had an idea what was wrong but was trying not to think of it right now. "I ate it way too fast." Liss got up and sat in a comfy chair in the antechamber. At least she was awake now and could listen to the conversation.

Karsis sat again and smiled at her, welcoming her with just his eyes. He was going to go to her, but Rhoe beat him. No surprise really, the way these two were fawning over each other. Karsis asked the air to bring him a decanter of wine and watched as it spun through the air like a top. Adrilian clicked his tongue in disapproval, but that only made the bard laugh. He had just grabbed the wine out of the air when Liss asked the most intelligent question he had ever heard.

"So why is it that humans can't cast magic, yet we've seen sorcerers use it?" It had been bugging her ever since the dry bridge. She just didn't understand the concept of *some can, others can't*. Something had to be missing.

Adrilian raised his eyebrows at the question and stood slowly. "Let me start by telling you about *why* the elves hate these sorcerers so much." He held up a hand to forestall Karsis's objections and gave his son a stern look. Though forbidden for any human to hear, these two needed to hear this. Besides, the unicorn wouldn't tell anyone and the little faerie was sound asleep.

"Long ago, when we had finally sealed away the Incarnation known to us as Dar'Krist, some of the elves saw that the humans had potential. Ill'lyth G'harr had taken a human as her lover and over the years taught him magic. His problem, however, was that he couldn't cast it. The reason is that millennia ago Syll made a pact between our ancestors and the elements; in return, we could cast magic by asking them for help. Ill'lyth found books on a very old cult called the Gramayre and how they used blood to cast magic—and it gave her an idea. You see, those with *any* elven blood can cast magic, so she cut her wrist and let her lover drink from her. It took three days of constant feeding, and ether to bind the blood to their bodies, but it worked. Others soon heard about her method, and after two weeks bodies were found drained of blood entirely."

Adrilian was silent for a long moment, then he looked directly into Allissana's eyes as he continued. "We tried to ban the practice, but it turned into a dark trend—some elves just had to have a human that could cast magic; it was considered fashionable. The problem was that humans didn't want to learn the correct way. It took years to get the right inflections and tone to be precise. They started getting sloppy, and that is when they realized they could just *force* the elements to do their bidding. They started to use "Obren"—*obey*— rather than asking. After that, it got even worse." Adrilian turned to Rhoe and fixed him with an even stare. The boy had to hear the ugly truth. "As more and more humans were fed, they learned to do it with less blood... but they were still killing elves. This was the true start of the last war, and why the upstarts were banished. We kept it out of all of the books because the fewer people who knew our blood could do this, the better."

"That is horrible," Liss said quietly. The room was so silent that you could've heard a quill drop. "So the people of G'harr are still killing elves?"

Karsis interrupted his father for this account. He knew personally why the G'harrans could cast magic. "Not in over fifty years," the bard began, casually taking out his hand harp and strumming idly. "They all have elven blood running through them at this point, being the children of those unions many years ago. Some of the assassins at the castle, however, are a different story. All the new sorcerers' apprentices you've encountered are being fed by the G'harrans. Othren probably keeps them on a schedule and makes them beg for it." Karsis ended with a look at his father and smiled. He had killed that traitor, and it had felt good.

Liss looked at Rhoe with unshed tears. She had asked to cast magic, but now that she knew what she would have to do, he probably hated her. He must know she would never do that! "Rhoe... I would nev—never..."

Rhoe was shocked to the core at the secret history of magic, but then he saw Liss's face and her eyes filling up with tears. He heard her start to speak and knew she felt bad about wanting to cast magic. He walked to her, pulling her to her feet and embracing her warmly. "You would never do that. I know you. It's all right." Then Rhoe jumped back as something shocked him. It was like a spark ran through his whole being from her body. He stared at her, then looked down to her stomach.

Liss couldn't believe what just happened. At Rhoe's embrace and the sound of his voice... the baby kicked! Strange— he even felt it, which would've been hard even *if* he knew she was with child. "Rhoe, I'm sorry. I wanted to be sure before I..." Liss cradled her stomach, which wasn't even showing all that much.

Karsis sat there and let his mouth hit his lap, his small harp falling to the ground and clattering with a horrid sound as the strings all hit together. He hadn't seen this coming at all, and now that it was here—well, he had no idea what to do. Wait! Yes, he did. "This calls for music!" Karsis exclaimed, pulling his lute out of his jacket and stowing the harp away until he could tune it again. Strumming a lovely spring tune, he wondered how much magic this young one would inherit.

Liss smiled and looked at Rhoe, letting her tears fall. "Karsis told us about the time difference in the Hidden Vale, and after I got sick I had my suspicions. I just wasn't sure."

Rhoe took only a second to digest all of this, smiling instantly. "It's fine, Liss. I'm happy! It was just a shock when I felt... that." *Whatever* that *was*, he thought. Rhoe would have to corner Karsis later and tell him about it; he wasn't going to worry her about it now. Rhoe stepped in and kissed her, holding her close. He couldn't believe he was going to be a father. *I'm going to be a father! I may faint.* His thoughts swirled, as they sat awhile still hugging each other.

Adrilian crossed his legs and drank deeply, then set down his glass. "Well, this is all fine and proper, but it's well past both your bedtimes and you need to get some rest before the dawn. The council meeting will be held when the sun sets, and we still need to go over the council members and their agendas." Adrilian couldn't stop smiling. Seeing this young wizard become a father was probably the second-best moment of his very long life; the birth of his son was the first. Adrilian led Karsis away as Rhoe and Liss started coming up with names and planning the future of their little one. It saddened him to know what was coming, but he would do everything in his power to change it. Thankfully, that was one thing he had in abundance —power.

"Well, those two are full of surprises," Karsis said as they walked up the circular staircase leading to Adrilian's workshop. They entered the glass room and saw N'vea seated and working on a painting. She got up to leave, mainly in embarrassment, but Karsis held his hand out to stop her. He looked at her painting and held his chin in his hands in a parody of the way snobby elves looked at art. "Don't think I've seen a better piece modeled after the sunset. Very nice work." She looked shocked, then laughed when she realized he was kidding. It was a painting of the moon.

"I don't want to be in the way," she said sheepishly, turning to leave.

Karsis wouldn't let her pass. "It's fine, N'vea. Stay. It's going to be just casual talk tonight. I can't handle anymore intrigue right now."

"I don't think I've ever heard you say that,' Adrilian said, going over to his table and opening the massive book that he kept there. It was night, and with the moon as high as it was he could see all the way across the city from way up here.

Karsis sat down on the cold marble floor, relishing in the coolness of the stone. "Adrilian, I don't think I've ever seen a more competent caster than that young warrior down there. He has amazed me at every turn and I swear, that is *not* easy." Karsis remembered sitting like this when he was just starting to learn magic from his father; the lessons would take hours, but the cold stone was always there for him. It was calming, and the gods above knew that he needed calm right now. He waited for the sarcastic remark from his father, then realized the elf was engrossed in his book once more., no doubt lost in another vision.

Being a Seer was a blessing and a curse, one that Karsis would never wish for himself. His father would stare at the windows, or his books, for hours on end. Adriliar would see all manner of things, from the past to the future and all the things in-between. When his father came out of his trance, he would then have to put it all together and see if what he'd seen was something pertinent—way too much work. Knowing that he had a little time to kill, Karsis looked over at N'vea and was pleased when he caught her looking at him.

Well, that *will pass the time at least,* he thought as he stood and walked seductively towards her. He knew his approach was working when she dropped her brush and fumbled while picking it up.

N'vea saw Karsis coming towards her and her breath caught. He wasn't supposed to catch her staring at him. She stood awkwardly and tried to get around him, but his hands caught her shoulder and spun her around. She looked into his eyes—eyes that looked just like Adrilian's—and saw the desire embedded in them; her master's eyes didn't look like that.

"Oh Karsis, we can't. I'm just his serving maiden. I'm no one imp—" She was going to continue but he kissed her then, a deep passionate kiss that made her knees weak.

Karsis led her out and onto the staircase, spiraling down until they came to the first floor again. He kissed her shoulders and neck the whole way down, quietly taking her robes off as he went.

"You know, N'vea, I don't think I've ever seen your room?" Karsis asked playfully. He chuckled as she turned a deeper shade of red, but she led him down the long hallway anyway. As Karsis started taking off his long coat, he thought of the sleeping faerie and how much trouble she could get into if she woke up. Then N'vea kissed his ear and that thought flew right out the window and onto the cobblestones.

OUTSIDE OF ADRILAIN'S TOWER, TIR-LANAN

Kilyan Lightblade skipped down the early morning street and stopped at the massive marble and glass tower. The first two floors were marvelously worked marble, wrought into a twisting pattern that turned to glass panes about sixty feet up. The clear windows made the rest of the tower see-through, though the glass was warded to keep the birds from crashing into it. The young elf smiled and brushed his short, white hair out of his eyes. He didn't hold enough stature to have hair down to his shoulders, so he grew the front as long as the back and kept it stylish. His clothes stood out as well. His silk shirt and breeches were dyed in reds and golds and his coat had silver ribbons flying in the cool summer breeze.

Kilyan had come to see if he could get an audience with the humans before the council meeting, but clearly, no one was awake as yet. Not that elves slept, but they did meditate for several hours when they needed to reflect. He looked up to shield his eyes from the rising sun and saw a bird spiraling down. *Funny,* he thought, *I thought no birds could get close to the tower.* Then the bird slammed into him in a blur of questions and babble.

LIANA AWOKE TO A VERY QUIET ROOM; THAT IN AND OF itself was dangerous. Add to the fact that the tower was home to one of the most powerful wizards in an entire city of wizards and it made for a very deadly problem: Liana knew that she shouldn't touch things in the tower, but she had to explore. It was in her nature... and she was bored. Rhoe and Liss slept on the floor, holding each other tight, and Avaryn was resting with his horn on the floor. Liana could've sworn he was snoring. "Healing that dragon must've taken a lot out of him," the faerie said to herself quietly. Liana fluttered here and there and looked out the many windows at the city below. It was so pretty! She didn't see Karsis anywhere, though she thought she heard some sort of low moaning downstairs. That's when she noticed Adrilian sitting at his bench reading a book.

"Goodmorning!" she rambled, as she flew over and landed next to him on the bench. He didn't move in the slightest, just kept staring into nothingness. "Ohnohehasbeenfrozen!" She was worried and flew around in a circle not knowing what to do. Suddenly Adrilian moved and Liana breathed a small sigh of relief; the wizard wasn't under a spell. "Are you all right?" she asked slowly, trying to calm down. She was the ambassador of the faeries and had to act like it; at least that's what she had told herself.

Adrilian came out of his *sight* and took a deep breath, then heard the faerie buzzing around him. He had seen what would get the elves out of their isolationist ways, and the Gods have mercy on poor Kilyan. His instincts were screaming at him not to do it, but he had been a Seer for a very long time and knew when he had to throw caution to the wind, so to speak.

"Good morning, little one. How did you sleep?"

Liana set down on the bench in front of the old wizard, slowing her wings so that she didn't blow away any notes. She was proud that she remembered to even do that, and so had a bright smile upon her face when she addressed him. "I'm doing really good today... what was your name again?"

"My name is Adrilian, but you may call me Ril if it is easier. Only you though." Gods above how he missed the faerie folk.

"All right, Ril it is. Is there anything I could do around here? I'm *awfully* bored." Liana knew she had to be a proper ambassador, but she desperately wanted to see this city.

"As a matter of fact, there is. There is an elf downstairs that wants help... and you are just the faerie to help him. Think you're up to it?" Adrilian shuddered despite knowing it was going to help. Unleashing this little ball of energy upon the elves would be hilarious, but would also draw attention to Rhoe and Liss before it was time.

"I'monit!" she exclaimed, launching off the bench in a flurry of wings and giggles, notes flying everywhere as she forgot this time. Liana flew up at the windows and went in circles before she found an opening to fit through. Then she was out in the summer air and twirling down the side of the glass tower. Liana saw a tiny elf standing in the front of the tower, shielding his eyes against the bright sun behind her. *How did that wizard know he was there?* she thought to herself as she came closer and closer to the ground. She beat her wings at the last minute, banking up and around at the elf, but didn't gauge her timing right. Liana slammed into his cloak with a slight *puff* of clothing. That didn't stop her from asking questions though.

"What'syourname?Areyouawizardtoo?   Mmmmmmmmm-mm!" The last bit was lost in a ruffle of clothes as the elf panicked and threw off his cloak.

"What in the name of Syll?" Kilyan threw the cloak and danced back, drawing his slender sword with steady hands. He wasn't sure what had attacked him, but as he calmed down he realized that it was *speaking* to him. He saw a tiny faerie peer out from beneath the cloak and his world turned upside down. The tiny thing was only about fourteen inches tall, with gossamer wings and curly hair. It was surely a faerie, though they had been gone for centuries. He had heard that the humans had come with a faerie and a unicorn, but he thought that was just a story made up to impress the younger elves.

Liana untangled herself from the cloak. She saw the elf staring at her and suddenly remembered she was the ambassador to the faeries. Drawing her tiny self up, she folded her wings and spread her arms out wide.

"You don't bow in greeting?" Kilyan asked, tilting his head to one side trying to figure out what the faerie was doing.

"We don't bow, silly!" She unfurled her wings and flew up to his face, watching him grip his sword tighter. These elves were all uptight. "Watch me again." Liana turned in midair and spread her arms out wide, exposing her chest to the elf-like she had done thousands of times. "See? We show that we have nothing in our hands to harm one another, and nothing over our hearts to protect us from another."

"Fascinating. How do you discern who is above everyone else? Are you important where you come from?" Kilyan couldn't gauge how important this faerie was without her hair or how deep her bow was; he was feeling a little lost.

"We're all the same where I come from—except the Queen, that is. She's the only one that is above us all. Well, her and the Trees." Liana thought that these elves were very strange. "You should come and visit us more often, then you would see some real fun! We've got games, and Revels, and dancing and drinks, andandandand..." Liana found herself babbling and tried to take a deep breath, but only succeeded in inhaling some of his expensive perfume, which made her sneeze.

Kilyan couldn't believe his luck. Here was the single most important thing to happen to his cause, ever. He was the head of the Ari'en Brekith, which meant "Song of the Free People" in the common tongue. His small faction wanted to see the rights to come and go given back to individual elves. If someone wanted to leave the city and venture out, they should be able to do so. Kilyan would call for slow migration by individuals over long years to get accustomed to open borders, and this excitable faerie was just the stepping stone he needed to finally make the council listen. "What is your name, great lady?

Liana just hovered there for a minute, unsure how to answer. He had called her a "great lady," but that was how one referred to the Queen. In the end, she just let out a big breath and looked him right in the eye. "Mynameis..." She stopped herself and took another deep breath, like Avaryn always told her, then continued. "My name is Liana. What's yours?"

"My name is Kilyan Lightblade, and I think you could help all of elven kind."

"That'swhatI'mherefor!" she exclaimed, then calmed down once more; just a bit though. "I'm the ambassador for the faeries! I can help!" She was so excited that she flew in circles around the elf as he walked and told her his ideas for a brighter future for elves and faeries. She wasn't worried about getting lost; she still had her whistle that she could use to call Avaryn.

Adrilian turned away from the glass window and reeled in his *sight*. The little faerie was off and onto her own tiny destiny. Little did she realize that she would save them all in the end.

I HOPE YOU KNOW WHAT YOU'RE DOING? AVARYN THOUGHT to the man, even though all the wards made him hesitant to do so. Now that they were inside most of the wards were gone, but Avaryn still wasn't sure. The unicorn knew that this man was something more than just an elven wizard, though he didn't share that with the others. He had seen something like this before, back when he first met Karsis—though on a much smaller scale—and again when he felt the power radiating from the Incarnation of Death. Except this didn't feel like Death. Oddly, the man reminded him of a... unicorn actually. *So what are you that you can see the future so well?*

I am a Seer, and as far as I know, I am the only one for the last seven centuries; I am also the Incarnation of Magic, but I suspect you already knew that. Adrilian smiled at Avaryn, then turned and went to see how Rhoe and Liss were doing. He had heard her run to the privy upon waking, followed quickly by her steadfast warrior... or wizard, or whatever this talented young man was these days. They, too, might save the land, but only if he could avert the darkness that was coming. For the first time in his very long life, he had a vision with two paths, and he would be damned to the Hells below if he let the dark path win. In fact, it was very surreal to him to have met the people responsible for so much change yet to come.

Rhoe held Liss's hair as she emptied her stomach again. He couldn't believe she was pregnant—pregnant with his child. His child! He did the math and it would put her at around twelve weeks, give or take a week. Liss wasn't showing a whole lot, but now that he knew, Rhoe could see a slight change. How could they go back to Everknight and war now? Rhoe shook his head and cleared his mind.

Let's take one thing at a time. Get through this council meeting and worry about the fighting later, he thought as she got up and straightened out her tunic.

"I'm tired of this getting sick nonsense already," Liss said, using a wet cloth on her face. She hadn't felt the baby move since Rhoe had hugged her and she wondered if it was because he was a wizard. Rhoe had told her that he had felt a literal shock, like a spark from the baby. She smiled—leave it to her child to be dramatic. Liss couldn't believe that just last winter, things like faeries, magic, and elves were merely stories in her books, and she herself was just a kid. Adrilian come over and she bowed slightly. As a guest in his tower she was unsure of the custom, but figured at least it might make him smile.

"You flatter me, young princess," Adrilian said, returning the favor, his long hair coiling to the floor with his deep bow. He rose and smiled, knowing that he would remember these two for the rest of his life. "We should hear from the council this morning as to when they will want to meet." Adrilian waved them ahead as he used magic to freshen up the air in the privy. "Let's head down to the antechamber and call for Karsis, I think a good stroll around the city is in order—that is if Rhoe can keep from attacking any more councilman." Adrilian laughed at the face Rhoe made and placed his hand on the boy's shoulder to let him know he was kidding.

He never got the chance...

—Adrilian was somewhere else, maybe outside of Everknight, and everything seemed blurry. He had never had a vision like this, and already he could tell that he would have a killer

headache after it was over. He turned slowly at the sound of battle and saw Rhoe leaping over a blockade with a grace that seemed magical. With him was Dar'Krist himself, looking almost as battered. It was clear they had seen their share of fighting. Rhoe's robe was slashed and cut, stained with blood from a dozen minor wounds, and he spun and kicked with a fervor that astounded the Seer, using the wind to speed his attacks and the earth to keep his steps measured and steady. Adrilian was torn between pride and being awestruck at the ease with which this young wizard combined magic and fighting.

Then the scene changed—Rhoe was on the ground, rotting away, a large man crawling to his side as he rotted as well. Another figure stood behind them, unaffected by the wasting power of Death. There was no sign of Dar'Krist anymore. He saw the big man die, his large body turning to ash next to Rhoe while he reached for the boy's hand. But they never touched. Where was Liss? Then he heard a scream and saw her running towards them both, starting to rot as well—

Adrilian let go of Rhoe's shoulder and stumbled, almost falling to his knees. That had definitely been a first for him. The Seer usually never saw things that vividly; his power brought only flashes, not entire scenes. He knew one thing though; he'd just seen the dark path he was trying to avoid. He needed to make the elves hear the princess and change their stubborn ways or all was doomed.

"Are you all right, Adrilian?" Rhoe felt him stumble and moved to catch him. It wasn't needed, but he held the elf's arm just the same.

"Yes, I'm fine. Just a bit too much morning wine, I suppose," Adrilian lied. He marveled at the boy's reflexes and vowed to look into the ways of these warriors later... if there was a later.

They came to N'vea's door and Adrilian knocked lightly, not wanting to alarm the poor thing.

"Why would Karsis be in... oh, never mind." Rhoe should've known. The only thing worse than Karsis around women was Tanan around a full purse, or so his mother always said. Funny. He used to hear those stories and wonder if the Companions of Everknight ever knew his parents. Then he found out his parents were part of that elite group and his whole world changed.

The door opened to reveal Karsis standing in his longcoat—and only his longcoat—and of course his extravagant smile. "Well, good morning. To what do we owe this visit to my Lord?" Karsis mocked his father as easily as he breathed air. It had taken a little while to shake off his mood, but now he was hitting his stride. One of these days he would regret it, but not this day.

"Oh, good Gods above! Get dressed. We're going out for a stroll to show the children the city." Adrilian shielded his eyes in jest and turned away, winking to Liss as he did so. "Avaryn is staying in; he would draw too much attention and he knows that. It will just be us."

"What about Liana?" Liss asked, looking around for the little faerie.

"She is running an errand for me. Don't worry." This last part was directed at Karsis before the bard could interject. Adrilian walked out and waited for his charges in the rising sun as they traded worried looks; this would be interesting, to say the least.

AS THE SUN CAME UP, BORIL'RAN SILVERLEAF WALKED THE streets and everyone rushed to get out of his way. The head warden had been dragging the young guard behind him for most of the night and they had one last stop. Boril'ran started out going to the Silversword Pass barracks and talking with

Ives'rhan Silkwood, the commanding officer. That conversation had been enlightening, as the official report had been discarded and never filed. Once they picked the commander up and he regained consciousness, he was promptly fired and replaced.

From there, Boril'ran went back across the city to the warden barracks. There, they talked to the other wardens and warned them of the humans and to not bother them if confronted. A couple of his wardens weren't here, but he didn't think that would matter as long as the main force understood. Now the head warden was on his way home to Silverleaf Villa, where he would interrogate the young guard even further.

Illiandral was exhausted. He hadn't been able to say anything for the entire trip. Every time he tried, the head warden shushed him with the veracity of an angry dragon—and he had seen a dragon, so he could imagine that look. The young guard's feet hurt and he was tired of walking this fast. Didn't the head warden use magic? Did he really walk everywhere? He tried once more.

"Sir?"

"Illiandral, not now." Boril'ran knew that, despite his wards, there were eyes and ears all over the streets, and this matter was too damned important to discuss out in the open. Once they were in his villa, the permanent wards would keep all but Adrilian out. Nothing seemed to keep out the Seer when he wanted to talk with you. Boril'ran was worried that someone might try and silence this young guard—permanently—for what he had seen; hence dragging him around until he could get him to safety. Then they rounded a corner and saw five elves with raised hoods obscuring their faces and knew his fears were sound.

"Well, what do we have here?" Boril'ran asked, placing his staff under his cloak and into a magical pocket and drawing his slim sword. It wouldn't do for this staff to break inside the city, and this fight could get ugly.

"All we want is the guard, Boril'ran. Just give him over and you can walk away." The hooded figure sounded calm and in charge.

"You all realize that I'm the Head Warden for a reason right? That I've dueled wizards for centuries?" They had to have something up their sleeve, otherwise, this would be a foolish fight for them... and they didn't seem foolish.

Another hooded figure stepped forward and spread his hands out. "Yes, I am aware. However, your weakness is that you can't deflect all five elements at once. Oh, some of the ancient archmages could deflect five elements, but on your best day you could handle... what three? Maybe four?"

Illiandral saw the five elves and knew this was going to be bad. The head warden was good, but if these were accomplished wizards, then even Boril'ran was outnumbered at this point. *So I'll just have to help,* he thought as he desperately tried to think of something. It hit him that he could do something akin to what that young wizard had done with the dragon—he had to think of something that just wasn't done.

All magic had its stereotypes, and wizards used the different elements in the same ways all the time. Air was used to hold people, earth was used to shake the ground and engulf others, water was used to batter opponents in range, ether was used to charm or control people, and fire... Well, fire was always used to ignite or freeze. Wizards also combined elements to create lightning, dust storms, even mud, yet there had to be more. He just had to think of something new. Something they wouldn't expect,

Illiandral concentrated and turned on his *sight*, looking around for anything that might help. He was still in training, but he was quite good at some elements already. He saw some rocks that were part of a sculpture. The rocks tumbled endlessly through water coming from a marble fountain, spinning over and over. Normally, wizards had a very hard time affecting things if they were already part of some other magic, but to his *sight,* it seemed that the water was enspelled, not the rocks—perfect. Boril'ran and the five assailants were still bantering back and forth when Illiandral whispered softly. "Ash'anti fir, fra halven lae sonn's an gli la car'cen!" Illiandral raised his voice at the end, pointing to the ground before the five elves to direct the magic. The young guard was taking a chance calling upon fire and air at the same time, but if this worked like he thought it might, it would give Boril'ran time to go on the offensive. Illiandral wasn't a strong wizard, but it might be just enough... he hoped.

Boril'ran knew he was in serious trouble and there wasn't a single patrol in sight. *They planned this well, one of them must know me personally,* the head warden thought as he scanned the area behind the five elves; Boril'ran needed a distraction. Imagine his surprise when he heard Illiandral chanting. *That's right—the young guard is in training to become a warden,* he thought as he caught the words Illiandral was using; his eyebrows rose in surprise. *That just might work.*

Boril'ran saw the rocks in the water soar over to a spot on the ground, and the elves tensed and shouted a counter for the ground enveloping them. When nothing happened, they all laughed and dropped their wards, ready to attack the head warden. Then the heated water in the tiny cracks started to evaporate and blew the rocks apart, pelting the elves with fragments that stung. but did little damage. However. they served as a wonderful distraction.

"Ash'anti fra, sonn's, shoran lae kith!" Boril'ran shouted to the air and the fragments on the ground swirled in a small wind funnel, flying at the surprised elves with the force of a catapult.

The fragments dropped one elf outright and took two others off their feet. Boril'ran was already chanting again. The elves fought back, raising a wall of earth to shield themselves, even flying up in the air to rain down small bolts of lightning. But without all five they never had a chance; they weren't strong enough.

In the end, four elves lay dead or dying and only one was left alive. Justice was swift when you attacked the wardens, never mind the head warden. "Please Bor... spare me?" The elf took down his hood and revealed the face of Boril'ran's own apprentice, Javier'ril. The elf was over two hundred winters and had his white hair tied up in a bun to conceal it under the hood. He was about to say something else when Boril'ran's sword slid into his heart quicker than the elf could fathom. Then it was over.

Boril'ran sighed and turned to the young guard he had been dragging around the city. "That was most impressive, Illiandral. I never realized you were so far in your studies." Boril'ran would be teaching that trick to his wardens over the next few weeks, as it was very simple. In fact, it was so simple he was angry. Not at the young guard for doing it, no. He was angry that, in over four hundred years, he had never thought of that trick himself; such was the poison of stagnation.

Illiandral was in awe. He had never seen magic used so fiercely in battle before, and he was truly afraid of the head warden at this moment. He wouldn't be pushing him any day soon on *any* subject. Then Illiandral realized Boril'ran was speaking to him and he almost fainted again. "Sorry... what?"

"I said, I didn't know you were so far in your studies." Boril'ran signaled the wardens with a small message using ether and started walking to his villa once more, this time just walking not dragging the young guard.

Illiandral walked along, trying not to look at the bodies

strewn all over the road. "Oh, well, I'm not really. I've got another twenty winters before I can try out for the wardens. I can only handle small things, and even then not very far." Illiandral felt stupid saying that to the wizard that just took out five trained assailants.

"Well, how did you come up with that little trick then? You know, the one that just saved my life—and coincidently yours as well." Boril'ran was dumbfounded. How on Syll's green world did the young guard just *come up* with something like that?

"I... That is..." Illiandral took a deep breath and decided to just go for it. "I remembered the young man using fire to heal the dragon and figured that maybe there was more that we haven't tried. So I experimented." There, it was out. Illiandral didn't want the head warden of Tir-Lanan to think he was just guessing at it, but that's exactly what he had done.

"You guessed. You *guessed* that it *might* save us?" Boril'ran didn't know if he should laugh or shout; so he did both. Boril'ran laughed so loud that the first warden to come upon them thought he was under some kind of spell. The head warden waved them off and continued on his way, leaving them to identify the bodies lying around the street. "So, Illiandral, I think your old job at the Silversword pass might be over. Your boss being replaced is not going to win you any favors." Boril'ran couldn't stop smiling. He had a very good idea what the young elf would end up doing.

Illiandral hadn't thought of that. He stopped in the middle of the road and stared at the head warden, not sure what he should even say. He was going to try a witty argument, but all that came out was, "But...I didn't do anything." Illiandral lowered his head into his hands and shook his head. Having that post was what got him into training so early.

"Well, the good news is that I no longer have an apprentice..." Boril'ran waited for the elf to get the hint, but it seemed to fall flat on the ground in front of him. "Illiandral, I was hinting that *you* could be my apprentice. You could at least raise your head and nod."

Illiandral heard, but his brain had registered the words as junk and filed them away with all the other clutter that he heard all day long from the other guards. Then Boril'ran kept talking and Illiandral actually *heard* what the head warden was saying. "Your apprentice? Honestly?" This was his dream come true! "I'd be honored, sir."

"Well, now that the matter of selecting an apprentice is settled..." Boril'ran stated as they arrived at his villa. He opened his door with a flick of his wrist and motioned for his young apprentice to go first. "You can start this new job by cleaning my wardrobe and finding your own new robes. We have a council meeting soon—and a very important one at that."

"I can go to the meeting?" Illiandral asked as he walked into the villa. He was going to keep talking but was caught breathless at the beauty of the dwelling. It was a mix of trees and crystal, grown around each other with an almost lurid functionality. Branches served as stairs and crystal ledges stored works of art and sculptures.

Boril'ran chuckled and patted the young elf on the back; he was starting to like this one already. It usually took years to warm to his apprentices, but this young one seemed special in every way. "Of course you can, but I need to know. What faction do you support, if any?" This was important, just in case his enemies ever found out.

Illiandral shied away and backed up. "The Ari'en Brekith, sir. I have always wanted to go and see the human cities." Illiandral was ready for the shouting to begin at any moment. While not a very large faction, the Ari'en Brekith was hated by certain elves in the city. Their position was less than the full migration that the Yaw Worl'aren wanted but would allow elves to visit and walk among the humans once more.

Boril'ran could hardly believe it. "As am I, good elf. My secret longing has always been to follow that fool Karsis on his adventures. You know that he and I trained together, right?" Boril'ran could see by the elf's mouth on the floor that he hadn't, in fact, known that. "Come, I'll fill you in on some politics and stories as you clean." Boril'ran led his new apprentice down the crystal hall with a lightness to his step that hadn't been there in centuries.

ELSEWHERE IN THE CITY, ADRILIAN LED KARSIS, RHOE, and Liss down the cobblestone streets towards the Gol' Roun. The elven Seer was in a mood that was hard to describe. Kind of like winning a test of magic, only to find out the prize was a swift blow with a really big hammer swung by an angry ogrann. The vision he had when he touched Rhoe still troubled him, and he felt distracted. Then he saw Lisa reacting to her surroundings and he forgot about his worry for the moment; she was a breath of fresh air. The sun arced into the sky, and as the hours passed the elves had come out to start their daily routines.

Liss looked on in awe—she couldn't believe how wondrous this city truly was. The streets were paved with gorgeous cobblestone, the buildings all interwoven with the trees around them. Even the decorations had an elemental presence about them. They passed fountains of fire that bubbled upwards like water, gazebos of air bouncing tiny water balls inside of them, and even an earth garden with cascading rocks like flowers.

Rhoe thought about the elemental fountains and how he had never seen a stationary effect before. He was curious so he used his *sight* on one and was confused by what he found. It looked like magic strings—or threads—were twisted all around them, holding them together. Rhoe wasn't about to ask Adrilian since he wasn't sure if he should even be using his *sight* in the city. He figured he would wait and talk to Karsis later.

Liss marveled at the change in culture, so different from what she was raised on, soaking it all in as they walked. She saw the elves staring at them with wonder and skepticism. Every elf she saw was armed somehow, just as Karsis had described. Liss knew she should be worried about the council meeting, but waiting for them to schedule it was the real drain on her frayed nerves. As they turned a corner, Liss saw children doing magic and stopped dead in her tracks. The others barely noticed, except for Rhoe, and of course Karsis; the bard rarely missed anything.

"Liss?" Rhoe saw her head over towards the children and smiled. She was a curious person, but he worried that might go sideways in this strange culture.

Liss walked slowly, like the children were wild animals that might run at the slightest movement. Once she was within reach, she stopped and just watched. There was one making little balls of water to roll on the ground; another child was braiding a third's white hair using the very air. The magic didn't hold together long but it was fascinating all the same.

Liss couldn't help herself. "May I?" she asked, sitting down on the lush green grass next to them. One of the children handed her a bunch of little sticks and said something in elven she couldn't quite catch. The sticks came alive and twirled delightfully in her hand. Liss decided to try and use the elven she had been learning to have some fun. "Ash'anti woden, bin ithin wan an...dance." Liss didn't know the elven word for dance but hoped it would still be all right. *It won't work anyway, I don't have elven blood,* she thought sadly, then her eyes went wide as the sticks entwined with a little water ball and spun around on the grass like a wooden toy. The children al_ clapped and bounced but Liss sat there frozen.

Karsis was enjoying the show... up until the sticks moved and combined with the water. Liss asked for them to do it and it worked. *How?* he wondered, moving quickly to her side, quietly whispering a spell to shield their conversatior_ from anyone passing by. "Allissana, come with me, quickly, before we have more visitors than I want to handle at the moment." He'd just figured out how she was using magic, and he was ashamed he hadn't seen it coming.

Rhoe was there in a heartbeat as well. "What happened, Karsis? Did Liss do that?" Rhoe was trying to see if one of the children had done it as a prank on her but they didn't seem at all mischievous. Then Rhoe noticed two elves pointing and whispering. This couldn't be good. "Karsis..." Rhoe started to say, but then he felt the ground pull out from underneath him. The elves weren't whispering to each other—they were casting at him!

The grass slipped out from under him like a rug and he fell on his back, but only for a second. He rolled backward and came up in a crouch, looking to see where they were. One had moved a little ways off to the left while the other stood there smiling smugly. The elf was right next to a fountain of earth, so Rhoe used what he could see. "Ash'anti dir, heath dosan kith," he asked gently, not wanting the earth to enfold the man too tightly and suffocate him. The other elf ran as his friend was engulfed in rocks and soil, but stopped fast as Karsis grabbed him with air.

"Not so fast, my little friend." Karsis was impressed with Rhoe's adaptation to a strange setting. The boy had pulled the elements away from their enchantment, which was very hard to do, and even kept his voice calm to avoid causing undo harm to his attacker, something Karsis wouldn't have bothered with.

"Just who wanted to provoke my friends?" Karsis asked the frightened elf. He guessed the attack hadn't been aimed against him—not many in the city would dare—so it must've been Maldren getting his revenge on Rhoe. Just then a warden turned a corner, striding toward them with purpose; she must've sensed the magic.

Delain wasn't supposed to be on right now, but she was covering a shift for a friend. The head warden had called a general meeting, but Delain didn't bother attending—today was supposed to be her day off, so she had hoped for an easy few hours. Then her wizard stone went off, alerting her to the casting of magic, and she cursed Syll under her breath. Off she went, her long legs making good time through the sparse crowd.

Delain was tall, almost six feet, and her shoulder-length white hair bobbed as she went, her hand already on her sword. Guard duty wouldn't normally be this intense, but with humans here and a councilman attacked already, no one was taking chances. Delain turned the corner and saw the infamous Karsis holding an elf with air, then noticed the struggling elf-shaped pile of mud. *Why me?* she thought as she put on her 'I mean business' face. Before she could say anything, there was a human standing in her way.

"We're sorry for the trouble—they were just protecting me. My name is Allissana Everknight, Princess of Everknight." That's all she got out before a sword was pointed at her chest.

"Stand aside, Princess. I know who you are and quite frankly I don't care." Delain was in no mood for nobles of any kind, especially humans.

Liss looked back at Adrilian and saw him nod slightly in approval. She didn't want to do this, but her father always said if you want others to listen, sometimes you had to be forceful. Liss drew Deathsong in one quick motion—the blade remaining quiet for once— and stepped back out of range of the warden's slender blade. She still took a cut on her check, but it was minor, the shock more invigorating than anything. It reminded her of her lessons with Carana.

"That's one," Liss said, as she fell into a strong stance. Blades clashed and rang, and Liss parried and spun, sweating already. The warden stepped back and whispered quickly. All Liss heard was air, so she over-extended and slashed at the elf's face to make the warden stop casting and defend herself. Liss knew she was too far away to actually hit the woman, but her blade was close enough to make her pay attention. The warden come at her more aggressively, knowing that Liss wouldn't let her use magic this close. The princess was fighting with everything she had and was only holding this elf at bay. Then she remembered one of her lessons and knew what she had to do. *This is going to hurt.*

Delain was surprised when this young whelp drew her sword on a warden. She didn't want to incapacitate her, so she thought to teach her a lesson. Delain looked to the Seer, Adrilian, and saw he was smiling. *Well, that can't be good,* she thought. Then she found out why. This woman was good. Not just good for a human—she had apparently been trained by an expert swordsman.

It didn't matter, though. Delain was over two hundred years old and a wizard. She backed up and quickly asked the air to hold her opponent, but never finished the spell. That dreaded blade came flying at her face out of nowhere. The woman had overextended herself, leaving herself vulnerable. It was risky but effective against wizards. *Who taught you, princess? Was it Karsis?* Delain wondered as she went at the girl even harder. It just wouldn't do to lose to a human on the open streets like this. Suddenly the princess swung hard and her sword went just a little too wide as Delain sidestepped the attack. The warden knew she would never bring her blade around in time and lunged quickly, looking to incapacitate the princess with a strike to her leg. It wasn't until Delain had committed to the attack that she saw the girl smile.

Liss let the sword go out wide and, right on cue, the elf lunged for the kill. Well, a little low for a kill, but it would do. Liss smiled as she spun without even trying to bring the sword around or block the attack. She took a cut on the leg, but not the full brunt of the attack, then grabbed the elf's wrist that held the sword. Liss didn't even try to disarm the warden; instead, she used her opponent for balance to complete the spin. The princess's other hand brought Deathsong around in a vicious arc and the pommel connected with the woman's temple, hard. The blow didn't knock the warden out, but the elf was staggered and dropped her sword.

"Yield," Liss said, completely out of breath. She was trying to hold her sword steady, but she couldn't even hold it up."Oh, Gods above—who am I kidding? I need a nap," Liss said, clapping the elf on the shoulder.

Delain tried to figure out why her head had rebelled against her legs—even her knees weren't speaking to her right now—then the end of the fight came back to her. Delain was far too dizzy to do anything about it, but at least she knew what happened. "Who...?" she started but realized speaking was a *really* bad idea. She sat down first.

"I'm Allissana, or Liss."

"Not who *are* you... who *taught* you that?" Delain asked as her head cleared a little more. She thought she had seen every move ever made with a sword, but that one was positively reckless; she *had* to learn it! Karsis came over with a wide grin and Delain knew she was going to loathe this conversation immensely.

"If you ever come to Everknight I'll introduce you to her," Liss said warmly.

Once they had started fighting, Karsis let the elf he had caught go and told him to let Maldren know he was displeased; that would irritate the councilman to no end. Karsis saw Rhoe looking edgy and went to forestall him from getting involved. "Let her have her fun, Rhoe. She will be all right."

"But.. .the baby." Rhoe couldn't believe he was saying that about Liss.

"That warden won't go for a kill—they abhor death on their watch. Too many questions from above. No, she will try instead to cripple or incapacitate, which won't hurt the child." Karsis knew that wouldn't help, but he couldn't resist. He saw the young wizard's face and chuckled. "It's fine, Rhoe. You've seen her face off against the Incarnation of Death."

"He took it easy on us."

"You're alive, right?" Then he saw Liss take out the elven warden and even he had to admit she was talented. They weren't blademasters, but wardens were still very skilled.

"I didn't see that one coming, and I'm a Seer," Adrilian said, whistling and walking over to the women. More wardens came around the corner, swords drawn, but the old wizard held up a hand to forestall them and sat down in the air next to Liss. "Now, do you think we can make it the rest of the way to the Gol' Roun without you challenging anyone else?"

"What does 'Gol'Roun' mean? I don't know that one," Liss asked, standing and clasping the arm of the warden to help her up. They nodded to each other and the warden moved off to confer with her fellows. She would love to hear the spin the warden would put on this fight.

Karsis brushed past her to crash the warden's meeting, calling out over his shoulder, "It means Trade Circle." Then he was among the wardens, flirting and being, well... himself.

Rhoe walked on, grabbing Liss's hand and pulling her closer. "So... you did magic and neither wizard is bothering to wonder why." Rhoe was concerned that Adrilian and Karsis weren't telling them something and that it was going to be bad.

"I know. I was expecting a talking to, at least from Karsis, but he basically ignored the whole thing. Think it could be that bad?" Liss had other things to worry about, but if it was something to do with the baby she wanted to know. Before anyone answered they arrived at the Gol'Roun and what little breath she had gained back went right back out of her in a rush.

It was immense. The Gol'Roun was a huge marble circle with a massive fountain of dancing crystal in the middle. All around the edges of the marble circle were beautiful benches made of roots and crystal, as well as merchant shops selling their wares to anyone passing by. It was almost the size of a small village. The entire circle was packed with elves, both commoners and what looked like nobles, their varying hair lengths standing out as badly as the expensive clothes and jewelry of the haughty nobles back home. Liss was so taken by the entire scene she never saw the little elven messenger run up to Adrilian and hand him a scroll.

Adrilian took the scroll and unrolled it, not bothering to tip the elf that handed it to him. The council had decreed that they would meet in five hours. *Hours.* They wanted to get the humans off of the streets and on their way, that much was clear. Word of the unrest they had caused had reached the council no doubt, and they weren't going to be in the mood for any speeches. Boy, were they in for a surprise. Adrilian sighed and rolled up the scroll, putting it in his robe.

"Don't get comfortable. The council called the meeting for five hours from now, and we will need all that time to prepare. Let's go kids—back to the tower." The Seer was expecting resistance, but Rhoe turned around and walked back without a word. The boy was lost in his own thoughts. *Probably on why nothing was said about the princess casting magic,* Adrilian thought. He knew exactly what was happening to the human princess, but he didn't think they needed the distraction at the moment.

Liss, on the other hand, was devastated by the news that they had to leave. "Now? Fine, let's get this over with so I can come back and enjoy some of this." She stomped after Rhoe, trying not to pout, and failed miserably. The princess was excited to meet the council, feeling that at least she would be in familiar surroundings; she had no idea how wrong she was. Liss saw Karsis still talking with the group of wardens and called for him as they neared, but he waved her on with a smile.

"Don't wait for me. I'll be there in an hour or so," Karsis said as they passed. He turned to one of the female wardens and kissed her on the cheek, playing with her hair, while Delain just rolled her eyes at her companion. Karsis had seen the runner heading towards the Gol'Roun in haste and figured it was bad news.

Adrilian shook his head and led the kids back to his tower, ignoring the looks of utter contempt on some of the elves they passed. Let them sneer and gawk—he knew times were changing and those that didn't want to change with them would learn the hard way. This council meeting was not going to go how *anyone* expected, and he couldn't wait.

CAS EN OREN, TIR-LANAN

She was somewhere called the House of Words; that was all she really knew about her entire day. Liana was in front of about fifty elves who fired questions at her non-stop. To the faerie's credit, she answered them almost as fast. It wasn't *her* fault if they couldn't understand her.

"So Ari'en Brekith means 'Song of the Free People?'" Liana asked, slowing her excited speech for once. There had been a break in the questions so she figured she would fire one at the group herself. After all, she *was* the ambassador, right? These people were going to lay out a plan to help her convince the elves to do... to... well, Kilyan had said something but she had forgotten with all the other questions.

Kilyan laughed and stood among his peers, flipping his shoulder-length hair out of his face and straightening his red silk shirt. "Yes, dear one, it does. We would like to see rights given back to the elves to come and go from our great city if they so choose. If an elf wants to leave the city and venture out, they should be able to choose that without having to petition the council. Don't get me wrong—we don't think building whole cities again is the way to go, but stagnation is killing our great race. We call for slow migration by individuals over long years to get accustomed."

"Wellthatseemsfair!" she answered, getting excited again. Liana saw an elven girl giggle at her and flitted over to buzz her hair, just for fun. "Why won't they do that now?" Liana asked the room once she landed again. She was trying to exert some control like Avaryn was always telling her to, but she kept losing focus.

"Because they want to stifle us!" someone called from the back.

Kilyan held up his hand for quiet, knowing that the entire room would join in if he didn't. "Friends, the council is scared and has become complacent, yet they think they are protecting us." Kilyan walked around slowly, keeping their attention. "Their ways have been the same for centuries upon centuries, but all that can change with this little one here." He pointed to Liana and the room went quiet.

"Me?" Liana was shocked but excited. *How am I going to help?* she thought. Liana was a little sad that for once Avaryn wasn't there, thinking back to her. She was truly on her own; that's when the fear set in.

"Yes, little faerie—you." Kilyan turned to Liana and smiled, fixing his jewelry as if it was in the wrong position or something. It was a nervous habit that he had never outgrown. "If we pitch that the faeries are willing to return to the world if the elves do the same, then I guarantee that we will get over half of the votes."

Liana thought of a devious plan then. Something that, if she had read the room right, would give them *all* of the votes. "I'll do you one better, but I will *only* tell Kilyan for now." Liana fluttered over to his shoulder and whispered in his ear. This was one of her favorite games back in the Hidden Vale, where others would have to guess or wait for the one that heard it to reveal it.

Kilyan heard her but he couldn't believe it. "You can do that?" He was utterly shocked at her proposal. Kilyan had originally thought to ask but figured it would be out of the question due to some of the answers she had given. This would be a major move, and one the council wouldn't see coming. He knew at least three of the five councilmen would probably cry.

"I can, and I have full authority of the faerie Queen. We're good friends after all." Then someone asked how she became friends with the Queen and that's when her resolve crumbled. "Ohwesavedtheoldqueenfromthisdarknessthatanelfreleased."
Her reply was lost in a cheer of gratitude at the chance to finally break free of the isolationist ways of the old nobles, even if they didn't know how it was going to happen.

He received word that the council meeting was pushed up and, despite being shocked at the timetable, Kilyan was ready for anything. Well, at least he thought he was. How could he have foreseen what two humans would do when they entered the council meeting, or the impact it would have on them all?

✦ 6 ✦

QUEEN TAKES ROOK

He strode across the barren field with cautious steps, his *sight* stretching out before him. Dar'Krist had been assailed at least twice by an unknown force, testing him at every turn with ancient magic. This last attack came just north of the ruins of Daelyn, where he fought that large man and the lithe woman,. Dar'Krist was crossing the river when he saw the water rise up in front of him—which brought back memories of his river adventure and angered him even more—and he had just enough time to fight through a wall of water and roll to the other bank, watching it collapse behind him in a rush.

The time before that he had been attacked by the ground itself. the earth trying to engulf him like the last time the elves had entombed him. Dar'Krist won through both attempts, but was hard-pressed to figure out who could be doing this, or why Surely, whoever it was knew those attempts had been made in the past, so why even try them? To weaken him? Pointless. Dar'Krist had been rejuvenated by his mountain journey and his reserves were almost limitless at this point, never mind that he could draw power from the elements around him.

Soaking wet, the Incarnation of Death wandered into the

abandoned town of Daelyn a little while later and smiled despite his aggravation. The town was truly ruined. Before Dar'Krist could really appreciate the destruction, he felt the wind pick up rather ominously. Guessing it was his mysterious attacker, he feigned indifference and wandered through the town as the wind howled around him, faster and stronger. After a few moments, he needed to shield his eyes, as the dirt road was whipped up into a little twister of air. Rocks and pebbles flew at him as he sought cover against a building. Dar'Krist turned his *sight* upon the air around him, searching for the tell-tale presence of his attacker. He always tried this, but whoever it was always pulled back before he could find them.

Just as he thought he had narrowed it down, he was hit with a focused blast of air and dirt, making him spin away or be hammered in the face. Dar'Krist knew the general direction this time though. "Where are you?" he called out, trying to deceive his attacker as he rolled onto his back and flipped up again into the street, right in front of where he had last seen the shimmering air. More attacks came and finally, he lowered his head and sent back his own attack.

Ill'lyth sent a blast of air at the Incarnation and smiled when he spun away, obviously foiled in trying to track her. Sweat poured off of her naked body as she furiously asked the air to attack the Incarnation over and over again. Ill'lyth watched as he came stumbling and rolling backward. She thought she had him, only to see him lower his head and send out a pulse of death all around him.

She saw too late what he was up to and the wave came right through her trance spirit, following the host back to the body. She fled after it, knowing what she would find. When she opened her eyes she heard a whimper—one of her servants was rotting away next to her. The wave of death had followed her spirit back but was deflected to another body. Ill'lyth breathed a sigh of relief and thanked Syll she had the foresight to anchor her spirit to another for just this occasion; one could never be too sure with Incarnations.

"He has become more resilient than before, but he won't stop me," Ill'lyth said as she absently stroked the dying women's hair, accidentally pulling some out. "Now I have narrowed it down to two elements that could incapacitate him." She had been present all those years ago when the Incarnation had been buried and she knew that the powerful beings were vulnerable to one of the five elements. Finding out which one was the key. Ill'lyth walked out of the room and called for food, not bothering to dress or even cover herself.

Dar'Krist stood slowly as he checked for the presence; it was gone again. He shook his head, still trying to figure out what this person wanted. He shrugged and once more set out down the same road he had taken not so many days ago. Soon he would come upon that little hold where that tricky little rogue had hurt him. After that, it was a straight run to that damned bridge and on to the capital. Death would come swiftly to any who opposed him.

HOUSE ULRYNTAR, TIR-LANAN

He sent out the fifth messenger bird this afternoon and smiled to himself despite his bruised ego. Maldren Ulryntar was calling in favors like children collecting stones near the river, and it would all work out in his favor at the end of the day. He had dirt on almost every councilman, and if he didn't someone else did. They would vote his way or else—then those despicable humans could go running back to their castle and cry. It was time to forsake the truce and truly seal themselves away, warding their city against intruders with powerful magic.

As for the reports of the faerie and the unicorn, he didn't

believe those anyway. After all, no one had seen a faerie for almost five hundred years. Creatures like that just couldn't stay hidden for that long without someone finding them. Maldren laughed, remembering how Jalafryn Silverleaf tried for years to find them, only to let the darkness into his heart and flee the city after killing the high king's daughter; no one ever heard from him again. Poor Boril'ran never got over losing his younger brother to the darkness within, especially since he had helped train him.

"Leave it to you to sit in the dark and brood, Maldren," a female voice said casually, startling the councilman. Magiciel Ash'ashlyn walked into the room like she owned it and no one could tell her differently, not even a pompous arse like Maldren. She was old, one of the oldest elves in Tir-Lanan. After the King and the Seer, that was. She wore her extremely long hair down, swishing by her waist as she walked, and her violet eyes matched her very pale skin. She wore a long purple dress with a deep black shoulder throw, and all of her jewelry was silver set with sapphires; even her sword, held on her slender hip, was decorated in the deep blue gemstones. At over five hundred and fifty years old she still looked like a beauty, albeit a dangerous one. "Now what did you want? That bird you sent must've flown through a cloud of pipe smoke because it was rambling about faeries and some sort of sorcerer." Magiciel knew exactly what he wanted, she just liked baiting him. Nothing quite entertained her like this man when he was livid.

Maldren looked up, taken aback that his assistant hadn't announced he had company; he would get him for that later. "Magiciel, the bird told you clearly what I wanted from you. It is time to call in all the markers. I want your vote." The councilman stood slowly, watching her smile fade as his grew wider. He had something on her and he could tell she didn't know what it could be; she was in for a surprise indeed. "There is only an hour left before the council meeting and they will vote once more to give this land to the humans and a pledge of silent truce. I say no more." Maldren paced back and forth, really coming into his speech, but she cut him off before he could get going.

"No," she said with finality. Magiciel didn't know what this windbag had on her, but it couldn't be bad enough for her to throw the vote against the king.

"Oh, I think you will change your tune when they find out that your daughter didn't just escape the city all those years ago by chance." Maldren waited for her face to drop, but it never did. *Impossible, she must think I'm bluffing,* he thought.

Magiciel kept her face impassive, though fear raced up her spine. He knew. Her daughter Illiyana was born without magic. Every elf was born with a connection to the elements—magic was in their blood—yet her daughter was born without any thread of it. Ask as she might, the elements ignored Illiyana every time. It was unheard of, an abomination. So before Magiciel's noble house could drag Illiyana in front of the city and call for her death, Magiciel helped her daughter escape into the night and watched her flee the city. Magiciel had done it in such a way that Illiyana would never know she had helped. She thought no one else knew either—until now.

"Maldren, my answer is still no. You can't possibly know anything about my daughter. Furthermore, if you insist on this line of thought, I will call for an Inquiry of Duel." Magiciel saw him blanch at the mention of the deadly challenge. She smiled and continued. "Yes, I see you remember who was an instructor for the blademasters for years. It will not be pretty."

An Inquiry of Duel. Maldren rethought his stance on blackmailing the old council women, but his source had said he could prove it. He pulled himself up and tried to smile even though his nerves screamed at him to run, run and never look back unless it was to scream that he was very, very, sorry. "I think you might want to meet someone first, Magiciel." Maldren turned and whistled. A slender elf came out, wearing a hooded robe that concealed his face. The hooded figure walked with the grace of a warrior in perfect balance.

Magiciel subtly shifted into an attack stance, barely moving her feet, yet the elf saw and stopped dead. She knew he was eyeing the deadly sword on her hip and wondering if he was far enough away from her, just in case.

"We meet again, Magiciel. I am..." The elf's words died in a gurgle of blood as he clutched his throat and dropped to his knees, his hand falling away from the hilt of his blade. *Turns out he wasn't far enough away,* Magiciel thought as she heard Maldren start screaming.

Maldren didn't even see her move. One minute his contact was talking to the woman, and the next she was right there in front of him, her sword through his throat and out again. She spun on the councilman and he screamed, running for the back room of his villa. Maldren could call for his personal guard but he had angered a blade master. He didn't have enough guards for that—no one did. He threw open the back panel of his study and slipped through a secret door, closing it behind him and whimpering all the way down the tunnel. This just wasn't his day at all.

Magiciel laughed and didn't bother to follow the councilman. "I take it our meeting is over, Maldren?" she asked the empty room. She casually flicked the hood back on the man she had killed. When she saw who it was, she had to admit that he would've had her. It was the very elf that she had bribed to let her daughter go. Magiciel thought that he was loyal, but Maldren must've gotten to him. Some days you just couldn't trust anyone.

Magiciel cleaned her blade on the fallen elf's robe, sheathing the weapon delicately. She left the body and walked away, not worrying that anyone would come after her. The body would be found in Maldren's villa, and so he would dispose of it himself or risk an investigation. *Besides, he will be frightened of me for at least fifty years after this. I may even be able to get a couple of things past the council with his votes if I keep scaring him enough,* she thought as she walked back down the road to her villa. She had just enough time to change into something that would flatter her skin and eye color. She had to look her best to meet Adrilian and his charges. Plus Karsis would be there, and he was always someone that she enjoyed flirting with, even if she knew it would never go anywhere. It was the game that she enjoyed, and he was a very skilled player. If she only knew that she would never sit on the elven council again after today.

NORHIL HOLD, NORTHERN LYTHINALL

He walked up to the abandoned hold and smiled. Dar'Krist was overdue for another visit from his hidden nemesis and if their pattern held true, they would try using the element of fire against him this time. Fire was the one that worried him, as it could really do some damage, but he would be fine—it wasn't his weakness. The Incarnation of Death had worked out that someone was trying to find his weakness so they could confront or control him. *Maybe it was that bard that wasn't a bard,* he thought. That one seemed powerful, though it didn't fit his style at all, not from what little he had witnessed of the man. No, this person liked to stay hidden and work from the shadows. The bard was too flamboyant for that.

Dar'Krist circumvented the empty hold and carried on his way until he saw a campfire in the distance. He used his *sight* and saw the fire was being used by one person who even had a tent. *Believable and tempting—someone really* does *know me,* he thought as he walked the rest of the way to the site. He scanned the surrounding countryside with his *sight* for anyone else that could be waiting for him and found nothing. His curiosity peeked, Dar'Krist walked right up to the person and touched their shoulder, focusing his power down into them. Nothing happened—except the body fell over. Whoever it was had been dead for well over a day.

The Incarnation stepped back, ready for anything, when the body exploded. Rolling with the blast, Dar'Krist hit the ground hard twenty feet away and rolled another ten feet before he stood up. His cloak had flown off of him and put itself out, but his robe still smoldered and his arms were badly burned. Patting the tiny embers out, he studied the site once more. Nothing seemed to curl in the shadows, nothing seemed to appear out of thin air;. There was just an exploding, dead body. He walked back cautiously, eyeing what remained of the body. *I'm glad it didn't get up. I don't know what I could do against the dead.* He chuckled to himself as he scanned the air for the telltale signs of his attacker. *Was that it? Was the test of fire just an exploding body?* He laughed and continued on, knowing that the next test would be different indeed.

Ill'lyth watched him go—the fire had done its task. She was far enough away he would never sense her, and since she didn't need to use magic, she could stay this far away. She saw the complete lack of fear in the Incarnation when presented with the four elements, so that only left ether. The problem was ether was a diverse element that could be taken in a variety of ways. You could heal with it, command the minds of others, change your appearance, even set and disable wards to protect yourself or others. There were a dozen other things you could do with ether and even more if you mixed it with the other elements. Ill'-lyth drifted closer and asked the ether for what she wanted. It was a complex casting, as she was asking it over and over for different things and weaving them together into a single thread pattern. Not many wizards—if any—could cast these thread spells anymore. Ill'lyth was confident that this was it. If it worked, the Incarnation of Death would be hers to command.

Dar'Krist sensed the disturbance and spun, but stopped cold. He couldn't comprehend what he was seeing, and it took his mind a moment to focus. Gone was the road and even the long stretch of grasslands. There was nothing but dense forest around him.

That's when he heard them: voices that tugged his memory in such a way that he found himself answering them casually, like he knew them.

But I do know them.

There were three of them, a woman and two small children. They were dressed in filthy rags and wore animal skins for cloaks. The children carried sharp spears that doubled as walking sticks and the woman looked at Dar'Krist as she spoke.

"Ra'gan, we shouldn't be here. I know that you want to start your own village, but to travel this far north is reckless." The woman seemed worried, constantly looking over her shoulder and into the tall trees. She was tall for a female, with black hair to match his, and deep green eyes.

M'ren. That was her name.

"Mother, the elves live far to the north. Father says so. Besides, I have been practicing with the spear. I will defend you from these mysterious creatures." E'gan smiled and spun his spear around and stabbed a tree, dulling its point but hitting true. The boy was tall, like his father, with raggedy black hair and dark eyes.

I'm his... father?

"E'gan, stop fooling around and stay on course," Ha'gan, the eldest child, scolded. The boy had his hair cut short but was obviously more skilled with the spear. "We have to follow this

'River of Serpents' to the north." The boy scoffed at the name, but he had to admit there were an awfully lot of snakes near the river.

He was called Ra'gan; he remembered this. This was during the dark times, centuries after the destruction of most of the land. The ancient scrolls the elders kept said the heavens had rained fire and death, crumbling mountains and forests alike. These sacred writings said the gods had waged war and their followers were paying the price, but Ra'gan didn't believe that at all. It was just nature rebelling for something these elves had done. The stories told around the fire said the elves were demons that had fallen from the skies. Surely, he thought, that was the cause of the devastation all those eons ago.

This was before any humans had migrated north above the great break, a cliff that appeared when the land was broken by the gods. Ra'gan was the first to attempt to cross the imposing divide.

Yet no one would remember that, as I never made it home.

He had been foolish, thinking that he could start his own tribe out here in the endless Dark Woods, the name his people had given this forest.

My people.

These humans were wandering nomads—barbarians, really —from the far southern plains. Ra'gan had argued with his chieftain and struck him. For that, he had been banished, but in his arrogance, he took his whole family and struck out for the north. It was his pride that lured him here, and his pride that ultimately led to his downfall.

"I still say this is reckless," M'ren, said again with a stern gaze.

"M'ren, it will be fine. You know I'm the best warrior in the tribe. No elf can stand against me," Ra'gan said with a mock thrust of his spear, drawing a smile from his wife.

My wife... gods above I loved her so.

M'ren still had a bad feeling about coming here, but she would accept his knowledge of fighting. She was no fighter at all, but she could feed them every day with what she could forage. They walked for another day and she started to get that feeling again, stronger this time though. M'ren peered into the canopy above them, as if she could see what was troubling her through the dark leaves. Before she could express her concern to Ra'gan, however, her children shouted in alarm.

No, please... not again.

E'gan rounded a tree to suddenly find a slender sword pointed at his throat. The sword was held by a tall being with long white hair and vivid blue eyes. It wore white leathers, decorated with small pouches and trinkets like the elder women in his village. Aside from the blade in its hands, the being seemed harmless, smelling faintly of flowers—he screamed nonetheless.

Hearing his brother scream, Ha'gan leaped towards him, only to find himself on his back with another slender sword pointed at him as well; he never even saw what tripped him up. The being pointing the sword at him was a girl, but her white hair was short and her cloak matched the color of the leaves.

"Father!" Ha'gan cried out in fear.

Everything happened so quickly that it took Ra'gan a second to register his own name.

That really is my name, isn't it?

Ra'gan grabbed his spear and walked cautiously towards the elves—if that was what they truly were—balancing his feet for an attack. He had never seen an elf before, despite his bravado, but they truly did resemble demons. "Leave them, demons! Your fight is with me!"

"Leven lea rien kithin." Jaldrien didn't want to kill these beings, whatever they were, but he would if they put up a fight. They had watched these barbaric creatures for days slowly move closer north, and the word from his superiors was that if they came deeper into the woods they would be dealt with harshly. However, his apprentice was not a lover of the unknown by any means and she would be the first to start a fight if he didn't take control soon. Jaldrien really hoped they would just turn and go back to the plains.

Ha'gan wasn't even being watched. The girl who had the sword on him was looking at his father, so he had a shot. He had dropped his spear, but he grabbed a rock with his hand. With a flick of his wrist, he shot it towards her face and rolled away, out from under her blade. She called out strange words but her tone said that he got her good. Ha'gan felt his side catch on a branch and grunted, but pushed on, standing quickly and dropping into a fighting stance. He felt his knees buckle. Why was he so weak? Then he hit the ground and breathed his last.

Pal'lyne was watching the tall being with interest. She had never seen anyone as tall as he was, nearly seven feet if he was an inch. Then movement caught her eye and a rock slammed into her face. "Gos, dosan ra wa deth!" she cursed, sliding the sword into the boy's side as he rolled. To his credit, he kept moving to stand and face her, but he was losing too much blood to fight. Pal'lyne had hit his heart with a single stab, right under his arm. She watched him drop with the satisfaction of a maneuver well executed.

"Son! *No!*" Ra'gan turned and thrust his spear at the girl while keeping the man in his field of vision. Predictably she parried with her sword, and that's when he lashed out with his leg, catching her in the chest with a powerful kick. She slammed back into the tree behind her and he spun towards the man, but he was too late.

My sons... No!

Jaldrien slumped his shoulders and shook his head sadly. It was too late. Pal'lyne had acted quickly in the face of an attack.

Jaldrien saw the strange being move, so he swiped his blade quickly across the throat of the boy he was guarding, bringing his weapon back to ready position to deal with the black-haired attacker. He saw Pal'lyne get hit and raised an eyebrow— not bad. That was when he heard the woman come screaming at him. The woman was out of her mind, screaming for her son, and Jaldrien brought his sword up and let her impale herself with her momentum. She grabbed his shirt and mumbled something in her crude language. Then, to his horror, he saw the tiny knife slashing at his face. Kicking her off before she could cut him, he stumbled back and hit a tree, just as the man lunged for him with his spear.

M'ren! My love!

Ra'gan saw his beloved wife die just as he saw his sons die, and something in him snapped. They would pay! Every last one of these demon-blooded, white-haired bastards would rot before his eyes. By the gods, he would kill them all! "By Krist, you shall all die by my hand!" Ra'gan cursed as he lunged at the elf while the demon was still unbalanced; he never got there.

Pal'lyne was livid. She couldn't believe that this crude stranger caught her off guard. Then she heard that name. *Krist.* No one was allowed to utter that name, and for some reason, it gave her pause. *So these barbaric creatures know of the gods. At least I know where they will go when they die,* she thought, as she righted herself. When the tall being made for her master, she leaped and slashed the tendon on his supporting leg, toppling him before he ever got near Jaldrien. Screaming, Pal'-lyne slashed and cut the fallen warrior, making him pay for his insolence with his life.

"Leven la Pal'lyne, vin fin." Jaldrien couldn't believe his apprentice was this cold-blooded. He knew she had a mean streak, but this was monstrous. She stopped and looked at him with a stare that could've slain an ogrann. Jaldrien walked away, turning his back to show his disapproval. He heard her follow quietly, and together they left the bodies to lay in the fading light of the sun shining through the dense canopy.

But I'm not dead!

Ra'gan stirred, lifting his head with sheer willpower as the life ebbed out of him. He heard a voice calling to him as the fading light started to wisp away like so many ccbwebs in flame. He thought it was M'ren, clinging to life and pleading for him to help her, but he heard it again and knew that it wasn't his wife.

Mortal, thou has called to me and I have heard thee. You shall be my hand in all things from now on, bringing swift death to those that deserve it.

The voice was inside his head and he could feel the presence moving around in his mind with dark fingers.

I remember this... I... I'm.. who am I?

Ra'gan stood alone in the forest, unharmed and whole. Gone was the voice and even the bloody clothes. That's when he heard them. Voices that tugged his memory in such a way that he found himself answering them casually like he knew them.

But I do know them.

There were three of them, a woman and two small children. They were dressed in filthy rags and wore animal skins for cloaks. The children had sharp spears that doubled as walking sticks and the woman was looking at him and talking.

&.

ILL'LYTH SMILED AS SHE WATCHED HIM THROUGH HER Trance. Dar'Krist was enthralled perfectly and showed no signs of fighting it. She flew back to her body and with a shudder and leaned on her alter. "Bring me a scrying bowl!" she called out to her servants in waiting. Three men came in, trying not to look at her naked body, and brought her the silver-lined bowl full of cold water; they spilled most of it trying to avoid her naked form. "Oh for the love of Syll, just look at me and stop spilling the water!" Ill'lyth had to hurry. The Incarnation couldn't be left alone too long or her thread spell might weaken. These spells had to be reinforced from time to time to keep them tight.

The servants bowed and took their leave quickly, grateful that they were still alive. Ill'lyth threw on a robe and asked the ether to show her the Incarnation of Death. The image in the water showed her exactly what she wanted. The big man was standing in a field and staring at the sun as it set on the distant horizon. Whispering again, she opened a portal and stepped through, her robe open and flying in the warm summer breeze. Ill'lyth fought the dizziness from the stress of casting and gazed upon her prize. Dar'Krist was stuck in a loop of a past memory; it would replay over and over again, keeping his mind locked down. Ill'lyth couldn't tell what the memory was, but it was always something very personal to the target. If he tried to break free, the spell would transfer him to another memory to keep him complacent—and someone that old had a lot of memories. When it came time to use him, Ill'lyth would send suggestions to him and the memory would shift subtly to what he had to accomplish.

Ill'lyth grabbed his arm gently, almost hesitantly, as she wasn't sure that his power would be locked with his mind, but nothing happened. "You will be my weapon against Everknight, and then we march upon the elves," Ill'lyth said as she guided him through the portal and back to the Golden Palace. She left him by her bed and went to the window to gaze upon her realm once more. She needed to let her body rest a bit before she traveled again, lest she risk fatigue. When she was ready she would take her prize and go to her troops and tell them it was time.

LOWER SHIELD MOUNTAINS, NORTHWEST OF EVERKNIGHT

She spied the column of ogrann and winced inwardly. They were indeed headed to Everknight, and she had no opportunities to try and divert them. Ellen hated to admit it, but there were too many. She kicked a rock and swore quietly under her breath; she had waited too long. Now there was nothing to hinder them except the plains, and there was nothing she could improvise in that terrain. Ellen had followed them for the last day and into the night before they had camped, looking for a spot to ambush them or lay a trap. Nothing looked like it would work, especially for a group that large. Hearing a noise behind her she spun, drawing her bow and almost loosing the arrow until she saw that it wasn't an ogrann.

"Please... don't... shoot," Thanier said, trying to catch his breath and failing miserably. He had half walked, half ran to catch up to her, worried that she would try something foolish. Thanier had gotten lost twice, turned around once, and fallen into a mud pit. He was filthy and exhausted, but he was here. Now he just had to live through spooking her.

Ellen couldn't believe her eyes. Thanier was a mess, but he had followed her all the way here. She had thought he would try but assumed that he would get lost. "Gods above, Thanier, how did you find me?" Ellen asked quietly, leading him away from her scouting position lest they be seen.

"I..." Thanier stopped and took a couple of breaths, trying to calm his breathing. "I used what you taught me about tracking. I followed the smaller tracks and when that failed, I followed the big ones." Thanier didn't think it was a big deal, but he was proud of himself for actually finding her. He was almost as shocked as she was.

"Well, that will be a hell of a story for later. Right now we have bigger problems." Ellen led his gaze over to the large group of ogrann exiting the lower hills and onto the plains. There had to be almost one hundred of the beasts. "They are heading straight towards Everknight, I just know it. And there isn't anything I can think of to stop them." Ellen was tired and frustrated; she just wanted to shoot something.

Thanier thought for a moment, then looked to the north. He had an idea—a terrible one, but an idea nonetheless. *Gods above, I'm exhausted.* "What if we lured them north to the bridge, then hid and circled back to warn Everknight? They will turn around eventually, but we could outpace them to the city, I'll wager." Thanier wasn't sure *he* could actually do that, but his coin was riding on Ellen to get there at least. He would just find a ditch and sleep for a year or three.

Ellen looked to the north then back at Thanier, her mind stunned by the simplicity of it. How did she miss something like that? "Than, you are a genius!" Ellen tried to keep her voice down, but she was excited by the chance to do something. "I know just the thing to distract them." She smiled as she lifted her bow like a child showing a present. "You stay here while I get them to the bridge, then I'll signal you when I come back through."

"No. I'm going with you. I can do this; I'm tougher than I look." Thanier was, in fact, exactly as tough as he looked, but he didn't want to be left behind.

"Tough? You can't even spell tough." She shook her head. She couldn't just abandon him here. "All right, you can come." Ellen hit him on the shoulder and gathered up her things, getting ready to sneak down around their left flank. She picked her path cautiously, trying to stay to the ogranns' left all the way down, instead of behind them. They had gathered down on the plains like they were waiting for something. Ellen felt her hair stand up on the back of her neck at the sight: these creatures never had this much patience.

Thanier followed her down the rocky hills, trying to keep his unsteady balance on the loose stones. His robe was tattered and the mud he was covered in had almost dried to a hardened shell. Thanier didn't even want to know what his face must look like. They made it down to the plains quickly and, once they were there, they headed north before Ellen turned and took aim. Thanier shaded his eyes against the setting sun and saw her arrows find their mark in the biggest creature there. He howled and looked around for the source, finally seeing them in the grass. He ran at them without giving the rest orders so the whole group followed after.

"Now we run, Than. Let's go!" Ellen took off at an even pace, wanting to see if her companion could keep up. She was shocked when he did. "You've gotten in shape on this little adventure," Ellen praised him, keeping her breathing even. Her companion wasn't saying anything, probably because he was conserving his energy. It was at least eight to ten miles to the bridge. She knew they couldn't run that far, but they had to get a good head start or they were dead.

Kragth howled as he ran after the littles that stung him. He wasn't really hurt, but those three arrows stung his pride more than anything. He was the leader and he had to look big in front of his group. So he charged after the two who had shot him, but they were fast. He might not be as fast, but he could keep up this pace all day; he would catch them and make them pay. Kragth noticed that some of the others had slowed down and were hanging back. He was losing them. "Keep running fools—there is our food!" He pointed to the fleeing littles. Just as he finished that sentence, two more arrows thudded into his shoulder. The ogrann next to him caught one in the leg. "Get them!" Kragth yelled, running even faster.

ELSEWHERE, IN THE PLAINS EAST OF EVERKNIGHT, AERIC Savar·walked his horse slowly, leading a train of new recruits across the high grass in single file. At least that was what he was trying to do. The young kids, ranging from sixteen to twenty winters, were all over the place. They weren't taking the exercise seriously, and it was all that Aeric could do not to flog one of them. He was attempting to be mindful of their age, but after an hour of them having fun instead of training, he had lost what little self-control he had. "Squad—halt!" Aeric yelled, watching them scramble to avoid running into each other as some stopped and others didn't. This being nice stuff wasn't working. *When all else fails, fall back on violence,* he thought as he stalked towards the lead soldier in training, almost dragging his poor horse. He strode right up to the boy's face and barked in his loudest 'I mean business' voice. "Do you think this is a picnic soldier?!" Aeric was going to treat them as men from now on; their lives depended on it.

"Well... I..." Gunter started, but his nerves got the better of him. He was only sixteen-winters old. His short black hair matched his dark brown eyes.

Aeric answered the question for him. "It is *Not!* Now, we are going to line up on file and walk steadily while keeping at least three feet apart. Do you understand?"

"Yes sir!" They called back—all except for Gunter, who just swallowed. It was right about now that he was thinking that he had made a terrible mistake.

Aeric turned on his heel and smiled once he was sure they couldn't see him. His plan to walk them to the lodge and then down to Everknight should go a little better now. Soon he would double-time them, once they got the hang of staying in file.

They weren't perfect, but Aeric's shouting had the desired

effect—the kids were much more orderly, and as a result, made better time. After an hour of marching, they spied the roof of the lodge, as well as a large, dark line on the horizon Aeric had seen a lot of things in his time, but he was honestly stumped as to what that line could be. He would approach with caution, keeping the group on straight time instead of double-timing, at least until he could figure out what was ahead.

Gunter tugged at his arm. "Sir? What is that line? It seems like a bunch of things are walking, but what could be that big that you would see them from so far away?" Gunter had really good eyesight, and although he couldn't quite make out the line in the distance, it filled him with dread. He knew it was something bad.

"Good eye soldier. What's your name again?" Aeric was impressed; he couldn't make anything out. *Looks like I just found my forward scout*, he thought as he sized up the young boy.

"Gunter, Sir." The boy walked faster to keep up with the Lord, who now strode with purpose. Gunter hoped they would stay away from the mysterious line, but he severely doubted it.

"Well, Gunter, you're going to stay up here with me." Aeric turned to his new recruits and walked backwards through the high grass, speaking to them as they marched. "All right, men! We are heading towards that odd formation on the horizon. Keep pace and I will tell you what we are heading into once I know for sure." Aeric spun and clapped Gunter on the shoulder. "We will give it another hour, then I'm going to send you on my horse to see what we are marching towards. You don't have to get close, not with your eyesight, but I need to know what it is." Aeric saw the boy was deathly frightened, but he knew that he would be alright, especially on his horse. The damn thing was good about staying out of trouble.

G'HARRAN CAMP, SOUTHWESTERN LYTHINALL

Lady Ill'lyth G'harr stepped through a portal directly in front of General Ellis, reveling in the pure shock from his guards and staff. Dar'Krist followed right behind her, still lost in the never-ending loop she had him entwined in. "General, how are my troops?" Ill'lyth asked once the initial shock left his face. She really wanted to give him a shot—he had potential.

General Ellis smiled and looked her right in the eyes, "The troops are restless, my Queen. They've been here for days and are more than ready to march on Everknight. Just say the word." In truth, the troops wondered why they had to wait; half of them blamed it on their queen's inability to lead, but he would never tell her that. Ellis had publicly flogged a couple of men who had been heard saying it, just to keep the rest in line. The chatter stopped after that.

"You wouldn't be lying, would you General?"

Now you're in for it, Franc's voice echoed in his head.

Ellis carried on as if he hadn't heard his dead friend speak. "No, my Queen, I've handled any dissentients. Things are doing very well now." General Ellis wasn't sure if she could read his mind, so he told her just enough to keep himself from being caught in a lie but not so much that she went overboard and he lost more men. He had heard the rumors of the Queen's deadly outbursts. He cocked his head to the side and looked at the very tall man dressed in tattered black robes and the flowing black cloak. The cloak seemed to be blowing in the wind. *Funny, there isn't any wind,* he thought as he turned back to look at his queen. "Is this your errand?" Something about the man made the hairs on the back of his neck stand up. Stand up, run in circles, and cry for their mother.

"You could say that. This is the Incarnation of Death and

Corruption, and I now control him. He will be unleashed against the city once they have been... softened up." Ill'lyth smiled at Ellis's horrified expression, unsure if it was because of who the man was, or what would happen to the people of Everknight. "Is that a problem, General?"

She's going to see right through you sir.

Ellis really wished Franc's voice would stop; it was getting a bit unnerving. "No, my Queen. I am just... worried that my men might not be able to pull back in time to get out of his way." Implying that she hadn't thought of her own people was risky, but he had to make sure his troops were safe. Ellis didn't want to be the kind of General who only thought of his own hide. If the Queen wanted a yes man, she could find someone else.

"I applaud your thoughtfulness, General. Have no fear— your men won't be anywhere near the gate he is heading for." Ill'lyth stopped as two men stomped over, angry faces barely containing their rage. "Ah! Generals Haldir and Kasson. So good of you to join us." Ill'lyth glare met theirs.

She wondered if they were tired of living, coming at her so full of hate.

General Haldir stopped one step closer than Ellis, aiming to appear in charge of the conversation. Haldir had dark hair that was obviously dyed to hide his grey and a fine mustache that curled up at the corners. He was livid that Ellis, a mere commander, had been placed in charge of himself and Kasson, two Generals. It was time his queen understood how valuable he was. "My Queen, I must insist that the command of these forces be handed over to an experienced General. A siege against the capitol city of Everknight will need constant atten- tion and stratagems that only years of formal training can achieve." He kept his voice controlled, but even so, his tirade ended with a squeak as the queen's gaze bore into him.

Ill'lyth turned slowly and General Kasson took a step back,

his face turning white. Gone was his bravado and anger, just like that. "General Kasson, please let the troops know they will be marching within the hour." Ill'lyth waved her hand and the man turned and fled, his medals on his field jacket jingling. Ill'lyth turned her cold gaze back to Haldir. "You think we only need five Generals in G'harr, General Haldir?" Ill'lyth stepped closer as she talked, stopping before she was almost kissing him. "You question my promoting this Commander to General in the field?"

Haldir swallowed and stood his ground; there was no backing down now. If he looked weak, she would devour him. He had heard the rumors. Haldir lowered his voice, as she was so close, but didn't back up. Not even an inch. "Not at all, My Queen. I just think he could learn from watching a real General at work." Haldir thought that he made a good case. How could he have known that he was horribly wrong?

Ill'lyth leaned in further and whispered in his ear, asking the water in his body to heat up rapidly. Haldir trembled, then his eyes went wide and he tried to strangle her. She backed up and slapped his arms out wide with a strength that not many knew she had, then punched him lightly in the throat, staggering him. Haldir fell to his knees, gasping and trying to scream as his body began to redden and blister. He took a while to die, and she never took her eyes off of him until he was dead. "Now, General Ellis—did we learn something from watching a *real* general today?"

General Ellis stood and watched the entire thing; when Haldir was dead he thought he heard a scream in his own head. A scream of Franc finally leaving him to the horror of becoming a General. When Ill'lyth addressed him, he was ready with an answer. "Yes, I did, My Queen. Never suffer a fool to live." It probably wasn't the answer she wanted, but it was the lesson he had learned. She made the tough call, and while her methods were barbaric and cruel, they were necessary in war.

Ill'lyth was shocked at his answer—it even showed on her face—but then she smiled and patted him on the shoulder. "I think we will get along famously, General. Now, go find General Kasson and tell him about Haldir. The men march in an hour. Be prepared for war." With that, she turned and went through her gate back to G'harr. She would look in on her other surprise once she was home.

NORTHERN RUN ROAD, NORTH OF EVERKNIGHT

Thanier couldn't breathe. They had run for miles, then jogged when he couldn't run any longer. Now he was fast-walking and trying to convince his lungs not to explode. His lungs weren't having any of that; they were sure he was guilty and wanted to make him suffer. "I'm never going to make it El. I'm sorry—I thought I could, but I can't." Thanier hit the ground mid-sentence, landing on all fours. His lungs gained more popular support from his stomach and his feet, and suddenly nothing wanted to work; it was a mutiny.

"Not happening. I'm not leaving you behind now." Ellen wasted no more words on him. Instead, she leaned down and helped him stand. Turning and grabbing his arms, Ellen spun and pulled him onto her back, bending forward and holding his arms around her neck. "Just hold on and try not to get sick all over me." With that she was off, jogging with him on her back, barely keeping ahead of the horde chasing them. This was not going as planned.

After another five miles, Ellen finally saw the Northern Run Road in the distance, but that was nothing to cheer about. The ogrann were too close behind for her to stop or even attempt to hide, and it was still another thirty miles to the bridge. Thanier was running next to her again, barely, but she was too exhausted to notice if he was doing well or not; she was spent. Being a tracker and guide had made her sturdy, but this trek was pushing her beyond even what she was capable of. She had run almost four more miles carrying Thanier, but when she stumbled, he had forced her to let him run again. Ellen couldn't fight him. She couldn't breathe, never mind argue.

Thanier knew that they were in trouble. No, scratch that. Trouble was so far behind them that he couldn't even see it from where he was. His lungs burned and his legs were wobbly, but he was still going. He was worried about Ellen though—she didn't look well at all. Thanier knew they would soon slow down enough that the ogrann would start to gain on them, then it would be over quickly. Thanier looked at Ellen again; the brave woman had always fascinated him. She was strong, independent, and sarcastic. He had never learned where she came from or anything else about her, and now it was too late. Thanier knew what he had to do. He just hoped her head could take it after her injury.

Thanier slowed down just a bit—too much and he would fall over completely—and as he did, he fell in behind Ellen. They had just gained the road and now running was a little easier than in the high grass. He looked back and saw that the ogrann were close, but still far enough away that the beasts couldn't clearly see himself and Ellen. *Now or never,* he thought as he raised his fist and punched Ellen in the back of the head as hard as he could. Thanier felt his fingers snap as he connected and Ellen pitched forward uncontrollably, spinning into the high grass off the edge of the road. Thanier ran on, hoping he had hit her hard enough so that she stayed down. Normally he wouldn't have been able to take her down with one hit, but her wound was still healing. He just prayed to Davalar that she didn't bleed to death out here all alone. Knowing that it would all be over soon anyway, Thanier put everything into a last-ditch burst of speed and led the brutes back into the high grass. The bridge was out of the question; now it was time to improvise. He led them northwest, away from the one person that he cared about. It was a shame that she would never know.

Ellen hit the ground hard. She tried to get back up, but her legs wouldn't work and everything was spinning. *What hit me?* she wondered, but even her thoughts were coming slower now. She lifted her head up a bit and saw Thanier running away. Ellen let her head fall back, more relieved than angry. At least he would make it. She had really learned a lot about the old scholar on this little adventure; a part of her was glad that he would go on to warn the city. Then the darkness came up and took her. Ellen never saw the ogrann run right by her body. Nor did she witness them catch Thanier not more than two-hundred feet away.

Kragth was losing the attention of the horde. They had chased these littles for miles and couldn't catch them. Now, however, it looked like they were slowing down. The littles veered towards the road, then ran off again into the grass. "Now you is my food, little!" Kragth called, running faster and faster as the little slowed. Now, Kragth wasn't entirely stupid, only mildly so, but even he could count to two. The little in front of him was only one, so where did the other little go? Kragth stopped as the others went by him and he looked around, but for the life of him he couldn't see any other littles. He shrugged and turned back, just as an ogrann slammed the little he was chasing down to the ground and stomped on him. Hard. To Kragth's surprise, the little tried to roll and keep going, but then the other ogrann got into the game, stomping him down until he no longer moved. Then someone ripped an arm off. Now it was a party.

"What are you doing this far North?!" As Ill'lyth came out

of her portal with Dar'Krist behind her, she couldn't believe where they were. She was expecting the ogrann gathered by the bottom of the Shield Mountains, awaiting her orders. Ill'lyth thought the charm she had cast on Kragth still held, but evidently it was lapsing. She whispered to the ether and gained control of his mind once more, this time with force. Ill'lyth noticed a little blood come out of his ears, but otherwise he was still up. Good. *Now get the others marching to Everknight before I rip your lungs out,* she sent before twirling around and leading Dar'Krist back through her portal. Now all of her pawns were on the board—it was time to take their King.

Kragth turned and hit the nearest ogrann so hard he almost killed him. "Let's go, no more fun. Time to kill King!" He started them marching down the road, as it was easier than the high grass—that was what Ill'lyth wanted, anyway—leaving Thanier's ripped and broken body behind. The ogrann marched to the capitol with bloodlust in their veins.

❦

GUNTER SAT ON THE HUGE HORSE AND STARED AT THE column of creatures walking down the road. He had no idea where he was, as he never had left River Vale before and hated geography in class. He wasn't going to get any closer, but he had a strong feeling they had done something bad from wherever they had come from. It was their shouting about blood and death that did it. Had he known of ogrann, he wouldn't have thought about it, but he had never heard of them either. Cautiously he brought the horse around North through the grass, staying away from the road until he was sure that they couldn't see him. The magnificent steed brought him right to the road and stopped, shaking his head as if something was wrong.

"What is it, boy?" Gunter looked around and finally saw

what the horse could both see and smell. It was the body of a woman! Gunter dismounted as best as he could without falling —he was still getting used to that— and rushed to her side. She didn't appear to be run through or anything, so he turned her over. He hoped she was alive and was rewarded by a slight groan from the woman's mouth.

Ellen came around as she felt herself moving. Her head wasn't talking to her anymore, so she couldn't be the one doing the moving. She opened her eyes and saw a young man holding her. This couldn't be good.

"How bad do I look?" she asked as she saw his expression.

"Not too bad. Where are you hurt?" Gunter helped her up and held her as she steadied her legs. Now he could see the back of her head was a little bloody.

"I'm fine. We have to find Thanier." As she became more coherent, she remembered her friend and the danger chasing them. She forced her legs to move despite the differences she was having with her head. Although she ached something fierce, she followed the trampled grass left by the ogrann. Her heart sank, fearing what she would find. Ellen heard the boy behind her, talking about his Lord and how they could get him to help, but she wasn't listening. Ellen had to find Than. Ellen knew the scholar must have hit her to knock her out, probably to lead the ogrann away. To save her. She cried silent tears as she saw a bloody trail and bits of robe.

Then she saw him.

"Than!" Ellen stumbled to his body, falling down next to him and cradling him in her arms. He was pale, white, and missing both an arm and a leg. His robe was torn to pieces as if it had gone through a lion's den, and his back felt broken in so many places that she couldn't keep him in her lap without effort. "Oh Than, why did you do that? Why did you try to do this alone? I would've fought with you... we could've figured something out." Ellen smoothed his hair and looked up at the sky, trying to work through the emotions that ran—more like galloped— through her. She knew she had to face them so she could get going to Everknight and work what vengeance she could. Ellen knew Thanier wanted to save her; she just hated she never got to tell him how great he had been with the people of Keragan Hold. And herself as well. He had saved them all and saved her. Twice.

She held his body and cried as fatigue dragged her down.

Gunter knew he was intruding on something private. "Stay here—I'll get Lord Aeric," he said. Aeric had said if anything urgent happened to get him; this had to qualify. Gunter rode hard, letting the great beast do all of the work finding its master. In an hour he had returned, leading Aeric and the entire group to where he had left the woman; he was ashamed to realize he never asked her name.

Aeric had taken the news gravely, wondering if an honor guard had got caught flatfooted in the plains. When he heard it was a woman, he worried it may have been the High General. So he was filled with apprehension as he rode over to see the woman. She stood slowly, lowering a body to the ground. It looked like she had cradled the corpse the entire time.

"Hail, King's Marshal," Ellen said, standing slowly and working the kinks out of her sore legs. She had dozed for about an hour while holding Thanier and now felt a little better. As well as anyone who has just lost an old friend can feel.

"Greetings, Ellen Falkwind—but I am no longer Marshal. Arian made me Lord of River Vale. But that is a story for another, lighter day. We made haste when my scout told us of the dire news. Was the man an honor guard out of Keragan Hold?" Aeric dismounted to clasp her arm and noticed the face of the body on the ground. "Thanier? The scholar? What befell you all that he came to be out here?" Aeric motioned for his trainees to check the perimeter while he talked with the Scout Captain.

"It is a long story indeed. But more importantly—we have to warn Everknight about the ogrann. They are going right for the North gate. We were trying to lead them away, but they caught us." Heat burned her face as she thought about Thanier's death. Gods above, they would pay!

The North Gate. The worst place for the ogrann to hit would be the lightest held gate of the capital. With an invasion from the southwest, the other two gates would be the priority. This was the worst-case scenario—and here he only had trainees and one horse. Some days things looked bad, then there were days like *this*. "All right. You three—bury that man with all of the honors of a knight. Don't shake your head at me, just do it! If you don't know how, ask around." Aeric looked at the rest of his "men" and sighed. "The rest of you, listen up. We have to accomplish something that will sound impossible. You will want to stop and say you can't, yet we have no choice. *This* is what it means to serve. Right here." Aeric had their attention now. N, and not an eye was looking at the ground. They were ready. "We have to double-time down this road and catch those beasts. When we do, we will try to engage them enough to draw their attention. Once we've distracted them, Gunter will ride around and race to the North Gate to warn the soldiers. Hopefully, they can call for reinforcements in time."

"I will?" Gunter was surprised to hear his name, and it showed on his young face.

"Yes. You have ridden the horse already and you have the best eyes here. Follow us in the grass, riding parallel. When you see the enemy turn towards us, make a run for the city." Aeric cleared his throat and stared at the others, his face more serious than ever. "It sounds easy, but you have never run that far. And when we do stop, you will face an enemy that is ready to eat you. Literally."

"I'll ride with the boy. I'm ready to travel again and I have five arrows left." Ellen wouldn't miss this for the world. There was no way she was backing down now. When the boy made his run, she would slide off and watch his flank with arrows. This was what she was made to do. Besides, she couldn't run anymore.

Aeric's heart soared at her courage. "Do you hear her? Do you see how bad she looks? This is what you will be called upon to do; this is what you will be remembered for!" Aeric was pumping them up, and they were taken on his enthusiasm, cheering and pounding one other on the back. "When we engage the enemy, we are not striking to kill. Our goal is to buy time for Gunter to get past them. We will engage them from a distance, so when I call the retreat, do not turn and run. Back slowly away and fight to get free. I'll be there, don't worry. Now form up!" Aeric called for attention and they rushed to get ready. They were eager, all right. That eagerness would last the first two miles. The next six would test them. The final few miles would either break them or make them heroes. He went around taking their packs off and stuffing his with rations and water. He would keep them light and unburdened; it was the least he could do. "Forward men!"

Gunter climbed up onto the horse and shook his head. He was worried that he would screw this up, but the men were doing this for him. For him to get through. He couldn't let them down. "All right, ma'am. Are you ready?" Gunter asked the rugged woman standing before him.

"I'm no Ma'am—I'm Ellen. But yes. Let's ride, Gunter. That's your name, right?" She slid right up behind him, trying to get comfortable without making him feel awkward in the process. She failed, as his cheeks flushed red.

"Ye... yes. Ellen, it is." He led the horse east into the grass and found a spot where he could still see the men. He followed parallel to them at a slow pace. He could feel Ellen snug behind him and, at sixteen winters, it was a long uncomfortable ride.

THE MIND OF DAR'KRIST

He was called Ra'gan; he remembered that. This was during the dark times, centuries after the destruction of most of the land. The ancient scrolls the elders kept said the heavens had rained fire and death, crumbling mountains and forests alike. These sacred writings said the gods had waged war and that their followers were paying the price, but Ra'gan didn't believe that at all. It was just nature rebelling for something these elves had done. The stories told around the fire said elves were demons that had fallen from the skies. Their fall had surely caused all the devastation those eons ago, he was sure of it.

This was back before any humans had migrated north above the great break, a cliff that appeared when the gods broke the land. Ra'gan was the first to attempt to cross it.

Wait, I've done this already. What is going on? Fueled by anger, he exerted his will and drove the questions deep down inside of himself, refusing to take another step. He could hear the voices around him ask what was happening, but he knew this was wrong. He couldn't say why, he just felt it somehow. The world seemed to *shift* slightly, then he was somewhere else.

He was stumbling through the Dark Forest, running into branch after branch in the pitch black of night. The canopy above refused to let any moonlight through so he was lost and wandering. He felt weak, but not terribly so, and was still crying

Why am I crying?

Ra'gan stopped again, leaning on a large tree to catch his

breath, but he didn't need to. He remembered now—he was running away from that voice. The voice had come to him when he lay dying and suddenly he was healed. Worse, he had lived when the rest of his family had been slain.

Ah, that's why I'm crying...

Ra'gan would make the elves pay with their lives, as soon as he could see where he was going.

You are now my instrument, human. In time you will forget your name, and I shall name you after myself. You will be the Hand of Death, Dar'Krist.

The voice was back, pounding in his skull louder than before. He pressed his hands against his head and screamed at the black canopy. He had no idea what was going on and he couldn't save his family! Ra'gan stumbled as the tree he was leaning on started to wither. He looked down as the tree softened and could faintly make out the forest around him.

In the dark?

No, he couldn't see still, but he could sense the area around him. "What magic is this?!" Ra'gan yelled, his question directed at no one in particular. He felt leaves falling on him from above and soon the canopy opened a little to reveal the brightly shining moon, a shaft of its light breaking through the thick leaves—leaves that decayed even as he stared at them.

That is your sight, my Incarnation. You can use it, like those terrible elves do, to see over a great distance or in the dark. You won't be able to discern magic as they do, but it will help you nonetheless. I have also given you the ability to draw power from the earth to fuel your strength and speed. Death will follow you where ever you tread; you will herald it with your very presence.

This voice likes to hear itself talk, Ra'gan thought.

"What is an Incarnation? Are you the god Krist?" he asked. He felt calmer now that he could see a little better. He marveled at the piles of decaying leaves all around him, spread out like a cloak of power.

The voice, if you could call it that, sighed and its power lessened, quieting inside his skull. *An Incarnation is something never before seen on this plane. The Gods have each placed a fragment of their power inside a chosen mortal. Those chosen will carry out our will upon the many lands of this world.*

How did I already know that?

And yes, mortal—I am He. As for the leaves around you, you are correct. They do resemble a cloak. And so it shall be... The dead leaves swirled around him in a funnel and when they settled he was holding a cloak of pure black. He threw it around his neck and swore he felt it move on its own.

You might want to feed it soon, else it may grow violent.

"Feed it? This thing is alive?" Ra'gan couldn't believe what was happening. He had the power of a god inside him? And the God of Death at that! But the voice was silent once more. He shrugged and started walking again, watching the leaves on the ground decay at his very touch. Yes, this could be fun. He would give himself a couple of days to master this power, then start looking for the elves. Suddenly, a sound made him snap around quickly—someone was coming. It looked like a man stumbling through the darkened wood.

He was stumbling through the Dark Forest, running into branch after branch in the pitch black of night. The canopy above refused to let any moonlight through so he was lost and wandering. He felt weak, but not terribly so, and was still crying

Why am I crying?

And so the magic of Ill'lyth contained Dar'Krist once more even as he fought for control. Little did he know that help would come from a very unlikely source, and very soon.

7

WAR

General Ellis watched as his men marched to the Serpent River Bridge. They had finally received their orders and were more than happy to oblige. The general expected the enemy to be waiting at the bridge—it's what he would've done, after all—but the scouts came back with odd news. It seemed there was only a small force feverishly working on the bridge. But to what end, they couldn't say.

Ellis had his suspicions. "Damn, I hope they aren't dropping the bridge," he said, then turned towards his squire. "Horse!" The squire brought him his steed and Genera Ellis mounted up, galloping away towards the front. He hoped he wasn't too late. He had wanted to lead from the front like he always did, but General Kasson mentioned that they would target him if he did. *Why did I listen to that old fool?* Ellis thought as he rode in and around his men. They were still fifty yards from the bridge, and he saw at least seven of his sorcerers waiting at the front of the army. Even if the foe did drop the bridge, the sorcerers could use magic to get his men across, but it would be slow going. He dismounted and strode up, ignoring the sorcerers altogether.

"Captain, how many on the bridge?"

Before the poor captain could answer, he was interrupted by a large man in the black robes of a sorcerer Head Theurge Axiom Caster was loud and obnoxious, a trait that he worked on daily. He had short blond hair and dark eyes and stood an intimidating six and a half feet tall. "General, why are we waiting? We can have that bridge cleared in no time. There is no time to waste on rank and file!"

General Ellis turned very, very slowly. Caster was intimidating to most, but not with Ellis. He looked at the man and ignored his rank and title by shoving his finger into his broad chest. "The next time you interrupt me when I am speaking to my men, Axiom, I will personally flog you in front of everyone present."

"Don't you threaten me!"

Ellis stepped closer and shouted right at the man even louder. "I am *not* threatening you! That. Is. A. Promise!" Ellis waited, and sure enough, the man backed down. The general counted to three and took a deep breath to calm himself before continuing. "Now, Axiom—if you think there is nothing wrong on that bridge, then I give you permission to clear it." Ellis smiled as he spoke. Let Axiom think he had won. Ellis knew there was something off with the bridge, even though now that he had a good view it didn't seem like they were taking it down.

Axiom turned on his heel, still fuming. He signaled to his sorcerers and they started walking to the bridge. He saw the small force on the other side working faster and faster to complete whatever they were doing, almost panicking as the men in black robes stepped onto the bridge. Axiom waited until they were about thirty feet in before he signaled the others to start casting; the Head Theurge wanted to see the faces of the enemy as they writhed on the ground at his feet. Axiom raised his hands to call upon the water under them, then paused as he noticed the bridge was a bit slick; he couldn't remember the last time it had rained.

It's a trap! As soon as the thought flashed through his mind, he shouted a warning to his men. "Shield yourselves!" Axiom called to his sorcerers, but it was too late. Fiery arrows came in low from the banks of the river and ignited the oil-coated bridge. The heat was immense as the flames roared to life, burning higher as the small vials which had been left on the railings ignited and added to the blaze. They were trapped; only the very talented could concentrate through the pain and get their shields up fast enough to stay alive. A few of the sorcerers shouted and commanded the fire to leave them alone, but many more screamed and fell to the ground, burning. Of the seven sorcerers, only two made it back to the main force. Axiom carried the other man, who sobbed in pain from the burns all over his body. The Head Theurge handed the man off and turned to put out the flames before they engulfed the bridge entirely. It would still be weakened after the fire, but even a damaged bridge would be better than using straight air to walk everyone over the river. It never occurred to him that there could be a secondary attack.

General Ellis saw Axiom go down under a hail of arrows and couldn't help but smile. The man did exactly what he wanted, spring the traps and tipping Lythinall's hand. Ellis signaled for shields and for another sorcerer to put the flames out. Then he sounded the general alarm for advance. He had his own archers fire back, but the other side was quiet once more.

"Not bad. They got seven sorcerers in that trap—I've got to remember that one," Ellis said as his troops pushed forward slowly. He knew that Everknight's forces would pull back for another ruse, but at least he could get across the bridge and split his forces with general Kasson. He would take the West gate and Kasson would head down to the East gate unless Everknight surprised him and met him on the field. Ellis doubted that though, especially with having sorcerers against them. No, they would settle in and repel the attacking army—well they would try at least.

Two hours later, he had his forces across the damaged bridge and he bid farewell to General Kasson—Gods take the man—as he made his way across the plains to the eastern gate. General Ellis would wait until he had the signal from Kasson to advance in order to hit the gates simultaneously. He had the men clean their weapons and do a final check, just to keep them on their toes. As soon as Kasson's force was out of arrow range he heard a shout in the distance. *Great, more surprises,* he thought as he sent out advance scouts to check his own path.

General Kasson was glad to be rid of the upstart Ellis. The man was the pet of the month and would barely listen to reason. Kasson yelled for double time, watching his men march across the plain. The general was as surprised as everyone else when the grass ahead of them lifted up and arrows came at them at point-blank range! *I should have sent scouts, damn them all,* he thought as he slid off his horse and used the animal for a shield. Kasson heard a great shout as the arrows stopped and blades rang out in the front ranks. The general called to his troops as he stood, trying to see what was happening.

"To arms men! Take these upstarts down!" Kasson didn't get far, as his horse had been hit several times by arrows and was trying to bolt in its agony. He spun around, trying to keep his horse, then let the steed go as the shouts became screams of the dead and dying. At the front was a small force from Lythinall, hacking into his wounded and surprised troops. Before Kasson could yell any other commands, a shrill whistle sounded and the attackers leaped back suddenly, dropping to their knees. To his horror, he saw a female lower her arm as the bowmen stood and loosed another volley over the heads of the infantry. "Down!" Kasson screamed just a little too late, as he took an arrow in the shoulder. By the time his forces had readied themselves again, the attackers had withdrawn across the battlefield in haste. General Kasson called for a halt and let the enemy go, worried about falling into any more of their traps. He had to assess the damage and casualties, then send out scouts. This was not going well at all. He spun, looking for an uninjured aide.

"You there, soldier," Kasson called. "Send word to Ellis that we've encountered the enemy on the field and will be longer than anticipated." He did not add that they had gotten the better of him. The general had to admit it had been a good tactic, but he still had the numbers; he would see that woman again, and the next time he would prevail.

HIGH GENERAL CARANA LED HER STRIKE FORCE BACK TO the gate, praising them the whole way. They had struck a telling blow against a much larger force with little to no casualties on their own. She could only guess that Lord Tanan had as much luck at the bridge since the enemy was taking their time getting here. They were still a mile out, but she didn't want to stop them until they were well away from the advancing host. *Still can't believe that the sorcerers didn't act in that engagement.* she thought as they started to slow. Carana looked back and saw that they were in the clear for a time. "All right men slow to a walk, you earned it." Carana made her way through the group, congratulating each individual man for their work, then went to the front. She had seen the puffed-up general on the opposite side and wasn't impressed in the slightest.

"High General?" The slight man in front of her shifted his feet as if he didn't want to ask what was on his mind.

"Out with it, soldier." Carana clapped him on the shoulder to show that she wasn't in the mood to be formal. She went through the mental file she had on her men and came up with his name; Evens, fourth-year infantry.

Evens cleared his throat and looked her in the eye. "How come we didn't keep attacking them? We had them flat-footed, even with the second volley. We could have rushed them again and taken out even more of them." Evens wasn't arguing, he was generally curious.

"Because, Evens, if we had tried one more time, they could've gathered their wits enough to keep us there. We retreated quickly, while they were still trying to pull arrows out of their arses so that we could get back and fortify the defenses. We now know who is coming to which gate, and we know how they fight; think of it as recon with some teeth." He nodded and she turned back to look at the distant city. It had been her home for many years and she would be damned if it fell on her watch. It had only ever been attacked once before in her history, and they had stopped the approaching army on the field. That had been over seventy years ago when they had been at war with the province of Miran to the Southeast. She turned to her men, got them in some sort of marching order, and started a cadence as they approached the city. That would increase morale a bit and if they sang loud enough, she might just irritate the opposing general some more.

On the other side of the city, Lord Tanan ran with his small force and tried his best to keep from laughing. The face of the sorcerers on that bridge when his archer fired those flaming arrows was priceless. Then he remembered that Carana had left surprises near this gate as well. *What did she tell me? Stay in line with the right banner?* he thought as the man next to him suddenly fell. He reached out with lightning-quick reflexes and grabbed the man before he toppled into the spiked pit.

"Hold, men! General rest," he called out before he lost any men. Once they stopped, he looked at what almost got the soldier and whistled softly. The pit was only three feet by four feet and about three-feet deep. The top was covered by the grass that they cut away to dig, held up by two flimsy leather straps. Tanan saw how they rigged it and, as the man counted his lucky stars he was by someone with reflexes that rivaled a hunting cat, Tanan reset the trap and settled the grass in place once more.

"Sir, how are we going to get back without setting these off anymore?" the soldier asked as he watched Tanan.

Tanan smiled and winked at the soldier. "That is the easy part. Now that I know where they begin, all we have to do is keep in line with the right banner of the gate." Tanan looked at the barely discernible West gate, where the banner flew in the summer breeze. The fifteen men he had lined up at his command started walking slowly. Actually, now that he knew what he was looking for, Tanan could see the lines of the cut grass easily.

"Sir, someone is following us," one of the men in the rear guard said. They could see a group of men trying to keep low and out of sight.

Tanan circled back, skirting one of the patches and looking with shaded eyes. Scouts. *This just won't do at all,* he thought. He considered his options—just as he'd worried, he didn't have any. If the men following them found the traps, they wouldn't work. "All right soldier, give me that bow." Tanan held his hand out without looking; after a couple of seconds, when he still didn't have a bow in his hands, he turned to look. The soldier was smiling at him with his arms crossed.

"Lord Tanan, I'm a much better shot than you." Mavren didn't want to sound cocky, but when that's all there is, you have to own it.

"You may be at that, but you can't get them all by yourself." Tanan looked around and picked the highest-ranking soldier. "You there, lead these men back. Eagle Eye here and I are going to take care of the scouts."

"Mavren, sir."

"What now?"

"My name is Mavren, sir."

"Whatever you say, Eagle Eye. Let's go."

The forward scouts approached behind them, moving cautiously amidst the grasslands. After the fire on the bridge, they weren't taking any chances. There were seven of them, spread out twenty feet apart, and all had long sticks with which to prod the ground in front of them. They kept their eyes peeled ahead of them as well, looking for any signs of an ambush. They knew they were expendable, but the hazard pay was too good to pass up. Narron, a very small man with long brown hair and squinty brown eyes, was in charge and he moved fluidly, like water flowing down the cobblestones, always finding the easiest path. Narron had spotted the fleeing troops and was keeping them in his sights when a couple of them move off from the group. *Damn*, he thought. *Where did they get to now?* Narron held his hand up in a fist to signal the others to stop and scanned the horizon for any movement. Nothing.

Narron heard a grunt off to his left and rolled quickly to his right, coming up with his sword out. Another grunt behind him had him spinning, ready for anything, but he still saw nothing. "What in the Deep Hells is going on here?" he whispered to himself as he looked around desperately for any signs of trouble. That was when he noticed he was all alone. Narron promptly forgot all about being alone though, as a dagger slipped carefully under his arm and into his heart, silencing him forever.

Tanan wiped his dagger on the fallen soldier's tunic and saluted him. There was no sarcasm in this—for once—as he valued the soldier's duty. He knew these men weren't inherently evil, only following an evil regime. Tanan couldn't say that he took no pleasure in killing them, however; it was a thrill to carry out that kind of maneuver against one so skilled. Tanan looked up as Mavren came to collect what arrows he could salvage, noting that the man had taken out four of the seven scouts. Not bad at all. "Nice shooting, Eagle Eye."

"Thank you, sir." Mavren couldn't believe he only got four of the enemy before Lord Tanan downed three using only a dagger. The man must have moved like a ghost. Mavren never even caught a glimpse of the lord until this last kill. "Time to get back?"

"Almost. I just want to leave our general a little present." Tanan smiled and patted Mavren on the shoulder. "Help me with these bodies. We must be quick, as more scouts will be coming soon."

Thus it was that General Ellis's second wave of scouts—sent after the first never returned—found seven bodies piled neatly with a piece of parchment that read, *No traps on the right side.* The second wave grabbed the note, looked nervously around, and ran back to the main force as quickly as they could. Two hours later, General Ellis arrived with the rest of his troops. While he waited for a sign from General Kasson, he looked at the bodies. They weren't stripped, mutilated, or treated improperly. They were even stacked according to rank, with the commander on the top of the pile. Ellis knew that whoever did this had respect for soldiers at least.

"What do you think it means sir?" Larr was one of his captains. She had risen through the ranks by being smart and capable. She was all of five-feet tall but had a voice that could be heard from miles away when she wanted to yell at her men. She had dark skin and black hair that was twisted into five braids that hung down her back. Her deep brown eyes didn't miss much, either.

"I think someone wants us to take the right side of the approach to the gate. Line up the men in left formation and wait for my signal." Ellis smiled when Larr walked away. She was a no-nonsense officer and would follow his lead no matter what she felt. She just wasn't Franc. It wasn't long before he saw the plume of smoke that was the signal from General Kasson. General Ellis gave the order to march upon Everknight—there was no turning back now. With the numbers he had, it would be no contest on the field but bottlenecked at the gates...that was a different story. Ellis was glad he had sorcerers left to clear those gates when they got to them.

"Sir!" Larr called as she saw three of the columns falter. Screaming came from the direction of the gates. She could see the forces of Everknight lined up before the great gate and thought that they were under attack.

Ellis looked and saw the men falter, falling into something as they marched. *More traps!* But it was too late to pull back now. "Damn them," Ellis swore. He looked back toward the city and saw a line of mounted knights getting ready to charge. "Brace for the charge!" the general called. He know half of his men wouldn't have time to set their spears in order to meet the cavalry. This was going to hurt.

WESTERN GATE, CITY OF EVERKNIGHT

Arian stood with Tanan and Storn as the knights thundered down the small slope to meet the advancing G'harran forces. They would meet them on the fields before the gate, then pull back to the gate itself and try to hold them for as long as they could. If they faltered or fell, it would mean fighting in the streets. Behind the king, by the gate itself, stood his wife, Maressa. She was playing rousing songs of victory—mainly about their own adventures—to inspire the men.

Head Priest Ralavin was even further back, getting ready to help with the wounded that would surely start filtering back as they met the much larger force. Tanan had done an excellent job at hobbling the enemy, thanks to his and Carana's ingenuity. Arian wondered how they were faring at the East gate, but he put that out of his mind and focused on his plans here.

"The knights have hit their front." Storn was looking with mixed emotions. He would've rather started with a volley of arrows, but he trusted his king's decisions. Storn watched as the knights charged from the safe side, where the ground was solid, then pulled back just enough to bait their foes into attack recklessly. The knights blocked blow after blow, slashing about with their swords as they cut down the infantry in droves, at the same time constantly backing towards the gate.

"There!" Tanan yelled, pointing to a man set apart from the host on the far right. The man, who had to be a sorcerer, held his arms up and used magic to seal the holes in the ground so the force could continue advancing. The sorcerer thought he was out of bow range, and he would have been correct if it weren't for the prowess of Storn Keragan.

"Got him," Storn said quietly, lifting his bow and loosing an arrow in the blink of an eye. In three quiet breaths they waited, then the sorcerer staggered and went down, his hands clutching his neck; two more breaths and he wasn't moving at all.

"Nice shooting, old friend! We don't have much longer, as the knights are almost here and they are starting to take losses." Arian turned to Tanan and smiled. "Is Janna ready?"

Lord Tanan squinted and looked to the knights as they

backed up the hill, fighting for their lives. "I think so, sir. If they try anything you should be all right. I'll hold here until you return." Tanan looked again at the men behind him, his to command when the king left to bolster the knights with Storn. It should be the Queen holding the gate, but she was busy lifting the men's spirits and providing backup with her spells.

"I still think this is unnecessary, Arian. I know you want to lead from the front—trust me, I do that as well—but to put yourself that far away...." He shook his head. Storn was worried the plan would fall to pieces before they could pull it off.

Arian laid his hand on the man's shoulder. "I'll have you with me, old friend. Besides, with that bow, I don't think we'll be in much trouble." The king knew it was risky. He was a little worried himself, but it was a good play. Arian would go down there with Storn to 'save' the knights, thus placing himself as the bait for their sorcerers.

"To me!" Arian yelled, pulling his horse into a rearing charge as he drew his sword, Chalice.

Storn kicked his horse after his stubborn king and smiled, despite the danger. He loved being back with his old companions. He'd missed the old days of fighting impossible odds—now they just had to live through it again. The pair rode down behind the knights, Storn firing arrow after arrow as he rode. He wasn't going as fast as the king because he wanted more time until he had to draw his sword. Storn saw Arian hit the approaching troops like a firestorm, men falling before him like twigs to a flame. Then the air started to crackle. Storn scanned the rear of the G'harran force for the sorcerers, but he couldn't make them out yet. Standing in the saddle with his bow in one hand, Storn frantically looked for any sign as to where they were hiding; then he heard the screams.

Turning his head to the far left, Storn saw one robed figure ignite into flames and another fall down and roll, trying to put out the fire. Two arrows and they were done. Another robed figure ran screaming back to the main line, only to sprout two arrows in the back of the neck as Storn took another breath. He was too close to the fighting now to keep firing, so he sat back in the saddle and rode hard, drawing his sword and laughing in the wind; Janna had saved them all.

Storn saw her sitting on a warhorse in the middle of the knights, her helmet finally discarded as their ruse paid off. Janna looked uncomfortable in the mock armor they put her in, but it hid her from the eyes of the sorcerers until the last minute. No one had noticed that one of the knights in the middle wasn't attacking. Then Storn had no more time to reflect as they were in the thick of it. Storn and Arian beat back the enemy, giving the knights room to turn and head back up the slope to the gate, then they too pulled back and made a break for it.

Janna was in her glory. She had thrown her *sight* out at the G'harran forces, looking for anyone attempting to control the elements. When she saw them, she threw off her helmet and had set the heat in the air around them to work. Her attack was so fast they couldn't counter it before they were aflame, and by then it was too late. It was hard to concentrate while in that much pain. Janna loathed fire, but at this distance it was manageable. She saw the robed figures drop, riddled with arrows, and knew Storn had seen her show. Now they just had to make it back to the gate.

Janna saw Arian and Storn fighting to turn around once the knights had broken free, and looked to the knight next to her. "You, sir knight!" Janna called out. She handed him the reins of her horse. "Take these and guide me back—I have to help the King!" The knight nodded. Janna turned her head and closed her eyes. "Ash'anti dir, yanel ubel an ceas lae kithen." She pointed at the G'harran soldiers and sent her *sight* in their direction to make sure she got them and not the king or Storn by mistake. Janna was rewarded by shouts from the front ranks as the very earth rose up and created a small wall to hinder them from chasing after the retreating pair. The southern sorcerers would be able to take it down easily, but it served its purpose. Janna slumped in the saddle, exhausted from the reach she had to make and the exact direction. Never mind the magic she cast at the sorcerers. As an Incarnation, she would be fine in a matter of moments but it was inconvenient while trying to flirt with the knights.

Arian rode up to Janna and took the reins from the knight, leading her horse himself. "Great work, Janna. You really turned the tide in this fight for us. You have my gratitude." Arian saw her try to smile but could tell she really wanted a nap. "We're almost back. Rest up while you can, as I'm sure those sorcerers will be here soon."

"No way, your Highness. I'll feel better with my sword in my hands anyway. Besides," she said and winked at the knight riding next to them, "I have to show this one here just how good I am with it."

Arian laughed and shook his head. The poor knight was in for a good time if he lived through all this. The king led them back to fanfare from the Queen, then arranged everyone in position to ride once more when the enemy came up the slope. They had to keep them from the gate as long as they could. If they became bottlenecked, it would be a much different game entirely. "Let's just hope Carana is having as much luck with Gareth and Tierra."

EASTERN GATE, CITY OF EVERKNIGHT

General Kasson and his force approached the East gate apprehensively. The rest of the way had been quiet, without any new surprises. His men had been on edge, just waiting for whatever was going to cave in or pop up and impale them, but nothing came. The anticipation alone was exhausting. As a result, the men were now nervous and jumpy. By the time they could see the forces of Everknight before the Eastern gate, most of his soldiers were constantly looking over their shoulders. General Kasson saw the knights arrayed in front of the slope and knew that they were about to charge.

"Front line—brace!" the general yelled, as the knights started down the hill toward them. The knights picked up speed and the first three ranks of soldiers set their spears to receive the charge. Kasson signaled to his sorcerers to hold while his footmen earned their pay. Once the knights were engaged, his men would pour around them and sweep them under a blanket of bloody steel. General Kasson noticed too late that the knights had not lowered their lances or readied their swords. He turned to his second in command just as he heard the shout of alarm that signaled his best-laid plans going out the window—out the window and smashing into the ground head-first at the speed of a raging dragon.

The knights of Lythinall split down the middle, veering off to either side. As they split, Kasson could see the small force of soldiers from Everknight coming behind the knights on foot. They had been hidden from view by the horses and now charged at the front line at full speed. *What are they...?* he wondered. Then he saw the heavy ropes the horses were dragging.

The twenty knights—ten to each side—had ropes tied to their mounts, stretched between the two groups that now rode on either side of Kasson's forces. As they passed the waiting G'harran troops, the ropes pulled tight and slammed into the front line with the force of—well, twenty horses. The knights braced for attack from the soldiers on the sides and rode on, using only their shields to parry the spears and swords of their enemies. They dragged the first two, then first three, lines of soldiers to the ground before the southern sorcerers finally used their magic to break the ropes, but by then the damage had been done.

The infantry forces of Everknight fell upon the prone G'harran soldiers and slaughtered them mercilessly. The confusion was so bad that those in the back rows couldn't even get to the front to help their downed fellows. Worse, with the ropes no longer hampering them, the knights drew their swords and wheeled back around to flank the enemy, cutting down any who got in their way. Kasson shrieked for the sorcerers to get to the fore to put an end to this debacle; that didn't go so well either.

Gareth was having the time of his life. He was part of the small force of soldiers to attack the downed G'harran troops and his ax rose and fell tirelessly. Next to him, twirling in a dance of death herself, was his wife Tierra. Together they had led the foot soldiers to try and put a dent in the approaching force while Carana got their troops ready to retreat. "Reminds me of old times, eh?" Gareth asked Tierra, his booming voice easily heard above the din of battle.

Tierra scoffed as she ducked under a feeble swing from a man that had gained his feet. Her steel balls came around at him and he dropped quickly. "Old times? Was I sick that day?" Tierra was calm and focused, punching and kicking in a rhythm that most could only gawk at. Another man came at her and he went down with her foot in his windpipe.

"I meant us fighting the good fight," Gareth called back. He was going to say more but he saw the men in black cloaks striding to the front of the line. "Bananas!" Gareth screamed the code word that they had come up with —ok, that *he* had come up with—and started to slowly pull his men back.

"Really? Bananas?" Tierra knew he had picked the word but had silently hoped he would change it to something better. Now, she just hoped their plan worked. Tierra danced back, saving one soldier from a spear and dragging another away that had taken a sword to the gut. She ignored the few cuts she had taken through sheer force of will, filling her center with calm and need. She would hurt tomorrow... if there was a tomorrow.

The sorcerers saw the retreating troops and smiled. They strode forward, ready to cast magic to assail the retreating forces from Everknight, but found the very earth hindering them. Dirt snaked its way into their mouths; the few that tried to counter the magic were smashed down by a gust of air from above.

Frenir threw off his cloak and smiled. "All right lads, let's get back in there and show them what for!" he called to Gareth, drawing his weapon and scanning the remaining sorcerers to see if any had thrown off his magic. Everknight's ruse of retreat turned into another charge, timed perfectly with the knights coming around to their aid. Frenir had hidden amidst the soldiers, sticking to the back and waiting for the sorcerers to show their hand. He was G'harran himself, but Frenir had lived in Lythinall for years, always trying to make peace for both lands. Then G'harr had betrayed him.

Frenir was sure that whoever was leading G'harr had counted on the King of Lythinall to kill him. Turned out, all those peace talks had done some good though—the rulers of Everknight trusted him. More and more he knew that Lythinall was his home. They could call him a traitor to his land; the truth be told, it didn't bother him one bit.

GENERAL KASSON WAS FURIOUS. HE SAW THE FRONT LINE get decimated and all of his commands were useless. He finally sent the sorcerers in—much to his displeasure—and even they went down. "Archers! Ready positions!" Kasson called out.

"Sir, our men are in the line of fire as well."

It was one of his captains, yet Kasson didn't recall his name; it didn't matter anyway. "I know this, Captain, but we have to take down this force before they get back to the Eastern gate." Kasson turned to the men hurrying to get in position. As soon as they were ready he let his arm fall. "Fire!" The general's eyes followed the arrows as they ascended into the sky, then arched downward towards the front line and the massacre there. The Everknight forces had slain most of the sorcerers as they tried to get up, and the rest of the soldiers were struggling to pull back from the onslaught of the knights. *I have thousands of soldiers, how are they doing this?* Kasson thought as he received yet another shock of this horrible engagement. The arrows stopped dead in the air above their heads... all of them! "That's it. Company! Full charge!" Kasson stomped the ground as he ordered the entire complement of soldiers to advance against the frontline.

"Sir! They will trample our own men, we can't—" The captain died with Kasson's sword in his throat.

"That's the last time you question me, captain," Kasson said coldly. He smiled as all of his men went forth to crush his enemies. He sat back and watched the scene play out, but soon he realized that the forces of Everknight were continuing to pull back with little losses. Then the Eastern gate opened once more; inside, soldiers lined the walls. He had been goaded into this and now there was no turning back. He ducked behind a group of soldiers in the rear as the arrows came down on his own men from the city.

Frenir was exhausted. He was no great sorcerer like Ran'-

cian, nor was he a skilled bard like Karsis. Frenir was a decent caster that had to do the impossible. Not only did he have to pin the sorcerers on the front line down with air, but Frenir also had to raise a shield of air above their heads to keep the arrows from slaying the soldiers. They couldn't move, because the shield was immobile, and if G'harr launched another volley Frenir didn't know if he could stop it.

"You all right, Frenir?" Gareth came back. The southern sorcerer was looking haggard all of a sudden. He wished he knew more of this magic stuff, but he'd never had a head for it.

"Aye. For now, I am. Just pray that they don't do that again before we can safely pull back to that gate." Frenir dropped to one knee as the last sorcerer he held with air fought back with earth and shook the ground under him. Any stronger and he would have lost his hold on the precarious elements altogether. "Do me a favor would you, Gareth? Go thwack that last one on the head a little harder?"

"Ha! Will do, milord." Gareth bowed mockingly and turned to do said thwacking when he saw the entire enemy force shifting towards them at a good pace. "On second thought, that may have to wait." Gareth brought both hands up to his mouth and bellowed. "Faaaaalll Baaack!" When he finished, he grabbed Frenir and started backing towards the gate, his ax in one hand in case anyone came at them. "Tierra! Now!" Gareth knew she wouldn't follow right away, but he needed to see that she was safe.

Tierra smiled at the sound of her husband's voice. *Listen to him, all commanding and official. Almost makes me want to listen to him. Almost.* She ducked another sword thrust. Tierra was getting tired but she wanted to help a couple more soldiers before she followed. She was much faster, and if she retreated now many wouldn't make it out. Then she noticed why her husband called for the retreat—this was bad. The G'harran forces surged forward with no concern for their own men, either their wounded or their fallen. The knights were riding rear guard and she would be cut off if she didn't move soon, but there were still ten men that had to pull back. *Just like old times, he says... Well, this is going to be a first,* Tierra thought as she took three quick steps and vaulted over the ten men to land among the soldiers. Correction. Soldiers... and one last irritated sorcerer.

"I will flay the skin from your—!"

That's all he got out as her foot slammed into his head, throwing him into his fellows. Tierra spun and kicked, keeping the sorcerers back more from the sheer audacity of her attack than anything else. "Run, men! Get back to the gate!" Tierra spun once more, taking a man in the throat and coming around with her other foot to knock a spear out wide. A sword got through and sliced into her leg, but she blocked the pain and kept fighting. Another down, then a third. Tierra was actually having a hard time catching her breath now. She hadn't fought these odds in over twenty years, if even then. Then her husband's voice sounded once more.

Gareth saw his wife flip into the group of enemies, holding the last of their men back, and frowned. He heard the gate open and knew that the time had come. They couldn't wait for her, no matter how important she was. "Down, love! Terafar!" Gareth called, hoping she would remember the flight from that southern city and the hail of arrows that followed them. He lugged Frenir into the gate as the arrows fell among the encroaching host and watched as the G'harran's paid dearly for their advance. As the enemy fell back in disarray, he scanned the bodies for his beloved. He knew he couldn't go to check until all the arrows finished, but waiting was killing him.

"There, lad!" Frenir leaned against the wall and pointed to

the sea of fallen men. He had started scanning the bodies as the last of the arrows fell and saw a hand reaching for the sky.

Gareth ran out of the gates. He heard Carana call for aid as well, but he wasn't waiting. Gareth barreled down the slope at a full charge, finally seeing what his southern ally had seen—an arm reaching out for the sky. "Tierra!" Gareth yelled through tears that he didn't know were falling. He plowed into the fallen bodies of the dead and dying and surged to her, pulling her into his arms. He gasped at the arrows sticking out of her. "Hold on, love. I've got you." Gareth ran up the slope and saw Caerlyn running down to them. "Go back, Caer, it's all right," Gareth called, not wanting her to get caught out here. He was inside the gate again in no time and handed Caerlyn a limping Tierra. Four men stood there, obviously tense with worry. "What's the matter, men?"

"Name's Hanlen sir. Is... is the lady going to be all right?" The man fought back tears, and he wasn't the only one; Tierra had almost died for them.

Gareth smiled, understanding their emotions. He turned, and the sight of his wife being tended to give him a pang of worry himself; they weren't in their twenties anymore. "Yes, soldier, I think she is. You see, she's too stubborn to give up just yet." Gareth winked at the men to relieve some of the tension and turned to see High General Carana coming over.

Carana had seen Tierra's valiant stand and came to see if she was going to be all right. Not just because she was worried, but because she needed to know whether her captains were still in the fight. Not that she would call the Companions of Everknight "captains," but they were the closest thing she had right now. They were her best weapons in an impossible fight and Carana couldn't afford to lose such a valuable asset this early. *Am I really thinking like this right now?* she wondered, but the grim truth was that she knew she had to. "All right, men, enough lounging around. Let's get those weapons ready for the next charge. Be ready to meet them on the slope." Carana turned to Gareth as the men meandered away and smiled weakly. "How are you doing, Gareth?"

Gareth brandished his ax and smiled at the high general. As they spoke, he watched the enemy reforming. "I'll be fine as long as you point me at an enemy and let me loose."

"How about all of them? Is that good enough?" Carana asked, pointing to the thousands of soldiers poised to assail the Eastern gate. They had to hold them on the approaching slope for as long as they could before they fell back to the gate itself. Things would get really bad when that happened.

Gareth laughed, a great barking sound that made one man jump. "They'll do. Frenir, you get some rest and come save me in a little bit." Gareth saluted Carana and bowed to Frenir, then trotted off to the front of the troops and started banging his ax against his chest.

"You know, anyone else and I may think they were bragging, but I would put money that he will take them all if he gets mad enough." Frenir laughed at the outrageous statement, but he saw the high general frown like she was actually figuring the odds.

Carana scrutinized the forces and thought of how he could do it. "He would have to take out the sorcerers first, then work his way through their flank." Carana stopped when she realized the southerner was staring at her and laughed to cover up her slip; she didn't want him to think she was serious. "Just kidding, old man. Now get some rest. You'll have the worst job if they get up here." Carana knew that he would be pushed to the limit if the sorcerers got to the gate and started working in close quarters. What he didn't know was that when that happened, she was going to let loose and tear into the enemy herself with a vengeance.

Caerlyn worked on taking the last of the arrows out of

Tierra and smiled at her old friend. Tierra was staring at her husband with a look that said volumes. "You know, I remember you always looking at Gareth like that, even when you were with Karsis," Caerlyn said lightly. The statement brought Tierra's head spinning around in shock.

"No...! I never. Did I?" Tierra hadn't thought about it before. Everyone in the Companions knew better than to bring it up, especially with how things between her and Karsis had ended so badly.

Caerlyn stifled a laugh. "Since the day I first met you all, I noticed that right away. You two were almost as bad as Maressa and Arian." Her work done, Caerlyn channeled healing into the woman's wounds and closed them up. "There. Now don't go charging into another arrow storm anytime soon."

Tierra smiled at the healer and flexed her arm to test it; no pain and full mobility. The healing power of the small priest of Davalar always amazed her. "Thank you very much, Caerlyn," Tierra said, laying a hand on the healer's arm. "I also never thanked you for saving my son. I heard that if it weren't for you he may have died." Karsis had told her how Caerlyn had healed Rhoe after his run-in with the wolvren.

"Thanks, Tierra. But Karsis helped. Besides, I helped bring that boy into this world. There was no way I was going to let him leave it on my watch." Caerlyn heard a bell toll and knew the enemy was coming. "You better get going. I'll be swamped in a bit." They hugged and separated, each going to where they were needed most. Neither of them noticed the man watching them from the shadows.

Graf stretched his legs quickly then settled back into the shadows of the pottery shop. It was the closest building to the eastern gate and afforded the best view of the open field beyond. He wasn't the kind of person to march out and fight in a field; not even close. No, Graf was best in the kind of situation that arose when all hells broke loose. Once they started to pile up in front of the gate, then he would find his way into the throng of fighting. He figured he could fight his own way and still help, but the size of the force arrayed against the city looked bad. Graf had looked around again for the elven woman that he ran into days before but still could find no trace of her. The woman was good at going unnoticed. Graf shrugged his shoulders with a sigh. She would show up when things got bad enough, he knew it. He had a good sense of people, even elves, and he knew that she would be here somewhere. *Maybe I'll go check on the kids at the Northern gate,* Graf thought as the forces clashed outside of the city. He snuck off slowly, with no one seeing him leave.

EVERKNIGHT CASTLE, CITY OF EVERKNIGHT

Sprout looked out the window and frowned harder. She had already been frowning but felt that she could do better, so she deepened her dislike of the situation and really put some effort into it. Sprout knew she was too little to fight in a war—she was eight, not stupid—but it still stung to be locked up in here with all the other folk while her friends got to run around having fun —she thought they were having fun, at least. What was even worse was that this boy kept following her around everywhere she went! Sprout turned around and looked at the boy, sticking out her tongue. "Stop following me."

"He told me to save you," Rythal said automatically. He screamed inside of his fractured mind and on into the endless void for his brother, but Innal was dead. Rythal's brother was just a pile of ash and dust and he wouldn't hear anything anymore. It didn't keep him from screaming though—that's all he did now inside this broken mess that was once his mind.

Gone was the fun, carefree life he had known with his twin. Gone, along with his sanity. Still, Rythal felt the time was fast approaching that he would finally be able to act on his own desires. Something about this little one intrigued him though. It's not like she gave him the clarity the healers had, but she filled in something that he had been missing: his memories.

When he was near this little girl, Rythal could finally remember the good times he had with Innal. That gave him something to focus on besides the endless screaming. So whenever she went somewhere, Rythal focused on the power burning in his mind and followed her. Instantly. Just like he had been doing ever since his arrival at the castle. No one could stop him from going anywhere now.

"Well, *I* don't need saving." Sprout stomped off and looked for something else to do. It was so quiet, what with most of the people down inside the castle. She got bored and wanted to explore, so she looked out the windows. The one thing Sprout didn't see when she looked outside was war. *Well then, it must be safe to walk the streets,* she thought. Sprout had always been a master at self-rationalizing, even if she didn't know what that meant, so she did what she did best. She snuck past the towns-folk standing guard and even grabbed a length of rope on the way out. She played with it as she walked— at least she could play with the rope if the city was as boring as the castle. The streets were empty as she skipped along, humming a little tune to herself. Then, as Sprout rounded a corner, Rythal was there.

"He told me to save you."

"*Ah!*" Sprout screamed, dropping her rope and all but falling over backward. "Don't do that, you little squirt!" Then she had an idea. "Wait. I know what we can do to make this quiet city more fun." Sprout walked slowly towards him and, as casually as a brick falling on someone's head, she reached out and touched his arm, bolting away as she yelled, "Tag, you're it!"

Sprout ran as fast as she could, but as she rounded another block, Rythal was there. This time though his arm was out straight and he was holding a finger out at her.

"Oh, no you don't," Sprout said as she slid under him and kept running. They played tag most of the way to the Northern gate.

"Tag you're it!" Illiyana knew that voice anywhere. What was more startling was that the city was supposed to be empty, what with the G'harran forces attacking. The elven blademaster stood on the roof where she was lounging and smoothed her dirty cloak out of habit. Illiyana had short, white hair that fell to her slim shoulders and her silver eyes sparkled in the sun. She was almost five feet and her slight frame was very lean but rugged. She moved with the sureness of a warrior, but as quietly as a master thief. Illiyana had been living in this city for decades, hiding in the alleyways and rooftops. She had watched over the homeless children for many years, starting with Sprout; Illiyana knew her by another name though.

Illiyana oriented on the voice as it called out again, then she was off across the rooftops. Why that little one was out and about she had no idea, but it meant no good... she could feel it. Illiyana had raised her since her untimely birth, though she wasn't her mother, and it had almost broken her heart to let her go off on her own.

Graf saw the woman vault over the alley and land quietly. He was impressed. He too heard a little girl and guessed that it was the wee one. Graf followed silently behind and kept to the side of the buildings. A light wind had picked up and it drove him into a nervous fit to not have his pile of rags to hide in. He could tell that they were heading towards the Northern gate, and he clicked his tongue at the revelation. It felt like something else was pulling them all towards something important. *Well, it's not like I haven't been in tight spots before,* he thought, running lightly through the darkening streets.

WESTERN GATE, CITY OF EVERKNIGHT

Ralavin spread his healing through the wounded soldier's arm and smiled at the poor man. He would live—until he took a spear in his back, or an arrow in the throat. The head priest looked up at the gate and shook his head. They had lost the slope quickly and had fallen back, but they were holding for now. Janna was exhausted, as she was keeping most of the remaining sorcerers busy, and the king had that look like he would love nothing more than to be doing this by himself. Ralavin stood and noticed, for the first time since this whole battle started, that he had no one to tend to immediately. Oh, there were injuries still, but they were either very minor or the those suffering from them were dead. As if his standing was a sign, Janna collapsed and the wall to the right of the gate crumbled, leaving a hole the enemy began flooding through.

"Breech!" Ralavin shouted, running to Janna's side before the enemy troops could swarm her. Ralavin saw Arian turn and start shouting orders, but it was Dren that came to his aid first.

"Cover her! The men and I will hold them off," Dren yelled as he ran past the head priest with six other soldiers. Dren and his men had just come off a healing rotation and were about to relieve some others when they heard the call. Dren came at the invaders swinging his blade in quick, efficient strokes. He fought to main, not kill, as that was quicker on the field of battle.

Ralavin got to Janna's side and held her head in his lap. She was all right, still breathing at least, but she looked like a pale version of herself. "Hang on, Janna, I'm here."

"Hello... Priest," Janna managed to croak out with a faint smile. She had been overwhelmed trying to battle ten sorcerers at once, but there was only one left. She should've known he was just waiting for her to wear herself out. She lifted her head and saw Dren standing before the breech with his sword with six men around him and knew they weren't enough "Ralavin... the G'harran's have a sorcerer still. Shield them... quickly." Janna's head fell back and she closed her eyes. *Nothing wrong with a tiny nap. I heal quickly after all, right?* she thought as darkness took her.

Ralavin knew the men were in trouble if the invaders still had a sorcerer with them. He closed his eyes and called out to his God. "Davalar, let us bask in your warm glow and feel your shield in all things." Ralavin spread his hands and directed the magic at Dren and the men around him. A soft glow encompassed them and settle around their weapons. *That should help them,* he thought. *And more than just a little.* The only problem was that he could only do that once a day, and it was exhausting. Not nearly as bad now that he had his youth back, but he wouldn't be able to heal anyone for a couple of minutes.

Arian saw that the breach was covered and went back to cutting down the enemy. His sword, Chalice, sliced through armor like it was cloth. The king took blow after blow on his armor and even though he was starting to feel it he was nowhere *near* done with this fight. This was his land, his people, and his city. Arian Everknight would be dead before anyone took any of those from him. "How are we doing, Tanan? Are they ready to surrender yet?" Arian called out to his old friend.

Tanan ducked a spear, gutted the man who held it, then spun and stabbed another in the thigh, kicking him back into the crowd. There were fifteen of them holding the gate, with reinforcements behind them to take their place if necessary. Once in a while, they would pull back to catch their breath, but after a quick rest, they would jump right back in. It had only been a couple of hours, but it felt like they had been doing this all day.

"I'll send another messenger to their general, though I fear I made him a little mad when I saw him last." Tanan feinted with his sword, then kicked a man in the knee. "You—go tell your general that I wish to accept his surrender."

Arian sliced a man's neck with a side stroke and shouldered another man away. "Wait. I want his surrender! I'm the King," Arian said trying to catch his breath. *Gods above, I'm not twenty anymore,* he thought.

Storn fired at the back of a robed man raising his hands. "Would you two stop bickering and fight this war? Honestly, you are like children with sharp weapons." Storn knew that once Janna was down the rest of the casters would raise their ugly heads. He waited patiently and looked for the first robe to pop up. Storn was about to fire again when he felt his bow heating up. "That's it—now I'm angry," he said as he dropped his bow and drew a dagger. He let fly at a smiling G'harran. The small blade flew through the air, embedding itself in the sorcerer's right eye. Storn's bow promptly cooled off.

Maressa watched all of this as she helped the healers in the far back stitch up soldiers who had taken minor wounds. She had this nagging worry in the back of her mind that she couldn't shake, but since things were a bit busy she didn't divert much attention to it. That was when Kari came running, shouting for the King from at least a block away. Maressa's stomach plummeted.

Arian heard his name and fought back a man with a hammer. Two cuts and the man was down. Quickly the king shifted to the back of the forces as two others took his place at the front line. He turned to see Kari running at a full sprint, completely out of breath. He didn't need to know what happened—he knew the Northern gate was in trouble. Arian held one hand up to the sky and *called* to his horse that he had left behind the fighting.

"Let no one tear us asunder," Arian said as he opened his eyes and started running. His horse brayed and he heard hooves galloping on the cobblestone; the king was off in an instant.

Once he was gone, Maressa finally figured out what had been bothering her. Her husband had been fighting like he always had. Fearlessly. Back in the day, he was unmatched in battle and could take any wound and recover... because he had his ring. His ring! Arian didn't have that ring anymore, their daughter had it! With no magic to protect him, his typical, headless approach was going to get him killed.

"Arian!" Maressa screamed. She was up and running, as no horse was left available after the loss of the slope. She only hoped that she could get to him before he did something stupid. *Hang on love, I'm coming!*

Kari stopped running and watched both the King and Queen go as her message went unheard. Men looked around in confusion and the Lord Tanan was a bit busy. As faces turned toward her, wondering what had happened, all she could think to do was... sing. So Kari closed her eyes and thought of a calming tune that Jerina had taught her, a little song that helped get one on the right track mentally and cleared the mind. Kari opened her mouth and knew these men had to know that everything was going to be all right. When the first note left her mouth, she *felt* it. Kari dropped to her knees and carried on through the tears that came, unasked, as she sang to the men who fought for the city—her city. She felt a hand on her shoulder and she looked up into the eyes of a smiling soldier.

"Thank you—but you better sing over there, miss. It could be dangerous for a bard to sit in the open like this."

Kari couldn't answer, just nodded as she stood and walked woodenly over to where Jana was lying down. It looked like there were two gates now, but one was just a hole in the wall.

"Nice pipes kid," Janna said as she started to come around,

She had to get up and stop those damned sorcerers from ruining the place. Janna felt better, but she had to watch herself. She got up and patted the girl on the head, heading back to the wall where Ralavin was helping. Kari watched her go and smiled despite the war going on around her.

NORTHERN GATE, CITY OF EVERKNIGHT

Lan paced back and forth in front of the closed gate, nearly beside himself with boredom. They had seen only three advance scouts the entire day and those they had dealt with rather easily. Even worse, his superior told him to simply "relax and keep busy." Keep busy! The fighting at the other gates had been going on for hours while Lan and the others had done nothing but sit here. He looked over at the old veteran knight in charge of the gate. The man had seen at least fifty winters and had short, grey hair with a neatly trimmed long beard. The man's deep, blue eyes had seen a lot of violence, and his smile said that he had learned from most of it. Angran Kolan was the best knight-trainer in the kingdom, and his boast was that he could train anyone with only one arm... mainly because he only *had* one arm.

Angran's left arm ended at the elbow, an old wound from his younger days during the border wars. He had a shield strapped to the upper arm and had learned to use it very effectively over the years—so much so that most knights still couldn't get in a hit on the old man. It sat a little higher than normal, but he moved quickly, despite his age.

"Sir Kolan, may I go up to the wall?" Lan asked, trying not to sound bored. He desperately needed to be doing *something*.

Angran sighed deeply and nodded. The poor kid was spoiling for a fight to prove himself and with his luck, he would get it. Angran had thirty soldiers and twenty knights under him at the Northern gate, all older veterans who were about to retire or had been disabled. They had only one horse, what with most of the men unable to ride effectively anyway. With them were the new King's Messengers, who Angran thought was a bit of a joke. He trusted the king, but at their age, they wouldn't amount to much in a fight. Still, he did like the young knight applicant though. the kid just needed to calm down a bit. The boy seemed vaguely familiar, too—but then again, at his age, didn't everyone? Angran looked over at the other children, all of whom were behaving nicely and talking with the other men. All but one of them. The young healer was off to the side looking like he wanted to be anywhere else but here. He had heard the kid was exceptional at his craft, but if this was his first battle that would explain his look.

Lan climbed up the ladder to the top of the wall where a soldier sat watching the plains for any movement. "Mind if I stand here for a while?" Lan asked.

"Suit yourself, young one. There isn't anything out there, nor is anything coming."

Lan huffed and walked the edge of the wall, staring out at the road as it wound its way north. He watched for a couple of minutes before something caught his eye. Lan swore the sun dipping below the horizon was playing with him because he saw a shadow crossing *sideways* across the grass in the distance. "Sir?" Lan turned to the soldier only to see the man stand and squint himself. Lan looked again and then he saw the black crowd on the road. "Sir Kolan!"

"Ware the rider!" the soldier standing next to Lan called out loudly, cutting Lan off in mid-sentence. The scout scrambled down and worked the gate with five other men, quickly opening it as the knights filed out to great whatever was coming.

❧

GUNTER RODE HARD FOR THE ROAD, HIS VISION BLURRED from the tears streaming down his face. He had seen his friends attack the ogrann to give him the chance to cross unmolested, many of them falling quickly. Behind him on the horse, Ellen swore but urged him to keep going. Gunter could feel her shooting her bow as he rode across the field, but at this distance, she only hit a few of the marks

"I'm going to have to wait until they get closer," Ellen said.

"Closer?"

"Yes, Gunter—I don't have any illusions that those beasts won't catch us in a little bit, possibly before we get to the gate. Ogrann can move fast when running."

"But why did the others sacrifice themselves then?" Gunter was confused and scared. He couldn't stop crying. Gunter held the reins tightly and guided the horse onto the packed earthen road, feeling the horse finally find an easy rhythm. The gate was in view but still a ways off— even moving this fast, it would take them a number of minutes to reach it. Minutes Ellen was saying they might not have.

"They sacrificed themselves because if they hadn't, we might never have made the road." Ellen looked back as she spoke and saw the ogrann running right for them. "They gave us a chance, at least. Which was more than we would have had otherwise." In a couple more seconds she could shoot the lead beast and try to hobble him. Ellen lifted her bow and took a deep breath, letting it out slowly, then loosed the arrow. She saw the beast stumble and slow, but he kept coming. "Faster if you can, Gunter; this is going to be close." Firing again and again, Ellen prayed silently to Davalar to watch over the fallen boys and the young one behind her.

Gunter saw they were gaining on the gate, and in his panic he started shouting, hoping whoever was guarding the walls could hear them. "Ogrann! Ogrann coming!" He saw the gate open as they came up the slope, their horse galloping at a speed that he had never thought possible; the wind wiped away his tears faster than they could fall.

Lan and Trav ran down the slope with a dozen soldiers to assess the situation. When they heard the rider start shouting, they looked at each other incredulously and rushed back to the gate. "Sir Kolan! Ogrann!" they both yelled at the same time.

Angran's eyes went wide as he heard the marauders were coming towards the city. He had fought ogrann before and he knew that they were in trouble if they couldn't brace the gates before the masters arrived. They needed to get that rider in here now! He pointed to two of his men. "Get the timbers ready to brace the gates!" he shouted, then turned to the kids. "All right, King's Messengers—time to earn your name. You there, girl." Angran had no idea what her name was, but he needed to get them working as a group or they were all in trouble.

"Kari, sir," she answered, quickly and politely

"Kari. Run to the Western gate and warn King Arian that there are ogrann at the Northern gate. Number unknown, but more than a few." Angran turned to the young man with the bow and handed him a much nicer weapon. "Vance, is it?" Angran saw the boy nod and tried to smile to make the young man more at ease, as Vance looked like he could throw up at any moment. "Take this and climb up on the wall. When you see an ogrann, shoot its eyes or its legs, if possible." That left the healer and the boy with the hammer. My, but he was a big one. "And you would be?"

"Tomas, sir."

"Well, Tomas, I need your arms to help with some lifting. We need to brace these beams against the gates to hold back those beasts, then we have to hold them in place when they start hammering on them. Think you can do that?"

"My father was a blacksmith, sir. I can hold." Tomas was

glad to have something to do, even if it seemed 'meaningless' as Lan would call it.

"Rider's in!" Lan called as he and Trav started closing the gates as quickly as they could. The ogrann were a mere fifty feet away as men piled on the gates, pushing harder to close them. As the beams were set in place they all breathed a little easier until the lookout called down.

"Sir! There must be almost one hundred of them!"

Lan heard the breath leave most of them men right there. *Almost one-hundred.* It was inconceivable. No gate could hold back that many ogrann.

"More like ninety—we dropped close to ten of them," Ellen said, dismounting and slapping the horse before Gunter could get off. "Live well, boy!" she called to the inexperienced rider as he held on for dear life. The kid would not be any help here—by the time that horse stopped, the fight would be over. *He's safer out in the city, for now,* Ellen thought, then turned to the knight who was barking orders. "I'm here to help, Sir knight. Point me in the direction of some arrows."

Angran pointed to where Vance stood on the wall, then turned to the gate as it groaned under the weight of the beasts. "More braces, men. Quickly!" Angran called. There was nothing else they could do. Ogrann hammered on the gates, and soon the first beams began to buckle. Soldiers arrived with more beams but they couldn't fit them unless the doors stopped buckling.

Lan saw what was happening with the gate, and time seemed to stop as he looked around. Kari had gone for the king, but it would take her a long time, even running, to get word to him. These men would all be dead and the ogrann would be inside the walls and at the backs of the defenders. There was only one thing to do. "Trav, I release you."

"What now?" Trav wasn't really listening. He was trying to

think of a way to stop a ravaging horde from blasting through the gates and eating them alive. He had never fought such a beast, but the sheer strength was intimidating.

"I release you from our bond." Lan drew his sword and started climbing the ladder up to the wall.

Angran saw the young one leaving the gates and called out furiously. "Get back on line, knight!" He strode over to the ladder, but another young knight stepped in his path.

"Sir, I know what he's doing." Trav was numb with the realization: Lan was doing something that scared the life out of him. Trav had seen frightened men before—hells below, he had frightened them personally half the time—but he could see the look on Lan's face. Trav knew he was going to his death. *How can he do that?* Trav wondered. Then, as if a weight had been lifted off of his shoulders, the brash knight suddenly understood. "The Code of the Knight."

"What are you babbling about, knight?" Angran had no idea what was going on, but it better resolve itself quickly or they would be in serious trouble.

"I never really believed in the Code before. I became a knight out of curiosity and as a boasting right, but now... That young knight applicant has shown me the Code really is something to die for." Trav looked Sir Kolan dead in the eyes. "Hold that gate and get ready the braces—we will buy you time." With that he was off, racing to the ladder to catch up with the young knight that had filled him with a purpose after a regretful life of shameless actions. Trav grabbed two shields off of a rack and climbed hard with one hand. "Wait, Lan!" Trav called, praying he wasn't too late.

Lan turned to see Trav climb up on the wall. The other knight tossed him a shield and smiled like he was going on his favorite hike. "What are you doing?" Lan asked. He'd never seen Trav like this before.

"I can't let a fellow knight charge into danger alone." Trav walked up and clapped Lan on the shoulder, holding back tears that would take too long to explain. "Now let's save that gate."

Lan nodded, a little confused but glad to not be doing this alone. At least they could go out together. He just hoped his father would've been proud. Lan walked to the edge and looked over, then lined his sword up to the biggest ogrann near the gate... and leaped off straight down on top of the beast, sword first.

"For Lythinall!" Lan cried, slamming into the beast, but he was thrown off to the side. The bards never got to *this* part in their stories. They always wrote that the knight smote the dragon or some such nonsense. In the songs, it was quick and easy. This was neither. Instead, Lan was rolling through their legs and stench, desperately trying to get to his feet.

"For Lythinall!" Trav copied Lan's cry and leaped down as well, but not sword first. Instead, he landed on the brute and wrapped his massive arms around the thing's throat, squeezing with everything he had. His shield dropped as the bands broke; he could hear the thing wheezing as he squeezed tighter. Blow after blow rained down upon his armor as other beasts tried to dislodge him, but he kept the pressure up.

Griff saw Lan climbing the ladder and knew that his fears were coming to pass. He'd had a dream last night that he was going to lose friends today, despite his ability. Griff knew this must be a part of his Oracle powers, but knowing that didn't make him feel any better about it. He closed his eyes and told himself that Davalar had foreseen this, that there was nothing he could do to help. Griff found a corner and sat, waiting until someone needed him. Then he heard Lan shout and started crying.

Ellen saw the young men drop into the throng of ogrann and

her mouth fell open. They would be bashed to pieces. "You there, boy! Any good with that bow?"

Vance smiled, fitted an arrow, and fired at the beast that Lan had dropped down on, taking it in the throat. 'I guess not," he said. "I was aiming for its eye." Vance chuckled and fired again, intent on saving his lifelong friend.

Ellen laughed and fired as well, taking another down with two arrows in its face. "That's all right—they die just as well with an arrow in the throat."

As he stood, Lan saw Trav, as well as his sword lying on the ground within reach. The ogrann were ignoring him for the moment, but that would soon change. As arrows rained down, he lunged for his weapon. As soon as it was in his hands he slashed another beast across the back of its legs. Lan struck low enough so that the thing fell to its knees, then reversed his swing, taking it across the throat. That was when the tree hit him in the back—at least it *felt* like a tree. Lan was pretty sure his spine was yelling at him, but he couldn't hear it over his head complaining. Instead, he decided to hit the ground and see if that helped. It didn't.

Trav saw Lan dropped by a massive punch from the largest brute in the crowd and let go of the ogrann he was holding as it fell to its knees. Once the arrows started, the other ogrann had stopped hitting him, thank the gods above. "Lan!" Trav swung his fist into the thing's head as hard as he could and made a dash for Lan. His back was very sore, but his armor had taken most of the beating. It helped he was a big man and could take a pounding. Trav reached down and grabbed the young knight by the arm, pulling him to his feet. "I got you." Trav smiled down at Lan. Then his world went black.

Lan got to his feet and looked at Trav just as an ogrann grabbed Trav's head and twisted with everything it had. *"Nooo!"* Lan screamed as Trav's lifeless body hit the ground. He scrambled to raise his sword and slashed wildly, anger directing his every movement. The ogrann beat his sword aside and bashed him hard in the chest, slamming him against the gate. Lan smiled.

"Why yous smile little?" Kragth asked, poised to smash this little thing to pieces.

"Because, you piece of filth, the gate felt sturdy when I hit it. You'll never get through it now." Lan knew he was done for, but at least the others would be safe until the king could get reinforcements here.

Griff heard Lan scream and something inside of him snapped. Davalar wasn't here. The God wasn't watching, waiting to tell Griff what to do. *That's not how this works, is it? It is all up to me.* Griff stood and ran to the gate. This was *right*, he could *feel* it. "Tomas, let go." Griff turned to all of the soldiers holding the braces. "All of you. Let go and throw wide the gates." His hands started to glow. The light traveled up his arms. Griff silently called to Davalar and offered himself completely for the power to save his friend. *Anything I have—for you*, he thought to the heavens; the answering warmth was all he needed.

"Are you *mad*, son? That young knight just died to get these gates sealed!" Angran couldn't understand what was going on.

"I can't explain how I know; all I know is that if we don't open those gates *right now* we are all doomed."

"I believe him, sir. Just listen to him." Tomas turned to Griff. "I trust you, Griff. You saved Sprout, and now you will save Lan. Hells below, maybe all of us." Tomas turned and forcibly pulled a brace off the door, shoving a bewildered soldier to the ground. That was when they all heard the call behind them: *"Throw open the gates!!"*

❦ 8 ❦

TO THE RESCUE!

Rhoe had been listening to Adrilian go on about elven customs for almost two hours. Not that he didn't find it all fascinating—he really did. It just wasn't what he wanted to discuss right now. He was in the presence of an elven archmage and wanted to talk about magic, but he didn't dare ask any questions for fear of sounding stupid. He glanced at Liss and smiled and how captivated she was about the unending list of council do's and don'ts. She was going to enjoy this a lot more than he was. Rhoe heard magical chimes sound through the rooms to let everyone know the tower doors had opened and excused himself, hoping the chimes meant Karsis had returned. Rhoe had a couple of questions that he had been thinking about, and what he had seen with his *sight* and felt more comfortable asking the man that trained him. He walked down the spiral staircase, which seemed slightly different than the last time he walked it, and turned a corner. The bard was flinging off a purple scarf that clearly wasn't his, along with something that looked to be a women's undergarment.

"Had a good time, did we?"

"*We*, my boy? No—*I*. I had a marvelous time while you've

207

been stuck here listening to my father go on about the council." Karsis laughed and patted Rhoe on the shoulder as he passed, intending to run right up and sit, but something made him stop. "What's the matter, Rhoe?" Karsis asked, turning slowly, in case he should be worried. If someone had infiltrated the house, this could get messy.

"I wanted to ask you a couple things. Without everyone here." Rhoe paused slightly, waiting for Karsis to nod his approval, then asked "Are you a wizard or a bard?"

Karsis laughed. He could see why the boy would be confused. Rhoe knew Karsis was an elf, so he likely assumed the 'bard' thing was a cover. "Well, dear boy... I'm both. I tested early as having the talent for being a bard, but my father trained me as a wizard as well. I can sing a room into a stupor with this voice." Karsis knew there was more Rhoe wanted to ask and wondered if the boy finally figured out his biggest secret. "What else is on your mind?"

"Well, I wanted to ask about what I saw around the city," Rhoe asked sheepishly. He felt stupid and almost didn't ask, but his curiosity was stronger than his humility.

"Go on. What have you been looking at with your *sight*, and what did it look like?" Karsis breathed a little easier. Common curiosity he could handle—divulging secrets was harder.

"Well, the fountains of the different elements looked like they were... *tied* together with some sort of magic... *string*?" Rhoe wasn't sure he was articulating the right words, but he hoped just the meaning came across.

"Ah, yes. Those spells were cast with Thread magic." Karsis saw the confused look on the boy's face and smiled. But the confused look went away in a flash, replaced with recognition.

"Oh! Like the sleep spell you placed on me in Daelyn?" Rhoe remembered waking up to being surrounded by threads of some kind, all weaving a silly pattern around and around him.

He had pierced the spell and woken up but hadn't thought about it again... until now.

Karsis stopped breathing. The boy was exactly right. "Yes, Rhoe," Karsis said very slowly, like he was testing the first ice on a winter lake. "I *did* use a thread sleep on you. I assumed it wore off early because you were simply waking naturally."

"No, I used my discipline and focused it into a single spike. Then I threw it at the threads, and after a loud, echoing snap, they dissolved." Rhoe didn't like the look on the bard's face right now; without realizing it, he even took a step back. "So what is a thread spell?" Rhoe asked meekly, trying to change the subject.

Someday Karsis intended to push the limits of this prodigy, but for now, he focused on what the young wizard wanted to know. "A thread spell is just like any other spell, except instead of letting the elements go off on their own, you use ether and weave them into 'threads.' With these 'threads,' wizards can make spells last longer than usual because the elements are tied to the spell until it is broken and don't have to be reigned in." Karsis saw the rapt look on Rhoe's face and laughed. "You're just soaking all this in aren't you?" The bard was amazed at the progress this young man had made since they left Daelyn all those months ago. *Months! Most wizards take years to accomplish what he has done in this time. And he's done things that only a rare few can do without pause,* Karsis thought, as he continued. "However, breaking a thread spell is almost impossible from outside, as they are set against such intrusions. It is far easier to attack them from within."

"You said *almost* impossible."

"Yes, I did. I always try to leave room for the unheard-of— like most of the things I've seen you do." Karsis heard his father coming down the stairs and rolled his eyes. "Looks like it's lecture time."

Liss followed Adrilian down the spiral staircase and went

over all the information he had given her. It wasn't so different than the court at the castle, but some deviations had floored her, mostly about etiquette and hair length. Then she noticed that the staircase seemed different, almost like it had changed since she had last walked it. *I must be overstimulated,* she thought as they came upon Rhoe and Karsis downstairs.

Adrilian walked up to his son and glared at him. "And did you bring me back a souvenir?" he asked playfully, then laughed at the look on Karsis's face. The wizard looked around and saw the purple scarf hanging on a corner table and plucked it up for his own. "Come upstairs—we have a bit more to talk about," Adrilian said and slapped Karsis on the shoulder. But as his hand touched his son's shoulder, the room seemed to vanish from his sight.

Adrilian was somewhere else again. This was the second time he had one of these strange visions, but this one felt even stranger. He was on a cliff facing the Sea of Irace, the waves crashing far below. Then he heard his brother's voice with others somewhere below him—maybe a ledge? Adrilian heard Dar'Krist mock someone he couldn't see and then the scene changed to a bird's-eye view. More importantly, Adrilian saw threads of magic surrounding him on the edges of his vision. This was Dar'Krist's mind! Not just any wizard could capture the Incarnation of Death and Corruption in a spell-like this, and that thought fell like a stone in his stomach. He was flung back then, as a deep female voice laughed over and over...

Adrilian stumbled and Karsis was there, holding his arm. "It's all right. It was just a vision." The old wizard said the words, but they just didn't seem to cut it right now.

"You've never had *that* kind of vision before—I could see you struggling." Karsis hadn't been worried about his father in well over two hundred years. Despite his general attitude toward his sire, it wasn't a feeling he relished.

"No, the sort of vision I'm getting now has been a new thing since you all arrived. It's by touch, so I think it's relevant to the current flow of time at least. Bad news, though—I think Ill'lyth has the Incarnation of Death in a spell meant to trap his mind. If she controls *him*, Everknight really is doomed... and we would be next." Adrilian straightened up and smoothed his red robes. "The good news is now we know about it and can work to correct it."

Karsis frowned. He had been reading his favorite book, *Dost Frein en Krist*, and it mentioned nothing about Ill'lyth trapping Dar'Krist. "I think we're in trouble. The prophecy doesn't mention this at all when it describes how Rhoe kills the Incarnation."

"Because he isn't supposed to kill him."

"All right, father—what did I miss this time?" Karsis knew he had to put aside his ego and get this right or they could all perish. Besides, his father hadn't been able to teach him anything in a very long time. He was intrigued.

Adrilian walked up the staircase in silence, smiling to himself. He knew this must be killing his son, but Karsis was wrong and they all had to know it before they went forth against this creature. Opening his door to the study, he grabbed a book off of the stand and flipped it open. He had his own copy of the prophecy. After all, one of his sisters had written it, even if she *was* human. "See here," he said, pointing to the open page. "The word 'Termin.' You're reading this in elvish as 'kill,' when it really is better translated to Auld tongue as 'stop.' You see, they never put in the ' in any of the elvish words they stole, and over time that's changed the meaning." Adrilian closed the book with a snap and looked at Karsis, but it was Rhoe who spoke first.

"So I'm just supposed to... stop him?" Rhoe actually thought that sounded worse. "Stop him from doing what?"

"Welcome to prophesy," Adrilian quipped. "Every answer brings ten new questions."

"First things first, let's get this council meeting over and get help to Everknight," Liss said. "If that woman can unleash the Incarnation of Death on the city, then it's even more imperative that we convince them to help us." She was feeling anxious now; she hated waiting.

"And as I've said before, it won't be easy to convince them, though I *do* have some things up my sleeves." Adrilian smiled at the looks on their faces, as if they just realized how quiet it was in the house.

"Wait... where is Liana?" Karsis asked in his serious tone.

Rhoe looked around. Avaryn was sleeping in the corner, but the little faerie was nowhere to be seen. "Yeah, this can't be good."

"The ambassador to the faeries is doing her job. And I think she must be doing it rather well if she still isn't back yet." Adrilian basked in the others' incredulous looks and then walked out of his study, putting the book back as he went. "Now, now—it's fine. Liana is with the very people that are going to be helping you. Come—it's a rather long walk to the council chambers and I want to take in some sights as we go." Adrilian brushed past them, whistling a merry tune as he went down the spiral staircase.

Liss couldn't believe that Liana was out on her own and there weren't any alarm bells ringing. She shook her head and followed the old seer, grabbing Rhoe's hand and dragging him along behind her.

Karsis stood behind in the room and waited till everyone else was almost downstairs. He had known that Liana was the key to getting the council, but he thought they were supposed to bring her. All these decades of learning and that old elf was *still* showing him how to do things. Karsis tossed his auburn curls and fixed his long coat before descending the stairs. He was ready for the council meeting... but were they ready for them?

MET EN KITH, TIR-LANAN

He looked out at the sea of faces and grinned. The room was full to capacity, a sight rarely seen at all in Tir-Lanan these days. Elves lined the walls, standing in the back of the hall and whispering to each other in anticipation of the events about to transpire. Some of the council members had pushed for a closed hearing, but Mas'ril wasn't having any of that. He was the High King of Tir-Lanan, and though this was a council, he could evoke the King's Right once per year, which gave him complete rule over one decision. Using that right this early in the year spoke volumes to the rest of the city. Hence the whispering and gossip that ran rampant throughout the city.

Mas'ril Moonriver was an imposing elf, standing over six-feet—tall for an elf— and weighing over fourteen stones. His long, white hair was in three braids which fell all the way to the floor, and the sword at his side shimmered in its sheath. Mas'ril was over six hundred years old and had become High King very young. Even with all those years of experience, with all he had seen over the centuries, this meeting still concerned him. The humans coming here was nothing new; they came every generation to pledge their fealty to the elves so that they might continue to prosper under their shadow. At least, that was the way it had begun.

Over the past few decades, the human kingdom had been thriving on its own, weathering every storm without assistance from the elves. Until now, that was. Mas'ril thought about his fellow councilmen and was saddened how they had all but forgotten these humans were the descendants of the heroes who had helped them all those years ago. The humans had stood against the sorcerers, fighting and dying alongside the elves, earning the right to co-exist with them. Instead of honoring that, the elves had secluded themselves and hidden from the humans, making them bow to the structures of old for a promise that was never fulfilled. True, he had been High King back then, but he was a different man these days. Over the last hundred-odd years he had watched his people stagnate, drowning in seclusion. With nothing new to learn or experience, the elves were wasting away—it had taken his daughter's death for him to speak out on the subject.

Lil'lin Moonriver had died at the hands of an elf who had let the darkness within consume him, all for knowledge that never helped him anyway. The day he found her body, Mas'ril pledged to set the elves free from their stagnant prison, even if it killed them. Mas'ril had tried every way he could imagine to overturn his own decree but had been thwarted by the council at every turn. The high king couldn't just change the law, and each time he had tried to end their seclusion the council had gathered support from the elves of the city, and even the King's Right couldn't help him then. Now, however, at long last, the day may finally have arrived. Mas'ril knew change was needed to save his people but he needed the council to be on his side for something this big.

That's why this meeting needed to be public. He didn't need the entire city to hear the humans ask for aid, but he needed them to see what the humans had brought with them. Mas'ril was not without his own eyes and ears within the city and the first reports of a faerie had swelled his heart. Well, that and the news of the human assaulting Maldren, Syll curse that elf. For the lost faeries to send a representative at a time of crisis like this could only mean that they were close to rejoining the world. Add to that the presence of a unicorn and it made for the sort of grand show the elves of Tir-Lanan desperately needed. At least, one could hope.

Mas'ril snapped out of his inner reverie as the council entered and took their seats. The hush in the packed room was almost palpable as they filed in quietly, scorn on most of their faces. They were used to getting their way, and this little turn of events had them pouting. *Do them some good once in a while,* Mas'ril thought as he smiled at them all in turn.

Maldren Ulryntar came in and sat, looking out of place and distant, like a child whose favorite toy had been taken away. Next came the lady of style, Ciril'ven Draken'ar, dressed in a long gown of deep-red scales with her hair in twin ponytails. She looked impassive as she took her seat—not upset, but rather on the verge of being disappointed. Sinaron Hana'ryr came in staring at the ceiling for some reason, then looked up as if he didn't know where he was. Sinaron smiled at the high king and took his seat, talking quietly to himself—or his God, whichever decided to answer him today. Magiciel Ash'ashlyn walked in wearing a frown but still seeming pleased somehow, like she had won a battle but wasn't sure that she'd wanted to win after all. Then came the newest member.

Galfren Duran'ryn had only been on the council for six months, joining after his father had passed on to twilight at the very young age of six-hundred and thirty winters. The young elf, only one-hundred winters himself, was the last surviving heir. Most of his family had died in the war of the Incarnation and had dwindled soon after that. His mother was lost, presumed dead in a magical accident while traveling the ether. Galfren was only five feet tall and wore his long, white hair hanging straight and unbound. He had crimson eyes and a pleasant smile that hid a saddened demeanor and restless spirit. He sat down last and actually jumped when the gavel hit the table to call the meeting to order.

"Greetings to you all on this day, Mas'ril said, rising to address the room. "Let it be known that today's council will be held in the common tongue for the benefit of the visiting humans."

The council seats were on a raised dais five feet above the main floor, behind a long, marble table that ran the length of the dais. The high king was seated all the way to the left, apart from the others and three feet higher. Mas'ril watched as the young human boy stood slowly.

"Ins zren dost kith an Jal," Rhoe said, looking directly at the high king. He bowed slightly and sat once more, ignoring the chuckles that came from both Adrilian and Karsis. He heard the back of the room start whispering loudly and smiled to himself. After the attack from that elf at the front gates, Rhoe felt the elves needed to know that he was not just any outsider, and he thought addressing the king in his own tongue would send that message loud and clear.

"I don't know what he said—some of those words were new to me. I heard 'we' and 'you.' That's about it," Liss said, leaning over to Karsis. "Did he insult someone?" Liss shifted uncomfortably in her chair, which seemed to be fashioned out of a mix of wood and crystal. Pretty, but hard on the backside.

He turned to her with a grin, placing his hand on her shoulder. "My dear, he *thanked* the elven people and their king on behalf of us all." When he responded, Karsis didn't bother to whisper in the slightest. In fact, he raised his voice slightly so the whole room would hear him

"Karsisendriel, to my knowledge you do not have the floor, nor are you standing. Can the humans please refrain from commenting until called upon?" Ciril'ven smiled the entire time she spoke, not angry at all, but she still wanted to put the person higher than her in society on the spot. It almost worked.

"Karsisendriel?!" Rhoe said it a little louder than he intended, but he couldn't help it.

"Not now, Rhoven." Karsis stood slowly and bowed deeply to the council, his auburn curls actually brushing the floor. "My apologies, dear Ciril'ven. I was unaware I offended you so much—maybe dinner later? Maybe some wooing?"

"Wait—let's get back to the fact you called him *Karsisendriel*." Rhoe knew he was so going to get in trouble over this, but he couldn't pass this one up. The glare from his mentor seemed like it could melt stone, but he was saved by the High King.

Mas'ril brought the gavel down again, a little harder this time, though truth be told he was enjoying himself. "Order in the council." The high king waited a second for the mumblings to die down before continuing. "Please sit, *Karsisendriel*, so we can begin the proceedings," Mas'ril said with a wink to Rhoe. The high king was relieved that the famed wizard sat without further prompting, leaving Ciril'ven blushing uncomfortably. Mas'ril would have to look into why that was later; he could always use leverage against that woman.

Maldren stood and brushed off his purple robes. "I call the first order of business. Frantril of the Sran'en kith." Maldren sat before anyone could object and a young elf stood and droned on about signatures and papers.

Liss knew that it was clearly a distracting move, and one she didn't have time for. Her people were in imminent danger—for all she knew could be fighting this very instant. Countering the move would take time though, and without more knowledge of the elven ways, she would just have to improvise. Liss looked around and realized that she should stick to what she knew. So she stood up, walked to the front of the room, and grabbed a chair from the front row, displacing the poor elf who was sitting in it with an apology and a winning smile. Murmurings and curious glances darted around the room, but no one could interrupt the poor elf who was talking as long as he held the floor. If they did, it would breach the whole meeting—although Liss thought that tradition seemed stupid, if they asked her.

Everyone in the room assumed she was going to merely sit in the chair, but the assembly erupted when she brought that very chair crashing down on the edge of the council table right in front of Maldren in a shower of wooden and crystal splinters. "Enough!" she shouted in a stern voice which resembled her father's. Elven wardens rushed in from every entrance, ready for anything, but Mas'ril waved them down. The rest of the council wasn't so inclined.

"Young lady, I don't know—" Maldren tried to sound outraged, but after being attacked in his own home, he was more than a little worried. She didn't give him time to finish.

"That is correct, councilman—you don't know." Liss turned to address the high king, ignoring the council altogether, but Galfren stood and pointed at her. "Ash'anti fra hadar dosit em'ren!"

Liss felt the air solidify around her. Panic welled up in her chest, but she heard Rhoe call out across the din.

"Ash'anti, fra rels ea!" Rhoe stood and countered the spell, then smiled condescendingly at the young elf who had tried to cast a spell on Liss.

Liss broke free and spun towards the elf that cast at her— who, despite his youth, was still hundreds of years older than her—and gave her best death's head grin, but a voice from the side stopped it from going further.

"Let her talk, Galfren. The princess has earned it," Delain said evenly as she walked towards the council table with three other wardens. "Besides, you'll hurt yourself if you keep pushing them." Delain nodded to Liss and told the other three wardens to start picking up the pieces of the chair. The young elf who was speaking for Maldren finally sat down, unsure what to do at this point. The room waited with bated breath to see what would happen next.

"I'm guessing that you are Princess Allissana of Everknight?" Mas'ril wasn't upset—on the contrary, he was thrilled she was upsetting the balance of power in this council meeting.

Liss took a deep breath and almost began reciting the speech that her father had told her to give. Somehow, though, it didn't seem right. Not with the danger looming over the city— her city, someday. Instead, Liss closed her eyes and turned toward the crowd. She spread her arms out wide, as the faeries did. "My name is Princess Allissana Everknight and I am here today to ask the elven people for help. A woman from your past has come back and is attacking our capital. She has under her control the Incarnation of Death. This being has already laid waste to several villages and slain countless people. We've tried attacking him—the faeries even repelled him, but their champion was slain."

Liss paused for a second to let that sink in, then continued. "Yes! Ill'lyth G'harr has returned to life somehow and is coming for Everknight. If the city falls she will have all of Lythinall. Then she will come here." Liss knew they were whispering about the faeries, but she didn't want to say more about them yet —let the bait dangle a bit more.

Maldren stood, shaking with rage. "And how do you, a mere girl of at most twenty winters, know what a powerful archmage will do or won't do? Have you talked with her yourself? Conspired with her perhaps?" Maldren saw his way in and took it without thinking. "And what of the faeries? I do not see any faeries here!" It was a risky move and backfired faster than he could've imagined.

Sinaron Hana'ryr, the oracle of Davalar, laughed out loud at the ridiculous accusation. Before anyone else could attack the pompous windbag of a councilman, he said, "Surely you jest, Maldren. Everyone in this room who knows that name can guess what Ill'lyth will do. And, lest you forget, the Princess travels with Karsis." The elves around the room nodded and looked at Maldren, disgusted at his attempt to smear a young girl. Sinaron's work done for the day, he leaned back and awaited his chance to escape this stuffy city. He caught Adrilian's eye and smiled; they both knew what was coming.

Kilyan Lightblade had never known what holding a bolt of lightning felt like, though he had some clue now. He had sat down in the back of the room with Liana safely tucked away in a magical pouch for just the right time. Kilyan thought that was going to be the easy part. Gods above, was he wrong. Since the meeting had started, Liana had wriggled and fought to get free in order to see her friends. It was all Kilyan could do to tell her that she had to wait. Once the princess smashed the chair, Liana burst free with a giggle, but Kilyan grabbed her quickly and held her back. Now they were actually discussing faeries he knew it was time. "All right, little one—time for your grand entrance."

"I don't want to now." Liana pouted inside the magical bag, her voice echoing out around him.

"Wait... what? Why not?" This was disastrous, and now the elves around him were looking at him again.

"You've kept me locked up in here and now I guess I'll just stay here." Liana wasn't really going to, but she wanted to teach Kilyan a lesson in manners; she felt Avaryn would be proud. Then she heard someone say "I do not see any faeries here!" and knew that he was right; it was time. "Oh, all right. I suppose I can go meet everyone." Liana heard an elf laugh and mention Karsis as she flew straight up and over to the table like a hummingbird. "You said something about faeries? I think you mean me!"

Collectively the room stopped breathing.

"There she is," Karsis quipped amidst the silence.

Sadly, Maldren was the first to recover. "Who is doing this... this... trick?" It couldn't be real. Faeries were gone. End of story. Then he was holding his nose as blood flowed freely from where Magiciel's fist had connected with his face.

"If you utter one more word, Maldren, I swear by the very faerie in this room that I *will* end your life before the High King himself." Magiciel was on the verge of tears. *Faeries*! Her dreams were filled with faint memories of good times gone by. All that came rushing back the moment this beautiful, tiny miracle flew up to them.

Liana flew right up to Maldren and stopped inches from his face, then smiled. "Do I look like a trick to you?" She tweaked his nose and flew back as Galfren grabbed for her. "Hey!" She saw the utter hatred on the young elf's face and knew that she was in trouble. She had heard Karsis speaking earlier, but now that everyone had stood up she had lost him in the crowd. Liana was scared for the first time in her life. Before the angry elf tried magic on her she did the first thing she could think of... Liana blew her whistle.

The very tiny whistle around her neck was special and had been around her neck for years. It had been given to her by Avaryn—she never asked how he got it—and when she blew it he was supposed to come to her aid. She'd had never tried it before; she'd never had a need. "Avaryn! I need you!" Liana called, her voice filled with fear as the elves crowded around her.

"Oh dear Gods, Rhoe get back!" Karsis called out as he heard the little faerie calling for Avaryn. He knew what she had done... and what was about to happen. Rhoe was already moving to get to Liana's side, but listened to Karsis and moved back quickly, telling others near him to move back, just in case.

Then it happened.

Avaryn appeared out of nowhere in a cloud of mist. The unicorn reared up on his hind legs and neighed loudly, warning all around him that he would use force if necessary. *Know this, all of you! This little one is under my protection—attack her at your folly!* Avaryn sent to every mind that he could sense in the room, even the ones that were shielded. Most of those he broke through and the few he couldn't would still have headaches for days.

"*Hold!*" Mas'ril stood and whispered to the air to ring the gongs on either side of the room. The loud bass sound of the gongs was a warning in the council hall that the wardens were ready. When the assembly calmed a bit and backed away from the unicorn in the room —he'd never thought he have to think about this particular scenario—Mas'ril slowly walked around the table and down to the floor, approaching the unicorn and faerie with arms wide open. The high king remembered the faerie customs.

Liana turned to the rest of the council. "See, he knows I'm real." Then she stuck her tongue out and flew over to Avaryn. "Thank you, Avaryn. I was so scared."

You've never blown that thing since I gave it to you. I thought you were dying. His sending would have been a laugh if he were capable of laughter. Then he turned his attention to the old elf, bowing his head slightly. He actually knew this man. *Greetings, Mas'ril. How have you been?*

Mas'ril froze, then recognition blossomed on his face. Could it be? Avaryn? From all those centuries ago? "As High King, I greet you in the name of Tir-Lanan. No harm shall come to either of you in this city as long as I draw breath."

"My High King?" Liana flew up with a serious face.

"Yes, dear one?"

"Are you going to help the humans?" This was the real part

of her strategy. She had baited Kilyan and his friends with what they so desperately needed, intending to force the elves, if need be, to help her friends. Liana could tell how much the elves longed for the faeries, so she figured she could lure out their help with the promises of the faeries return. Liana was excitable, not stupid.

"Well, no decision has been made as yet. Why do you ask?" Mas'ril had a feeling that his council hall was about to get exciting again. *Maybe I will even get to see Maldren cry. Wouldn't* that *make my century?* he thought.

Liana puffed out her tiny chest and landed on Avaryn's back. "I have been given leave to assure you that if you help the humans and open your doors to let the elves visit the world once more, then the faeries will return to not only the world but this city as well." It wasn't *exactly* what the Lurien had said, but it was close enough.

The room exploded in shouts and exclamations, all of them positive. Many who had only dreamed of this day now wept openly. Maldren sat back— he had to admit that he had been outmaneuvered spectacularly. The best part, of course, was that he didn't much care. Faeries were his weakness, which is why he was so upset by the thought of being tricked by someone using them against him. During all the years he'd grown up, he had loved faerie stories and still—to this day—loved to read about them. Maldren raised his hand slowly, eyeing Magiciel carefully as she slowly turned towards him. "May I speak, High King Mas'ril?"

Mas'ril flinched but waved the elf on. "As long as your heart does not speak in anger, Maldren, then yes." The high king eyed Magiciel and she sat down. a smile on her face.

"I say we help." The words, spoken plainly and without pomp and circumstance, floored every single elf in the room, up to and including Karsis.

Karsis walked forward and cleared his throat. "What say you, High King Mas'ril? Will the city of Tir-Lanan come to Lythinall's aid?" The bard knew that they needed a vote and that the vote couldn't be taken until all cases were brought to the table, but after the way this council meeting had gone so far, he was positive some of the rules could be bent, if not shattered outright.

Mas'ril rubbed his hand on his chin in contemplation. It *was* against the rules, but in dire times a vote of consequence could be called for in an emergency. But was it an emergency? "I would like to actually see the city if you wouldn't mind. Warden's?" Mas'ril sat back as the head warden stepped forward with his new apprentice following in his wake. Both stared openly at the unicorn and faerie. "Oh, and Boril'ran? Thread the portal." The high king knew they wouldn't need the portal for just a quick glance; he had a bad feeling about this.

Boril'ran raised his brow and looked around for Adrilian. "Care to help me with this, Seer?" Boril'ran knew a threaded viewing this large would require a large amount of both power and skill, and it would be easier with the two of them working together. That way, if anyone tried anything he could still defend himself. People always called him cynical, but you could never be too careful. As Adrilian came over, Boril'ran turned to the unicorn. "If I may ask, majestic one—how did you get in here past the wards?"

Avaryn turned to the man and bowed his head. *I am magic, wizard. Nothing can technically stop me from going anywhere I choose, except knowing where it is I have to go,* Avaryn sent to both him and the High King.

"But how did you know where to go?"

The whistle.

"Ingenious."

I know.

Then Adrilian was ready and they worked the casting. All they needed was a large body of liquid—there was a pool for just this reason in the council hall, usually used for viewing parts of the city—and a lot of skill: hence the need for the Head Warden and Seer to work together. Everyone inched forward and pushed to get a better look. When the scene came into focus, what they saw made every elf on the council raise their hands simultaneously in favor of rushing to Lythinall's aid right there on the spot.

The city was besieged on two fronts by thousands of men; on the third, a host of ogrann was approaching fast. Behind the beasts, watching beside a companion clad in tattered, black clothes could only be Ill'lyth G'harr. The view of the skying was high enough that she probably couldn't sense it, but Boril'ran pulled it back further just in case as Adrilian tied the last thread. Every elf recognized her from their history, and some knew her personally—all those gathered knew how bad this was.

"Gods above! Father..." Liss was devastated at the sight of her city under attack, and her body moved involuntarily towards the pool of water. Rhoe was there in a second, holding her and turning her away from the sight.

"It's alright, Liss. We'll help them." Rhoe looked to Karsis. The bard's face was serious.

"We need to go now, Rhoe. If Ill'lyth is left unchecked, she will unleash the Incarnation very soon." Karsis turned to the high king, who studied the scene with a trained eye. "How soon can help arrive?"

"It won't take long—maybe a few moments." His heart went out to the defenders at the odds they were facing. Before Boril'ran pulled back, he had seen mere children fighting at the northern gate.

Sinaron stepped down from the dais, a smile on his face and a bag on his shoulder. "And about the decree, High King? Will you accept the offer from the faeries? Will you let the city be open once more?"

Mas'ril turned to the rest of the room and to the tiny ambassador of the faeries they all loved and missed so much. "How could I say no? How could *any* of us say no?" Mas'ril saw Magiciel stand and step forward as well and knew what was coming. At her side, she wore her father's sword—not her regular weapon of choice. She favored daggers when in the city, so Mas'ril knew what she must be thinking; both her and the Oracle.

Karsis hadn't planned on leaving now—or through a portal, at that—but after what he had seen, they had no choice. "Rhoe and I have to go and confront Ill'lyth, hopefully to stop her and possibly end her life once more, though the latter's a bit of a stretch." Karsis laughed at the absurdity of it. He was very good, but even *he* had limits.

"I'm coming as well," Adrilian said as he motioned for the young apprentice of Boril'ran to come take his place. "Together we can distract her long enough for Rhoe to stop the Incarnation."

Illiandral gulped but didn't dare to second guess the famous Seer of Tir-Lanan. He stepped up and, using his *sight*, gently took the threads of magic from the red-robed wizard. Illiandral glanced over at his master and saw Boril'ran was smiling at him. His confidence swelled and he focused on holding the portal open, letting the head wizard guide him. With the thread tied, it was just a matter of concentration, but even he could feel the pull from the sheer size of the portal.

"If that woman *is* controlling the Incarnation, how am I supposed to set him free?" Rhoe asked. He knew this would be the fight of his life. He had not faced the thing that only looked like a man since the beach near the Hidden Vale. Rhoe felt more confident now but still knew that he was outmatched.

Rhoe knew a few tricks he hadn't tried yet, but he would only use them if he absolutely had to.

Karsis turned to his student and looked directly into Rhoe's young eyes. "Listen, Rhoe. You're going to have to do what I did with Caerlyn. You're going to have to go inside of his mind and free him from her control from within." Karsis saw the incredulous look, not only on Rhoe's face but on the faces of the elves nearby who had heard. He ignored them and went on. "Unfortunately, it is more than likely a thread spell. You will have to slip through it, then unravel it once you're in. I have no idea how you are going to accomplish this, but I do have faith in your ability to figure it out. After all, you've been taught by the best."

"Well, the second best," Adrilian said as he walked by, saying his goodbyes to N'vea and some others.

"You keep thinking that," Karsis muttered without looking the old elf in the eyes.

Liss stepped up to follow them, but Karsis stopped her. The bard stepped in front of her with such sorrow in his eyes that she actually took a step back. 'What? What's wrong?"

"You can't come, Allissana. We are going to travel through the ether a great distance and the forces that pull at you on a trip like this will more than likely kill the baby." Karsis was trying not to cry; he knew how this was going to hit her. An impossible decision lay in front of the Princess of Everknight, but her parents would understand... if they lived through this.

"What? No! But..." Liss was at a complete loss for words; her heart torn asunder. Rhoe was leaving her for a fight that could very well end his life and she couldn't come? She couldn't go to her father's side and help her own city? Tears instantly crept down her face, like rivulets of anguish, and some of the elves found themselves crying despite not knowing why.

Tiny splinters of wood and crystal floated off the ground without any apparent reason. Some elves noticed and started backing up. No one but Karsis and Adrilian knew what was causing it, and both knew there was absolutely no time to get into it. "Rhoe, say goodbye, and let's go—fate of the land and all that," Karsis said as he wiped away his unfailing tears.

Sinaron stepped up and laid his hand on the Princess's shoulder. "I will protect your city with all that I have. Fear not, brave girl. If we succeed, I see a great future for you and your family." Sinaron moved on next to Rhoe. He began chanting quietly and pointed to the Western gate. He passed through the viewing portal, disappearing in a quiet flash.

"I, as well, will spend what life I have left defending your city, brave girl," Magiciel said as she looked at the city with trepidation. Illiyana could still be there, or she could be dead. Either way, Magiciel would defend the city that had sheltered her blood all these years without fail. Magiciel pointed to the Eastern gate and passed through. As she did, a great flash of brilliant light came from the North gate

Rhoe embraced Liss with his powerful arms and kissed her on the forehead. "I love you. Always remember that." Then he turned to leave as Karsis and Adrilian lined up to pass through the portal as well. He pointed at where Ill'lyth was and chanted softly.

"You *will* come home to me, Rhoven Whiteheart!" Liss cried out as she felt a pulse of magic surge and the air snag at his robe. It was like her very presence was casting magic to hold him there. It didn't last, but it shocked Rhoe enough for him to turn, then look at her belly with a smile. Then he was gone; they were all gone. Tears swelled and ran down her face, like the spring-fed river she had fallen into those many months ago. Liss ran from the council hall in frustration and anger. She fled down the cobbled streets without purpose, angry at the gods for keeping her here while everyone she loved faced certain death. Liss never heard Liana yell after her that she knew what to do.

Liana was drowned out in a sea of noise. Liss couldn't hear her after the devastating news she couldn't go home through the glowy portal thing. Liana flew up and shouted but no one even acknowledged her. Liss ran off, and as she went by Liana screamed, "LissIknowwhattodo!" But Liss didn't stop.

Hold on, dear one. I can get you to her, Avaryn sent as he moved through the sea of elves. The High King was calling for the wardens to gather in the defense of Everknight and there were no shortages of volunteers. Avaryn cleared through the mess and out the main doors, galloping after the princess.

"Can you poof her there, Avaryn?" Liana asked, even as was scared of the idea that had entered her head. She knew that it could work—there was nothing faster in all the world, or so she was always told—but it was dangerous.

Alas, Liana, I cannot. For the same reasons that she couldn't go through the ether, Avaryn answered sadly. With a final burst of speed, Avaryn passed the princess and turned, rearing high on his back legs. He had an inkling as to what Liana was getting at—it would be interesting, to say the least.

Liss saw Avaryn and Liana and skidded to a stop, collapsing in her grief. She hugged the unicorn's leg as if she was a child holding a teddy bear. "They're gone, Liana! I can't lose him. I can't!"

"I know what to *do,* silly!" The tiny faerie spoke slowly to get her point across.

"What Liana? What can we do?"

One word, spoken by the smallest of faeries. One word, yet it had such an impact on all their destinies that it seemed to reverberate around the city with tiny shock waves.

One word: "Dragon."

NORTHERN GATE, CITY OF EVERKNIGHT

"Throw open the gates!!" King Arian bellowed with everything he had. He saw the failing gate and knew they didn't have much chance of holding back whatever it was on the other side. So, element of surprise it was. Arian also could tell someone was in trouble on the other side. Obviously, that's where he needed to be.

Soldiers threw the gates wide, and Griff caught Lan with one hand as the young knight fell backward out of the ogrann's grasp. With the other hand, Griff pointed at the brute in front. "Davalar's light take you!" he called and felt the warmth cascade down his arm. A brilliant light flashed out from his hand, cutting through the first ogrann and the five beasts behind him, burring them all to cinders.

As the flash faded, Arian rode right into the sea of ogrann, slashing about him with perfect form. He had seen Lan pulled from the other side of the gate and longed to hear that story later. In fact, Lan's bravery inspired him. "For Lan! For Everknight!" Arian called, rallying his troops to his side. To his surprise, his call was answered from *behind* the host of ogrann.

Aeric Savar was alone. After his new recruits had drawn the ogrann away so Gunter could get to the city, things had gone from bad to horribly wrong. One young man stumbled, and when two others stopped to help him up they all died, crushed by ogrann fists coming down on them. Aeric had rushed in, but it was too late. The rest of the retreat was a mess, as most of the young men who remained were crying, desperately trying to keep the brutes away with frantic swings. Once the ogrann had given up and chased after the horse and rider headed toward the city, Aeric had gathered the remaining recruits and brought them off the road. Heed faced a difficult decision: head back to River Vale with them now, or carry on alone and leave them behind. Aeric could just make out the city where they were, but with the fighting as fierce as it was, he didn't think the recruits would live through any engagement.

As he debated his course of action, Aeric had heard the distant call from the northern wall. "For Lythinall!" His hair stood up on the back of his neck; he made up his mind right then. He was needed. Aeric drew his sword and made his way quickly towards the gate, trying to keep a low profile until he could strike. He saw the big knight's brave death, then saw the other young one slammed against the gate by the large ogrann. Aeric was at the bottom of the slope, preparing to rush the enemy's flank when he heard his king. *His King!* Aeric answered with his own rallying cry as soon as Arian shouted his: "For Everknight and glory!"

Aeric leaped into the fray, slashing the backs of the knees of the ogrann closest to him as he fought his way to his king. The brutes, once a controlled group, were falling apart, but they were no less dangerous as a disorganized mob In fact, it may actually have been worse. Aeric dodged and rushed in, coming up under a smaller ogrann and stabbed upward into its throat, then stepping away as another grabbed for him. The Lord of River Vale took hit after hit on his armor. He felt every blow but kept fighting toward Arian. The arrows helped—he thanked the gods for whoever was up on the wall shooting—and soon he stood beside King Arian near the gates, daring any to try and pass them.

Arian had no choice but to dismount as an ogrann grabbed his horse's head and twisted viciously, killing the animal instantly and throwing the body aside. Arian took the ogrann's head off with Chalice and attempted to rein in his rage; he needed a calm head if they were to hold this gate. *And I stationed the children here! I could have killed them all. How did they know? And where in the* Hells *did all these ogrann come from?* His thoughts flashed through his mind quickly before he finally saw who had answered his call—it was Aeric Savar!

Arian marveled at The Lord of River Vale as the man fought like a dervish through the throng of ogrann, finally making it to his side. "Well, well. Fancy meeting you here," Arian said shortly as they worked to keep the beasts back. It wouldn't be long before the ogrann were brave enough to band together and storm the pair, but for now, the chaos seemed to be keeping them hesitant.

"I figured you may need an extra sword. Or three." Aeric was already winded. It was a long run behind these beasts, and he sorely missed his horse. This fighting on the ground was for stronger men.

"Throw open the gates!!"

Sprout stopped dead as the voice echoed all through the city. She knew that voice and it sounded like it came from the northern gate. "The King!" Sprout turned and touched Rythal on the shoulder and ran for the gate. "Tag your it!" Sprout had to see what was going on. *Maybe it is a real-life war!*

Graf, too, heard that proclamation, and his heart sank. It was indeed from the north, and that meant that the gate the kids were guarding had been hit after all. Not only hit, but badly enough that the king was now there. The Incarnation of Shadows gave up on stealth and went for sheer speed, rounding the corners like a man who had trained all his life to run. The wind rushing by him made his skin itch and his eyes water more than normal, but he plowed on. After three blocks it started to physically hurt but he was almost there. Graf passed Sprout and Rythal, but a moment later Rythal appeared ahead of him, smiling as he held out his hand to touch the Incarnation of Shadows.

"He told me to save you."

"Thanks, kid!" Graf called as he passed. Then he dodged to the side as a form landed beside him and started running in step with him. He caught his balance and ran next to the white-haired elf, smiling devilishly. "I knew you'd show up," Graf said as a matter-of-fact.

Illiyana smiled. "I'm not here for *you*, dear man. I'm here for the children." Illiyana ran breathlessly next to this human, impressed at his control and speed. They had left Sprout far behind and now ran on towards the gate.

"Not the children—just her. Am I right?" Graf could see the worry on her face; this was personal for her.

"Shut up and get ready to fight," Illiyana said with a scowl. Damn this man to the Deep Hells for seeing into her soul like that. Who was he anyway? The scene that met them as they approached the gate was pure chaos. Knights and soldiers gathered around the gate, preparing to face the host of ogrann that were on the verge of storming into the city. Soldiers hauled barricades from the side to the front of the gate, while others handed out extra weapons. The two figures who stood in the ogrann's way were bleeding and battered but gave no ground. Illiyana looked at Graf and nodded gravely. She knew that by going to their aid she would be exposed for what she was, but if she didn't, Sprout and the other children might die.

Graf smiled. He looked at the men fighting to save the city and back to the elven woman. He could see the worry on her slim face. "They will be grateful and will welcome any assistance."

"And afterward?" Illiyana called over the din of battle.

"We have to live through this first, right?" Graf drew two daggers and launched them over the king's shoulder. They buried themselves in the eye of an ogrann who was advancing on the man. Graf was impressed—Arian never lost a step. He and Illiyana slid right past the soldiers and lined up with the King and the Lord so the four of them together held the gate. For the time being, at least.

Griff had healed Lan and now was trying to keep him down. "Listen, I've done what I can but those bones will still be sore. You need to rest now." The young man's body was whole but still fragile for the time being. He had taken quite the beating out there.

"I've got to get to the king." Lan was so surprised to be alive that he was in shock. Add that to the king being here—and using his name as a rallying cry!—and, well, he just *had* to get to his feet. Then he saw Graf and a new lady speed through and join the defense of the gate. With a groan he lay back down, giving into the blackness of rest. "I'll just..." he began. Then he was asleep.

Angran walked over and smiled down at the young healer. "I'm sorry son—we have to move you back. This could get bad soon if they get past us." The old knight was impressed with the young ones, he had to admit. That Tomas kid was a powerhouse when it came to moving things and the archer was proving invaluable since all their marksmen were at the other two gates.

"Thanks, we'll move back over—" Griff stopped dead as two familiar figures appeared around the far corner. Sprout and Rythal! Griff felt his entire world shift sideways in that instant. He knew that everything hinged on this moment. It was one of those moments that is key not only to this world but to the shape of *everything*. He had no idea how he knew, but as sure as the sun rises it was right at that instant that everything went wrong.

The ogrann made a concentrated push at the four defenders, trying to isolate them and get through the gate. They slammed into the barricades, impaling themselves on the sharp beams, the ones behind them pushing them out of the way even as those who were impaled struggled to get free. The soldiers and knights met them with steel but were a feeble defense against the gruesome tide. Within seconds, Tomas was down with a blow to his head and Griff lost sight of him in the chaos.

Ellen saw the ogrann break through and turned her bow back inside the walls, taking shot after shot but doing little amidst the throng of enemies. She saw the boy next to her go rigid and followed his gaze. A little girl stood about fifty feet in front of the rushing monsters and the look on the girl's face was one of pure horror. Ellen fired arrow after arrow at the ogrann heading towards her but it was too late. Or it seemed as if it was until the boy leaped off the wall.

"No!" Ellen called after him, but he was already rolling on the ground and running with a limp towards the girl.

Vance saw Sprout and knew *this* was what had made him feel so awful. He knew saving her meant his doom, but he owed her. In fact, Vance owed her *everything*. He had to save her—there was no one else who could. Tomas was down among the soldiers; Griff was tending Lan, who still seemed out of it; and Kari was gone. That left Vance. He threw his bow aside and leaped down off the wall, hitting the ground and rolling to his feet. As he landed his ankle twisted, but he ignored the pain and ran as fast as he could to get to Sprout. The ogrann weren't going for her specifically, but they would trample her underfoot if she stayed there. Vance dodged their big legs and crushing feet as he sprinted past them and tackled Sprout, managing to cover her body with his just as the first of the feet started trampling around her. She looked up at him with shocked, tear-filled eyes, and Vance smiled at her in a moment of peaceful acceptance.

"Close your eyes, little one—I don't want you to see this." Vance saw her close her eyes tight, just as the first foot came down on his back. After the third foot on his back and legs, he passed out. After the fifth one hitting his head and back, he was gone.

Griff was frozen with shock. He knew the moment Vance covered Sprout that he was expecting to die, but he couldn't believe it was actually happening. Then he heard Sprout's muffled whimpers and snapped out of his shock. Pushing himself forward, crawling through the sea of trampling feet to get to his friends, Griff grabbed the body of his friend and rolled him off of Sprout.

"I'm sorry, Vance," Griff said quietly as his tears ran down his freckled face. More ogrann were coming toward them; they were doomed. Just as he was about to cover Sprout himself, Sir Kolan was there, holding his shield above Griff and taking a beating.

"I've got you, kid—grab her and get back!" Angran shouted as another beast came at him. He bashed the ogrann on his left with his shield and quickly followed up with a sword thrust, then kicked out high at the new ogrann, catching it in the groin. He knew he was alone here, but these kids were his responsibility and he would protect them no matter what it cost.

Griff dragged Sprout back and started sending healing energy into her bruised and broken ribs. He felt them move slowly back into place. He looked up as Sir Kolan took a punch to the chest and fell like a rag doll to the cobblestones. "*Stop!*" Griff had had enough. It was then he heard Davalar's voice in the back of his mind.

You don't have to touch to heal...

Griff stood defiantly, glaring at the ogrann stalking towards him, and smiled. He raised his hand and three tendrils of golden light flew out like writhing snakes, slamming into the chest of the fallen knight. Griff staggered back, almost spent. *Won't be doing that every day,* he thought as he sank down to Sprout's side.

The ogrann laughed. "Yous missed me, littles."

"He wasn't aiming for you," Angran Kolan said as he stood on shaky legs. He knew he was dying, drowning in his own blood as he tried to force air into his ruined lungs. Then he felt a hand reach into him and he was whole once more. Angran leaped to his feet and thrust his sword up through the ogrann's back, piercing it through the heart. He shouldered it to the right so it wouldn't fall on the young healer. "Now heal that little one," Angran said, standing on wobbly legs, amazed that he was alive. He saw the young boy—no, young *man*—kneel and finish healing the little one of her breaks and cuts. Angran had seen the young archer sacrifice himself for the little girl and knew she was important to these kids. Now she was important to him as well. "Knights to the King's side!" Angran cried out as more ogrann came at them. "Soldiers to me! Rally for Everknight!" He felt a flicker of hope stir in his breast. It was still unlikely, but they just might make it.

WESTERN GATE, CITY OF EVERKNIGHT

Sinaron stepped effortlessly through the transition from Tir-Lanan to Everknight, as if he had been using magic portals for centuries. After all, he had been. Soldiers whirled towards him, thinking that he was an enemy, but he held his hands up to show no hostility. "Tah dwoen." Sinaron said slowly, "I am a friend of the Princess and am here to help." He saw the distrust on their faces when they heard him speak in a foreign language, but a shout from across the way freed him from suspicion.

"He's an elf! Let him be," Janna called as she defeated another sorcerer's attempt to decimate the troops. Despite being rested—and almost immortal—she was ragged and weary. When

Janna heard the elven words for 'calm down,' she knew they were going to be all right.

"Janna, who's your friend?" Tanan asked from the front line as he fought side by side with Storn and the other knights. They had taken horrible losses but were holding the enemy at bay once more. With both the king and queen gone, morale had slipped, but then that girl started singing and spirits had risen a bit. If only Storn had arrows or the room to shoot, they would be in a better spot. Tanan bled from a dozen or more wounds, some of them quite serious, but there were few others in better condition to command.

"And can your friend fight?" Storn parried so fast he was acting on pure reflex. It was a miracle he was still standing with the wounds he had taken. He was sure that the blood on the ground was mostly his.

Sinaron stepped in quickly, relieving the dark warrior and all but shoving him back towards the healer, his thin blade a virtual bringer of death to all who came at the elven Oracle. Sinaron whispered a prayer to Davalar and a shield sprang up in front of Tanan to help deflect some of the incoming attacks—some, but not all. The men near him cheered and he smiled winningly at them between dispatching enemies. Here and there he cast spells to help others and generally bring some stability to this side of the city. It wouldn't last, however; even he had his limits. Sinaron was pushing himself in the hopes that the other elves arrived before those limits were reached.

"Well come, sir elf," Tanan said in a daze. He hadn't seen an elf since he was young. The sight of one right here helped boost his own crashing morale. Then the Lilac Lord had an idea. "Can you hold off the sorcerers for a couple of minutes?"

"I may be able to do that, though it will tax me far quicker if I do. Why do you ask?" Sinaron already liked this dashing rogue and knew he had to be a friend of Karsis. The bard always surrounded himself with people like this.

"I want to borrow Janna to help me take out their general." Tanan looked back at Janna and knew that it would be the last thing she did today, but if it worked it could save them all.

"You've got a couple of minutes—go now." Sinaron concentrated and strengthened his magic barrier to take even more of the attacks, at the same time looking for signs of enemy magic so he could start countering their spells.

Tanan limped over to Janna as quickly as he could. "We have a couple of minutes—can you get me to the general?" He had faced the man on the field by Keragan hold, but he was in worse shape now. But he couldn't help it—this had to be done. Luckily, Tanan still had a few tricks up his sleeve; he just had to be fast.

Janna sighed and turned away from casting to look at him. "Only if you let Ralavin heal that wound. You're a mess." She knew she could open a small gate for herself, but she'd only taken someone with her once, a long time ago in Sirr, and it had almost been a disaster.

"No time. New guy is taxed already and if we don't hurry he won't live long enough to be 'old guy' anytime soon." Tanan wiped his blade clean on a cloth and stood, ready.

"Well, he is an elf, so in theory, he is already an old guy," Janna quipped back. She used her *sight* to search the field for the general. She saw a man with grey hair and broad shoulders barking orders and yelling at a dark-skinned woman who was now running away. "Get ready, Lord," Janna said. "I have to go with you, but I'll be using everything I have left to keep the doorway open," Janna whispered to the ether and opened the door, grabbing Tanan in a tight embrace before jumping through. The magic would try and pull them apart but as long as she held tight she could force the magic away; this was going to drain her almost completely.

They came out of the ether behind a tent, a few yards from General Ellis. Tanan shook his head to clear the dizziness, then ran and placed his sword at the general's throat. "I've been asking for your surrender all day, General—care to give it to me now?" He was expecting shock and surrender, but Ellis somehow beat Tanan's blade away and drew his own in a blink of an eye. Then the general attacked.

Ellis was furious! How dare this upstart Lord think he could just pop in with magic and try to kill him? He swung his great blade in two hands, the sword cutting great swaths that would cleave the man in two... if he ever connected with him! As it was, The Lord of Everknight almost broke his own blade when he tried to parry Ellis's sword. Parrying was out of the question; the only option was to dodge as if his life depended on it. Because it did.

"How about I take *your* surrender, Lord—I could just show your troops your headless body and ask someone else?" Ellis had him now. The lord had tried to roll but caught his foot on something. His eyes looked up meekly, begging to live. The general stepped up and raised his sword for the killing blow. He expected to see fear in the lord's face, but instead he... smiled?

Tanan grinned. He pulled out his long dagger and brought it down on the man's foot with everything he had. Tanan had tried this trick against the Incarnation back when he lost Morlan, his sword, but General Ellis didn't have the power of Death. The dagger went right through the hard leather, through his foot, and into the dirt, pinning the general in place. Tanan stood quickly, hefted his blade, and stabbed at the man's heart.

The men around General Ellis realized what was going on too late. By the time they knew what was happening they didn't have time to react. Captain Larr, however, was there at the last minute. She saw what the devious man was up to and called out a warning. "General!" She didn't have time to stop him, so she did the next best thing. Throwing herself at the general, she took the sword meant for him in the side and threw Ellis down, ripping the dagger out of the ground. Larr screamed once, then locked down her pain with sheer discipline even as she started to lose consciousness. This somehow snapped the others into action, but her enemy was already on the move. Larr gave into the darkness and closed her eyes.

Ellis cried out in pain as the dagger ripped free from the ground, nearly slicing his foot in two. He was in shock and confusion, lost as to what had happened, but his first concern was for Larr. "Hold on Franc! Don't die on me."

Her name isn't Franc, the voice in his head said quietly, returning after a long silence.

Ellis frowned as a healer pulled Larr off of him and helped him stand. He had said the name without thinking. Maybe he was going crazy. "Godspeed, Larr," he called as they took her away to be tended to.

Tanan stole a sword off of a stunned guard, then sliced two others as he rolled back to where he left Janna. He raced behind the tent and found Janna huddled on the ground, her eyes closed, her body shaking. He grabbed her tightly—like she had held him earlier—and turned to leap through the shimmering gate. Tanan never noticed the guard behind him until he was halfway through. The sword pierced his side even as he fell through the gate. On the other side, strong hands caught him before his world went black.

EASTERN GATE, CITY OF EVERKNIGHT

Magiciel came out of the gate more disoriented than usual, more than likely because she wasn't focusing enough. The scene here was worse up close than it had appeared from afar. Men fought in the streets and bodies lay everywhere. Spells slashed through stone and flesh alike and only a few stalwart men still stood to fight. "Who leads the gate?!" Magiciel called out in the human tongue. It felt weird using it out here in the wide world. A big man with a bloody ax turned and smiled at her.

"I do—for now. You must be an elf. Name's Gareth. Come and join the party." Gareth spoke quickly and to the point, swinging his ax in deadly, efficient arcs. The gate had fallen and Carana had waded out into the sea of G'harran soldiers to try and take out the enemy general, leaving him in charge.

Just then a woman with long braids tipped by steel balls came spinning through the air, kicking. She landed with the force of a small mountain, killing a sorcerer as he came through the shattered gate with the metal orbs that swung from her braids—dangerous hair indeed! Magiciel had never felt out of place before; this was a first, and that's saying something when you're over five hundred years old. She noticed two breaches in the outer wall and called out to the earth. "Ash'anti, dir sran lea kithin!" The earth rose up and shielded the men near the breaches, acting as a makeshift wall and burying the enemy soldiers in the way without mercy.

Tierra was exhausted but at the sight of an elf, she knew they were saved. "Our own sorcerer is out cold, so if you could help clean up this mess inside we could go back to holding the gate." Tierra looked at Frenir and saw that he was being tended to by Caerlyn, but he was barely breathing and looked as if he would be out for the rest of the fight. The man had earned her eternal respect.

Magiciel looked at the men fighting, closed her eyes, and whispered to the earth under them. The ground shook violently —the stone walls cracked and trembled, but held. The soldiers lost their balance, but at that moment Magiciel took three of the enemy cleanly, allowing the remaining defenders to kill their opponents quickly and take a breath.

The woman with the braids twirled around, her dangerous hair taking out another soldier even as she waved and went back to defending the gate. The big man, Gareth, came over to help as the men rushed the gate.

"You must be from that elven city Karsis brought the kids to. All went well then?" The big man seemed casual despite the ordeal they all had endured. Still, his endurance didn't seem dented in the slightest, either that or he hid his exhaustion well.

"Yes, Princess Allissana was most compelling. I and another came early while Karsis, Adrilian, and the young man have gone to the north of the city to fight the Incarnation and archmage that controls him." Magiciel would've said more but the man took off at a dead run, leaving his ax behind. Magiciel shrugged and went to look for wounded to help and sorcerers to fight.

NORTHERN GATE, CITY OF EVERKNIGHT

Outside the walls, Graf knew they were all in trouble. Canny fighters or not, when you're surrounded by creatures this big and deadly, it spelled disaster. He dodged a fist, snuck around an ogrann, and slashed quickly, ducking another swing that came from behind. He saw the white-haired elf dispatch an ogrann, but as she turned she took a heavy blow to her back as another came at her. Graf rolled under two ogrann and past the king, then came up and pushed her out of the way, taking two hits by the ogrann that were on her. Graf healed quickly, so he assumed it would hurt, but wouldn't be that bad. He never saw the ogrann behind them take apart the barricades to use as weapons.

The thick beam went right through his chest and sprayed the ogrann in front of him with blood. Graf struggled weakly to raise his daggers, but he couldn't feel his arms. He spit blood at the huge face looming at him, then opened his mouth to say something witty, but the light faded from his eyes before he could. The Incarnation of Shadows was gone.

King Arian the Brave swung his sword in a wide arc, knowing they were surrounded. His companions had been pushed aside by the fighting, and he was starting to slow down. His wounds were getting the best of him—it wasn't until this moment that he remembered that his ring was on his daughter's hand. He had never worried about injuries before, but now he knew he was in trouble. Aeric was hard pressed as well, cornered by the other side of the wall behind the white-haired woman, and there was no help coming from them. Then he saw Graf roll past him and he used that hole to shift towards the right of the gate. Here, he could get the wall to his back and see from both sides. That's when he saw Graf skewered by the sharp beam.

Arian cried out in shock and anger, hacking furiously to get to the man, but a moment later Graf's lifeless body slid down off the beam. Arian was stuck now—he was unable to get back to the wall and he was spinning around every few seconds, slashing at the ogrann all around him. He knew this could only go one way. The king saw two more ogrann lifting beams up as spears. He tried to get behind some of the brutes for cover, but it wasn't working. *Well, if death is coming for me I will greet her like the old friend that she is,* he thought, taking out another ogrann with two quick slashes. He saw the two ogrann with the beams coming and moved to shift sideways so that, when they hit him, the wounds wouldn't be mortal at least, when he saw a blur come through the gate and slam into him. Hard.

"Be safe my love!" the blur called as he flew back to the ground.

MARESSA RAN AS FAST AS SHE COULD, HER HEART POUNDING in her chest and her head. She had to get there in time. Without his ring, Arian would be killed, she just knew it. Her husband had taken risks before, but after he had that ring and discovered what it could do, he had become reckless. Maressa rounded a corner and her heart fell. Before her was a sea of ogrann, at least sixty of the beasts. They were already inside the gate and soldiers were falling faster than she could count. Then she saw Arian and her heart stopped.

Just outside the gate, her beloved was surrounded by ogrann —two huge beasts were rushing toward him with beams that looked like massive spears. She closed her eyes and sang a song to Ollian. The bardic spell increased the bard's speed—typically to get *away* from harm, but there was no avoiding what she must do. Maressa raced in and around the fighting, her movements a blur as she picked up speed, pushing herself to her limit. In what seemed like a moment of frozen in time, she was there. Maressa slammed into her love like a hammer from above, shouting at him as she did.

"Be safe my love!" Maressa called as the massive spears slammed into her back and sides, passing through her body to erupt from her stomach and chest. The queen spit up a fountain of blood as the ogrann pulled in two different directions to claim their prize. One spear ripped free, but the queen was still impaled on the other. The ogrann hoisted her up as a standard, and she slid down the shaft toward him. The beast seemed disgusted at his prize and shook her off into the dirt. The last thing she saw was her love crying out her name and killing the brute who still held the beam. Queen Maressa faded and was gone.

Arian stood and cried out in pain and loss, his voice echoing to the very heavens. A hole in his stomach formed as he saw Maressa thrown to the ground and his anger was cut loose. In a fury too violent to be restrained, Arian was suddenly right there, hacking at the beasts in a flurry of sword strokes, rage, and tears. The king dropped the remaining ogrann around him, taking hit after hit and not caring in the slightest as his blood flew through the air and pooled on the ground. When the monsters were dead, he dropped to his wife's side just as a cheer went up among the defenders. White-haired fighters emerged through magical doors, slashing at the beasts inside the gate and repelling them with magic.

Arian spared no time for them or victory; his wife was all he could see. "Oh Gods, Maressa. Hold on baby, just hold on." Arian looked around for the young healer who was stationed at the gate and finally spotted him through the crowd of ogrann. "Griff! Help me!" He saw the young man was healing Sprout, and Angran stood guard over them both. There was no way Griff could reach Maressa. The king of Lythinall looked down at the love of his life, his soul mate and partner in all things, and saw her lifeless eyes staring at him. With tears falling and a heavy, vengeful heart, Arian closed her eyes. "I love you, Maressa…"

He appeared in a grassy field and had to duck instantly as a bolt of ice flew over him. "What—is she not going to tell us her evil plans first?" Rhoe asked as he rolled away from the three wizards who stood facing one another. The bad guy always did that in the books he read; he just expected Ill'lyth to be the type of person who would do that.

"Gods above, Karsis—he gets that from you doesn't he?" Adrilian asked as he focused and whispered to the earth to shift under Ill'lyth's feet. He knew that she would simply float in order to avoid it, and waited for Karsis to counter that; the elven archmage was three steps ahead of them.

Ill'lyth laughed as the ground shook. She asked the ground to take her as part of itself. It was an unorthodox use of magic, at least in battle, but some wizards of old had used this trick to slumber in the wild without worrying about being attacked. Quickly, Ill'lyth cast a mix of air and ether at the foppish bard even as she melted into the earth like a ghost and disappeared from view.

Karsis reinforced his mental shield as the mini-cyclone of thought assaulted him. He threw up a defense as fast as he could, but the attacking thoughts blew apart his shields and forced him to fight back her mind with nothing but raw power. "Well I didn't expect her to do *that*," Karsis said, slightly out of breath. Keeping up with this woman had already proved daunting to say the least. It was a running battle between the three wizards, with this being the only breather to speak of; it had been less than a minute since they'd begun battling Ill'lyth. If this took much longer, they were done for. "Rhoe, get in Dar'Krist's head and get him out—we can't hold her for long!" Karsis flew backward as Ill'lyth came up out of the ground again like a shot, hurling gale-force winds laced with fire like it was nothing.

"Fools! You do not stand a chance against me!" Ill'lyth mixed air and water and sent a bolt crashing down on Adrilian's head, watching the old elf roll to the side at the last minute with a shield of earth to protect him. The flippant one was floating in mid-air and calling upon the wind to funnel her up. *Foolish!* Ill'-lyth countered the wind and the fire the other one sent at her, then sent another bolt of ice at them both to spread them out. They were good, she would give them that, but she had some old tricks they had never seen before.

Rhoe saw the fight and snuck quietly over to the man who stood stock still. He was still dressed in tattered robes and a cloak that moved like it was rippling in a breeze that wasn't there. As Rhoe neared, the cloak actually moved to intercept him. Rhoe pulled back quickly to avoid contact as the cloak struggled to get free and attack. Rhoe wasn't sure *what* would happen if it touched him, but better to be safe. He sat down at the Incarnation's feet, just out of reach of the ominous cloak, and touched Dar'Krist on the leg.

Rhoe used his *sight* to perceive the threads around the Incarnation and whistled softly. This wasn't going to be fun. They were woven in a spiral pattern and seemed to be very tight... except right on the edges. "Ash'anti ether, sistren ea ent dosit id," Rhoe asked quietly. As he felt the magic start to work, he carefully found his center and focused it before him, aiming the force at the edges of the spell. He felt the gap widen slightly, just enough to let him through; then he was somewhere else.

Karsis saw Ill'lyth's face when Rhoe went through her thread spell and knew that the fight would get serious now. He closed his eyes and called upon both fire and water, throwing a cloud of steam at her and dropping to the ground. He rolled backward as another shard of ice flew aimlessly by, and called out in pain, hoping to mislead her.

Adrilian saw the steam and floated up higher, calling upon both earth and water, softening the ground under her to the point of near liquid. Ill'lyth could pass through it, but it would slow her descent just a fraction of a second. Adrilian felt the heat around him gather and used a cool shield to protect him while he flew over her. They had to protect Rhoe so he could break the Incarnation free. If they didn't, they were all dead. "Now, Karsis!" Adrilian called as the heat intensified around him, singeing his robes despite the shield. He calmly asked the ether to make him resistant to flames—not something every wizard knew how to do, but he was the Incarnation of magic after all—and flew even higher.

Ill'lyth couldn't see, and she couldn't spare the time to call upon her *sight,* not with both these wizards on her. They had been holding back in the beginning but she now realized that they were very powerful. Still, she was better. Ill'lyth heard the elf above her call upon the earth and figured that he was bringing it up at her, so she countered with wind, focusing it straight down in a tiny funnel. The small wind spout also cleared the steam the curly-haired human had created, which was hot enough to sting her skin. Still, it wasn't anything she couldn't handle.

Ill'lyth heard him call out to his companion and knew that they had some sort of plan. Tricky elves and their allies! She heard the human try and take control of her wind funnel and actually laughed. Ill'lyth let him have a little control, then snapped it forcefully away again, leaving him reeling... or so she thought. That was when she felt the wind from above. She never heard the other one cast!

The two funnels connected and sent her spiraling towards the ground, tumbling head over heels until she splashed down. *Splashed?* Ill'lyth barely had time to think before she heard the human calling upon the element of fire. They were going to try to freeze her!

Karsis fell to his knees as Ill'lyth splashed down into the massive mud puddle. "Ash'anti wan, fros!" he shouted and saw the liquid earth start to freeze solid around her half-submerged form. *This won't hold her very long, and if I were a betting man —which I am—I would put five gold that we're dead if Rhoe doesn't hurry,* Karsis thought as Adrilian dropped beside him, calling for the earth to harden even more. It would be like frozen stone at this point, but that would still give them two minutes, tops. Karsis looked over at his pupil, sitting on the ground in front of the living embodiment of Death, and a wrinkle formed on his brow.

"What is it, Karsis?" Adrilian asked. Seeing his son frown was never a good sign. It usually meant he had missed something.

"The cloak is moving. It wasn't doing that when we showed up." *Could that thing be reacting to Rhoe's invasion?* Then the thought was lost as the sound of shattering stone shook the plains. Karsis stood and cracked his knuckles, knowing that this was going to be the fight of his life. *The stuff stories are made of,* he thought. *Now I just have to live to write them.*

THE MIND OF DAR'KRIST

He was in a very alien place. The air was heavy with the scent of salt and the wind roared past his ears. Rhoe had read about the ocean but had never dreamed that it would be so vast. At least he assumed what he was looking at was the ocean. It had all the aspects he had read about: crashing waves, a field of blue all the way to the horizon, and the call of birds trilling away above. The huge cliff he was on was new though, and not entirely pleasing. Rhoe stepped back and tried to get his bearings, knowing Dar'Krist had to be here somewhere as this was his mind. That's when he heard fighting. Rhoe oriented on where he thought the sound was coming from and sprinted towards it, following the ocean and keeping the crashing waves on his right. He followed a winding path until he saw a number of figures struggling on a small landing. One of them was clearly Dar'Krist. The others all looked elven, with long, white hair and slim features. It was four against one.

The young wizard felt conflicted. For the first time in his life, the line between good and evil wasn't black and white. Rhoe knew he had to stop this evil man, but he'd been told specifically that he wasn't supposed to kill him. *Do I let his mind play this out? Or am I supposed to help him?* He shook his head, then shrugged and ran down the path towards the incredible fight. In the end, he would do as he was raised to do—help others in need. Rhoe was worried the four elves would see him before he got there, but they were oblivious as he made his final approach. Interestingly enough, he heard the big elf with a familiar sword ask the earth to hold his steps steady. *Where have I seen that blade?* Rhoe thought as he made a quick mental note to try that spell when he was out of here, then focused on the fight once more.

"You can't win Death. You are outnumbered," one of the

elves growled, clearly irritated. She didn't seem suited to a battle of any kind.

"Oh, I'm sorry, was I supposed to *let* you kill me?" Dar'Krist said, kicking out and landing a solid blow to another elf's back. A third elf stood once more, ready to attack.

They all spoke in perfect elvish, albeit with a strange accent; all except Dar'Krist, who spoke a weird mixture of elvish and common. *Auld Common.* Rhoe smiled to himself and decided to do something reckless instead of coming in slowly. When he was almost upon them he jumped and hit the big one with a flying kick that should've knocked him back right off the landing; it didn't. The elf grunted, took two steps back, and looked at Rhoe with contempt. *Well, that grounding spell really does work well.*

"You dare to interfere with War?"

Rhoe looked up and brushed the long, white hair out of his eyes. "War? Isn't that a little silly for a name?" Rhoe asked in the common tongue. He rolled back as the elf stomped the ground where he had been moments before. Then the elf kicked out twice, hitting Rhoe hard and sending him flying back into the cliffside.

A beautiful elven woman, holding a white, wooden staff, spoke up. "Who is this interloper, Death, an ally? I thought you despised all life?"

"I don't despise *all* life, just all *elves*," Dar'Krist replied. He turned and grabbed Rhoe pulling him to his feet. "I know not why you are here, but I thank you for the help." Dar'Krist positioned himself back to back with this new fighter and squared off against his brethren.

"Oh man, do you *all* have such silly names?" Rhoe asked, feeling out of his depth. He ducked two swings and hastily raised a shield against cold as one of the elves drew the heat out of the air around them. He felt Dar'Krist—or 'Death' as they called him—shudder behind him, so he extended the shield to encompass the both of them. He had never tried that, but it seemed simple enough to ask the elements to widen the area. Rhoe heard the elf in front of him gasp and clutch his robes in horror.

The elf asked the air to speed his attacks, then cried out, "For the love of Syll, this young child knows magic!?"

"Did you think you were the only one that could, Time?" Death asked coldly, extending his foot straight out and catching a small elf in the chest, sending him spiraling over the landing. The solid hit sent the little elf flying out well beyond the cliff, spiraling down to the water below. It was over two hundred feet to the crashing waves and the gods above knew he wouldn't survive *that* impact. "One down, three to—"

"Murderer!" the female elf screamed as she went at Death with all she had.

With one of the attackers down, Rhoe shifted and took advantage of the moment, kicking out at the one called Time with a pump kick. The hit lifted the elf and slammed him against the cliff wall, then Rhoe lunged and followed up with a quick, two-hit, punch-knee combo that had the elf on the ground. Rhoe whispered a quick plea to the earth and encased the man's hands and feet, then turned to see Death finish off the other woman with the staff before facing War. They never had a chance to finish the fight.

The world blurred, shifted to the right a bit, then dumped a mountain on Rhoe's head—or at least that's what it felt like. Rhoe tried to get his bearings, but he was somewhere else again. This time he was in a lush forest, facing hundreds of troops, and Dar'Krist stood at his side. The Incarnation looked shocked to see him and jumped back in surprise. From the size of the army facing them, Rhoe knew he did not have a lot of time. "Listen—I know who you are and I'm here to help you."

"Why would you help me kill hundreds of helpless fodder?" Dar'Krist asked, clearly confused. He didn't want to kill the humans, but there was no other way to get to the elves.

"No. I'm not here to help with that. That happened hundreds of years ago. I'm here to help break the prison that has you trapped in your own mind." *That was stupid. He will never believe you,* Rhoe thought as the first wave of humans started running at them.

Dar'Krist looked at the rushing humans and smiled... he had felt *something* was off, but his anger had clouded his judgment. Ether was his weakness and it made sense that if this *were* a prison, repeating his mistakes would keep him locked in here. As Dar'Krist looked at the young man, twinges of memory started to surface, but he didn't have the time to think about that yet. "All right, then we must change history. What did I do last time?"

Rhoe had read books and Karsis had told him the story again with more detail, but he still didn't know *exactly* what happened. "You killed hundreds of them but lost in the end and they entombed you in the earth."

"Do you know *where?*" Dar'Krist had an idea, but it was tricky.

"Roughly. Why?" Rhoe thought he knew where this was going, and he wasn't sure he could pull it off.

"Go to where they will be bring me and free me there. That should end this loop and start a new one." The Incarnation of Death smiled. Whoever was holding him was in for a surprise once he was free. He wondered again who this young man was and why he had the hair of an elf. Clearly, he was a talented wizard if he had gotten into the mind of an Incarnation—that was no small feat by itself!— but he had to focus on the hundreds of warriors coming at him. Regret heavy on his heart, Dar'Krist went about slaughtering the hapless slaves by the droves with his corrupting wave as he began the fight for his life and his freedom.

Rhoe took off running for the northern woods. He wasn't sure where Dar'Krist had been entombed, but he remembered seeing him attack Wyndral. He had been running for about an hour before he realized that he wasn't in the real world; there was no reason to go all the way on foot. Rhoe stopped and concentrated on the far northern woods above Wyndral—suddenly he was simply there. *If that worked I wonder what else I can do?* he thought. He closed his eyes and tried to tap into Dar'Krist's mind; he was already inside of it, why couldn't he use it to his advantage? "Ash'anti ethir, reva dosit a'ren," Rhoe said closing his eyes. An image of a statue formed in his mind and he traveled to that area instantly.

Rhoe appeared behind a massive oak tree and heard chanting. He peered around the tree and saw a distant group of people, all similarly robed like Dar'Krist. They were chanting in auld common; he caught the words "death" and "gods," but it wasn't enough to convince him they might help. From behind him, he heard the sound of elves chanting and the choice was taken from him. Rhoe thought about what he wanted to say and hoped that this weird mind world would translate his words from his will alone, in much the same way it moved him from place to place.

"Dar'Krist needs your help!" Rhoe called out, running lightly into their little circle. "The Incarnation of Death has been captured by the elves and they are coming this way!"

"And who are you to intrude upon the gramayre?" one man asked, but an arrow took whatever else he was going to say and laid him to rest.

Rhoe ran for the huge statue of what appeared to be a man holding a scythe and hid behind it as the elves rode in, slaughtering the robed men, shouting at them in their elven tongue and calling them the "Cult of Death." *Well, that would've been nice to know ahead of time,* Rhoe thought as he desperately tried to think of a new plan. He heard the remaining cultists gasp and peaked around. There, floating through the woods, was a huge coffin of earth, roughly man-shaped and vibrating with power.

All right, new plan. Rhoe smiled as he looked up at this huge statue. He waited and tried to time the exact moment when the coffin of earth would pass under the statue. When it was almost there he closed his eyes and concentrated on the wind, calling out for it to help him shove the statue.

"Ash'anti fra, sho dosit sonn!" Rhoe pushed with all his might as he finished, helped by the wind, and was relieved as it crashed down on the earthen coffin, breaking it in two. The elves leaped back in alarm and ran towards Rhoe with swords drawn and magic on their lips, but they never got three steps.

Dar'Krist was free, and as he felt the cool, outside air rush into the damp, earthen casket, he unleashed a wave of death so strong he felt the very trees shudder and wither around him. The Incarnation of Death crawled to his feet and saw the only person still alive and breathing was that strange young man. The boy had a look of horror on his face and Dar'Krist knew that they were somehow on opposite sides of a conflict. "It is killing you to help me, isn't it?" the Incarnation asked, struggling to force his way through the fog in his head.

Rhoe didn't know what to say. He had just watched all these elves disintegrate before his eyes. He knew that this was all in Dar'Krist's mind, but had the Incarnation done this before? "I can't let that woman control you. She would use you to destroy an entire land full of innocent people. If you are free, then at least I have a chance to stop you myself." It was the truth, hard as it was to admit.

"You have the power to… kill me?" Dar'Krist looked at the young boy and sensed power— indeed, a great power—along with intense control. It wouldn't be enough to defeat him, though. That thought was followed quickly by the realization that the boy was somehow untouched by his rotting power. Before he could ask how the boy was unaffected, the world shifted and flew sideways, flinging them both to another part of the dark man's mind.

Rhoe was in a familiar village. After the dizziness of wore off, he realized he was back in Wyndral. He heard a commotion and turned to see Dar'Krist walking into the town with murder in his eyes. Rhoe knew what was coming next; he had witnessed this first hand when he first tranced. He ran through the gathering crowd and waved them back, skidding to a halt before the man in black, tattered robes with the twisted smile.

"Stop! This is where it will change again. If you spare these people, however, this might be the final scene." Rhoe felt it was all down to this. But could he get through to the man underneath all this death?

Dar'Krist had reclaimed most of his memories now and knew this boy was, indeed, one of his enemies. The young wizard—if indeed that was what he was—had thwarted him time and again, and impossibly so. *Still, if I listen to him it may set me free,* he thought as he slowed to a stop. "And remind me, insect—why would I listen to one of my enemies?'

Rhoe hung his head. Dar'Krist was right back to where he started. What was different? The two other times he had interacted with him in this mind-space, the Incarnation had been complacent, even helpful. *What am I missing? Listen to me, I sound like Karsis now,* Rhoe thought, then laughed out loud at his own quip. His laughter set the Incarnation off again.

"Do you *try* and anger me on purpose, young one?"

It all suddenly clicked. "That's it!" Rhoe had it. Dar'Krist wasn't angry in the other scenes. It was his anger! The Incarnations all had a weakness and if Ill'lyth was using ether to imprison him, she was *half* right— she just wasn't using the *right* kind of ether. "Ash'anti ethir, tah dosit a'ren." He prayed that calming the Incarnation's mind would work, as that was all he could think of this quickly.

Dar'Krist felt like he had been hit by a mountain. He dropped to his knees and grabbed his head as the pounding continued rhythmically over and over, driving into his brain. The magic tried to snake its way through all the parts of his mind and he felt it seep out of him and into the very air like water from a broken dam. Dar'Krist screamed soundlessly and looked to the sky for some sort of help from his god. What he saw instead were large snake-like threads, dissolving one at a time, falling apart like a tree rotting from his touch. He also felt his power draining slowly away slowly, and he couldn't hold onto it. "What... what have you done?" The question wasn't asked in anger, but rather in wonder. He felt so... free.

"I'm not entirely sure myself," Rhoe answered as he, too, watched the thread spell unravel in the open sky above them. The crowd started to disappear, then the village as well, until he and Dar'Krist were left in a black void of nothing. "How do you feel?" Rhoe asked, still ready for an attack in case it hadn't worked, but he relaxed when the nearly seven-foot-tall Incarnation of Death started laughing. *All right, that's not the reaction I was expecting...*

"You have freed me from unrelenting anger. You have no idea how much I've missed feeling like this! *I* had no idea how much I've missed feeling like this. Ever since my family..." Dar'Krist stood slowly—something was still siphoning off his power. "We're almost out, and when we are, I'm going to kill that bitch. Be warned—someone or something is stealing my power. After I use what I have left on her, I won't be much better in a fight than you I'm afraid."

"It's fine, I've got some friends keeping her busy." Rhoe

looked down and realized he was almost transparent. He smiled at the man in tattered robes one last time and was shaken to the core when he smiled back.

Then Rhoe woke up.

PLAINS NORTH OF EVERKNIGHT

Karsis rolled again, putting out the flames that were crawling up his longcoat. He flung another blast of cold at the elven archmage who floated just above the ground and saw it smash against another of her shield. *All right, mistakes were made,* he thought as he rolled again and tried to stand. Karsis was out of breath and—more importantly—almost out of ideas. What was worse was his father was doing better than he was, and that *really* ate at him. Adrilian flew around Ill'lyth, parrying her slender sword with a shield of grass that he had formed out of the field. Suddenly, she blew the Incarnation of Magic straight down into the rubble she had broken out of, then rolled the rocks slowly on top of the wizard.

"One down..." Ill'lyth said as Adrilian screamed and went limp, his arms falling among the rubble.

'Father!" Karsis cried out, but before he could go on the attack, something out of the corner of his eye grabbed his attention. More like slapped his attention and pushed it off a cliff. The bard spun and saw Rhoe stand up on shaking legs. Karsis knew he still had to keep Ill'lyth busy... and now he was alone. He summoned air as a distraction, then whispered to the grass around him which lay trampled and broken because of their fight. Karsis flung the grass at Ill'lyth as she dispelled the air that he had used as a feint, and nearly caught her off guard. Nearly.

Ill'lyth caught the air easily—she knew it wasn't the real attack. Then she saw the grass coming at her and frowned; this man was serious. She slipped sideways as she tried to burn the blades with fire, but only got half of them. Those that made it past her spell lacerated the back and legs with dozens of small cuts. As she spun, she saw what had pushed her opponent to desperation. The young boy was up! Ill'lyth called out to the rubble and threw a deadly shower of rocks at the young wizard. Rhoe rolled quickly backward and tried to shield himself with earth, but he still took a pounding.

"So—I see that you are back," Ill'lyth taunted, floating towards him. She sent a powerful wall of wind at the flippant human in the ridiculous coat and sent him sprawling. The Incarnation of Death was still standing stock-still. Ill'lyth laughed. The boy must have failed in his attempt to break her thread spell. She checked her spell, and with a shock realized it was gone! *Impossible, but that means...*

She threw herself to the side just as the Incarnation reached for her. She pelted him with the rocks that had fallen short of hitting the young one. The stones tore through his already tattered robes, spinning him around. She stood and stopped the young one in mid-strike as he was poised to kick her face. The boy stood like a statue before her, leg in the air and terror on his face.

"Almost. That *almost* worked," she hissed, "but I am not an archmage for nothing, young one. I commend you for the effort. It isn't easy to unravel my work, but this is where you all die." Ill'lyth would've carried on for another moment or two—after all, she *did* like to spill her plan once her foes were broken in front of her, not before—but then a gag of air slammed into her mouth and her arms were held behind her back by the very earth under her feet. "Mmm!" She tried to scream and failed.

Adrilian stood behind her, a triumphant look on his battered and bloody face. It wasn't the first time he had feigned defeat in order to achieve victory, something most wizards, in their arro-gance, never considered. He had bound her mouth with air and watched as Karsis silently made the earth under her come to life. He hoped that Rhoe had succeeded in stopping the Incarnation, but he had no way to tell for certain other than his vision of them together at Everknight. Adrilian was relieved as the man in tattered robes stood and smiled at his former captor.

Dar'Krist smiled and reached out for Ill'lyth, grabbing her by the throat gently, almost like a lover. The Incarnation of Death let his failing power flow into the woman—the last of his power in fact—devouring her from the inside out.

"Well..." Rhoe didn't know what else to say.

"Well said, my boy. Well said." Karsis dusted himself off and walked slowly towards the Incarnation of Death. He bowed slightly and then went to Rhoe's side, checking him for major injuries. He didn't trust that Dar'Krist wouldn't snap and attack them all in a moment, but he tried and have some faith.

Adrilian walked up unflinchingly and nodded to the being that he considered his brother, misguided though he may have been. "Thank Syll you finished her—I couldn't hold her much longer." Adrilian turned towards the city in the distance. "Now, I think we have a city to save. That is if you're tired of being the bad guy."

THE GOLDEN PALACE, G'HARR

Ran'cian felt it, an almost imperceptible vibration in the very metal that shackled him for all these...*These what? Years? Had it truly been that long?* Then the very air started to shimmer, growing in intensity and his hope swelled. Could it be!? The concussion that had slammed him against the wall had broken his arm and lower leg, almost taking consciousness from him as well. Ran'cian slid down the wall, screaming; not in pain but in exaltation. "Free! The Bitch Queen is dead!" Power flowed around him as the metal rusted away in seconds. He shouted to the ether to heal his leg and arm, as well as his strength and vitality. Standing straight and tall for the first time in countless days—if not years—he commanded the very moisture in the air to form in a pool at his feet, holding the element so tightly it stayed in a perfect circle. At the same time, he whispered to the ether once more to show him Everknight and almost lost control of both spells when the sight was revealed to him. The city was under siege and barely holding its own.

Normally, this wouldn't bother the Sorcerer King of G'harr, but over his long imprisonment, he had learned the value of life and truly had a chance to reflect on his own deeds during the many years he had been a tyrant. Besides, his daughter could be there. Shifting his stance, he closed his eyes and started yet another casting, this time opening a portal for travel. Ran'cian was weak, but his power was returning faster than he ever imagined it would. He would go and personally command his forces to stand down. He just hoped that King Arian was in a forgiving mood. Stepping through the portal, he closed the gate behind him. He never saw the pool of water break and flood the throne room, nor did he see the servants shake their head and dutifully clean it up. Just another day as a servant in G'harr.

Ran'cian came out behind his forces to the east of the city and saw the bloody mess in front of him. At first, he thought his own men were attacking each other, but it soon became apparent they were all trying to take down one woman. She stood on a pile of bodies, bleeding from more than a dozen horrible wounds. The worst part, however, was that she was obviously winning. He spotted his general, Kasson, though it was hard to tell it was him with only half of a head to go by. The woman held the general's body in her off-hand as a shield—and quite effectively, at that.

Ran'cian shook his head and tried to focus. He commanded the ether to amplify his voice and shouted over the din of battle

and the screams of the dying. "Hold G'harran's! Stand down—
the war is over!"

CARANA WAS ACTUALLY NEAR EXHAUSTION FOR THE FIRST
time in decades. The Incarnation of Protection had waded into
the eastern forces with nothing but her sword, shield, and determination. Hundreds fell to her prowess; no one man could stand
against her. Hells below, no *five* men could. By the time she had
reached the general, her shield was split and she was covered in
wounds that would've stopped lesser beings. Thank the gods
above she wasn't a lesser being at all. As an Incarnation, she was
so well versed in warfare that she could switch fighting styles
between three different attacks, all the while keeping her focus
on opponents not even within reach yet. Still, after all this time,
she was finally slowing down. Sweat ran down into her eyes,
mingling with blood, and she had to keep wiping it away as she
fought, parried, and riposted for her life. That general had to
die. Not that he was that good—he was rather slow, truth be told
—but with him gone, the eastern force would fall apart quickly,
which would, in turn, save lives at the failing gate.

When Carana eventually reached him, she brought her
sword down on his head with a force that made the men around
her back up and retch, then she grabbed the falling body and
used it as a shield against the spearmen who made up his body-
guards. She fought and killed men by the hundreds, eventually
climbing atop a mountain of soldiers who had all rushed to their
deaths. Just when Carana thought she might actually fall in
glorious battle, her eye caught movement in the rear of the
G'harran force. Someone had come through a shimmering
portal. *Great, just what I need. More magic to deal with,* Carana
thought as she shifted her grip on the body of the dead general

and prepared to throw him. Then the man who had come through shouted to the forces to stand down and she almost dropped the body in shock.

"Ran'cian?" Carana asked incredulously as the men stood down in bewilderment. Carana walked forward and smiled a bloody smile at the Sorcerer King of G'harr. "Is that really you?" It almost seemed like a trick, but that wasn't his style at all. She hadn't seen him in years, not since the last treaty session, in fact.

"Hello, dear High General. I always knew you were good, but this has to be some sort of record for you." Ran'cian opened his hands to show he held no weapon and smiled nervously. No fighter in all of his many years had been this dangerous. He would have to look into her very soon. She looked tired and hurt, but most animals became angrier when wounded. Before they could say anything else, a cry went up from the gate, and indeed, around the entire city as the defenders gained hope. From here. Ran'cian could see others stepping through portals; even at this distance, he could see the long, white hair of the elves. "It appears the fight may truly be over, but let me make it clear for the rest of the troops. Will you accompany me to the western gate?" Ran'cian held out his arm as if they were attending a ball at the finest court.

Carana dropped the dead general like a rag-doll and walked forward, sheathing her notched and dripping sword. She knew the fight was over and besides if he tried anything, her martial arts were as deadly as her sword. "I would be delighted," Carana answered pushing men out of her way.

Ran'cian called to the blood on the ground to serve as a portal and used his *sight* to bring up the western gate. The blood formed a pool and the image became clear. It was harder to use blood than water, but it would do for now. Ran'cian stepped through with Carana and the soldiers left behind watched as the blood fell back to the ground in a splash. They gathered their wounded, saved who they could, and gave silent thanks to the gods above that they were still alive.

ABOVE THE CLOUDS, CENTRAL LYTHINALL

She was hanging on for dear life. After hearing the word "dragon," Liss gained a renewed sense of purpose. With the help of Avaryn and Liana, it didn't take her long to get out of Tir-Lanan and into the Silversword pass once more. She recalled the dragon's name and shouted it to the heavens... but to no avail. Then Liss felt a little kick and somehow she knew she had to use magic. "Ash'anti ethir, sirin Kanthalianar!" she called to the ether and within moments the great dragon soared down towards them to land in a cloud of dirt and stones. After telling him about her plight, the dragon offered to bring her to Everknight. Her, but not the others.

"Hang on, little one—it's going to get bumpy!" Kanth called back to his passenger. Passenger; the word was ridiculous to him. He hadn't had a rider since the end of the dragon war and it felt awkward and uncomfortable to be worrying about her.

Liss nodded out of habit, unable to respond with words with the wind whipping by her this fast. Thank the gods above he had told her to guard against the wind before they really got going or she would be in a small crater on the ground somewhere by now. Karsis had remarked on the speed of dragons here and there in his stories and sarcastic remarks, but she never thought his comments were anything other than the bard's normal flippancy. Being magical creatures, as well as probably the first creatures ever created, dragons had a connection to the elements that could never be explained. When they focused their will, they could fly at unbelievable speeds, but doing so meant losing the ability to maneuver quickly. Thus they used their fastest speeds primarily to get from one point to the next very quickly, then they would drop back to a more regular speed. Even so, they almost never used this unless in retreat as it left them physically exhausted.

"The city lies below the clouds!" Kanth called back after a couple more minutes of nerve-wracking speed. They had covered over two-hundred miles very quickly. He couldn't think of another time he had traveled so fast. Thanks to that young wizard, however, he still felt like he was in the prime of his long life, though he had to confess he was a little winded.

Liss had asked the air to ignore her for the trip and had to keep asking over the course of the flight, lest she get blown off of the dragon's back. That was fun, mainly because she had a hard time concentrating while going that fast. Even though the wind wasn't hitting her, it was still going by her and as such, it stole her breath from time to time. Liss was tired and sore from holding on, but Rhoe needed her. She remembered her vision and the pit of her stomach rolled like boulders down a slope. She knew she *had* to get there, and soon.

Suddenly, they angled down, breaking through the clouds and into the sky above Everknight. With a mighty roar, Kanth announced their presence. Liss saw tiny figures, ants to her eyes, scurry and run from the sound, but one spectacle drew her gaze: a large bubble of multicolored light with darkness inside it struggling to escape. The dragon slowed, banking its wings, and Liss freed Deathsong as they came close to the ground. Her heart stopped as the sword made a mournful cry akin to a mother losing a child. *Hold on Rhoven... I'm coming*, she thought, fighting the growing dread in her stomach as the dragon came in for a landing.

WESTERN GATE, CITY OF EVERKNIGHT

The gate had fallen and Tanan was backed into a corner. Behind him was the girl, Kari, now wielding a dagger she had taken off of a fallen soldier, and an unconscious Janna. Tanan tried to protect them both as best as he could, but he had taken that sword to the side and knew he was losing too much blood to keep fighting effectively. Last stands really weren't his thing.

Tanan tried to call out to Storn, who was fighting his own final battle with Sinaron back by the now destroyed pottery shop, but he couldn't find the strength to shout. He parried another blade and ducked a second spear, taking yet another boot to the ribs, then a knife to the leg. Tanan dispatched another soldier, but two more took their place.

"Sorry... Kari," was all he could get out before he was parrying again, this time an ax blow that came overhead. The ax drove him to his knees and then two swords came at his gut. Tanan closed his eyes and heard the ringing of steel... yet there was no pain. *This is what they must mean when you feel nothing when you die,* he thought, opening his eyes peacefully. There on either side was a beautiful, white-haired warrior, all pointed ears and smiles. "Well, isn't that just the best timing I've ever seen," Tanan said weakly, then decided to pass out before they could answer him.

Kari stood in wonder at the sight of the elves, then shook herself out of her stupor to tend to the fallen Lilac Lord. "Help! I think he's dying," Kari called out to the majestic beings she had only heard about in fairy tales. The elves rushed over to help. They also aided the other man, the dark-skinned warrior, and soon the invading forces were pushed back outside the gate. Kari started crying, great heaving sobs that wracked her body. She had stared death in the face, and the experience would be with her for a very long time.

"You did good, kid," Janna said weekly from behind her. The Incarnation of Beauty crawled over and called to the ether to heal Tanan. She would have a headache the size of a dragon tomorrow, but maybe he could owe her.

❧

RAN'CIAN AND CARANA EMERGED FROM A PORTAL AT THE line of retreat. He used his voice again to command his troops to stand down. Immediately a call came out from the command hill to ignore that order. Ran'cian looked toward the voice and saw Ellis giving orders. "How good are you with the spear High General?" Ran'cian asked nonchalantly.

"I'm better than anyone you have ever seen. Why do you ask?" Carana smiled at the prospect of killing another general. *That* would actually be a record.

"I need you to let that man know I mean business, and we can't get to him in time." He took a spear from the soldier next to him and handed it to her with a stern look. "Not to kill him— just let him know we mean business."

"You're no fun." Carana took quick aim and threw a high arc, using the drafts to send it soaring down directly at the general's feet.

General Ellis couldn't see who was issuing the retreat, but he figured it was the enemy caster again. He'd been pretty sure she was out for the fight, but apparently, he was wrong. Someone shouted a warning, and a moment later a spear landed right between his legs, startling him. He leaped back. Looking up he saw the distant figure of his liege, free and restored—and looking rather perturbed.

"Stand down!" Ellis called, then turned to his captain. "Send word that Lord Ran'cian is back and has ordered a cease to fighting. I need to go see if I still have a head."

General Ellis walked towards the Sorcerer King with slow, measured steps. He saw the enemy general standing beside him and tried to smile. "My Lord, I am glad to see you free at last."

"Relax, Ellis—the promotion suits you. Now, bring the men back and camp at the bridge. I want Arian to see that we're actually leaving, not just done fighting." Ran'cian felt a power growing in the north and frowned. That much power spoke of magic being used in great amounts. *What could they be fighting that they have to use that much power?* he thought with growing dread.

Carana felt a prickling on the back of her neck; she could tell Ran'cian felt it too. Of all the times she had occasion to meet with the Sorcerer King, she had always thought him ruthless, but he seemed... *different,* changed somehow. Carana looked up as a sound echoed across the entire region. She had heard that sound in ages past, but not in at least seventy years. The clouds parted and a massive shape came into view, hurtling down upon the city at a tremendous speed.

"Great, just what we needed today. A dragon." Carana turned to Ran'cian but he was already casting another portal. How he could do that so soon after making the last was a mystery to her. From what she knew about magic, it should be impossible. *They always said he was powerful,* she thought as she took his arm once more and stepped through the gate.

General Ellis let out a breath that he didn't even know he was holding. He turned to see Larr striding towards him with a half-smile on her face. She had taken a nasty cut to her left side in saving his life, and now half of her hair was burned away.

"General Ellis, I've called off the sorcerer and pulled our men back." Larr was trying not to seem too wounded, but it was getting harder with each step.

"What about the other two that were with him?" Ellis asked,

already knowing the answer. The new wizard that showed up was quite good and reports said it was an elf at that.

Larr shook her head, her braids swinging slowly. "He was the only one left, sir, and I had to convince the elf not to kill him." It had been mostly fighting for her life, but Larr had succeeded in keeping the sorcerer in one piece. She herself, not so much, but she was still here at least. That elf was talented.

"Let's pull the men back and tend to the wounded. We're done here." Ellis waited a second for some rebuttal from the voice in his head, but nothing came. Just as well, really, Franc would've been pissed that they were pulling back.

NORTHERN GATE, CITY OF EVERKNIGHT

Rhoe leaped over one of the blockades gracefully. His robe was ripped and torn, as blood from a dozen minor wounds soaked through the cloth, yet he spun and kicked with a fervor that scattered his opponents. Behind him came the Incarnation of Death himself, looking almost as battered. Experimenting with what he had seen in the Incarnation's mind, Rhoe asked the earth to hold his steps steady and the air to speed his attacks as he took out the ogrann that came at, him one after another. He couldn't believe that these beasts were attacking in numbers like this; it seemed like a story right out of one of his books. Rhoe also couldn't believe the number of bodies he saw littering the ground outside and inside of the gate. Luckily, he had no time to recognize any of them.

Rhoe ducked and hit another ogrann in the knee, dropping it so Dar'Krist could finish it off. He couldn't believe he was doing as good as he was against these beasts. The elves were here too, and even though the fighting was almost done, the ogrann weren't going to surrender, not cornered in the city like this. He and Dar'Krist had charged into the Northern gate ahead of Karsis and Adrilian, as both wizards were spent from their fight with Ill'lyth. Rhoe was shocked to learn they had been fighting her for almost an hour without rest. He couldn't imagine casting magic for that long and still being able to think.

Rhoe sidestepped another feral swing by an eight-foot giant and backhanded it, spinning the ogrann towards the dark Incarnation by his side. It felt weird fighting next to the man that had tried to kill those he loved, but after seeing what he had seen in the Incarnation's mind, Rhoe felt he knew him a little better. *At least he isn't rotting things anymore,* Rhoe thought as he caught sight of the king once more. Arian was yelling and hacking with abandon. A chill went down Rhoe's arms at the sight; he couldn't imagine what could make the calm, resolute king lose his composure like that.

"Best fun I've had in days!" Dar'Krist yelled over the commotion, launching a spinning kick that caved in the chest of an ogrann that tried to charge him. His power over death may be gone, but the fighting prowess and strength were still with him. Then he heard a shout outside of the gate and sprinted that way, bounding over the bodies of the fallen toward the sound. A white-haired elf was pinned under the body of an ogrann while two more advanced on her with murder in their eyes. An elf. Dar'Krist paused for only a fraction of a second, then realized that she may be someone's wife. *Like my M'ren,* he thought as the memory of his fallen love came back to him. Then he acted.

Illiyana was pinned under the body of an ogrann she had slain. It had crushed her legs when it pinned her, and now she was a sitting duck. She saw the two ogrann coming for her and swore softly to herself; Illiyana didn't want to die. Just when she was going to give up hope, someone was there to fight them off. The man was tall, even for a human, and dressed all in black. That was when she heard the voice in her head.

Child, take my power and become my vessel

I'm broken and of no use to you....get out of my head! she thought at the voice. At least she had saved Sprout.

With my power, you will heal. Take it and dwell in the shadows forever more. Beware the wind though; it will ever be your enemy.

Why me?

Because of your talent with the shadows, and more importantly your immunity to magic.

I'm not immune, I just can't cast it. Illiyana was confused. How did this mysterious voice know anything about her? *Who are you anyway? What would I be getting into here?*

You are *immune, and I am the God Norar. Serve me as my Incarnation and I promise you a life of adventure.*

Fine. Just get me out of this and I'll do it. As soon as she had the thought she was somewhere else. Illiyana recognized the place immediately; it was the hovel where Sprout grew up in. She laughed and searched for a piece of scrap paper. She furiously scribbled a note down the leaped down to the alley. She knew that had to deliver this and leave quickly.

Rhoe saw the Incarnation leap the bodies at the gate and followed, not out of concern but responsibility. No matter how much the man seemed reformed, Rhoe couldn't take that chance. He saw Dar'Krist kick one of the ogrann back and roll under the other, coming up to punch it in the stomach. He was protecting the fallen woman! Rhoe launched himself through the air and kicked the ogrann in the chest, sending it backward into the dirt.

"Help her—I've got these two," Rhoe called, facing two hurt ogrann. He feinted and spun, kicking the knee of one and the groin of the other. He was startled when an icicle burst out through the chest in front of him, dropping the ogrann flat.

"I would, but she's gone," Dar'Krist said evenly. He turned to help the young man but saw the two wizards drop the ogrann and knew that he wasn't needed. He had saved the elven woman at least; small redemption, but it was a start.

"Miss us?" Karsis said weakly, heaving air into his lungs. He hadn't been this worn out since those triplets in Lyr that winter. He had just arrived at the gate with his father when something appeared behind him out of nowhere. Spinning, Karsis saw that it was only the damaged child, Rythal. He almost discounted him, but something in the young boy's eyes made him look again. "Hey, why don't we...?" That was all Karsis got out before the explosion threw him into the city. he rolled over and over again, landing against the young healer Griff. "Fancy... meeting you... here." Karsis climbed to his feet to see all of the ogrann lying on the ground and foolishly thought it was over.

Then Karsis heard the scream.

Adrilian stopped because he could see his vision coming true before his very eyes; his head throbbed and his vision blurred. A quick charm and those were gone... but then he was hit by a concussive blast. He was thrown back, and when he stood he saw a child walking purposefully towards Rhoe and Dar'Krist. The Incarnation of Magic stood—knowing in his very soul that this was the pivotal point of his vision—and prepared for the battle of his very long life. "I Love you Karsisendriel," he whispered to the ether so his words would be carried to his son. Those would be the last words he ever spoke.

Rhoe came up from his roll on his knees as Dar'Krist reached down to help him up. The blast wasn't as bad for them as it was for Karsis and Adrilian, but it still hurt. "Thanks—" Rhoe started, but then he saw Rythal behind Dar'Krist and his breath stopped. The child looked right at him with evil in his eyes. Rhoe felt the power come off of his childhood friend and immediately knew intimately it was pure death. "Wait!" Rhoe screamed, but it was too late. Dar'Krist turned to ash before he could even scream; Rhoe felt himself weakening considerably as well. *I'm not immune to it this time,* he thought. He tried to speak to Rythal, to no avail. He only got out one word: "Why...?"

Rythal looked down at his childhood friend and smiled. "Sweet Rhoven. The Incarnation of Death may be to blame for killing Innal, but it was *you* that caused the worst pain I have ever felt. Because you embraced me and not Innal, I have been forced to live without a piece of my soul. And for that, the gods have granted me the power to kill you before I have to leave." Rythal walked slowly closer, scuffing his feet as if he was bored. "You see, I've been groomed to play this part ever since Daelyn. Ever since that voice came and gave me the task of saving your parents, I've heard them in my head: the gods. Now I am the new Incarnation of Death, Tar'Krist." Rythal was going to say more, but a strong wind pushed him back and kept him from touching the young warrior he had grown up with.

Rythal turned to see an old elf, another Incarnation by the feel of him, keeping him away. He closed his eyes and focused his power outward in a radiating circle, hoping to kill the elf where he stood. But some force stopped his power at the clearing around them and a glowing bubble of magic kept him contained. It was coming from the same elf! Rythal could tell the spell was draining the elf, and not just sapping his strength; somehow, Rythal knew the wizard had tied the spell to his soul.

GARETH HADN'T SEEN HIS SON ARRIVE AT THE BATTLE. HE had rushed to the North gate and started fighting the ogrann, but hadn't found his son yet. He had heard Rhoe was out on the plain, but his eyes couldn't make him out from this distance. So he shrugged and helped Arian deal with the problem at hand, cutting down ogrann and saving what soldiers and knights that he could. The king looked in bad shape but was still standing. Gareth was about to drag him away when he heard the scream. He knew that his son was in trouble.

"Karsis!" Gareth called out desperately. He ran to the gate only to see his son dying before his eyes. "Help him! Please!"

Karsis skidded to a stop, seeing the destruction with his own eyes. His father stood there, defiant, against an overwhelming force.

"I love you Karsisendriel." The ether silently delivered his father's words to him, and Karsis knew right then this was the last time he would ever see him. The field was awash in pure death—he could see Rhoe slowly rotting away within the magical bubble. A tear falling down his cheek, Karsis pulled out the Vial of Eternity and cradled it. He closed his eyes and held it out towards the bear of a warrior, not looking at him.

"I can't, Gareth," Karsis said slowly, despair creeping into his voice at the thought of losing those he loved. "I would, and gladly, but the vial won't work if used on family." Karsis turned his head and met the man's eyes with a look he hadn't used in centuries—not since his mother died. "I'm sorry."

Gareth went cold. He'd always known it was going to come down to this someday. He nodded and took the vial gently, knowing the pain Karsis must be going through. This secret had been a rift between them for many years, and avoiding the truth had eaten away at them both. "It's all right, Karsis—I understand." Gareth saw the death field and knew he wasn't coming back from this one. "Watch after her, will you?" Gareth saw Karsis nod and knew that for all of his faults—and there were many—the bard would honor this one request till death. That was the type of man he was.

"Gareth, wait." Karsis held the big man's arm for a second longer. He had to tell him. Gareth had a right to know before the end. "Allissana is pregnant." Karsis said it gently, smiling through tears he never thought he would shed for a man who had always caused him grief.

The big man smiled and laughed, happy that his boy was going to be a father. His boy! Gareth stalked towards the bubble and felt the wind blowing off of it. He had raised Rhoe from birth, loving him as if he was his own. He had known Karsis was the father from the beginning; Tierra had never kept that a secret, and he didn't care. Now it was his duty—privilege actually—to give his life for the boy he loved. Gareth smiled as we strode into the field of death, and with grim determination, started the excruciating path to his own end. "I'm coming, son."

Adrilian saw the big man pass into the field and tried to protect him too, covering him with the healing wind he was using on Rhoe. He felt Karsis start a spell to help and used a blast of air to thrust his son away. This was too tricky to risk losing him as well. *Time to earn this whole Incarnation thing I guess,* Adrilian thought as he felt his own life slowly ebbing away. Then he heard the dragon overhead and smiled. Good—she had made it in time.

The dragon banked his wings, slowing before he hit the ground. "Go, little one. And may your family survive," Kanth said as he saw Karsis blown backward. He wasn't going to get involved in war again, as much as he wanted to help the young wizard who had saved him. Those days were done for him.

"Thank you, Kanth!" Liss hit the ground and ran for the bubble. When she saw Rhoe laying inside of it, she screamed and broke into a sprint, only to be caught by gentle threads of air, then the soft hands of a caring friend.

"You can't Liss—the baby." Karsis was still numb from being

pushed out of the conflict by his own father, but he daren't try again and distract him from protecting Rhoe and Gareth.

"Why can't *you* save him? They are both going to die! I've seen it!" Liss was frantic and couldn't catch her breath.

"Because the vial that is going to save him can only be given by someone who is not related to him," Karsis said. It was time that she knew as well, especially with the baby she was carrying.

"But Gareth is..." Allissana stopped dead and faced the bard. In the heat of the moment, her brain fired and caught up to all the little things that she should've seen. The hair, the magic, the fact that *she* could use magic now *Because of the baby with elven blood...* "Oh, Karsis! He's *your* son."

Karsis nodded and looked back as Arian walked over, his own tears coursing down his cheeks. Everyone was watching now, knowing this contest was up to those few able to play it out. The bard saw Gareth on his hands and knees now, crawling as the roiling power from the new Incarnation of Death ate at his flesh and sapped his strength. Karsis saw Rhoe move, his own flesh slowly flaking away. He had never felt more powerless in all his extended life. He knew why his father had pushed him away, and it was killing him that he hadn't been able to say goodbye.

"I always loved you, father," Karsis whispered into the air. He could've used magic to make his father hear it, but for once he didn't have to.

Rhoe fought with everything he had. He tried spell after spell, but nothing could stop the pain and rot eating away at him. He cried tears of ash and thought of his baby, the child he would never see. Then he heard the one voice that gave him both hope and dread.

"I'm coming, son!"

Rhoe rolled over and saw Gareth stumble into the field that would surely kill him. He held a glowing red vial in his hands and had a smile on his rugged face. Rhoe saw the flesh start to blacken around his father's arms and with his dry throat cried out for his father to go back, but he couldn't make noise. Gareth fell to his hands and knees but kept crawling, a look of determination in his eyes Rhoe had never seen. *Rythal, please! That's my dad... Stop... Take me.....* Rhoe tried to project, hoping that the young boy he had grown up with could read his thoughts, but if he could, Rythal gave no sign. Then Gareth was there, his hair gone and his skin mostly black ash, impossibly still fighting to get the vial to Rhoe's lips.

"I love you son..." Gareth whispered through ashen lips, tipping the vial into the mouth of the bravest boy he would ever know. Instead of a liquid, the contents came out like a fine mist, winding its way into the boy's mouth on its own accord, unaffected by the power of Death. Gareth was sure he was going to die before he got to Rhoe, but the magic flying around the bubble had come to heal him little by little. It sounded like a whisper of voices, but he couldn't understand their words. His vision went dark as the last of the vial passed into his son and he passed quietly, never knowing that he had succeeded.

Adrilian was barely holding on. He had poured his life essence into the magic needed to both keep Rhoe alive and keep the big man going until he could save the young prodigy. His grandson! *This* was what he had seen in his vision and he had vowed to keep that dark path from coming to pass; he knew he had to wait until he saw Gareth give Rhoe the vial. Once he did, Adrilian poured all of his life into his spell, knocking the new Incarnation back against the wall and away from Rhoe. The young Incarnation's concentration broke and the field of death shut down. Adrilian felt light and airy and looked down to see his own form unraveling quickly.

And so the darkness falls. Adrilian smiled at his own son, then faded away.

Rhoe's blackened flesh healed, his withered bones hardened again, and strength flooded his arms and legs.

"*No!*" Rhoe jumped up, revitalized, and raced towards Rythal, murder in his eyes. He had fought so hard to get rid of one threat only to lose more people to a new one. He hit a wall of focused air and dismissed it angrily, only to hit a second one. He turned to see his mentor, tears winding their way down his cheek, holding Liss with one hand and directing the air with his other. Behind Karsis, the defenders of the city stood with a mix of fear and sadness on their bloody faces as they held their breath, waiting to see the outcome of this battle.

"No, Rhoe—he *will* kill you." Karsis stood defiant and glared at Rythal. "Go. You have your revenge on your killer. Leave it at that for now," the bard said, feeling power trickle into him. He knew he was inheriting the mantle of Incarnation from his father. They had arranged the transfer a decade ago when last he visited, just in case something were to happen. *That* was what they had fought over. Karsis welcomed the new power and it came just in time, too. He wouldn't be able to stand much longer without it.

Rythal straightened his shoulders and looked from Rhoe to Karsis. "I'm not going to lay waste to any land or kill needlessly. That said," Rythal turned to look directly at Rhoe, his smile gone, "I *will* see you die one day, Rhoven. But not this day." Rythal bowed and walked away north, fastening a familiar cloak around his shoulders.

"*Gaaaretth!*" Tierra came running out of the gate, screaming and was picked up by a funnel of air, which spin her and kept her from the large pile of ash that was her beloved husband. After the elves had taken control of the gate, Tierra had searched for her husband and had learned from the elf, Magiciel, that he had come here. But she was too late—Tierra had lost him. The warrior went limp and sobbed, hanging in the air, then felt herself slowly lowered to the ground. Then Liss was there, wrapping her arms around her and crying into her shoulder.

"Gareth saved Rhoe... He saved him!" Liss had no idea what to say but held the other woman anyway. She didn't see her father walk over to them, tears still streaming down his face.

"Liss..." Rhoe knew something else was wrong by the way the king stood. He walked over to his grieving mother and wife and stood there, not knowing what to do.

Liss looked up at her father and suddenly the wailing of the sword made sense. It wasn't because of Rhoe. The sword had been mourning its former wielder. "No... Please, no daddy..."

"Allissana, she fought bravely and saved my life," Arian said, choking back fresh tears. "Your mother was proud of the warrior you have become and you need to know that she always loved you." He broke down fully, falling to the cobblestones and sobbing openly, hugging his daughter as she fell onto him.

"Not too hard there, Arian," Karsis said through his own renewed tears. If Maressa was gone, then this truly was going to be a lonely world. Karsis used his *sight* on Liss to make sure the baby was all right. It was something he should've done in Tir-Lanan, but things had been hectic. The bar's eyes widened as he saw not one but two heartbeats.

"Oh! Are you hurt?" Arian quickly scanned her before he remembered that she was wearing his ring. "Wait..." Arian looked from Karsis to his daughter and tried to figure out what they were talking about.

Liss wiped tears from her face and couldn't help but laugh. She could hear her mother laughing and knew that if she were here she would smack him. "Not hurt... but you might hurt the baby if you crush me." Liss winced, waiting for the yelling. Instead, he started laughing through falling tears.

Tierra heard and was on her feet in a heartbeat, her tear-streaked face staring at her son and her daughter-in-law. "A baby?"

"Twins, actually," Karsis announced. Then they were all interrupted.

"My King," Carana called softly from the gate. All the soldiers had their weapons out at once as Ran'cian cleared his throat next to her. Carana had seen the queen's body off to the side, then heard of Gareth's sacrifice, and was gripped by a sadness that she hadn't felt for decades. Everyone she had grown close to died. It would never change. *This is why I usually keep to myself... will I never learn?*

"King Arian, I have called off my troops, as they are under my control once more. Know that I was held prisoner and *believe* me when I say that I *never* wanted any of this." Ran'cian bowed his head and heard the king stomp over to him. The Sorcerer King looked up, his eyes neither defiant nor weak. "There has been enough fighting and death for the time being. Can we save the arguments for another day?"

Arian felt a warmth from the sun behind him shine on his tattered armor; a peace came to him from that warmth, calming his anger. He knew his god was still there. "By Davalar, I think you're right." Arian looked around at all of the people that had come to his city's aid and even though he had lost the one woman he had ever loved, he knew that she would kick him in the shins if he didn't act like a King. *She would, wouldn't she?* he thought, laughing quietly at her memory. "Stay the night and we will meet on the morrow and discuss what we can do. Let me grieve the night, please."

It dawned on the Sorcerer King that Arian grieved for more than just his people and his kingdom. "Not Maressa...!" Ran'cian was truly devastated. Of all the Companions of Everknight, he had respected her the most. He saw the king nod and bowed in turn. Ran'cian turned away, walking back to the Western gate to make sure his troops behaved. Unexpectedly, he felt a tug to the side. It was a slight tug, almost like a wisp of magic that brushed his face. Ran'cian turned and saw a young girl sitting next to a red-haired boy in blood-stained, white robes. She looked like she had fallen down a long hill and had hit every rock there was on the way down. His smile grew wider as he felt the tug pull him in that direction. Ran'cian walked over to the young girl and smiled down at her. "And what is your name, little one?"

Sprout was lost in a deep well of sadness. Vance had given his life for her and Griff had saved her with his magic. They had hidden over against the stables with Lan, and once the elves had shown up everyone had forgotten about them. Sprout looked up at this man and something like a shock ran through her. He was familiar in a weird way; weird since she knew she had never seen anyone that looked like him, yet he was familiar. "My name is Sprout. Who are you?"

"My name is Ran'cian, and I would *very* much like to talk with you tomorrow if that's all right." Ran'cian would tell her everything and then wait as long as it took for her to forgive him. If she even understood most of it at this age. He was done being a tyrant; he would much rather be a father.

"Sure, but I've got to warn you—I'm going to be sad for a long time."

"Me too, child. Me too." It was then that he did what he had been putting off for a very long time. Ran'cian searched inside himself and let the darkness within fall away like so much dead skin from a healing burn. The Sorcerer King was whole at last.

CASTLE EVERKNIGHT

Days later, after many talks and meetings, both between The Sorcerer King of G'harr and amongst themselves, the remaining

Companions of Everknight watched the forces of G'harr fade away back to the southwest. A new treaty had been hammered out, a solemn discourse that benefitted both parties. Ran'cian was taking with him a small contingent of elven wardens to ensure he stayed in power and to solidify his new rule. There would be opposition, but it would work itself out. Carana announced her retirement as High General and Dren was promoted to General. It was something he didn't want but was really good at.

Most of the other elves filtered back, much to the dismay of the humans who had thought them only a myth. They wanted more. A few of the elves chose to stay behind, including Magiciel, who had asked to join the council of Everknight as a representative of the elves. She had never found her daughter, but after the fighting reports had placed a white-haired female fighter at the north gate before the arrival of the elves, so there was still hope.

As for the children, the loss of Vance was devastating. Lan was made a full knight, but the promotion he had always dreamed of seemed hollow in the face of all the loss. He was assured that it would get better, but that would take time. Trav was buried with full knightly honors and his sword was laid to rest with him. The Knights all looked at Lan very differently now.

Kari was taken aside by Jerina, now the ranking bard in Everknight, and trained further, but for a long time she would only sang sad songs. Tomas was the luckiest one, as he had taken a blow to the head and missed most of the horrible scenes of war. He comforted his friends and was there for them but never truly knew what they had gone through. Griff was taken to Caerlyn Hold to train with the healers, though he was assured that there wasn't much left to show him. Sinaron elected to go with him and provided additional training to both the young Oracle and the healers. With the extensive knowledge of healing he had learned over the centuries, there was much he could teach them.

Sprout locked herself in her room for days after talking to Ran'cian. She would never tell anyone what they talked about, not for many years, but at least she had a sense of where she had come from. He had offered her a place if she ever wanted one without pressuring her at all. All in all, Sprout was very confused. She had seen the white-haired female fighting with the king, and a name flashed into her head: *Iya*. Sprout never found out who she was. However, the next day she found a letter placed under her door, proclaiming his true name. It said her name was Lhana, but that, too, she kept to herself for many years.

The remaining Companions of Everknight met in the council chambers to say a final farewell to Gareth and Maressa. Caerlyn and Ralavin weren't present, as they had finally met to discuss what had been growing between them. They were locked in the Temple of Davalar for hours, and only the gods above knew what they were doing.

Stories were told and many drinks were downed, and Karsis sang rousing songs dedicated to their memory. The friends clung to each other, like sailors clinging to a broken mast in a storm. Of them all, Tanan was the most inconsolable. He had secretly loved Maressa, ever since they first met all those years ago. Losing her was like a hole in his heart.

"Tanan." Arian saw him at the table and knew what he must be going through. "I want you to know something."

"Arian. It's all right. I'm just still sore from... that sword in my spleen," Tanan lied, averting his eyes from the righteous man. He wasn't really in the mood to hear it gets better with time. It never had.

"It's not the wound and you know it. Everyone here knows

it," Arian said, letting his angry voice escape a little bit to get the man's attention. When Tanan looked up, the King's face softened again. "She loved you."

"Excuse me?" Tanan was sure his feet had just run out the door, and his knees may be next.

"I said, she loved you." Arian looked around the table. Everyone else nodded in agreement. "We always knew how you felt. It was no secret." Arian was crying again; he suspected he would be doing that for many years.

"But you... And you never..." At a loss for words for maybe the fourth time in his life, Tanan felt lost and unsure. It was not a feeling he relished at all. He sniffed and closed his eyes. These were truly his friends. "Thank you, Arian," Tanan said simply and cried silently himself.

"I, for one, need another drink!" Karsis said, trying not to feel sad. The loss of Gareth weighed heavily on him and he knew Tierra was never going to forgive him. In fact, he hadn't looked her in the eyes since that day.

Arian wasn't done though. "Karsis." He waited until he had the legendary bard's attention, fleeting as it were sometimes. "It wasn't your fault."

The glass the bard was holding shattered in his hand as he slammed it down, although he hadn't used much force at all. The new powers he'd inherited from his father would take a while to get under control. "Really? That's funny because I'm fairly certain that it was. *I* couldn't go in there. *I* couldn't be the one to save him. I think that constitutes blame rather squarely." Karsis stood up so abruptly that his chair slid across the room. It should've hit the wall, but there was no sound. The bard spun, half disappointed it hadn't—he had a flair for the dramatic after all—and saw Tierra holding his chair in one hand. *Gods above, she was still fast.* "Tell them, Tierra," Karsis said, choking up finally. "Tell them that because I couldn't go in, Gareth lost his life. Tell them it was my fault."

"You're missing something, Karsis," Tierra said with lowered eyes. She had wanted to blame him *so* badly, wanted to shout it from the high walls, but in the end, she knew who was to blame. When Karsis didn't say anything sarcastic and angry, Tierra knew she had him. The rest of the Companions sat quietly, waiting to see what would happen between the old lovers. It was something they had been through before. "Gareth..." Tierra sobbed, then focused her center and breathed deeply, opening her eyes and looking right into the soul of the man that she had loved once upon a time. "Gareth always knew that he would be the one to raise Rhoe. He may have hated you for hurting me, but he never hated the fact that you were the boy's father. Not. Once."

"Listen, you don't have to..."

"*Shut up and listen!*" Tierra screamed, losing control for the briefest of seconds before reigning it in. "Gareth was saddened by it, but he always wanted you to be a part of Rhoe's life. *That* was why he was so willing for you to take Rhoe and train him." Tierra's legs finally gave out and she sat down on the floor and looked up into Karsis's eyes. "I remember it shocked you when Gareth conceded that day, but I never knew why until now. You two may have had your differences, but fathering that amazing boy *wasn't* one of them." Her resolve broke then, and she was crying so hard that she almost couldn't breathe. *And Gareth is going to miss being a grandfather...*

"I... Thank you, Tierra." Karsis took a deep breath and bent down, wrapping his arms around the warrior and holding her tight. He the power flow out and into her—warmth and solace from the earth and ether, as he held the crying woman. It was Storn who broke the silence.

"So... who remembers that time in Terrafar?" Storn asked, knowing full well that they all did.

OVERLOOK BRIDGE, CASTLE EVERKNIGHT

The sun shone on Rhoe's face as he looked out at the city and closed his eyes. His father was gone, yet, according to his mother, Gareth hadn't been his father at all. Rhoe should've seen the signs growing up. The whispers around town, the differences between Gareth and the boy he was raising. But he had loved him so much... What his mother didn't know—could never understand—was that it also meant he was half-elven and his children had elven blood. Rhoe remembered the faerie queen, Irilyn, remarking that he didn't have a house insignia on his neck. That had come up when he confronted Karsis about being his father. The answer was not what he had thought of at all. Rhoe could still hear Karsis's voice, spoken low but precise: *It's simple, dear Rhoven. I'm not fully elven. I'm the child of an Incarnation, and as such belong to neither elf nor Incarnation. You are the same, except a step further removed. You are neither elf, nor Incarnation, nor even fully human. You are the child of Prophesy.*

An arm draped around his shoulder. "Are you all right? Having second thoughts about being a father?" Liss was teasing him, but deep down she was a little concerned; it had all happened so fast.

Rhoe laid his head on her arm and held her tight. "Never. I was just thinking about all of it. My dad, Karsis, Maressa." Rhoe looked at Liss. He saw the tears for her mother still in her eyes and he held her tighter. His gaze went back out over the city and he realized at that moment that he didn't want to raise his children here. It wasn't that Everknight was a bad place, but he wanted them to have the same upbringing he had: a simple life.

When they were older, they could all come back and live the courtly life. Besides, the future King or Queen should know the simple folk. "Liss, I would like to rebuild Daelyn and move there with you." Rhoe was worried about telling her, but waiting would just make it worse. He should get it out now so they could argue about it where no one else would hear them.

"All right."

"I mean, I know you want to stay... Wait, what?"

"I said, all right." Liss smiled at the stupefied young wizard in front of her and had to laugh.

"You don't want to stay here? You're the Princess—don't you need to be here?" Rhoe really thought this was going to be harder.

"I want to raise our children in the country. Somewhere far away from the intrigue of the court and the Lords of the city. Father will be fine and I can learn to 'work the land' with the best of them." Liss also wanted freedom away from the heavy responsibility of being the princess, if only for a while.

"We weren't just farmers, Liss."

"I'm just saying it would be nice to see our children grow up like you did. Besides, I already have a nanny coming with us." Liss averted her eyes and smiled. She had told her father that she would be traveling north with Rhoe and Tierra to rebuild Daelyn and had conspired with him to get a nanny.

"A nanny? Liss, I don't think we really need a nanny."

"It's Carana."

He shook his head and smiled. "Hell of a nanny, don't you think?"

"All right, more of a trainer. She hasn't left the castle in a very long time and, according to her, she has to move on soon or it will start to look suspicious that she isn't aging." Knowing that her childhood friend and trainer was an Incarnation had been a revelation. She wanted the best for their child and Carana was it.

"So it's settled then—the frontier life?" Rhoe smiled at the woman he loved and the twins inside of her and thought things couldn't get much better. He looked over the city again, this time letting his gaze linger on the clouds above the rooftops. No one had seen the dragon leave, nor even noticed what it had done after it had landed with Liss. Kanth was out there somewhere and he made a mental *not* to find the dragon and thank him. Rhoe turned his head as a page ran up, out of breath. *I swear they come out of nowhere,* he thought.

"Princess Allissana, the king said to come quickly." Barris was trying to breathe and not doing a very good job. He couldn't believe the news, but it was his job to report it, not believe it. Maybe it was code of some sort. It *couldn't* be real.

"What's wrong?" both Rhoe and Liss said at once. It was something that was happening more and more with them, ever since they had come together that first day once the war was over. Liss assumed it was the twins' doing, as they were also responsible for her being able to cast magic. Gods above, she would miss *that* once they were born.

"King Arian says that a *unicorn* just walked in through the northern gate with a tiny *faerie* riding on its back..." Had to be code for something. Definitely.

Rhoe and Liss looked at each other with broad smiles. together they ran down to the courtyard, leaving the page standing on the bridge, all by himself high above the city. Their laughter could be heard throughout the castle and it brought a smile to everyone that heard it.

❦ 10 ❦
EPILOGUE: ... HAPPILY EVER AFTER

The Village of Daelyn was thriving once more. Three years had passed since the attack on Everknight and the northern roads were safe once again. Rhoven Whiteheart had married Allissana in a town ceremony, so it was official. Even the Companions of Everknight had shown up for their wedding. The people of Daelyn were in awe of the guest list, but in the end, they were all just people. Liss had given birth to a healthy set of fraternal twins, Brinn and Braelyn. They both had the same tell-tale white hair that Rhoe had been born with, and no one ever said anything about it.

Elves and faeries had come back into Lythinall—now every town and village had tiny sprites or dryads living among the trees outside. Elves mingled with the folk of the land once more, learning the ways of the steadfast humans and teaching them tricks they had learned after hundreds of years of working with nature and the earth. Magic, however, was never a subject of their lessons. The Holds that once protected the land functioned once more, again ruled by their Lords. Tanan, the Lilac Lord, ran Norhil hold. The lady Caerlyn Whitestaff—now married to Ralavin Whitestaff—ran Caerlyn Hold, where she was raising her beautiful daughter, Shaera. Finally, Keragan Hold was rebuilt and run once more by Storn who had lightened up a bit but still had no love for his southern neighbors. He took Ellen with him and she erected a plaque for Thanier, in honor of his bravery.

Word of the Incarnations had spread, regardless of how many times King Arian denied they were involved with the war, and soon sightings were everywhere. Janna had silently walked away from the city after her battles at the gate. Her time there had scared her in ways that she would never forget. After her adventures in Sirr all those years ago she had tried to never allowed herself to care about anyone, but the Companions had left their mark on her heart—for better or worse. Janna wasn't heard of for years after that, as she spent her time in the lands near the ocean, far to the south of G'harr. Illiyana, the newly appointed Incarnation of Shadows, had slid her note under Sprout's door and traveled to the land of Miran in the southeast. She wouldn't be heard again until ten years after the war, but she never once forgot about her little Sprout.

Carana—or Caralann, as she was now going by—moved to Daelyn and taught the local people to defend their home, as well as trained the twins when they were of age. She became close with Tierra, and soon they were teaching people from all over Lythinall the way of the Changing Wind style in a small temple they erected just north of the town.

No word was heard of the new Incarnation of Death. Rythal, or Tar'Krist as he was going by now, had traveled to the Valley of Kherl, then over the mountains to the nation of Sirr. He would not be seen for almost fifteen years.

Karsis, as the newly inherited Incarnation of Magic, was everywhere. If someone needed help, he was there. If the king was in trouble, Karsis to the rescue. More importantly, he was there for Rhoe, Liss, and the twins. When he wasn't traipsing across the many lands he was in Daelyn, telling stories and singing songs; every child there awaited the great traveling bard to come to town. Karsis was determined not to miss this part of his son's life the way he had missed all the rest. He vowed to be there for the twins, regardless of what else he was doing.

Avaryn and Liana still visited, but stayed mainly in Tir-Lanan, as Liana was still the official ambassador of the faeries. And even though Lurien missed her, the queen had to stay in the Hidden Vale to protect the Council Tree. The Land of Lythinall thrived and prospered under King Arian for many years, with peace between all the lands, thanks in part to the new adventuring company called The King's Messengers. At least that's what all the stories said...

MEETING PLACE OF KRIST, SOMEWHERE IN THE HEAVENS

Not really a place as such, more of a constructed reality, it was brought into being the moment he thought of it. This place was created by the will of the being called Krist, God of Death and Corruption. While there, he kept his usual form—an ebony-skinned elf with long, white hair and eyes that blazed a vivid blue. The god wore gleaming mail and carried a scythe that seemed constructed of bone.

Krist was the darkest of beings, reveling in the death of all things and coveting power for only himself, yet he knew that death was necessary and came to all beings. Krist despised the undead and people who tried to cheat death, sending his Reapers to take care of wizards and sorcerers that tried to upend the balance of things. The Reapers were large and horrible, with leathery wings and rotting hair that grew from dark, dead flesh. They could only be thwarted by Fate, and that one weakness irritated him to no end. Almost everyone saw Krist as heartless and cold—those that said so weren't wrong—but he was not *wholly* evil, as most would assume. True, his cults had razed towns and started plagues, and done so in his name, but he never prompted them to do so. Krist controlled where souls went, and where they passed on to, yet he never got along with his fellow gods.

It was his turn to host the Gathering, as this was the last time they would meet. He knew the others would behave, as the rules still held and most of them were very conscientious gods. They couldn't fight amongst themselves and they couldn't use their powers against each other. They had been working on a project for years now, the first time they had worked together since they had created the Incarnations, but it was finally finished. Krist chuckled to himself. It had actually been over for years, but what was time to beings like them? To the gods, a decade was no different than a blink of an eye. Once the project was complete, they had sort of lost track of things; and as most dreaded this final meeting, it had taken some time to finally occur. The others would be here soon, and then they could sit and end things. As host, the meeting place was his form and consisted of a large dragon skull—it's top missing and filled with black liquid—fifteen feet in diameter that rested in a clearing of rotting trees. Bone seats were positioned around it and the sky was filled with dark ominous clouds. A single vulture spiraled above over the skull. The ground was covered in dead leaves and ash, and from time to time small things scurried under the blanket of leaves.

Every time they had these meetings (and this would be the fifth since they had since the plan began) the host would stylize the meeting place to their liking. Krist smiled at the notion that it would bother some of them to be this close to death—especially Syll, who had a special hatred of it.

Ah... much more to my liking, Norar thought as she stepped into this new realm. She was known as the God of Thieves and Shadows and this time had chosen a female form. Norar was hooded and cloaked in darkness but had a slender black cane for garnish. Long, white hair spilled out of the hood and her boots made no sound. She sat at the skull table and though her face was concealed, she scowled nonetheless. Norar was a secretive being, loving whispers and hidden truths the way some people loved sunsets. She relished sarcasm and nothing out of her mouth was ever direct.

I thought it might please you, Krist replied warmly. Of all the gods, he liked Norar the best. Krist sensed the others as they quickly approached his new domain.

Leave it to you to come up with a place such as this, Davalar thought as he sat in unison with his eternal mate, Ollian the Fair. Davalar was the God of Protection and Honor and disdained meeting with the others like this. He preferred they come to him, but alas, none of them could afford to do so during this whole mess. Davalar had chosen a form in line with healing this time, lean and toned with long, golden hair falling over his white robe. A golden rope tied the robe at the waist and a marble staff was in his hand; his other hand never left Ollian's. Davalar was generally a good being, guarding all life as sacred and having a flair for rules. He never broke his promise and always came through in the end.

Let's just get this over with so I can cleanse myself of this filth, Ollian thought, clearly disturbed at the scenery. She was the Goddess of Beauty and Love, and her form this day was stunning, even for a being such as her. Ollian had flowing black hair laced with silver bells and a cape of cascading water which covered a gown of pure lace. The lace showed off her perfect form, even though it had no need to do so. Ollian's pale skin was a perfect contrast to her dark eyes of purple hue, and her smile— when seen in this dismal realm—could melt any heart. She was a haughty being, not really caring about the needs of others. It was all about her, all the time, and twice at night.

Trust me, I am just as disgusted to be here with you all as you are to be here, but this needs to be finished by all of us. Am I right Davalar? Krist knew the God of Protection and Honor would adhere to the rules they had devised, but he asked out of spite. Truth be told, Krist looked forward to these meetings, if only to see the others squirm at being near each other. *It's their fault—they drove me out,* he thought to himself, knowing the powerful shields he had in place would keep his thoughts shielded. The room lighten a bit then faded like a sunset, as if a surge of power flooded through it. Krist concentrated and strengthened the reality of the place with but a thought, and laughed; his sister was finally here. Krist *did* like her, in his own way. After all, she was the only one who seemed to understand he was necessary.

Syll, Goddess of Nature and Magic, stepped into the realm through a veil of mist. This time she assumed a form with long, green hair entwined with twigs. Her cloak was covered in bark from a birch tree. Pine needles fell off of her as she walked, even though there weren't any on her at all, and her eyes were a deep brown. She was a kind being, loving all creatures big and small, and was as old as the very stars themselves. Elves and faerie folk all worshiped her, as did most wizards and sorcerers. Syll said nothing, still in mourning at her servant who had given his life for this little project. Out of all of them, she cared about those little beings the most.

Thank you for coming. The plan has succeeded, and we all have what we were looking for. My rogue Incarnation was stopped without divine intervention, and the rest have been scat-tered once more. He would miss the vengeance of Dar'Krist, but it had been a mistake to make him an Incarnation. He was too driven, too focused on killing. He had missed the fact that death was natural and that had twisted most of his powers. This young boy would be so much more malleable.

Yes, but I lost someone I had been working on for a while. Norar wasn't really upset, more frustrated that she had to choose another goody-goody. The elf was very good at keeping secrets and all, but she still had way too many feelings inside of her. However, being immune to magic was a hidden bonus that the others hadn't seen as yet. Syll would no doubt be complaining about that little problem soon.

Syll rose, defiantly slamming her hands down on the skull and sending waves across the surface of the black liquid. *Stop! It is done. Now that elves and humans are living together in harmony, they will possess elven blood as they procreate with one another. This means magic will move more freely amongst the races and war can be avoided. It will take generations, but the elements will be free for all.* A single tear rolled down her cheek, and all those gathered held breaths that they didn't have. If allowed to fall, that tear would cause storms that would ravage the lands. But Syll caught it deftly and wiped it on her arm for later. Rain always helped heal.

Krist raised an eyebrow at her emotional outburst but kept his sarcasm in check for once. *Well said, sister. And I am sorry for your loss. Ollian, are you satisfied with the newborns?* Krist turned to her and caught Davalar staring at him with a stunned expression. It seemed he wasn't prepared for the God of Death to be kind. That kind of made his eon.

Yes, the twins are exactly what I needed, even if they are both going to be looking to other Gods. A sideways glance at Davalar betrayed her feelings in this manner.

Let's not forget that I get that boy's soul, Davalar said sternly. His part in this was to protect Rythal and ensure that Innal's soul arrived in his realm, even as his twin worked for the God of Death. Davalar had plans for that soul.

Yes, yes. I have already sent him ahead of this meeting. Krist was a bit perturbed about that, but easy come, easy go. *Then I think our business is concluded at long last. We have evaded another long and bloody war and ensured peace for the next couple of generations.* He saw Davalar scowl and had to laugh. *Surely not all war, my militant friend, but at least the kind that would wipe out our beloved creations.*

And just like that, they were all gone. The powerful beings that would be gods vanished, as did the rotting forest around them. Only the lone vulture was left circling in the void of nothingness. It smiled to itself, as a bird cannot, and reflected upon his children once more. They had succeeded in doing what he had pushed them towards and he couldn't be happier. He grew larger and more distant, then vanished as if he were never there. And with no one to witness it, who was to say that he really was?

THE END OF THE DARKNESS TRILOGY

APPENDIX I: TIMELINE OF LYTHINALL

The events in the Darkness Returns happen without any mention of what year it is or how they keep track of the years at all. Originally I didn't want to include this because it was one more thing for the reader to follow along with—and one more potential mistake in continuity. So for the first time in print, you can now see how the years have fallen and which books happen when. The system is simple. The elves use T.R. for dating—"Tir Reckoning," which means "time" in their language—and they reset the roll of years after the God's War that devastated much of the continent. No one alive today knows how many years happened before that or how long the dark war lasted.

&

- **T.R. 0**—The God's War ends and the elves and southern Barbarians rebuild slowly, and separately from each other. The elves, crippled by the devastation, also rebuild.

- **T.R. 50**—The Gods create the first Incarnations, investing a bit of their own power in these first mortals. They were mostly elves, except for Krist's human Incarnation.

- **T.R. 135**—Plagues and death scour the northern part of the great forest as elves feel the brunt of Dar'Krist's revenge. He soon departs and travels southeast after this. He hits the dwarven cities, decimating them for some unknown transgression and the remaining dwarves flee to the south near Tir-Miran and take up residence in the high mountains.

- **T.R. 360**—The humans of the southern plains begin to migrate slowly outward, north, and east, staying away from the "cursed" woods of the elves. They settle in these lands and some make friendly trade with the elves that live there.

- **T.R. 490**—The elves in the southeastern city of Tir-Miran all disappear mysteriously overnight. The humans that remain take control of the city and start their own nation. The new rulers blame the elves' disappearance on their magic and ban it from their land under pain of death, No other elves are permitted in this fledgling nation after that. Any half-elves are hunted and slain outright in a great purge. Disgusted by this, the surviving dwarves head south and build ships, sailing for the far southern continents. They are never seen again.

- **T.R. 750**—Adrilian Everence is born.

- **T.R. 840**—Humans finally venture into the great forest of the north and treat with the elves for the first time. They help against the dragons and encroaching organn from the mountains.

- **T.R. 850**—Mas'ril Moonriver is born to High King Zen'ril Moonriver.
- **T.R. 900**—Dragons and elves reach a truce and the dragons allow them room to flourish with many of the great beasts slumbering the centuries away.
- **T.R. 901**—Magiciel Ash'ashlyn is born on the turn of the year to Lys'lyll, General of the Southern regions
- **T.R. 978**—The city of Tir-Novran is destroyed by a massive plague started by the Incarnation of Death. The other Incarnations chase down and imprison Dar'Krist in the Sea of Irace, losing two of their own in the process. Time and War help the survivors of the ruined city settle on the newly named Island of Novrantir.
- **T.R. 1050**—Beginning of the first elf/human war
- **T.R. 1054**—Faeries step sideways into the moon and disappear from the world because of the violent fighting between the humans and elves. They refuse to participate and leave altogether in a mass exodus. Avaryn is now the Last Unicorn after his mate sacrifices herself in the battles.
- **T.R. 1080**—The war ends with the elves enslaving the humans. They treat them kindly, teaching them their ways of nature and harmony.
- **T.R. 1100**—The Island of Novrantir defends the three sacred treasures used to power the prison of the dark beast from a sect of followers called the Gramarye. The evil cult is wiped out by the elven archmages.

- **T.R. 1209**—Adrilian becomes the Incarnation of Magic and marries Sherial'lan Ashgrove.
- **T.R. 1215** Mystanshir Nightstar born to House Nightstar on the Isle of Novrantir.
- **T.R. 1232**—Karsisendriel Everence is born. Sherial'lan dies in childbirth despite the healing magic of the elven healers and Adrilian.
- **T.R. 1300**—The Isle of Novrantir is attacked by the Gramarye arisen and three heroes race to stop the breaking of the seal set centuries ago by the Incarnations. They fail and Dar'Krist is released once more, heading towards Lythinall for his revenge against the elves once more.
- **T.R. 1305**—Dar'Krist is finally taken down in a massive effort by Khaerl Brightblade, a brave elven blademaster that sacrificed himself to bring Dar'Krist to his knees while the elven archmages entombed him in earth. The western part of the forest was destroyed and became a wasteland of death, renamed the Valley of Khaerl after the brave elf's sacrifice.
- **T.R. 1307**—Elves take human lovers and the first half elves are born in Lythinall.
- **T.R. 1310**—Ill'lyth G'harr teaches her lover magic and is banished from the Great Woods of Lythinall and settles the region south of the woods. She renames it G'harr and starts the second war between the elves and humans. The human slaves revolt at the same time and the elves are hard-pressed to maintain their hold on the forest.
- **T.R. 1329**—Most of the great forest is destroyed. The war is turned by a group of slaves, led by the

warrior Drennel. and after Ill'lyth's sorcerers are turned away, Drennel settles near the south of Lythinall and takes the surname Everknight. The elves of Lythinall retreat north to Tir-Lanan to seal themselves away.

- **T.R. 1345**—Golden palace of G'harr is finished and Ill'lyth is officially crowned Empress of G'harr

- **T.R. 1370**—Ill'lyth G'harr is slain by her own grandson as he usurps the throne.

- **T.R. 1371**—Illiyana Ash'ashlyn is born to Magiciel. Surprisingly, the child is cut off from the magic normally inherited by every elf.

- **T.R. 1390**—Cara Annalan is made the Incarnation of Protection.

- **T.R. 1403**—Karsisendriel adopts the persona of Karsis the bard and leaves Tir-Lanan to roam the human lands.

- **T.R. 1495**—Illiyana escapes from Tir-Lanan and flees to Everknight, hiding among the dark streets and alleyways. Grafton Jalmes is born.

- **T.R. 1500**—Janna Suris is made the Incarnation of Beauty and Song.

- **T.R. 1502**—Ran'cian Ashren is born.

- **T.R. 1520**—Grafton Jalmes is made the Incarnation of Shadows. Ran'cian Ashren slays the King of G'harr and takes the golden palace as his own. He declares himself Sorcerer King of G'harr.

- **T.R. 1522**—Grafton is captured in G'harr and has his mind broken by the Sorcerer King Ran'cian Ashren.

- **T.R. 1523**—The dark vampyre, Den'ath, enslaves most of the ogrann in the mountains and begins to decimate the land. The temple of the changing winds falls as —his minions flood the walls and all the warriors are slain except one: Tierra The Companions of Everknight are formed by the end of this year.

- **T.R. 1524**—After many battles, the dark vampyre is thrown down and the oran minions are broken. What's left of the oran flee west into Sirr and board ships to travel south.
- **T.R. 1531**—Companions of Everknight retire. Arian Everknight is proclaimed King of Lythinall. Allissana Everknight is born at the end of this year.
- **T.R. 1532**—Rhoven Whiteheart is born in the village of Daelyn. Karsis the bard discovers the faeries of the Hidden Vale and marries the Queen by accident.
- **T.R. 1540**—Allissana hears about the fable of the Tortoise and the Hare.
- **T.R. 1542**—Sprout is born on the streets of Everknight
- **T.R. 1543**—The sorcerers' cabal raise Ill'lyth G'harr and she imprisons Ran'cian in magical irons.
- **T.R. 1550**—Dar'Krist rises once more thanks to an arisen Ill'lyth G'harr and starts his path of destruction. Illiyana is made Incarnation of Shadows and Karsis inherits the powers of the Incarnation of Magic when Adrilian dies.
- **T.R. 1552**—Caerlyn Verasin marries Ralavin Whitestaff. Their daughter Shaera is born at the end of this year. Brinn and Braelyn Whitestaff are born to Rhoven and Allissana.

- **T.R. 1560**—Illiyana the Incarnation of Shadows returns.
- **T.R. 1565**—The Incarnation of Death visits Lythinall. Rythal, or Tar'Krist had travelled to the Valley of Kherl and then through the old woods to the west into Sirr. He came back changed, but still a force for Death.

APPENDIX II: ON ELVISH

A BRIEF INTRODUCTION TO THE
LANGUAGE OF THE ELVES OF LYTHINALL

The simplicity of elven is that it actually follows a basic syntax of word for word. Very few things change when speaking; the language follows a straightforward approach to its verbal understanding. Rather than having different words for run, ran, or running, the language simply has one word for run and surrounding words provide context to clue the listener as to how it is being used. In the structure of the elven language, adjectives are generally placed before nouns. In some rare cases the adjective can be after, but only in very rare conversations with some ancient elves. Below is a quick guide on how to pronounce some of the words as you read through.

PHONETICS

Ae is pronounced *ay* (hay)
Ah is drawn out long (aaahh)
Ay is pronounced as a soft *a* (air)
C is pronounced as a hard *c* (Car)
C if with *a* or *e* is pronounced soft (ice)

Ch is pronounced with a hard *ch* sound. (church)
Ea is pronounced *eeah* (leah)
En is always pronounced like *n*
Eu is pronounced soft (eew)
Ie is pronounced *i* (eye)
J is pronounced as a hard *j* (jar)
Ly is pronounced *l-eh* (list)
Ov is pronounced *au* (nod)
Oz is pronounced O (doze)
Ri is pronounced *re* (real)

A SELECTED GLOSSARY OF ELVISH WORDS

All-close/near
Alar—away
Ansis'ren—barrier
Amran—mountains
An—and
Ari—song
A'ren—mind
Ayre—blood
Ashanti—pleased
Ash'anti—please
Balen—steady
Balt—belt
Bin—bind/tighten
Blai—sword
Bli—knife
Boun—restraints/manacles
Braken—shatter

Brek—break/free
Car'cen—there
Cas—house
Cav—tunnel
Ce—a
Ceas—stop
Chal—blade
Col—cold
Cra'del—help
Crean—monster/creature
Dal—arm/arms
Dar—hand
Deth—doom
Dir—earth
Dosan—that
Dost—the
Dosit—this
Doz—sleep
Draco—dragon
Dren—end of
Dwoen—down
Ea—me/my
Eae—mine
Elien—fair
Em'ren—women/human
Ethir—ether
En—of
Ent—into
Eu—us
Faer—faeries
Fer—inside

Fin—over/ended
Fir—fire
Fra—wind/air
Frein—fall
Fros—freeze
Gli—fly
Gol—money/trade
Gos—filth/scum
Gra—bring
Gram—demon
Gres—grass
Hadar—hold
Haeth—encase/enfold
Halven—heat/warmth
Hary—hurry/fast
Haryen—faster
Hir—warrior
Icael—snow
Ice—good
Id—soul
Il—light
Ilkith—children
In—I
Ins—we
Ithin—with
Itim—treasure
Jren—from
Jal—king
Jera—evil
Jol—back/return
Ki—him/her

Kin—brother/sister
Kind—kindred
Kith—people/elven
Kithen—person/human
Kithion—half people
Krist—death
La—them
Lae—those
Lai—love
Lea—these
Leven—leave
Lith—risen people/elf
Liv—alive
Lok—control/enslave
Lythin—heaven
Lyst—lost
Ma—yes/agree
Mas—no/no more
Met—hall or chamber
Miran—isolation or alone
Mist—clouded or cloud
Misten—unclouded
Mith—shadow
M'ren-men/human
Nov—hide/hidden
Novran—secrets
N'roth-high
N'rothen—highest
Oa—the
Oren—words
Obren—obey

Ovra—over
Per—feet/foot
Pera—steps
Pire—cursed
Por—portal/door
Pry—force
Ra—was
Ranen—hills
Relin—rain
Rels—release/let go
Rien—forest/wood
Rienon—stick/branch
Reva—show/reveal
Roan—horse
Roun—circle
Rule—power
Sat—staff
Sellare—protected place
Seren—Land/kingdom
Shir—heart
Shiran—life
Sho—shove/push
Shoran—attack/fight
Sirin—watch/look for
Sistren—take
Sonn—stone/rock
Spir—tower/large structure
Sran—shield
S'ren—safe/holy
Ta—to
Tah—calm

Tann—Song

Tar—will/doctrine

Ter'min—kill

Tol—tell/communicate

Tow—at/towards

Tir—city

Travar—travel/walk

Tur—spin

Ubel—up

Unda—under

Urbis—come

Urn—war

Vi/vin—it/it is

Val—ever

Vam—the dead

Van—orb

Var—voice

Vessan—body

Vew—see/look

Wa—your

Wal—wall

Wan—water

Wanel—float/afloat

Worl'—world

Ya—you

Yanel—rise/lift

Yaw—open

Zat—here

Zren—thank/thanks

ABOUT THE AUTHOR

Born in the usual way, Michael D. Nadeau found fantasy at the age of 8 with Dungeons and Dragons. He loved being different people and casting magic. By the late 90's, he discovered his love for reading. His favorite teacher gave him her personal books to bring home, and he couldn't get enough. He had even more ways to explore the great worlds out there, and it was harder and harder to come back. When he was much older, and had created and destroyed more worlds than he could count, he decided to delve into the literary realm. He created Lythinall, a place where he could tell epic stories and invite his readers on the journey with his characters. The Darkness Returns is the start of that journey, but certainly not the end. You can learn more about his works at SkullgateMedia.com as well as his personal website, KarisTheBard.Wordpress.com.

 twitter.com/Salen_Valari

 instagram.com/michael_d_nadeau

 amazon.com/Michael-D.-Nadeau

"Discover New Worlds"
Skullgate Media

Tales From The Year Between

From the giant ants of *Achten Tan* to the sentient spaceship of *Under New Suns*, every volume of Tales From the Year Between pushes genre fiction to the limit! Each book in this anthology series entails an original, collaborative world filled with short-stories, flash-ficiton, poems—even recipies. *Edited by C. Vandyke*

"I loved this. Written by a collective of writers but is a fully imagined world."
Emma, five-star Goodreads Review

Loathsome Voyages

Cursed writing desks and monstrous beings that defy sanity, Loathsome Voyages brings together 14 of today's most talented writers for an anthology of original weird-fiction inspired by masters like Lovecraft, Leiber, VanderMeer, and Matheson.
Edited by C.D. Storiz & Chris Durston

Skullgate Media's official podcast. Get a behind the scenes look at Tales From the Year Between, hear contributors read their own stories, and generally fill your ears with all the bits and bobs of speculative fiction goodness we can't cram into our books. New short audio fiction drops every other week.
Produced by Chris Durston and Diana Gagliardi

 skullgatemedia

The Lythinall Books

An ancient evil loosed upon the land. A young warrior swept into a perilous journey with a legendary bard. They will be tested as hidden forces watch with bated breath, knowing this could be the end. Discover the epic fantasy Ed Greenwood calls "a series to fall in love with."
By Michael D. Nadeau

14 Tales of
Madness & Horror

Inspired by the work of weird fiction masters old and new–from Lovecraft to Miéville, from Hodgson to VanderMeer–this treacherous, eldritch volume brings together fourteen of today's best authors of speculative fiction.
(Edited by C.D. Storiz and Chris Duston. Available NOW wherever books are sold.)

Join Skullgate Media as we embark on our most... *Loathsome Voyages*